IF THESE WALLS COULD TALK

IF THESE WA
COULD TA

JAMES D. CROWN

FIVE STAR
A part of Gale, a Cengage Compan

GALE
A Cengage Company

Farmington Hills, Mich • San Francisco • New York • Wa
Meriden, Conn • Mason, Ohio • Chicago

Pri
1 2

GALE
A Cengage Company

Copyright © 2018 by James D. Crownover
All scripture quotations, unless otherwise noted, are taken from the King James Bible.
Five Star™ Publishing, a part of Gale, a Cengage Company

LIBRARY OF CONGRESS CATALOGING-IN-PUBLICATION DATA

Names: Crownover, James D., author.
Title: If these walls could talk / James D. Crownover.
Description: Waterville, Maine : Five Star Publishing, 2018.
Identifiers: LCCN 2017047955 (print) | LCCN 2017060631 (ebook) | ISBN 9781432838102 (ebook) | ISBN 9781432838096 (ebook) | ISBN 9781432838201 (hardcover)
Subjects: LCSH: Murder—Investigation—Fiction. | Quarantine—Fiction. | Western stories. | BISAC: FICTION / Historical. | FICTION / Westerns. | LCGFT: Historical fiction.
Classification: LCC PS3603.R765 (ebook) | LCC PS3603.R765 I38 2018 (print) | DDC 813/.6—dc23
LC record available at https://lccn.loc.gov/2017047955

First Edition. First Printing: April 2018
Find us on Facebook–https://www.facebook.com/FiveStarCengage
Visit our website–http://www.gale.cengage.com/fivestar/
Contact Five Star™ Publishing at FiveStar@cengage.com

ted in Mexico
3 4 5 6 7 22 21 20 19 18

To Brian

FAMILIES OF *IF THESE WALLS COULD TALK*

Beavers

    Tucker Sr., father, born 1833.

    Mary, wife, born 1845.

    Tucker Jr., born 1865.

    Eda B., born 1869, Married Joe Meeks.

    Sue Ellen, born 1874, married Bud Stone.

    Zenas Meeker Stone, son, born 1886.

    Nathan, born 1877.

Nealy

    Robert, husband.

    Presilla, wife.

    Lucinda, born 1868.

    Joshua, born 1880, father of Dempsey.

    Green, born 1878.

Brown

    James R., husband.

    Sue, wife.

    Parmelia, born 1862.

    Rance, born 1865.

    Polly Ann, born 1875.

Hicks
Conly, husband.
Eledina, wife.
Ana and Cepa, daughters.
Tucker, son.

Vaqueros of the Ranch of the Carizalillo Hills
Conly (Con) Hicks
Bill (Slim) Hardy
Porter (Gabby) Geer
Ira (Shorty) Ingram
Nava, Benito, Lupe, and Sergio (The Muchachos)
Eledina (The Muchacha)

PREFACE

The old-timer saw it coming when the first telegraph lines were strung. No longer could the long riders outrun the news. Now they had to avoid places where the lines ran and that web was growing, shrinking their territories more and more. Trains added to their problems. They brought riches for the taking, but they also brought the law in its many forms, constricting the "wild" of territories and men more and more. And, if that were not enough, here came the telephone, connecting neighbor with neighbor. The web of civilization grew tighter with the advent of the three T's.

There has been much discussion about where the last western frontier was. Was it in Arizona, was it the Tularosa Basin or southwest New Mexico? It could have been Brown's Hole, Colorado, the Powder River basin in Montana and Wyoming, or any other of a number of nooks and crannies of the west. All of them have a valid argument for being the last geographically, but I say it was none of them. The western frontier ended in the minds of men. The law came and began weaving its web, and it has grown and grown until it thinks it has the authority to tell us how to fry our eggs, paint our houses, dig ditches, or dry our clothes. It begins to suffocate. Still, glimmers of the old self-reliant pioneer glow, sometimes brightly, sometimes faintly. Pray it never dies.

When the old west was tamed is another debated question. Most of us born in the twentieth century would say it was 1900, but that isn't so. It, the Wild West, lasted long after that, into the 1920s or '30s and it was nearer mid-century before it crept into the realm of modern society.

Along the Mexican border in the early 1900s, Pancho Villa and the unrest in Mexico extended the lawlessness of the older west. It was war, pure and simple. The flames of war and lawlessness flickered along the border, fought and mostly contained by local citizens defending their own properties. The inadequate Army was largely impotent, tied by a weak president, red tape, conflicting purposes, national and international politics.

Dempsey Nealy and the men of the Mexican Beavers Ranch are thrown into the conflict when lawless men invade their range and threaten the very existence of the ranch. The story is woven around a remarkable woman who grew up on the pioneering ranches among the mountains and Indians of southern New Mexico, bordering the Tularosa Basin.

But first I want to tell you how the talking walls of an old ranch house eventually helped two young men, while they were quarantined during the 1918 influenza epidemic, solve the mystery of a thirty-year-old murder.

A note on the format of the story is necessary. Two languages are used by the characters of the book, Spanish and colloquial English. The colloquial English is obvious. When the dialogue of the story is proper English, the characters are speaking Spanish. Many times, Anglos used Spanish in preference to English when talking to each other. It was the custom of the times.

—James D. Crownover

Chapter 1
Old Pinetop

The old towns are melting away too fast as it is.

—Anonymous

1916

"Dempsey Barnes Nealy, round up that Cooper boy and come to the house, *now!*" Aunt Cindy hollered from th' back stoop. I leaned the pitchfork aginst the wall and went to find Saint Cooper. That's th' name he goes by, though I think it was different t'other side o' th' mountains. When he asked Aunt Cindy for a job, she asked him, "Haven't you got a better imagination than that?" meanin' t' name himself "Saint."

He had looked at her kinda sideways and grinned—just a little—and said, "No, ma'am."

"Well, I'm not going t' call you *Saint*. Saints are for Catholics, and I'll bet you are far from either one."

"Yes, ma'am, I 'llow you're right there." He grinned, but Aunt Cindy hired him, anyway. He slept that first summer on a cot in the tack room, but when it got cold, she made him take a bath and gave him a room 'cross th' hall from me in th' house. He made to move out to the tack room or bunkhouse come spring, but Aunt Cindy made him stay. He wanted t' go out b'cause she made him take a bath every week, sometimes two if th' work was dirty.

"Shore wish I could go back to th' tack room, this bathin' an' changin' clothes every week is 'bout t' wear out my skin *and* my

11

clothes," he grumbled.

I found him shoveling out th' chicken house. "Com'on, Coop, Aunt Cindy wants us at th' house."

He grinned and leaned the shovel on the wall, "Bet she makes me take my shoes off at th' door. I'll empty this wheelbarrow an' be right there."

I waited for him at the back stoop and we both left our shoes outside. She was at the front, holding th' screen door open a crack and fanning flies out with her dish towel.

"Thank you for coming by, Lester, I appreciate the information," she said. Turning to us without so much as a "howdy," she said, "That CF outfit has a hundred head or more in the Pinetop pasture. I want you boys to head up there and run them off my land. Fix the fence as best you can and make one of those old houses fit to live in. I want you to stay up there and ride line. I'm going to send you a load of wire and posts and I want that fence horse high and bull strong by fall. Go pack up and you can leave right after breakfast in th' morning."

"They wouldn't be comin' back if we just shot every one of those old cows," I said.

"Don't want you startin' a range war, Dempsey. Besides, I don't want their old bony carcasses stinkin' up my land, and you can't kill them t'other side of the fence, either. Now, git!"

"Yes'm."

"Let's go up t'night," Coop muttered as we retreated down th' hall.

"You go tonight and you go without any grub, Cooper," Aunt Cindy called.

"Yes'm."

My aunt is Lucinda Nealy Brown, sister to my pa, Joshua Nealy. She married Rance Brown, a merchant in Pinetop, New Mexico Territory. So long as I knowed 'em, they got along like dogs an' cats. They both had good business heads and did well. When Uncle Rance's health started failing, they closed the stores and moved down here to Piñon to be closer to town and th' doctor. Aunt Cindy took over the family business and ran three ranches—and did right well. Uncle Rance died in 1901 or '02, I forget which.

Pa runs the old ranch, which is half owned by th' Beavers estate. One day he says, "Demps, your Aunt Cindy's getting along in years and someone should be looking after her b'sides old Nap. You go down there and live with her and help her everywhere she'll let you, maybe some 'help' where she won't let you." That's how I come t' be th' second year-round hand for Aunt Cindy.

Pinetop town just kinda dried up an' blowed away. The homesteaders starved out and little ranches were absorbed into larger ranches—and only a few of them—until there was just no business left to keep folks busy an' fed. They drifted away and Aunt Cindy bought up th' place. It sits 'bout th' middle of what we call Pinetop Pasture. Folks took lumber out of their houses as they left and all that's left of the town is a few 'dobe houses, mostly without roofs.

"We're gonna hafta fix one of them up for a line shack." Sometimes I think out loud.

"One of what?" Coop asked.

"One of those 'dobe houses left at old Pinetop's got t' be our castle for th' summer."

"Ain't there only four of 'em left, an' two without roofs?"

"Yep, guess we gotta piece somethin' together."

"Ain't a door or winder left in any of 'em."

"That's right, we'll tell Nap t' scrounge us up a door and a couple of windows an' bring them up when he brings th' fencing."

Napoleon Witt is an old stove-up cowboy who worked for old

Uncle Zenas Meeker on th' Rafter JD. When Zenas sold out and moved to Culp Mountain, Nap came t' work for Aunt Cindy. That was before I was born and he's been here ever since.

"What are you takin' up there?" Cooper asked.

"Everything."

"Ever'thing I got'd fit in a shoebox 'less I stripped off an' stuffed my clothes in."

I grinned, "That's not a vision I want t' take to my dreams with."

"Me, neither. Well, I'm packed, let's go."

"I like to eat too much t' give up that grub, 'sides they ain't no corral fit for holdin' horses up there. We'll have to stay tonight and gather us up a cavyyard t' drive up tomorrow."

"Shucks an' darn, you're right, I'm just too anxious t' get goin'."

"Well I'll tell you one thing, if you are gonna quit takin' baths an' wear dirty clothes, you ain't gonna sleep in a closed-up house with me."

Nap's voice came down th' hall, "You boys gonna eat or you gonna stay there and yap all night?" Nap and Aunt Cindy took turns cooking an' one was as good as the other in a kitchen.

"We'll be there as soon as you calls dinner," I hollered back.

"Just did."

We sat down to what would be a chuck wagon meal except for the black-eyed peas and sweet milk. Where some people put milk in their coffee, I sometimes put coffee in my milk. Aunt Cindy says coffee, beer, whiskey, and wine are acquired tastes and something we could live without. She usually said that as she sipped some of Nap's coffee.

Coop was already up movin' about when the noise of dishes rattling in th' kitchen woke me up. Breakfast at that hour would be chuck wagon variety, since Aunt Cindy would sleep later than th' rest of us. We helped set th' table while Nap finished up cooking and ladled out sausage gravy on our biscuits and steak.

As we finished, Nap plopped a couple of boxes of .44-40 shells down on th' table. In a low voice, he said, "You two keep your guns loaded and handy, those Fereday boys won't take kindly to your chousin' their cows or buildin' fences and Old Man Fereday is worse'n them."

Coop's eyes got big, but he didn't say anything. I expected trouble and was grateful that Nap understood our situation, also. "I'll stay around here and watch after Miz Cindy, but if you need help, send Polo Pony down an' I'll come 'round. Jest don't shoot me when I does."

"Thanks, Nap," I said, "I s'pect you're right about those Feredays an' we'll keep our eyes open."

The British remittance men that came out t' play cowboy brought th' game of polo with them and cowboys took to it like fish to water. It got so popular that some ranches started raising horses and training them to play th' game. A good pony fetched a high price back in th' States. Bill French, a remittance man who became a good rancher, gave me Polo Pony when he got too old t' play. He's my favorite mount because he's so smart. It didn't take him any time to pick up on cattle herdin' an' I only had t' show him once how t' cut a herd. His body may have been too old t' play, but his want-to was runnin' full blast. The first time I rode him to a match, he trotted right out there on th' field, ready t' play. I can't take him to the matches; it upsets him that he can't play.

He was fidgety when I saddled him and I had t' do a runnin' mount. We rounded up ten horses and herded them up th' mountain. The horses liked the cooler air as we climbed and it was no trouble to move them. I opened the gate to Pinetop

Pasture and the cavyyard moved on through. Pinetop is our hay pasture and the hay was belly deep to a tall horse. The herd laid it over and it looked like a road through the grass. Soon we started picking up other trails where cows had walked and I spotted several bunches here and there.

"I'll bet we find considerable more than a hundred head in this pasture," I called.

"It won't be hard t' find them, will it?"

The only way we could tell where the old road went was by the darker colored grass and how much taller it was than the grass around it. A thousand trips by horse and oxen had left it pretty fertile.

"Won't be long until that haying crew starts t' work on this grass—hi you, get back where you belong," Coop called as he waved a straying horse back to the straight and narrow.

The road wound around the 'dobe walls of an old saloon at the foot of Main Street and, as we rounded th' corner, I heard hoofbeats retreating westward. "Someone's here, Coop, watch th' horses!" I spurred Polo down a narrow aisle between two ruined adobe walls. As I reached open ground, I glimpsed a horse just dropping under th' hill. Someone was layin' on his back an' quirtin' him pretty good. I couldn't tell who he was, but th' direction he was goin' pretty much told me what his family name was.

The Saint had the horses rounded in front of th' most likely looking house and he was leaning on the door facing when I rode up. "This'n has a dirt floor, but th' fireplace is lit right inviting-like. Looks like those ghosts knowed we was a-comin'."

"That there 'ghost' was ridin' a real horse an' encouraging him with a real quirt when I saw him," I said as I dismounted. The area around the front of the house was well trampled and I found several sets of boot prints and one set of moccasins. The youngest Fereday boy affected t' be an Indian and by th' looks,

16

I would suspect he was occupying the house when we rode up.

"You watch th' horses an' I'll check on th' condition of the corral fence." I walked around the corner of the house to the corral. Polo stopped grazing grass tops and followed, thinking something might be going on without him. The gate poles were down and the grass had been grazed some, makin' it obvious there had been more than one horse kept here.

You're thinkin' a man ought to be pretty mad about someone runnin' his herd in on his property, but I understand where ol' man Charlie Fereday was coming from. He had been a hand hereabouts when th' range was open and *bobwar* was a dirty word. Even if a man had deed to a piece of property, the open range philosophy was that land could be owned, but grass growin' on it was free. The coming of the wire fence changed all that, but there were some—most of 'em livin' on th' raw edge o' ruin an' starvation like Charlie—that held to the old ways. Whether they had arrived early to the area or were latecomers, they were men that didn't foresee changes coming. When he looked across his overgrazed pastures and saw belly deep grass on the other side of the fence, it was more than he could withstand.

It wasn't too hard t' find a weak place in the three-strand fence and encourage hungry cows to lean on the fence a little until the wire gave or enough posts broke over to lay th' fence down. Where one cow goes to good grass, more will follow, and if a man was t' bunch up those cows near the gap, why, that grass would just naturally suck them through like soda through a straw. The thing that galled was that they had nerve enough to put someone on the property t' watch. Well, th' watcher was on his way t' complete his job and we could expect company soon.

Back at the house, Polo Pony and I rounded up the horses and hazed them into the corral. I had just closed th' gate when I heard horses comin' on the run. There was the rumble of an angry voice, and we rounded the corner of the house t' see four riders in a semicircle around the shanty door and hear Charlie Fereday tell Saint Cooper, "Yo're meddlin' in man's business here, kid, an' you ain't gonna touch a hair on my cattle."

He got down off his horse and there was no guessing his intent as he strode toward Coop with his quirt slapping his trouser leg. So intent was he on his mission that he did not see me riding up behind him, and as he raised the whip high over his head, I grabbed it and jerked hard. Instead of coming free from his hand, the loop around his wrist held and jerked his arm further back into an unusual position, and I heard the pop as his arm came out of its socket. The man fell over backward, yelling in pain as he fell, his hand striking the hard ground first, and the shoulder popped again as it was pushed back into place.

Cooper had his gun in his hand and yelled, "Look out, Demps!"

Polo Pony saw the action before I did and without command whirled to face the horse bearing down on us, intent on knocking us to the ground. I felt his muscles tighten and he stepped quickly toward the rushing horse. At the last split second, he dodged the other horse's shoulder, and as he passed behind, Polo let him have it. The smack of shod hooves on leather and horsehide made two distinct sounds, and man and horse went down screaming.

It happened so fast that I hadn't had time to grab the horn, and all that held me on was my feet in the stirrups. Even so, I was so far over that I kicked free and fell softly to my hands and knees. Polo looked around at me and his message could not have been any plainer if he had spoken, "What are you doing down there, don't you know how to play this game?" With a "whuff" of disgust, he whirled the rein out of reach and trotted off a few steps, head high.

A shot rang out and Cooper shouted, a little shakily, I

thought, "Sit there, boys 'til we sort things out a little."

The fallen horse struggled to his feet and limped off a little ways, head low. His rider lay where he had fallen, his leg laid out in an unnatural position. It was Macel. Charlie sat up where he had fallen, holding his arm close across his stomach.

"It popped out of socket, Charlie, and then back in when you fell on it. That's gonna be sore for a few days," I said as I offered my hand to pull him up.

"Git away from me, I can take care of myself!" he growled, struggling to hold his arm in place and get his feet under him. "What's wrong with you, Macel, git up from there!"

"My leg's broke, Dad."

"It ain't broke, you little sis . . ." He stared at the misshapen leg, "Dammit!" The bluster and anger seemed t' melt, and he asked in a whisper, "What'er we gonna do now?"

It took less than a minute to put half th' CF crew out of commission, thanks to me an' Polo. Hardscrabble outfits can't afford such luck, and I'm sure that was running through Charlie's mind as he held his useless arm and looked down on his oldest son.

If Macel hadn't been hurt, I would have been obliged t' attempt t' whip him and any outcome o' that set-to would have been much in doubt. Macel was a head taller and thirty pounds heavier than me. As it was, he was layin' there sweatin' bullets and hurtin'.

I leaned over him and asked, "What can we do t' make you easy, Macel?"

"Puttin' a bullet in that there horse's head would ease me a lot," he gritted, "but there ain't *no one* touchin' that leg." His hand moved to th' hilt of his butcher knife hung on his belt. "An thet goes fer you too, Dad."

"Well, you cain't lay there forever, Macel; want me t' treat you like we treat a horse with a broke laig?"

"Ain't funny," the boy muttered.

I stood up and The Saint bent over Macel with his canteen, "Take a long drink of water, Macel."

While he drank, I looked up at the little Indian. "Rich, ride down to the ranch and ask Miz Cindy t' telephone Doc Shetley to come set a broken leg. Then wait for him t' get there and show him up here."

"We cain't do that . . ." Charlie started and I stopped him with a look.

"I don't want my gizzard carved out, do you?"

Little Richard looked at his dad, "Go on, son, and don't kill that horse doin' it." The boy turned and loped off.

"Macel, Doc'll have something t' kill th' pain and he can set that leg better than we can," I said. He was shivering and Coop was already bringing a blanket.

"Junior, catch up Macel's horse an' let's see what kind of damage that horse done t' him." Charlie had his hand tucked under his belt. Every time he moved the arm much, he grunted in pain. "Shore could use that jug o' corn at th' house," he muttered.

"Wouldn't be good for either one of you right now," said Coop.

"Whut air you, some kind o' doctor?" Charlie growled.

"Could be."

"Then why don't you hep th' boy?"

"I like my gizzard where it is an' I don't have any painkiller."

"Some welcome to a neighbor this is, not here five minutes and you jerk my arm out of socket an' that horse breaks my boy's leg."

"Neighbors don't cut fences and eat his neighbor's winter hay, and they shore don't take a whip to th' neighbor's hands," I shot back.

Charlie just glared at me. There wasn't any use going over

those same arguments he had made a hundred times with one rancher or another about fences and free grass.

Macel's horse limped up behind Charlie Junior and stood. "He's got a big frog on his muscle and th' skin's broke a little, but I don't think any bones are broken, Dad."

Charlie looked the horse's leg over good and nodded, "Leastwise there's *some* good news out'n this."

"There used t' be some horse liniment on one of th' rafters in there," I said. "It's in a yellow can."

Junior found it and rubbed it on the knotted leg. The horse flinched a little, then limped over to some tall grasses and grazed. I couldn't help thinking that this was th' best grass he had seen in some time. The CF range was grazed down to the dirt in lots of places and not much better in th' rest. They say that's what much of the range looked like back in th' winter of '85-'86 when they had such a die-off up north. Some of those cows drifted from Montana clear down to th' Gulf in Texas. The range saw its first fences when some of the cattle associations put up miles and miles of drift fences. Sure stirred up a lot of controversy all over the open range.

We made Macel as comfortable as we could without being threatened with a slicing. He even drifted off t' sleep some, but just th' slightest movement brought pain and woke him up. "Doctor" Cooper made a sling for Charlie's arm and tied the arm down with a rag around his middle.

We fixed a little grub and sat around drinkin' coffee. I got antsy knowin' there was so much t' do. Finally, I got up an' rode over to th' fence line. There must have been a full quarter mile of broken posts and wire. Our first job would be to rebuild fence and add a couple of wing fences t' funnel th' cattle back to their own land. I could see a lot of work for two; maybe I could convince Aunt Cindy t' send us another couple of boys.

Seeing all th' damage those CF cows had done sure made me

mad. I got back to Pinetop ready t' tear into old Charlie, bum arm or not, but he had left to fetch a wagon t' carry Macel home in.

We heard th' rattle of that ramshakle CF wagon long before Rich and Doc Shetley arrived. The Missus Mary Fereday was driving while Charlie sat humped over his arm. He was looking peaked. I handed the lady down and led the mules to the side while she hurried over to Macel.

She was typical of the hardworking ranch wife of the time, old beyond her years, thin to th' extreme, her hair pulled back tight against her head and rolled into a bun. By th' time she got to fifty years, she would be worn out. Most women were lucky to live that long and few got much older. "Charlie, why in the world didn't you carry this boy inside where he could be more comfortable?"

Charlie surprised me by his soft answer, "The boy wouldn't let us move him, Mother, so we had to make him as comfortable as we could where he lay. I'm just wondering where that doctor is, shore don't want him t' take all night findin' us."

"I share your sentiments there, Charlie," I said. Saint Cooper had brought a folded blanket for Mrs. Fereday to sit on and she made herself comfortable beside Macel, feeling his brow for fever and making him drink water.

"I'm 'bout t' float away now, Mom," he complained.

"Never you mind, son, you need all the liquids you can take," she said.

CHAPTER 2
DOC SHETLEY'S MAGIC

A country doctor's practice offered two distinct
challenges: how to get to his patient, and what to do after
he got there! Often the former was the more difficult of
the two.

—*Doctors of the Old West*

A red sun was just settling down on th' shoulder of Culp
Mountain when Richard and Doc Shetley rounded th' corner. I
heard another wagon and, directly, Nap rounded the corner
with his team of mules pulling a wagon, its cargo covered with a
tarp. Nap sat high on the seat and I noticed he was wearing his
gunbelt.

Doc was just on th' lower side o' forty, but already his hair
had gray streaks at th' temples and he stepped carefully like he
was walking on glass an' didn't want t' cut his feet. He snorted
when he saw his blanket-covered patient laying on th' ground in
that chilling air. "Too far to the house t' get him inside?"

"He preferred layin' right where he fell an' convinced us it
would be unhealthy t' move him," I explained. Macel threw
back th' covers with his left arm revealing his hand on the hilt
of his knife.

"Mighty convincing argument," Doc said. "Macel, I have
some medicine here that will make you easy and we can fix that
leg." He pulled a vial from his bag and started loading a syringe.
The vial was labeled "Morphine." Doc knelt b'side Macel op-

posite Mrs. Fereday and swiped his arm with a cotton ball dipped in alcohol. Quickly, he inserted the needle and applied the soothing liquid. It was almost magical t' see Macel relax so soon after the shot. While he slept, we moved him to a bunk inside and Doc got busy fixing his leg.

Instead of cutting his pants leg, they took the pants off and Doc snipped off Macel's long handles above the knee. Mrs. Fereday took the pants and folded them. I took them and laid them with the butcher knife well out of Macel's reach. That morphine would eventually wear off and it would be healthier for us if Macel couldn't reach the knife. Doc set the bone, wrapped the leg, and began building a plaster cast. By the time Macel stirred a little, Doc was done and sitting back observing his handywork over a cup of coffee. "You're fixed up, Macel; in a couple of days you'll be ready to go home."

"Couple o' days?" Charlie sputtered, "We brung th' wagon t' take him home t'night."

"You can take him t'night if you want, and bury him tomorrow," Doc replied. "That leg may have a blood clot in it and if it shakes loose in the wagon, he'll be dead in ten seconds."

Old Charlie sputtered, "Why, I never heard . . ."

"We *will* leave him here 'til Doc tells us he can go," Mrs. Fereday interrupted, and the tone of her voice ended all further discussion on the matter. "Doctor Shetley, when do you think he will be well enough to move?"

"I would not want to see him moved before the end of the third day. If he develops any discolored, swollen, or sore spots on that leg or runs a fever during that time, I don't want you to move him at all until I look at him. Blood clots and infections are nothing to treat lightly."

Mrs. Fereday looked down at her folded hands in her lap, "Doctor, I don't know how we're gonna . . ."

"I called you out, Doc, and if you write me out a bill to th'

Two Beavers, we'll send you a check," I interrupted.

"Fine, Dempsey. I don't relish going down the mountain in the dark and I would like to look at that leg in the morning, so if you've got a bunk empty, I'll stay here tonight."

"Take your pick, Doc, me an' th' boys'll sleep outside. Mrs. Fereday . . ."

"I'll be right here by the boy all night," she said and the matter of guest accommodations was settled.

Nap brought in a big armload of firewood and Doc found a place in one of the bunks. Mrs. Fereday wrapped herself in a blanket and settled in a chair beside the bed and we quietly left the house. It wasn't gonna be very warm in there without windows and a door. We hung a tarp from Nap's wagon over the door and that helped some.

Charlie and the two boys mounted up and rode for their own ranch and th' rest of us crawled under two wagons and slept.

I awoke to the aroma of coffee and cedar smoke and found Nap squattin' over a skillet full of fatback bacon and eggs. "Load up a plate an' eat, Demps," he said, and I was more than willing to comply. Saint appeared and filled his cup. He sat and sipped and when he filled it a second time, Nap handed him a plate. A shaft of light fell from the doorway as the tarp was lifted and Doc Shetley came out. Nap was halfway to the house with two plates and coffee for patient and mother. "Hep yoreself, Doc," he said, motioning to the fire with one of the plates.

"Believe I will," he said, and filled a tin with coffee. Taking a sip, he sputtered and blew. "Hot enough to scald a hog and strong enough t' float a horseshoe!"

"Nothin' beats fatback, frijoles, and coffee on a frosty mornin', Doc," I said.

"I don't see the frijoles."

"Nap substituted eggs in honor of our guests." Coop spoke for the first time.

"Then eggs it is," Doc said with some relief. He filled his plate and stood at the wagon tailgate and ate.

"How's Macel's leg?" Cooper asked.

"Couldn't see too good, but I didn't feel any lumps or hot spots on his leg or foot. He may have a little fever, but that's to be expected. I gave him a couple of laudanums and he's resting good." After a cautious sip of coffee, he asked, "How'd it happen?"

"Macel set his horse t' bowl me an' Polo Pony over an' Polo took exception to it," I explained. I pointed out Macel's horse standing with the tip of the hoof on his sore leg just touching the ground.

Doc chuckled. "If he'd been a polo horse himself, he wouldn'a tried it."

"Bet he doesn't try it again," Saint grinned.

"He won't if'n he's smart!" Nap stirred the coffee and poured a cup.

"Nap, when are you heading back down the mountain?" Doc asked.

"Soon's we're through with breakfast and unloaded," he replied.

"I need to get back down as soon as I can, and I'll bet there's a load of messages for me at the house. These telephones sure make following me around easy enough."

Nap shook his head, "Sho was nice an' peaceful without 'em. I jist cain't get yuster listenin' t' someone without seein' some part of 'im too."

"I know what you mean, Nap, but it also saves me a lot of miles and wear and tear to be able to travel from one patient to another without detouring back to the office first. Lots of my visits aren't necessary if I can talk to someone about a problem."

"Next thing we know, you'll be drivin' one o' those horseless carriages an' scarin' ever' critter in th' county," Coop said.

"As a matter of fact, I've been contemplating that very thing. If the county keeps improving our roads, one of those buggies would come in awful handy."

Nap gave me a head nod and we walked over to the ranch's wagon. "I've got you a load of grub and posts and there are about four miles' worth of wire reels under there. Next trip, I'll have you a door and frame and some windows. How many windows do you need?"

"There's two windows in this house and th' other house has three."

"T'other house has a wooden floor an' rattlers dennin' under it. Wouldn't sleep in it afore th' snow flies a couple o' times."

"Why don't you bring two windows an' we'll fix up this house for our summer home an' we'll take our time fixin' up that winter palace."

"Sounds good, Demps, that'll give me time to scrounge up a second door and windows. I drove th' old wagon so you could use it buildin' fence. I'll ride one of your horses back an' bring you a replacement with th' next load o' posts." He pulled his saddle from under the tarp and I saddled Doc's horse while Nap caught up and saddled his. We led both horses up to th' doorway and we could hear Doc giving Mrs. Fereday parting instructions on the care of her patient.

"Never saw such fuss over a broke leg," Nap whispered. "If there wasn't much blood or bone showin' we usta give th' victim a good bait o' whiskey, hold him down, an' set his bone. A few stitches when necessary, a bunch of splints, an' a few days in th' chuck or wreck wagon 'til we got to a ranch was enough for anyone."

"I know, doctors in th' country has sure spoiled us an' made us soft, ain't they?" I grinned.

"More than *you'll* ever know, you softy!" Nap slugged my shoulder and peeked in to see if Doc was ready.

"I'll be right there, Nap," he called. In a moment, he pushed aside the tarp and handed me his bag. When he was mounted, he tied his bag to th' horn an' with a cluck to the horse was on his way. Nap flipped Cooper with his rein and followed.

CHAPTER 3
GHOST OF THE LONGHORN

The Texas Longhorn made more history than any other
breed of cattle the civilized world has known. As an
animal in the realm of natural history, he was the peer of
bison or grizzly bear.

—J. Frank Dobie, *The Longhorns*

Mrs. Fereday appeared at the door with th' water bucket and hesitated, not knowin' where th' water was. "I'll fetch your water, ma'am." Cooper reached for the bucket. "It's a ways to th' spring."

"Thank you," she replied and abruptly turned back through the curtain.

Coop gave a crooked grin, shrugged his shoulders, and headed for the old springhouse with a bucket in each hand. Apparently, there had once been a goodly flow out of the spring, for the acequias that radiated out of the little streambed ran in several directions. It flowed strong and the water was sweet.

I stepped into the house and the Fereday matron turned from her ministrations and asked, "Now what do *you* want?" as if I had invaded her home uninvited.

"I just wanted to tell you that Cooper and I would be out workin' fence and roundin' up cattle. If you need us, just fire Macel's gun an' we'll be back as soon as we can."

"Don't know as I'll *ever* need help from such as you," she growled.

I didn't bother t' explain that Macel and Charlie were both t' blame for the situation they were in. It would have only made her madder.

It only took a minute or two t' catch up th' wagon mules and I was hitching them up when Coop came back with both buckets brim full. "Want I should give th' lady both buckets?"

"Yeah, don't spill any on her, it might curdle."

"Or steam up th' place 'til you couldn't see," he grinned. When he came back, he asked, "What's up?"

"Yuh gotta stop th' bleedin' first; we'll mend fence so no more critters come into our pasture. It's for sure no cow in its right mind would voluntarily *leave* th' place."

"Pretty bad, huh?" Coop hadn't been down to the line, didn't know how th' range over the fence was.

"You'll see." Coop had saddled his horse and as an after-thought tied his reins to the tailgate. I clucked and slapped lines on mule backs and we rattled down to the gap. Coop gave a whistle. "Must be a quarter mile o' fence down, an' look at those broken posts!"

It was hard not t' get mad at th' unneeded destruction of property Old Man Fereday had caused. Good fence posts in that country had t' be hauled a long distance and they were costly. "Those are locust and cedar poles we had shipped in here from Indian Territory. Cost a pretty penny." We had set a sturdy cedar post every quarter mile and strung three strands between with locust poles set every twenty feet. The wire was strung fairly tight, but there was enough give in it that a leanin' bull wouldn't break it. 'Course, we never planned on a horse hookin' his lariat onto a post and pulllin' it over. Coop was right; there was a quarter mile of fence down between two cedar posts that were yet in place.

We propped up the fallen posts that weren't busted and spliced th' two top strands that had by some coincidence "broken" in th' same span. The bottom wire had just laid over on th' ground.

"That bottom wire ain't too far off th' ground," Coop observed.

"That way t' keep rabbits out," I muttered through a couple of staples in my mouth.

"Don't do a bit o' good keepin' rattlers out."

"It's those damned two-legged rattlers I'm interested in keepin' out." Somethin' caught in my throat an' I almost swallowed those staples. *Keepin' two-legged rattlers out* echoed in my head. It wasn't only two-legged rattlers, but *all* two-leggeds that were kept out. Here I was closing off land to people who were used t' riding anywhere they wanted t' roam and welcome to do it. Now, this fence I was putting up was limiting where they rode, directing their paths and advertising that this was someone's property where he may or may not be welcome. The occasional gate would most likely be closed to keep out and to keep in cattle on either side of the fence.

In a more subtle way, it told of the captivity of the cattle. No longer had they freedom t' choose their range or seek greener pastures or good water. Now they must depend on the provision by their overseers. The independence and self-reliance of the open-range-bred Longhorn was no longer necessary and the wise rancher sought other breeds of cattle that would yield more meat and in less time. It didn't matter so much anymore that these domestic breeds required more supervision and were less hardy to weather. The rancher built windbreaks and loafing sheds for his herd, dipped them for ticks and flies, and watched them much closer. Calves from some breeds were harder to birth, more valuable to keep.

Closed range meant closed breeding and the rancher had the new problem of avoiding inbreeding and degradation of his herd. He had to keep records, periodically change his bulls, introduce new blood. Railroad construction shortened cattle drives and even the short drives required less manpower since the cattle were driven down roads enclosed in fences on either side.

The old open range vaquero watched helplessly as the need for his services dwindled all over the west. *Oh well*, he thought, *there's plenty other things I can be a-doin', tendin' bar* (in the face of a growing prohibition movement), *running a gambling hall or table* (that was being restricted by legislation and opposition to the institution), *operating a stable* (that would gradually be replaced by garages and gas stations) . . .

I became aware that Coop was talking to me. ". . . could put up a fence gap ever so often."

"What's a fence gap?"

"Well, I guess you could call it a gate made out of barb wire."

"What for do we want that?"

"It would allow you to go from one side of th' fence to th' other for any number of reasons that you would run across without cuttin' th' fence, Demps."

"I don't see th' need . . ."

"When we build this fence back, how you gonna get those cows outa here?"

"Well, hell's bells, Coop . . ."

"What about running them through a gap? You ain't gonna build th' Wall of China t' keep barbarians out and lookin' at that Fereday land, it's a pretty sure thing you'll have new neighbors you might get along with or you'll add a few used-up acres to what you already have. Either way, you *will* need gates from here to there."

"You sayin' we hafta stop the fence at a post, leave a gap and start another fence from another post, brace both posts agin th' tension, and then put up a gate?"

"Looky here, Demps, here's th way t' do it without a lot o'

bracing an' such." He drew in th' dirt. "We get two tall poles, set 'em deep, and tall enough that a wagon load of hay would go under them, run a tension wire b'tween 'em at the very top, an' there ain't a need for bracin' agin th' pull of wire on either side. You could either swing a gate in th' gap or just throw up a wire gate, which would be no trouble t' build."

I leaned back on my heels an' studied the drawing some. "Where'd you learn t' build fence?"

"Sorry t' say I was sentenced t' fence th' world out from that XIT range on th' Llano."

"You did that?"

" 'Til I got sick of it. They got more money in their fences than they got in land. Demps, they got ten two-man crews that does nothin' but ride fence, splicing places where wire cutters have worked and putting up new posts. They have a reg'lar highway around the fences."

"You right sure we need a gate?"

"Sure as sunshine. We'll have t' cut a couple of tall poles strong enough t' take th' pull and tall enough to clear what might go through th' gate."

"Well, first things first, let's get this fence up and then we'll worry about a gate."

We plumbed posts that weren't broken, replaced broken ones, spliced and nailed up the wires. I planned to come back later and plant a post halfway between the existing posts when we added another strand of wire. It took us the rest of the day t' repair the damage. I stayed mad th' whole time. Sundown found two thirsty mules and two hungry men climbing up to Pinetop. I tended animals while Saint Coop looked to round up some grub. To our surprise, we discovered that Mrs. Fereday had cooked up a mess of beans and rice and she even had steaks frying for us.

Macel was sleeping fitfully and her concern showed. Coop

felt the boy's forehead and looked his leg over as thoroughly as he could without touching him. "A little fever is to be expected, Mrs. Fereday. I would worry if it ever shot up high. He's going to hurt for a few days regardless of what we do. You can give him enough laudanum to keep him easy without hurting him."

She seemed grateful for the advice and even talked with us some as we ate. I grabbed the water buckets and filled them at the spring. By full dark, I was watchin' stars from under th' wagon bed until I fell into a dreamless sleep.

It took us two days to build the gate like Coop had planned, but when we were through, I could see how efficient it was in transferring the tension through the tops of the poles and not requiring a lot of bracing and such. We put up a five-strand wire gap and strung it tight across the opening. It looked good and strong enough t' hold. Later, Little Richard Fereday was our first customer when he drove through to the house to take Macel and his mom back home.

"Tomorrow, we're startin' a roundup, Coop," I said as we rode to the old town.

"Good. That'll give my blisters and scratches time t' heal afore we get back to the fencing," he replied. I didn't mention added scratches he was going to acquire popping some of that brush along th' branch.

Macel remained pale, but he had rallied some and was anxious to get out of the bunk. We measured him and spent the evening carving a pair of crutches.

It was dark when we rode out t' find cows. By high noon, we had gathered a good sixty head and moved them toward town. We let them graze around the house while we ate a cold dinner.

"Those cows sure look slick, don't they?" Coop observed.

"You can give Two Beavers grass th' credit for that."

"They look good enough t' take to market, don't they?"

"Uh-huh, they do—wonder if ol' Fereday would consider

such a thing."

Coop balanced his cup on a rock and dug out his makin's. "It's for sure they aren't gonna be in better shape than they are right now if he turns them back to his pasture."

"Let's ask Macel about it," I said as I stood." I peeked in at Macel and he was awake and auguring with his ma about getting up out of that bunk. "Mrs. Fereday, I need Macel to look at something out here and it might do him good to move about a little. How about me an' Cooper gettin' on either side of him and lettin' him see how those crutches work. All I need is for him to walk to the door and look at something."

She turned and looked at me, "No, I don't think he should." As soon as she turned away from him, Macel swung his cast over the edge of the bunk and by the time she looked back, he was struggling to stand. "Macel . . ."

"I'm getting up, Mom, *I have to go.*" And there was some urgency in his voice.

I hurried over and handed him his crutches. As he stepped away from the bed, I slid behind him and grabbed his belt. "I've got you, Macel, try walking to the door."

He took a tentative step, holding his broken leg clear of the floor, and teetered a little. If I hadn't been holding him, he would probably have fallen. It was slow going across that dirt floor, but every step he took gave him confidence.

Mrs. Fereday fussed after him and I think he would have done better if she had left him alone. When he got to the door, he said, "Mom, you stay here. I won't go far past th' door."

And he didn't, either. Two steps out the door, he fumbled with his pants and took the longest whiz I ever saw. "Whew, I don't think I could have held that another second. Now what is . . ." he was looking at the cattle and stopped in mid-sentence. "Those cows sure don't look like the ones we turn—that broke in here!"

"I'm thinkin' they aren't gonna be any better looking after we turn them back to your pasture," I said. "Do you think your pa would want us t' keep them bunched so he could drive them to market? They could fatten even more in th' ditches along th' road to the tracks."

"S'what we otter do, ain't it?"

"He won't do it, Macel, you know he won't." Mrs. Fereday stood just outside the curtain.

"Well, it sure is a golden opportunity to profit from good feeding," I said.

"He won't do it," she said again.

Macel wilted down on his crutches, "She's right, Dempsey; Dad is depending on those cows to build his herd on."

"Build it on Longhorn blood?" I caught myself blurting and clamped my jaws shut. It wasn't my place t' question what others did, especially my elders, but that was incredible.

Without another word, Macel turned and followed his mother back into the building. I helped him back to the bed and when he lay back down, he was near as pale as the sheets.

While we rested a bit, Coop asked, "Demps, how many ranches still have Longhorns an' Longhorn crosses like this bunch?"

"You're lookin' at th' only ones I know of. A feller would have to work at keepin' a herd like that around here. I guess Longhorns and open range go together like bread and butter. People like Charlie haven't noticed that th' range ain't open anymore. I hear that Charles Goodnight has a small herd in th' Palo Duro. He keeps them and his buffalo herd for old times' sake."

"I seen his buffalo herd on th' way out here. They sure were pretty grazin' across th' valley."

"Let's see if we can poke these cows through that gap of yours and start a new circle up north in th' morning."

We had our hands full keeping those critters together and moving th' right direction, and when Coop rode around to open th' gap, I had t' stop drivin' them and let them graze. "Get all you can, you bone-bags, th' pickin's fixin' t' get slim." I couldn't help feeling sorry for them. Charlie needed t' sell off all his stock and let th' land recover for a couple of years. That wasn't likely t' happen an' we would have t' keep our eyes open for "strays" as long as he kept cattle.

We had a heck of a time herding those cows through the gap. First of all, I don't think they had ever seen a gate and they were naturally spooked by running up against that fence. By th' time that last cow ran through, we were *all* in a lather. "Let's push them a good distance away from th' fence," I called, but it was a useless effort; the cows scattered like a covey of quail, each heading for his old stomping grounds.

Our north circle turned out sixty-three head in two days of hard riding. In all, there were a hundred twenty-three trespassers in the hay field and it was no little damage they did to the areas they grazed in. Nap appeared a couple of days later with another load of posts and wire. "What you two been doin'? Layin 'round town an' visitin' th' saloon?"

"Guess an observant man would see that the saloon has done gone dry," Coop replied.

"And we don't play with those card sharks that hang around there," I added.

"How many 'strays' did you get out?"

"There were a hundred twenty-three—so far."

"So far's right, I seen five or six head down near th' south gate a while ago."

"Nap, did you ever try herdin' guinea hens?" I asked.

"Nope, but I did get in on runnin' a herd of jackass rabbits once. We got to th' corral with two an' they were growin' cold layin' across saddles. Made good eating, even if they were a little tough and gamey . . . come t' think of it, they weren't all that good. The hay crew will be up tomorrow. Wes plans on cutting and baling it all in eight, ten days."

"It's good and tall but we better plan on less hay b'cause of those trespassers."

"I wouldn't think it would be all that much less than usual," Coop said.

"They've been in here a while. Did you notice how slick they were? I'll guarantee you they were just a bag of bones when they got in."

Nap threw a pebble at a grasshopper on a stem, "Charlie oughta take them right out an' sell them while they're good and fat."

"Not likely t' happen," said Coop. He looked t' be a good judge of character.

We rode down to the south gate and gathered up seven head of what went for pure Longhorn. Nap met us on his way out and sadly shook his head. "That shore looks like th' ghosts of a Longhorn herd I took up th' trail t' Dodge a lo-o-o-ng time ago. I swear that brindle with th' cocked horn was our lead steer on that drive."

I guess you could say that I was one of two green cowboys that made the last Longhorn drive in our part of th' country. Even in that short distance, they showed us some of th' reasons the Longhorn breed was so right for those long trail drives of not so long ago. It made me wish—but that's gone forever and I'll never experience what it was like.

Chapter 4
Fourteen Tons o' Hay

Grass is the Head Chief of everything.

—Old Indian Chief

The first thing we heard from the hay crew was the clack and clatter of a mower makin' its first pass on an eighty-acre patch on th' south end of Pinetop Pasture. We rode down to the north edge of his swath and watched the second mower approach. Wes Lemley was driving. "Whoa, there you, Ned, whoa, Nipper." The mules stopped and lowered their heads to graze the newly mowed grass. " 'Don't muzzle the ox on th' threshing floor.' Not near th' trouble stopping them than it is t' git 'em goin'," he grinned. "How ya doin', Demps? Is that th' new guy, *Saint* Cooper there with you?"

"He's the 'Saint,' awright, how you doin' yerself, Wes?"

"Finer'n hair on a frog, only way I could be better is if I had 'bout a thousand acres o' hay in th' sheds—say, why's this hay so trampled down around?"

"Ol' Charlie Fereday's been applyin' th' free grass rule to our hay fields. He couldn't hep it that th' wind blowed down a mile of fence an' his cows didn't know th' meanin' of 'property line.' "

"Them ol' mossy Longhorns do all that? They oughta be in a museum somers."

"I guess they could be grazin' on that extinct open range in th' next exhibit," Coop said.

"Not if'n they put th' bobwar exhibit atween 'em." Wes

chuckled. "Got a real funnyman there, Demps."

"He's a hoot. How long do ya think hayin' th' pasture out'll take?"

"Oh, ah-b-o-u-t th' reg'lar two weeks, I would guess. I got new hep on th' baler an' if th' thunder bumpers hold off a little an' I don't run out of pitchfork handles, we should be on schedule. I swear one er two o' those boys could break ah anvil!"

Aunt Cindy's gas-engine-powered balin' machine was a new thing in our territory and really changed th' way hay was handled. We could stack a whole winter's supply of hay in one hay shed where loose hay would take a half dozen sheds or stay in stacks in th' weather.

The hay would be raked into piles and the baler pulled up to it. Two or three men would feed hay into the hopper and a big old goose-necked ram would push it down to the chute where it would be compressed into bales. There was a trick to learning just when t' feed th' bin an' if you were a little off, th' ram would grab your fork an' most of th' time it meant a broken handle, maybe a busted chin or arm if you were not too fast. New boys broke a lot of handles.

"You don't know where I could find a couple o' fence builders, do you?"

Wes tilted his sombrero back and wiped sweat off his balding head, "Those danged Sanchez boys showed up t' work th' baler after I hired my crew an' I couldn't use 'em. If I could persuade those handle breakers that fence buildin' was more fun, I'd let you have them an' git my men back."

I thought a moment. "What if I hired th' Sanchezes an' we worked out a trade somehow?"

"What a good idea!" Wes enthused. "You git them an' I'll trade so fast they won't get t' drive a staple—tell you what, I'll go down th' mountain an' see those boys tonight. I'll bet they come back with me in th' mornin'."

"If you see any of those cows, let us know. We've sent a bunch back to Charlie, but I doubt we got 'em all."

"I'll do that and tell th' fellers t' be on th' lookout. We'll be stayin' in th' old town, th' 'dobes in good shape?"

"Yeah, we got a couple o' spare bunks in th' dirt floor one."

Wes nodded, "Me an' Jed'll claim them, th' rest will havta make do fer theirselves."

"I wouldn't recommend they sleep on that wood floor," Coop laughed.

Wes grinned, shook his head, and clucked to th' mules, "Hi you, Ned an' Nipper! Wake up an' earn your oats!" The clack and clatter wound up to speed and Wes and outfit mowed off in a cloud of dust and bugs. Scissortails and swallows sailed in for a harvest.

By sundown Wes and Jed had almost half the hay down. Wes hopped on Nipper's bare back and rode down the mountain, and Jed hauled two bedrolls to th' house and plopped them down on an empty bunk. He said, "Save me a bite o' supper, boys; I'm gonna take a bath afore I itch t' death." And he headed for th' spring.

"Don't you fowl our drinkin' water, Jed," Coop called.

Jed made a sharp reply, questioning Coop's ancestry.

It's always good t' have someone new in camp and we sat outside in th' dark and caught up on happenings around town. Jed had t' hear all about our adventures with the Feredays and we filled out dull parts with more interesting fabrications.

"It's a wonder they didn't take Polo's antics personal an' go after you two."

"It was touch and go there for a minute, but Quick-draw Cooper got th' drop on 'em and calmed things down a bit."

"Good ol' Quick-draw. Say, what was Wes goin' t' town fer? He jist hopped on that mule an' left without a word."

"Gone t' see if he could talk th' Sanchez boys into buildin' fence 'til we could trade them for those hay pitchers."

Jed laughed, "We 'most always break a handle or two ever' year, but those boys average a handle a day. Wes had t' order more from Alamogordo after th' store here run out of 'um. Two or three times they had t' break open a bale t' git th' iron end back."

Talk tapered off to an occasional word and I jumped when my head doddled. "I'm off t' bed, boys," but soft snores from two bunks inside told me I had been talkin' to th' wind.

About sunrise we heard a mower crank up an' Jed hurried down t' catch up with Wes. We built fence all day and when we got to the house that night, Wes and Jed had supper cooked.

"We finished that eighty an' got a good jump on th' next one," Wes said, "Our rake'll be here in th' mornin' and they should be done balin' down th' mountain by day after tomorrow."

Coop was drainin' blood out of a blister where the hammer had strayed onto his finger, "When are those fence builders gettin' here?"

"I sent word for them t' show up with th' balin' crew an' we'll make th' trade then."

"None too soon for me an' Coop," I said.

Two days later, the dried hay had been raked into windrows and piled on three forties, and the baler and crew arrived. We had a powwow and told them about th' swap. I was t' get three hay pitchers for the two Sanchezes but th' three novice hay men balked on us, threatened t' quit if they couldn't stay on th' hay crew. Wes offered t' keep them if they bought new handles when they broke one. It didn't take a genius t' figger th' economics of that an' his offer was turned down.

I nudged Wes and said, "Well, let's just leave things like they are an' we'll talk about it later. You fellers go on like you are today."

They left and I said to the Sanchez boys, "You go on up to th' house, me an' Wes have a little palaverin' t' do."

We watched them leave and Wes said, "Those boys ain't gonna be happy buildin' fence when I hired them t' pitch hay."

"I know, but we ain't gonna have fence builders th' way things are now."

"What d'ya pro-*pose* t' do? An' another thing, where air we gonna put this crew? They ain't room fer all of us in th' dirt 'dobe."

I thought a minute, "We have t' convince th' boys it's to their advantage t' swap jobs and I think I know how." I explained my idea to Wes. We wooled it around until it was full blowed an' decided t' put it into action that evening. I went to the house and told th' Sanchez boys our plan and they agreed t' go along with it—just so far. I didn't blame them there.

They helped with the fencing and we returned to the house late in the afternoon. Jed had let the rest of his crew except the three pitchers in on the plan and he and I didn't have to do a thing but watch as they took over and played it out.

Near sundown, they came in driving the mules to the corral and drove the wreck wagon into the yard. Th' three pitchers hopped down and grabbed their bedrolls, "Where d' we put these?" pitcher Aaron Evans asked as he peeked into the house.

"This here's th' fence crew house an' we'll be stayin' up yonder in th' other house with a roof," Jed said as he hauled his roll out of the wagon and headed up th' hill.

"Hurry up or he'll get first choice on th' bunks," pitcher Jessie Fenton whispered. He hurried after Jed and passed him halfway to the house. Aaron and J.S. Denny, another hay pitcher, followed.

"Hah," Aaron exclaimed as he crossed the porch, "this one has a wooden floor. Wonder why they didn't pick this one for theirs."

"Roof probably leaks," J.S. said as he crossed the room to a bunk.

"That's Wes's bunk, an' th' rest are taken too; you boys'll hafta sleep on th' floor."

"S'ok with me," Jessie said, "it'll probably be cooler there." He tossed his roll down and turned back to th' door. "What's fer supper?"

"Same as breakfast an' dinner, beans an' steak washed down with coffee or creek water," Aaron said.

"No, Aaron, iss not beans, iss *frijoles* and steak!" Sebas Sanchez corrected.

Being young, growing, and perpetually hungry, the trio hurried back for supper while Jed and Sebas lingered in the house. The boys had just sat down with their plates when a gun boomed at their house. Everyone froze as the echoes bounced back from the hills and gunsmoke drifted out of the door. In a moment, Jed stepped through the smoke and broke his shotgun down, removed the spent shell, and reloaded. It was still, very still. Even the cicadas had stopped singing.

Jed turned back to the door and Sebas stepped out. "We got one!" he called, holding up a headless snake by the tail. "Twelve rattles!" Sebas was a short man, only about five foot four, and he held the snake high over his head to keep it from dragging the ground.

Nasco took a large bite of his steak and said, "Not as big as the one we got last year."

"Where did he find that thing?" Jessie asked, his fork suspended in midair.

"Oh, they den up under that floor an' come out ever' once in a while," one of the crew said.

"We gotta sleep *on th' floor* with th' likes o' them crawlin' through th' cracks?"

"They won't bother you if you don't thrash around too much;

they just want t' get warm," someone said.

"Not aginst me, they ain't."

"Whatcha gonna do? Sleep out on th' ground with 'em?"

"I'll come up here an' sleep on that dirt floor," Aaron said, eyeing the newly hung door.

"Cain't do that," Nasco said, "Thees is thee fence crew house an' we got enough bodies een thee house."

"Don't the same person sign our checks an' own this place? I can sleep there if I want."

"Iss only for fence crew," Sebas said as he plopped the dead snake in the middle of our circle. The carcass twitched and writhed.

"Remember that one that tried to bite even after you chopped his head off last year?" Sebas asked Jed.

"Yep, would have, too if he could move." Jed stabbed another bite of steak.

"I ain't sleepin' on that floor," J.S. threatened.

"Sleep anywhere you want—*except* th' fencing house," Sebas said, to the affirmative nods of th' rest of us.

"This is a hell of a note, expectin' us t' sleep with rattlers," Aaron said.

"We don't expect you t' do anythin' of th' kind; you can sleep anywhere you want in this pasture."

"*Except* th' fencing house," Coop repeated.

"Think I'll quit," J.S. said.

"Ya cain't quit, you owe more for pitchfork handles than you've earned," Jed said, hiding his grin behind his coffee cup.

"*I* ain't payin' for those puny little handles. If you bought good ones, they wouldn't be breakin'."

"It'd hafta be three inches around," someone muttered.

"I ain't payin' fer 'em."

"Hows come you guys are sleepin' in there?" Jessie said accusingly.

"Rattlers don't climb up into bunks," Coop said, "s'long as you don't go stumblin' 'round in th' dark, you're safe—just make sure your bladder's empty afore you go to bed."

"Ya know what?" Aaron asked, "I don't believe *anyone* sleeps in that house; you're just hurrahin' us!"

"Hows come th' fencin' crew gits th' dirt floor? They's more of us on th' hayin' crew."

"We got here first," said Coop.

"Let's vote on it."

"This ain't a de-moc-racy, it's first come, first served."

"You're just tryin' t' make fencing look good." It seemed Mr. Denny was th' thinker of that gang.

"Eet not look good to Sebas."

"Well said by a man with a weak bladder," Jed laughed.

"Sí, sí, Señor Jed."

The argument went on and on until the three pitchers began negotiations with the Sanchezes for swapping jobs. First, they tried an even swap, but Sebas and Nasco were adamant about any trades. The more they said no, the more determined the trio was to make a trade. The objective of th' trade lost importance. The pitchers conferred in whispers and Aaron sat back and asked, "How much boot t' make th' trade?"

Nasco shrugged, "We not need monies."

"Ever'one needs money."

A long silence ensued, then Sebas said, "To not cook would be worth more than monies to me."

"You don't want t' cook?" Aaron brightened, "I'll cook in your place if you trade with us."

"Ev-er-ry time?"

"Ever' time."

"But I like thee cooking," Nasco objected.

"Would you trade thee cooking for a bedroll?" Sebas asked.

After a moment's thought, Nasco said, "May-*bee* I would."

"So, you would trade jobs with us if we cook in your turn and gave you a bedroll? That's too much." Aaron walked away in frustration.

Jessie made a counteroffer. "We can't give up a whole bedroll, but we could give you . . . a tarp."

"Wee must sleep out on thee ground on thees high mountain, rain or shine. Eet weel not bee possible without a bedroll and wee are poor amigos." Sebas shrugged, palms up.

"Maybee a tarp and a soo'gan?" Nasco mused.

Aaron slapped his knee in frustration, "I'll give them a tarp if one of you gives them a sougan and lets me sleep with you."

"Ain't sleepin' with me," J.S. muttered, "I know you slumber in your bed."

"That's a lie, you cain't say that and get away with it!" Aaron yelled and advanced menacingly until Jed stepped in front of him and whispered something.

"O-o-h . . . Are you sure?" He was doubtful, but sat back down.

Someone snickered and I couldn't hold it anymore. We roared with laughter while Aaron grinned foolishly and the Sanchez boys looked puzzled. "Slumber means th' same as sleep," I explained.

"Ah-h-h! It ees joke, very funny." Sebas and Nasco laughed with us.

It was settled then that for a tarp and sougan and cooking in the Sanchezes' place, the three pitchers would trade jobs with them and get to sleep in the bunks in the dirt adobe. We never told them that was what the brothers wanted all along. I think before the summer was over, they knew. The Sanchez boys only had blankets to sleep under and the addition of the bedroll was a Godsend to them.

Aside from the usual pranks and jokes, the summer went smoothly after the swap. Sebas and Nasco could pitch more hay into the baler than the three novices could and there wasn't another broken fork handle that year. The three found that fence building wasn't all that bad and a lot less dusty and dirty. They became quite good at the work, toughened up, and ended up enjoying themselves. By October, we had the entire line between the Pinetop Pasture and the Fereday ranch built with four strands of wire on posts set ten feet apart. Saint's gate did come in handy later on.

Only occasionally did we see a Fereday and then it would most likely be Macel or Junior. Charlie didn't sell his fattened herd and because they were in good shape, he had a nice crop of calves come early spring. After a couple of dry years, Charlie sold out to Aunt Cindy and they moved to Alamogordo where Charlie and both older boys went to work for the railroad.

We rounded up the Longhorns and Aunt Cindy donated the ones that looked purebred to the college at Alamogordo, and they kept them on their experimental farm for several years. I don't know what happened to them after that; hope someone preserved them somewhere. We fattened the mixed breeds and sold them for nearly nothing. At least they weren't eating grass that the better bred cattle could eat.

CHAPTER 5
THE FEREDAY RANCH AND THE
EPIDEMIC OF 1918

What's become of the punchers
We rode with long ago?
The hundreds and hundreds of cowboys
We all of us used to know?

—N. Howard (Jack) Thorp

The flu epidemic hit the United States in the fall of 1918. The *Socorro Bulletin* published the arrival of the disease and the first death there. Aunt Cindy called a meeting of all the ranch employees, which consisted of Nap, Cooper, and me. "We're going to deal with this flu thing," she said. "I've decided that since it seems to be hitting the young people hardest that you two, Demps and Coop, are going up to the old Fereday place and spend the winter. Nap and I will stay here and we'll keep you stocked. Nap will take two weeks' worth of grub at a time and leave it at one of the houses at Pinetop. You can pick it up there. I don't want you to allow anyone into that house and don't have contact with a soul, do you hear?"

Twin "Yes, ma'am"s answered.

"Good, now git packin'—and don't 'forget' a washtub and soap!"

Twin "Yes, ma'am"s.

We spent the afternoon packin' and thinkin' of things we would need until the wagon was stacked full.

Aunt Cindy kept naming things we needed and when she

came out to look at the wagon, she put her hands on her hips and said, "I swear, Nap, did they empty th' bunkhouse?"

"Not quite, ma'am, I made them put back my bed and nailed down a chair an' th' table." He chuckled.

"Well, I should say so. I want you to leave first thing in the morning. If you're here when I get up, you will be late."

"Yes, ma'am."

"Tardiness is the mother of sloth."

"Yes, ma'am." She turned and the screen door slammed b'hind her.

"Never wonder who it is when *she* goes through that door," Nap muttered.

We hitched up and pulled the wagon into th' barn hall. "Better put a tarp over that 'er th' chickens'll roost on it," Nap advised.

We put two of our horses each in th' corral with our mules and headed for the house. Aunt Cindy had cooked us a bang-up meal and we had steak, mashed taters, canned green beans from th' garden, and a pecan pie for dessert. We sat around th' table and talked until we topped off the dessert sides of our stomachs with th' rest of that pie.

Aunt Cindy kept askin' us if we had this or that and we pretty much had it all. Presently, she got up and left th' room. When she came back, she carried a heavy bag. "Well, here's something you never did think about—and you will certainly need." The bag was full of books. "I want you to read every one and both of you write me a summary of each book you read. That'll be your schooling for the winter."

So long as I lived with her, I never graduated from school or got too old t' be her student. I didn't always like it, but I have to admit I enjoyed th' learning—most of the time.

Up early, Nap cooked us eggs scrambled in crumbled-up sausage, biscuits with lick, and his scalding coffee. We were ahead of time when we went to the barn, but wouldn't you know it, two of those infernal horses slipped through th' gate and left when we got the mules out. While we hitched up th' wagon, Nap caught one of the horses left and rode out to retrieve the runaways. We waited and waited and finally started out of th' yard without him when it got too close to Aunt Cindy's get-up time.

We were turning into the lane and Nap was coming through the barn with the horses when we heard the boom of a gun and the leaves overhead were peppered with birdshot. Something whizzed by my ear and one of the mules flinched when a stray shot hit him. "Ouch!" Coop yelled beside me. I didn't have t' urge much t' get those mules moving. Th' stung one would have pulled his partner and wagon all by himself. Over my shoulder, I saw Aunt Cindy standing on the porch smoke drifting away from her shotgun.

"That thing's got two barrels, don't it?" Coop asked and slipped down b'tween th' seat and the dash.

"Don't matter how many barrels it's got, she knows how t' reload!" I hunched my shoulders and slapped reins on rumps. We had barely gotten started when we heard that screen door slam. Coop peeked around the side. "She's gone in, you can slow down now. Looky, Nap's stayed in th' hall with those horses."

"He'd better stay for a while and what makes you think she ain't gone back for buckshot?" I kept those mules at a trot until we were out of range. Aunt Cindy never showed agin and Nap got those horses turned around and drove them out of th' back of th' barn. He started them toward a gap to th' lane down th' fence a ways. We got there first and opened the gap for him and helped him tie the three horses to the tailgate.

"Ya gotta know those cayuses run clear to th' back o' th' pasture. Anyone git hit?"

"Me an' th' gee mule," Coop said. He pulled his shirt up and there was a red spot on his right shoulder blade but no blood on him or th' mule. "Crazy woman."

"Crazy as a fox," I said.

"What's she doin' shootin' at us—and you her blood kin?"

"Ain't no harm done an' she got her message over without yelllin' at us."

Nap snickered and we had to laugh.

"You see that little woman standin' there in her nightgown, her hair down, and with a shotgun near as tall as she was?" Cooper asked.

"I'm just glad she was strong enough to hold high until she pulled th' trigger," I laughed.

"Wonder what a *two*-barrel offense would be?"

"I don' know, but I'm gonna step around her, for sure," Nap grinned.

"If she'd pulled both triggers, she would probably have gone through that screen door without openin' it," I said.

We laughed about it all th' way up th' mountain. At Pinetop we checked out the houses. "Still got doors an' windows, guess no one needy has come by," Nap said.

"We can store the plunder you bring up on the wood floor," I said.

"D'ya think you could hear a gun from here to th' Fereday house?" Nap asked.

"Just shoot at th' house with Miz Cindy's gun an' we'll hear shot hittin' th' tin roof," Coop said, straight-faced.

We drove down through Cooper Gate and followed wagon tracks to Fereday's old house. It had been a log house with a dogtrot down the middle until someone closed in the middle hall and made rooms out of it. We got a surprise when we opened the door. Except for a little dust, the house was clean as a pin. "Miz Mary left th' place in good shape, for shore," Nap exclaimed.

There were a few pieces of furniture left, mostly things not worth carrying off. Coop moved the washstand off th' back stoop for a kitchen table. There were four built-in bunks in what must have been th' boys' room. It had an outside door to the front porch, which made it convenient. There once had been a stove in front of the old fireplace. We could open the hearth and burn our meals there. The house seemed to be pretty tight with a couple of layers of newspaper for wallpaper. Even the interior partitions were papered.

"I remembers some of that paper bein' up when th' Feredays bought th' place, but it sure wasn't as nice and neat as this." Nap rubbed his hand across the wall. "Nice an' tight."

The parlor and kitchen had a ceiling, but the rest of th' house was open to the rafters. The room could be closed off and kept comfortable in the cold winters. All in all, the house was well built and the handywork of Mrs. Fereday was obvious.

The wagon was unloaded and the plunder piled in the hall floor until it could be sorted out. After lunch, we drove the wagon up to one of our sheds and loaded it with hay. What little hay the Feredays left was usable and there was enough t' last us awhile. Nap would make it home by dark if he hurried some.

"You might throw your hat in th' door first and see if it sticks afore you commit yourself," I called as he drove out of the yard.

"Think I'll jist go to th' bunkhouse an' test those waters in th' mawnin'," he called over his shoulder. "*Andele*, you mules, time's a-wastin'."

We spent the rest of daylight putting things away an' makin' th' place livable. I sat on the front porch bench and watched the eastern sky as the stars winked on. Presently, Coop came out and sat. "Gonna get cold up here this winter."

"Yep, they's gonna be times Nap won't be able t' make it up

th' mountain. We'd best stock up good while weather's agreeable and be ready t' hole up any time after Thanksgiving. Hope Aunt Cindy and Nap think of that."

The next several days were busy, cleaning out the barn and cuttin' firewood. Wood was stacked under th' eave by th' back door and filled a couple of stalls in th' barn. Coop was afraid that would not be enough for th' winter and kept haulin' in deadfall where we could chop it up. The corral needed a little attention and we fixed it up.

Even after laying fallow two years, the grass had not recovered a lot from overgrazin' and we were feedin' hay almost from th' start. The week after I left him a note, Nap left us a hundred pounds of mixed grass seeds. We harrowed out long strips here and there, raked the seed under the soil, and rolled it so it would hold. Hopefully, it would sprout in the spring.

The snow line kept creeping down from the mountaintops and there was frost every morning. It snowed a skiff one night the third week of November and melted off the next morning.

"Won't be long now, 'til it sticks t' stay," Coop said.

"I guess we're as ready as we can be, aren't we?"

"I think so." Saint Cooper was anxious about getting stuck up here and running out of things. I let him worry, because the possibility of that happening was real. It didn't hurt at all to keep alert to things that we might run short on. That little snow spurred us to bring in more firewood the next several days.

Nap would leave us the newspapers that had accumulated since his last visit and we read of the progress of the flu epidemic. The papers began calling it a pandemic, meaning it was spread over almost all the world. Sadly, most of the news about it was inferred from the obituaries. It seemed that the old and the young were hardest hit. All the schools and even the churches were closed and people didn't mix much. Aunt Cindy kept me informed about th' family's health. It seemed that they were staying isolated and well. I noticed that Coop got quiet whenever we heard about things. I guessed he had family somewhere and he was worried. He never talked about them and I couldn't ask. He just got awful quiet at times.

Things got slower as th' weather got colder and we found ourselves by our fireplace more and more. It became obvious that we were not going t' do a lot of riding, so the next time he came up we met Nap with Polo Pony and another horse.

"Looky here what I brung ya, boys," he called and held up two grain shovels. "Thought you would need these to toss snow around when th' time comes. Try t' save all of it ya can, we'll need it fer moisture next summer."

"Drive on up t' th' snow line after we unload and we'll send you back with a load today."

"I ain't haulin' no green snow, you gotta wait 'til it gits ripe, Demps."

"How are things at the ranch, Nap?" Coop asked.

"They's jist so-so, Coop, we got th' word Mister Bob caught th' ep-i-dem-ic an' brought it back to th' Beavers Ranch. He holed up in th' bunkhouse and threatened t' shoot anyone who came near. Miz Cindy determined t' go up there in spite o' my objection. When she saw Uncle Bob was too low t' git out o' bed, she marched right into that bunkhouse an' took over."

My stomach did a flip and I feared for both of them. Grandpa was getting on in years, but took an active part in running th' ranch. I knew he had insisted that he be the only one to go outside the ranch, but I couldn't figure why he went to town. They should have been pretty self-sufficient. "Have you heard from them?"

"Miz Eda called me yesterday on the tell-a-phone an' said all was as good as could be expected. Miz Cindy had taken over th' gun an' was holdin' off ever'one jist like Uncle Bob did."

We had to grin. "She didn't take th' shotgun, did she?" Coop asked.

"Nope, she left it with me with instructions an' a list of who t' use it on."

"Bet it was a long list," I laughed.

"Jist one page, said she was feelin' charitable 'cause of th' season."

"Who . . ."

"Don't ask, Coop," I interrupted, "We might be on top o' th' list."

"You two was down towards th' bottom an' I proudly says my name wasn't on it!" Nap swelled his chest and ran his thumbs under his imaginary galluses.

"Don't you worry about bein' left out," I said, "I got a list of my own."

"But you ain't got th' shotgun."

"I don't like her bein' up there in harm's way, Nap, she's no spring chicken."

"They wasn't no stoppin' her, she's awful fond o' her father. They always been awful close."

Nap was right. Those two had always been very close. Grandma Presilla had once told me that they shared experiences none of the rest of us knew about. I figgered Grandma was in on th' secrets too, but she never said any more about it and I let it drop. It was none of my business. There might some day be secrets I kept that I would not want anyone t' know. As a matter of fact, I may already have had a couple of them back then.

"D'ya think I should go over there, Nap?"

Coop punched me in th' ribs. "Ain't you th' one Miz Brown shot at just fer bein' late, an' you her own blood kin?"

"Coop's right, Demps, all you gonna do up there is go in an' out of that .45's sights. Th' folks up there can take care of what's needed. I got things under control at th' ranch an' they's plenty of help I can hire if I need it. No use throwin' away all this trouble we went to t' keep you two healthy."

Of course, they were right, but it didn't do away with that empty feelin' in my gut. It was beyond my ability t' help and I would just have to leave it to Aunt Cindy, Grandpa Bob, and the Lord.

Nap sat on the wagon seat and me and Coop sat on th' stoop and talked for some time. Th' three of us felt pretty isolated and it was good to visit. The sun was well past its zenith when Nap left and we started packing some of our plunder back to the Fereday house by shoe leather. Next trip we would bring a packhorse.

It was just accidental that I rode through Pinetop a few days later and saw the newspaper on the floor of the 'dobe house. I picked up the paper and started to fold it when I noticed an article on the front page bordered in black. Its headline read:

LOCAL PIONEER RANCHER PASSES

This paper received word as we were going to press that Robert Nealy, well-known owner of the Beavers Ranch, has died. Bob had contracted the influenza in spite of all precautions. He passed to his reward on the evening of November 15, 1918, isolated from his family with only his daughter, Mrs. Lucinda Brown, attending. Interment will be in the family plot at Pinetop Cemetery. Funeral services will be in the spring when the epidemic has eased and the scattered family and friends can be safely gathered.

I knew some of them were going to come to the Pinetop Cemetery to bury Grandpa, so next morning we went over and dug his grave. The ground was frozen only about six inches deep and the rest of the digging was rocky but easy enough. Four days later I rode over and there was a mound of dirty snow and dirt over the grave. A note was stuck to the cabin door. All it said was, "Thank you."

That night it snowed thirty inches and blowed up big drifts. We were bound.

CHAPTER 6
AN UNEXPECTED TREASURE

Word comes from Texas that a hoard of silver dollars had
been found in the ruins of an old barn. A crowd of
searchers harvested from 150 to 300 dollars, depending
on who was telling the tale.
—*The Pinetop Crow,* March 4, 1880

Layin' around th' house was awful and we finally were reduced
t' reading Aunt Cindy's books when there was enough light.
Our reading was confined between sunup and sunset. Coop
gave in first and he was reading Pat Garrett's *Authentic Life of
Billy the Kid.* I dug around and pulled out *Ben-Hur,* which was
written when Lew Wallace was territorial governor.

The snow line kept creeping down our mountain and the
third week of November a blizzard blew down on us. It lasted
three days and the snow line made great strides past us. We had
enough warning to string a rope from the back door to the
barn. Our horses made out well in their stalls and when the
storm was over, we shoveled snow out of the center hall so they
could move around some. The only exercise they would get for
a while was plowin' snow and we rode them around the place
doin' that. It kept them in decent shape.

Sunshine days and cold nights put a crust of ice on top of the
snow and when it was thick enough to hold them we walked the
horses. We didn't go far with them for if they broke through, it
was a real struggle for them t' get back on top. Sometimes they

couldn't and we had to break a path for them. That's all th' work we had t' do and even that got awful troublesome and dull; sometimes it got so bad I would walk circles in th' house until Coop yelled at me t' settle down. If I didn't feel like it— settling down, that is—I would go out and mess in the barn some, but it was too cold t' stay long.

"You're like a caged lion, Demps, can't you sit down and read while there's daylight?"

"I cain't see how you can sit there fer hours at a time and stare at that book," I shot back.

"Isn't it interesting to you?"

"*Ben-Hur* was good, but I don't know about any of the others."

"Well for Pete's sake *look* at some of them. You'd like *Billy the Kid*, know a lot of the people in it."

"Someone else must have checked that book out," I said and stood at the door and watched snow fall and blow and frost build on both sides of th' glass. My eyes strayed to the wall beside the door casing and there on the paper stood a lovely young lady in her underwear! When I quit staring at her, I read the advertisement:

LADIES' SUMMER UNION SUITS
42C PER SUIT
THIS SUIT IS OUR BIGGEST SELLER

And is accounted for by the fact that we have been able to secure an exceptional garment to sell at this very low price. This garment could not be duplicated at any other retail store for less than 50 or 60 cents each. It is made from very fine cotton yarn. The low-cut neck and armholes are finished with mercerized silk tape. The large umbrella bottoms are finished with wide lace of a very pretty design. Color is white in sizes 4, 5, and 6, to fit bust measure from 32 to 40 inches.

"Coop, here's a naked woman!"

Coop jumped up, pressed his nose to the window, and steamed it over with his breath. "Where?" he asked, swiping at the fast freezing moisture.

"Here, not out there."

"Aw-w-w fer gosh sakes, Demps, she's not naked, she's got on longhandles."

"Not longhandles, union suit."

"Well, she ain't naked."

"May as well be, you can see all of her."

"No you cai . . ."

"Look at her legs, Coop, they go *alla th' way up!*"

"Shore they do, that's natural."

"How you know?"

"Demps . . ."

"You tell me you know, *I* haven't seen legs on any female over two years old, how you know they go all th' way up after they're two? You *seen* 'em?"

"An' if I had I wouldn't tell you."

I tapped the picture where her belly button would be. "This is th' first positive proof I've had that a woman's legs go all th' way up, you tellin' me you knowed it afore? Lookee here, it says these suits come in three sizes, four, five, and six, an' they fit bust sizes thirty-two to forty inches. You ever seen a bust that big?"

"They don't mean th' bust's that big, they're measured around th' body. You aren't that ignorant, are you?"

"I think I'd like my girl to be a size four with a forty-inch bust."

"Go on an' read th' paper, Demps, you might get ed-u-cated; I want t' read my book." He returned to the fire, threw on another log, and sat back down with a grunt. It was a lot of fun pulling his chain an' about all I had left t' look forward to.

The top of th' page with the union suit advertisement said the paper was *The Eddy Argus,* December 5th, 1907. The next paper over had a long article that took up all of the left-hand page of the paper and some of the right-hand page. The headline of the article caught my eye:

ALAMOGORDO SANDS
February 21, 1908
JUDGE BURNETT "TESTIFIES"

As promised earlier on these pages, this reporter has "deposed" our retiring Judge J.G. Burnett and this is his "testimony" of his life and career.

A long series of questions and answers followed. It was interesting reading until I got to the following question, then it got very personal.

Reporter: Judge, you have told us about your more famous trials as a lawyer, what was your most disappointing experience in the courtroom?

Judge: That one is an easy question—it was the murder trial of Tucker Beavers, Jr. in October of 1888. Young Beavers had returned from a two-year stay in Mexico and was arrested in the summer of '88 for the murder of Riley Giddens on the night of Beavers's disappearance in April of 1886. He was indicted for the murder by the Otero County grand jury in April and his trial set to begin October 25, 1888. I was hired to defend him by Bob Nealy, partner with the Beavers estate in the old Beavers Ranch.

Tucker Beavers had gone alone to Mexico to locate the killers of his father and ranch hands and retrieve cattle stolen from the ranch. He was wounded in a battle with the ranchers in posses- sion of his cattle and spent some time in hiding recuperating from his wounds. He was on his way home when the earthquake of May 1887 struck that region and he returned to the town of Bavispe to help the victims of that disaster.

The quakes caused the downfall of his enemies there and he was able to establish a second Beavers ranch on the vacated range. He was a fine, honest young man and I became convinced that he was innocent of the crime, but there was no positive evidence that would exonerate him.

The trial began and we were able to refute the testimony of one of the two prosecution witnesses and cast serious doubt on the other. Court was adjourned for the day when the prosecution rested and I was ready to put Beavers on the stand. Things were looking up for my client.

There was a sealed envelope on my desk that evening when I returned here to my office and the note on the outside, written in a neat female hand read:

Dear Mr. Burnett:

Please do not open this unless there is an urgent need for an alibi for Tucker for the night Riley was murdered.

The very presence of the note convinced me that my client was innocent and we went to the courthouse confident of a victory.

Reporter: *Here the good judge paused, gathering his composure and arranging his thoughts.*

Judge: *Of course you remember the following events: how young Beavers and deputy George Ryles, who would later become our sheriff, were shot down on the courthouse steps by John R. Giddens, the deranged father of Riley.*

All of us were very shaken by the incident and it was some time before Judge Webb called court into session. I had gotten myself somewhat together and motioned that the trial continue in absentia.

I suspect that the good judge knew my purpose in making the motion; he knew the state's case was on shaky ground. If the jury voted not guilty, the officials of the county would have to continue their investigation of the murder, which was two years old and there were no other suspects.

The prosecuting attorney made little objection to continuing, but did note that the events of the day may have prejudiced the jury. After some moments of deliberation, Judge Webb denied my motion. Then and there the trial was ended without giving Tucker Beavers a chance to be exonerated.

Reporter: *Did the investigation of the murder continue?*

Judge: *No. And the prosecuting attorney did not seek to have the indictment withdrawn, the result being that Tucker Beavers remained accused of the crime. It gave the county reason to close the case.*

Reporter: *It seems wrong, doesn't it?*

Judge: *Yes, and I am certain that the real murderer is yet to be found.*

Reporter: *You mean still free?*

Judge: *After twenty-two years, he could be dead.*

Reporter: *What did you do with the envelope?*

Judge: *Remember, the note asked me to open it only if there was an urgent need for it. The need was gone with Tucker's death. I held in my hand a piece of paper that would have cleared my client and possibly revealed the true murderer.*

Reporter: *You didn't open it, did you?*

Judge: *No, I burned the unopened envelope.*

Reporter: *Do you have any ideas as to who might have murdered Giddens?*

Judge: *Any speculations on my part would not be productive.*

The interview continued, but I didn't read more. Tucker Beavers, Jr. was the son of the original owner of Beavers Ranch.

Grandpa Bob was the ranch foreman when they made him partner in the ranch. When the senior Tucker was killed in the fight over the cattle, Grandpa took over the running of the ranch.

I had heard stories about Tuck, as they called him, all my life, though it wasn't often his name would come up. I knew that he had gone to Mexico and fought the thieves and was wounded, and that the earthquake had destroyed the ranch and killed the rancher. Tucker had made an agreement with Mexican sheepherders to share the range with them and had made Conly Hicks foreman of the Mexican Beavers Ranch. Con is still foreman there and the ranch had been a very profitable part of our ranching operations. I knew that Tuck was murdered in Tularosa, *but I didn't know that he was on trial for murdering another man!*

Uncle Nate Beavers and my Uncle Green Nealy worked the ranch now and had as long as I had knowledge of it. They ran th' ranching part of it, but Grandpa had last say in th' business part an' where money was spent. You could tell when they talked about Tuck that they thought the world of him and often when they were out working together on a problem one or the other of them would ask, "What'd Tuck do?" and there would come a long discussion of "what Tuck would have done in this situation." Sometimes the discussion got heated, but they would always come to some sort of agreement. If whatever they tried t' do failed one of them was sure t'say, "See, I tol' ya Tuck wouldn't of done that!"

But the name of Tuck rarely came up in family gatherings and I noticed even more rarely in Aunt Cindy's presence. Any time I had been around her and the name had come up, she would get mad and try t' bite someone's head off; then she'd get real quiet or leave the room.

"Whatcha thinkin' 'bout?" Coop's question made me jump, I

had been so deep in thought.

"You heard tell about a man named Tucker Beavers, Jr.?"

"Don't guess I have," Coop replied as he lay down his book, "who is he?"

"He *was* the son of th' man who built th' ranch."

"Th' one who got killed?"

"Yeh."

"What about him?"

"He was shot in Tularosa back in '88, but I never knew that he was on trial for murder at the time."

"Who tole ya that?"

"That wall over there."

"Walls can't talk, Demps."

"Well I can tell you that one sure did—and it told me more than I wanted t' know!"

"How come that bothers you, he weren't blood kin."

"May as well been if his name was Beavers. You don't want t' bring his name up in conversations with Aunt Cindy. She must hate him."

"Who did he kill?"

"Riley Giddens, I guess. His lawyer says he was innocent, but never got t' prove it afore he was killed."

"Who killed him?"

"Don't know, th' wall didn't say."

"That wall don't talk."

"Go over there an' see for yourself if that wall don't say something. It's right by th' naked lady."

Coop got up and stretched and walked over to the wall. "She ain't naked, either." He read the article a long time. "Says here that John R. Giddens shot Tucker an' th' deputy."

"*Says?* I thought you said walls couldn't talk."

"You know what, Demps? You could make a wooden Indian cuss."

I sat and stared into the fire a long time, thinkin' about all th' things I had heard about Tucker Beavers, Jr. and realized I didn't know much about him at all. A log fell in the fireplace, sending up a cloud of sparks, "Like Angel souls goin' to Heaven," Grandma Beavers used t' say.

"Say, Coop, when was that article written about th' judge?"

"U-h-h-h, February, 1908."

"When did it say th' trial was?"

"October, '88."

"Wonder if they's any papers that old on th' walls sommers."

"Best way t' find out is t' look, Demps, don't bother me, I'm readin'."

The living room walls looked like they had been papered last. That 1908 paper was th' oldest I had found and they ran from there up to August of '17. Older papers would have t' be somewhere in the other rooms, if at all. I wandered around the two enclosed rooms looking at dates on the papers. None of them here were any older than 1907. I noticed in a couple of places where the flour paste had let go that there was a layer of older papers underneath the newer ones. It was a frustration that the wall paperers had not paid enough attention to chronology when they pasted. Things were scattered haphazardly. I wandered into the hall. My eyes were drawn to an image of a beauty in a corset doffing her blouse:

SATISFACTION

When Ferris's Good Sense Corset Waist is on the form, the wearer is satisfied she looks right; she knows she feels right; she has the physician's assurance that she is dressed right for health. All who have worn them express their satisfaction with

FERRIS GOOD SENSE CORSET WAIST

Always superior in quality and workmanship. Made high and low bust, long and short waist, to suit all figures. Children's 25 cts. to 50 cts. Misses' 50 cts to $1.00. Ladies' $1.00 to $2.00.

"Hey, Coop, commere!" I heard the front two legs of his chair hit the floor. In a moment—I envisioned him finishing that paragraph—he stomped across the floor and came down the hall. I could tell he wasn't planning on staying long.

"What now, Demps?"

"Lookee that girl in th' corset, you think they really wore such things?"

"Says they did."

"Says they put them on children too, but I hardly b'lieve *that*."

"How do I know what they did in 1881, Demps? I wasn't 'round then."

"Wonder what she looks like *without* a Ferris corset? Reckon she's shaped something like a toad?"

"Well if she is in th' natural, where's all that go when she's all trussed up like that?"

"She wouldn't be breathin' deep, that's for shore. Coop, what's a high bust?"

"Don't know, an' I shore don't know what a low bust is, lessen it's old droopy wimmin."

"Then I suppose a high bust'd be them that stand out on young wimmin?"

"Beats me. I think I know what a long or short waist is about."

"Yeah, they's on both genders."

"Girls these days got that wasp waist without corsets, ya suppose their mamas an' grandmas wore them things so long it got in their blood some way an' got passed on down in th' nat-u-ral?"

"I don't know, Coop, but I shore like a waist I can reach around without usin' both arms."

"Me too. Don't call me less'n you got somethin' big." He turned and shivered back to th' warmth of our fire.

The back rooms were cold and it didn't take me long to go back and put a coat on. I took one of the lamps back with me. If there was a pattern to the papering, it was that the older papers were on the exterior walls and the partition walls inside had newer papers on them. In one corner of the back bedroom on the outside wall, I found a paper called *The Pinetop Crow* dated May 13, 1880. One of the articles was about some preacher who preached at the Pinetop Union Church and they had dinner on the ground. Another article was about th' local baseball team:

Pinetop 2, Cowboys 3

Gene Rhodes's cowboy team invaded town last Sunday afternoon and gave our boys a lesson in how to play baseball. It was a close game and wasn't decided until the last inning. Gene got a single with a line drive too hot for Tucker Beavers to handle at second base. With two outs, Riley Giddens ran the count to 1 ball and 2 strikes on Jeff Bransford when he left a fastball right down the middle and Bransford sent it to the back forty beyond center field.

The loss leaves the Pinetop Nine at six and four for the season. The Cowboys make the claim that they are undefeated. They must have forgotten their first game with Pinetop and the loss they suffered at the hands of La Luz afterwards.

"Hey, Coop!" I hollered, "Pinetop had a newspaper in 1880 an' Tucker Beavers and Riley Giddens played on th' same baseball team!"

"Is 'at right?" came the muffled reply.

I could tell he was greatly impressed. "Devil take ya."

Below that article on the same page was a little article about Beavers Ranch:

THE PINETOP CROW
Thursday, May 13, 1880

The Nealy, Brown, and Beavers families gathered recently for dinner on the ground and doughnuts. Adults visited while the children swam in the creek. A good time was had by all.

Below that page was another page with different print and I could barely read through the overlapping paper:

THE EDDY ARGUS
May 21, 1880
ARMY TAKES OVER RESERVATION

The Army has taken over the Mescalero Reservation and the Apache agent and his staff have fled. There has been unrest on the reservation for some time and an Army investigation of conditions found that the agent had distributed foodstuffs that were in essence inedible. There hasn't been a cattle disbursement in two weeks although records show that sufficient cattle had been received to make distribution . . .

It went on to talk about the missing cattle and the fear that the Indians might prey on the general population. Green and Nate had talked about their first cattle drive and it was to the reservation to feed starving Indians. I wondered if this was it. The last paragraph read:

It would be healthy for the fugitive agent to turn himself over to the Army before angry civilians find him and tie his neck to a cottonwood limb.

I hoped the civilians found him first.

There were several editions of *The Eddy Argus,* but there was nothing of interest there. The next row of papers started at the top of the wall and from the floor I could see that the top paper was *The Pinetop Crow.* I had to stand in a chair to read it. The date was June 17, 1880:

Yesterday Tucker Beavers and sons passed through Pinetop on their way back to the Beavers Ranch. They are returning from a cattle drive to the Mescalero Reservation where the Indians have been in a state of starvation and unrest. Mr. Beavers stated that the arrival of the cattle avoided serious consequences. The Army is efficiently seeing that the Indians are properly taken care of.

The drive was successful in spite of attempted interference by the rough element from Lincoln. Young Green Nealy was injured in a confrontation with the gang, but has now recovered. One would think that the proud possession of a fine .22 rifle went a long way toward healing the young man.

The Army has arrested the gang on a number of charges. We only hope they are not tried by a civilian court in Lincoln or Santa Fe, where justice would most certainly be perverted.

"Hey, Coop, here's a story about Nate an' Green's first cattle drive. They had a fight with a gang of the Santa Fe Ring from Lincoln, I remember them talking about it."

"Demps, what was the Rock Salt Sale?" His voice came from the hallway and startled me, he was so close.

"What's that?"

"A Rock Salt Sale."

"I don't know; people talk about a rock salt window, which means th' glass is broken, and they talk about rock salt shirts and union suits an' they mean they are full of holes, but I don't know where all that comes from."

"Here's an article from *The Pinetop Crow* for April 20, 1882. It says:

THE PINETOP CROW
Thursday, April 20, 1882
ROCK SALT SALE A SUCCESS!

The proprietor of Brown's Mercantile wishes to thank all those who participated in the sale last Saturday. All the damaged goods have been sold and a large quantity of rock salt retrieved.

"So it happened some time before April 20 in 1882 . . ." Coop seemed to be musing to himself.

An article in the January 13, 1881, *Pinetop Crow* caught my attention:

THE PINETOP CROW
January 13, 1881

We have noticed the absence of one of our prominent young men and upon investigation found that young Riley Giddens has gone east to further his education. His father, John R., does not know when his son will return. He will be missed by his friends who are eager for his return.

Grandpa Bob never had any good t' say about the Giddens. If the name came up, he would not talk about them. The only thing I ever heard him say was that Tucker Jr. gave Riley a good whipping after they came back from the cattle drive to the reservation. That seemed to give Grandpa much satisfaction.

Aunt Eda B. says th' fight was because Riley had telegraphed little Jimmy Dolan at Lincoln that the Beavers Ranch was making a cattle drive for the Army to aid the Apaches and Dolan sicked his hounds on them. That was when Tucker Jr. almost caused a gun battle by pistol-whipping the man that had roughed up ten-year-old Green.

After he got whipped, Riley left the country for a time but "back east" was only to Lincoln where he worked for Dolan and learned how to cheat . . .

"I found more!" Coop interrupted. "Here's an advertisement for the sale!"

"Dang, Coop, I'm fryin' my own bacon . . . what you talkin' 'bout?" I walked around the wall to where he stood in the hall.

"Read that!" He pointed to an April 12th advertisement on a page of the *Tularosa Sands:*

SALE   SALE
THIS FRIDAY AND SATURDAY
APRIL 14 & 15, 1882
BROWN'S MERCANTILE, PINETOP

Due to an incident Tuesday, April 5, several cartons of dry goods were damaged. These goods will be sold from the cartons at a 10% discount, first come, first served. IN ADDITION, A further penny will be discounted for each salt crystal found in the purchased garment!

The advertisement went on to list the items for sale: ladies' union suits, shirts, and muskrat hats.

"Well, I'll be darned," I said, "wonder if they's anything more said about it."

"What was th' date on that page?"

"It was . . . April 12, 1882."

"*Tularosa Sands?*"

"Yeah . . . here's another *Tularosa Sands* page."

TULAROSA SANDS
April 17, 1882

MYSTERY SOLUTIONS SUGGESTED

There has been much speculation about the Mystery rock salt victim and what could have precipitated his wounds. General consensus is that since it is too early for watermelon patch raids, the victim must have been in pursuit of the Forbidden Fruit and encountered an irate father or husband.

"Here's the front page of th' *Sands* paper from April 12th," Coop called from down th' hall a ways. "It says,

TULAROSA SANDS
April 12, 1882
A PARTIAL SOLUTION

Mystery partially solved. The arrival at this office of an advertisement from Brown's Mercantile in Pinetop (see ad, page 2) has partially solved the mystery of the rock salt victim. Only his identity remains unknown."

"There must be more to th' story," I said, but search as we could, we didn't find any more about the rock salt sale. It was always dark in the hallway, but when we looked out th' back door window, it was completely black outside. I hurried off to see to the stock and Coop rustled up some supper.

CHAPTER 7
A DECODING

What matter where the road goes?
The beauty is in the journey.

—Josef Muench

Supper was ready when I got in from th' barn and we sat down to more talk than food. Coop was so curious about this rock salt episode that he had made notes in the composition book Aunt Cindy had provided for each of us to write our book reviews in. I looked at what he had written:

April 11, 1882 Mystery Solutions Sands.
April 12, 1882 The mystery partially solved Sands.
April 14 and 15, 1882 The Sale Tularosa Sands.
April 20, 1882 The Rock Salt Sale A Success Pinetop Crow.

"Look, Demps, on the 11th, people were speculating on a rock salt *victim*. It must mean someone was hurt with rock salt."

"You don't suppose Aunt Cindy had rock salt in her shells, do you?"

"This was 1882, Demps."

"Shells'd last that long."

"Quit interruptin'. On the 12th, the advertisement from Brown's Mercantile came to the Sands. Then the sale was on the 14th and 15th."

The puzzle got my attention, "So something had t' happen before the 11th for the fellers t' speculate about . . . wonder what that was."

"Probably the only way we will find out is if it says something on the walls."

"Walls can't talk," I mimicked. "I sure would like to know more about Tuck's story. Maybe the walls will have something for me."

"Get your composition book and start making a list like I have," Coop suggested.

It was too dark and cold to start the notes so I rounded up the book and laid it out where I would find it in the morning. When we went to bed, it was snowing. When we got up it was snowing. We shoveled out the path to th' barn and hauled in more wood.

I took my notebook and started all over again. My first entry was the judge's interview from the living area. "February 21, 1908, Judge's interview *Sands*."

I called the exterior wall in the back bedroom "The 1880 Wall." While looking for my first articles, I found some more of interest and put them in chronological order. It was obvious that the judge's story did not fit in this group of articles.

March 4, 1880 Tuck registers brand and cut Pinetop Crow.
May 13, 1880 Preaching and ball game Crow.
May 20, 1880 Dogs used in Roundup Crow.
May 21, 1880 Army takes over reservation Eddy Argus.
June 27, 1880 Beavers return from drive Crow.
January 13, 1881 Riley is gone Crow.

The numbers penciled in before and sometimes after an article puzzled me. I had no idea what they meant. "Cooper, do you know what those numbers someone has written on the walls mean?"

"Nope, but I'm workin' on it."

Whoever wrote those numbers had grouped the different subjects they had read, indicating the location of the previous article on the walls by adding a code at the top of the article and placing a code at the bottom of that article to indicate the location of the next article. It took us a while to decipher the code, but we figgered it out, finally.

"We broke th' code, Demps, things'r gonna be easier from now on."

"Only if we read th' things he read, won't be any codes for other stories."

"Guess you're right there. We'll have t' make our own codes."

"Come spring, we might have all these walls memorized," I said.

"Not me, I'm reading books." And that's just what he did.

I sat down and drew up a plan of the house in my book. I knew the codes for the living room, hall, and back bedroom, but didn't know what the code writer had called the bunk room yet. It was interesting that the reader had linked Riley Giddens's leaving Pinetop to the cattle drive. He—or they—must have known about the whipping that Tucker had given Riley and linked the events. Pretty smart. Of course, it was a small community, so there would be few secrets. *And* I realized with a start, that rumor would pop up when Riley was killed, more fuel to fire the suspicions of Tucker's guilt.

Cooper suddenly stood up, whispering a code over and over again.

"Whatcha doin', Coop?" He only answered with an impatient wave of his hand. I followed him to the back room where he began looking for his article.

"Here it is." He was on the north wall by the window there. I looked at the story; it was titled:

James D. Crownover

TULAROSA SANDS
Monday, April 10, 1882
A STRANGE VISIT

*Doctor Tom Rice heard a knock on his door in the wee hours of
Saturday morning and receiving word through the door that
one of the two men there had gunshot wounds, directed them to
his office door at the side of the house. When he opened the door,
he was startled by the presence of two masked men. The younger
man was obviously in great pain and the good doctor immediately began treating him. It was obvious by the damage to
his clothes that he had run afoul of a shotgun and when he was
disrobed, the doctor counted a good two dozen places where shot
had penetrated the skin on his lower posterior. There were many
more whelps and bruises where the shot did not penetrate.*

*Imagine Dr. Rice's surprise when the first "shot" he extracted
was a lump of salt! The removal process was aided by the
administration of morphine and the patient dozed quietly while
the doctor worked two hours to remove all of the rock salt from
the man's body. When the procedure was finished, the older
stranger thanked Dr. Rice, paid him a very generous fee, and
staggered into the early morning light, half carrying the groggy
patient.*

I skimmed the article and hurried off to find Cooper. "Hey,
Coop, here's th' first rock salt article," I called.

"No need t' yell, I'm standin' right here," came from behind
my left ear.

"Danged if I'm not gonna put bells on your shoes."

"So . . . April 10th someone went to a Tularosa doctor with
rock salt in his hide . . ."

"Mostly in his ass hide, I'd say."

". . . he got trying to rob Brown's store on April 5."

It took me most of the afternoon to find the first article on the walls about the burglary. It was in *The Pinetop Crow:*

THE PINETOP CROW
Thursday, April, 6, 1882
BURGLARY THWARTED

A burglary of the Brown Mercantile was averted last night when Rance Brown surprised an intruder trying to make off with merchandise. One blast from young Brown's shotgun convinced the would-be robber to drop his plunder and flee, leaving his boots behind and taking three jacks from the game with him, supposedly buried in his bare feet.

Unfortunately, the shot did considerable damage to the merchandise the thief was carrying and the building, which took a considerable amount of rock salt from the gun.

The Browns were gratified at Deputy Ryles's prompt response to the situation. His only advice for them was that they should obtain new glass for the front door and more rock salt for Rance's shells.

"Someone tried to burgle Brown's store at Pinetop and got shot with rock salt and it also damaged some merchandise. They had a sale of the damaged goods, and the victim went all the way to Tularosa t' get de-salted so no one would know about it around Pinetop. Hacks and jokesters had fun guessing what the culprit did t' get shot until the Browns put that thank-you ad in the paper."

"All you need to know now is who th' culprit was," Coop added.

"A-h-h-h I don't care so much t' know that, probably never will know who *that* thief was. I'm gonna go warm up an' read." He wrote information about the article in his book and disappeared into the warm room. I pulled my earflaps tighter and continued searching the walls.

New papers I hadn't seen before began to appear. One of them was called *The Socorro Bullion:*

THE SOCORRO BULLION
September 1, 1881

Auditors and tax collectors from Santa Fe have descended upon local businesses to determine that they have complied with the new taxation on Texas merchandise. We wonder why they come so heavily armed.

It was curious that the tax collectors would "descend" on businesses and I had never heard of the tax on Texas merchandise. Just across from that article, I found something else about it:

THE ROBINSON BLACK RANGE
Monday, September 5, 1881

Tax collectors and auditors from Santa Fe were surprised and dismayed to discover that the books and records of our local merchants have succumbed to a tragic fire that destroyed the office of Martin & Samson, bookkeepers for virtually every business in town. The books had been gathered for audit to determine taxes due from each company. Mr. Samson said the visit by the state officials was entirely unexpected and the unfortunate fire has made their visit unfruitful and unnecessary.

"Sounds like some chicanery was goin' on back there. I wonder what *that* was."

"What you talkin' about, Demps?"

"Musta been talkin' to myself, quit buttin' in." On a new page, I wrote: Sept. 1, 1881, Armed tax collectors Bullion. Sept. 1, 1881, Fire burns records Black Range.

This had t' be a separate incident from Tuck's murder story, but it looked interesting. I was at the end of the hall and turned around to the opposite wall and the first thing I saw was *The Pinetop Crow Special* about the raid on the Beavers Ranch. Grandma had a copy of it folded in her Bible and I had seen it there long ago, but was too young to pay attention to so much writing.

THE PINETOP CROW SPECIAL
Friday, October 24, 1884

We issue this Special to give our Readers more Information on the Battle and Cattle Theft that Occurred last Wednesday on the Beavers Ranch.

MURDER ON BEAVERS RANCH

The Particulars of the Fight and Theft of Cattle as Related by Witnesses and Participants.

About noon on Wednesday, October 22, Bet Sommes, a cowhand, discovered the trail of a cattle herd being surreptitiously gathered and driven toward a remote section of the Beavers Ranch. Tucker Beavers, Sr., Bob Nealy, Bet Sommes, John Crider, and Pete Kidd trailed the herd to the area near a line shack in what is called the Far Pasture.

The Battle Reconstructed

Two old-time scouts and frontiersmen, Oliver Lee and Zenas Meeker, have visited the site of the gunfight and the following is how they have reconstructed the events:

The five ranchmen found the gathered herd in the Far Pasture with no one around them. While Bet Sommes stayed with the herd, the other four rode on to the line shack.

As they approached the shack, they were caught in crossfire from the woods to their left and the shack. Tucker and Pete turned to attack those in the woods and their horses were shot down before they had gone twenty yards. Pete took a grazing shot to the head and was effectively out of the fight, though he was wounded once more. Tucker had cover behind his horse and signs show that he did effective battle with the occupants in the woods, wounding or killing at least two. Unfortunately, he could not get cover from both combatants and the occupants of the line shack peppered him with long-range shots until he collapsed.

Meantime, Bob Nealy and John Crider charged the line shack, Nealy losing his horse in the process and arriving on foot. They shot through the cracks between the logs and several inside were hit, one is suspected killed, though the body was carried away. Bob Nealy fell by the shack and, though wounded, John Crider rode through the woods to the herd where the two hands tried to drive the cattle away. They were caught by ten or twelve riders on unshod horses and the herd with the two hands was driven south.

Posse Organized

Sheriff Garrett with Deputy Ryles organized a posse but they were unable to catch the stolen herd. They returned with the body of Bet Sommes, found beside his dead horse along the trail.

As best can be determined, the thieves were Indian, though what tribe is unknown. It is logically believed that they are Apache. There has long been a close and warm relationship of the ranch with the Mescalero Apaches and they are not considered to be the culprits in this incident.

Casualties

Tucker Beavers, Sr. and Bet Sommes were murdered in the fight or shortly thereafter in the case of Sommes. Bob Nealy and Pete Kidd are seriously wounded but Doctor Hutto expects that both will recover. John Crider is still missing, his fate unknown.

Funeral Arrangements

Funeral service for the two decedents will be held at 10:00 AM, Tuesday, October 28, 1884, at the Pinetop Union Church. Interment will be at Pinetop Cemetery.

Cattle Bound for Mexican Ranch?

There have been rumors of a ranch in Mexico that uses the Beavers brand as their own. Cattle, stolen a few head at a time from the Beavers Ranch, bear a brand that cannot be altered; therefore the thieves do not bother to change it. Cattle thefts prior to this occasion have been small and largely unnoticed.

The murders and size of the herd stolen are sure to draw attention from the Beavers Ranch owners and from state and federal authorities.

Other Cattle Stolen

Beavers Ranch is not the only ranch suffering losses by the thieves. Ranches all along the border from Texas to California lose cattle that are driven across the border. Some assert that cattle stolen south of the border and driven north might exceed the stolen southbound herds.

The situation is ignored by federal authorities of both

countries and control of the activities is left to largely
overwhelmed and ineffective local enforcement.

I read the article carefully for the first time and learned a lot
I had not known about the raid and the ranch. It had always
been a puzzle to me that Bet Sommes was buried in the family
plot beside Mr. Beavers and it put a lump in my throat to finally
understand and realize that "the family" included the ranch
hands. It isn't quite that way anymore, though we still care for
the permanent hands on the ranch more than the summer help.
Only four or five years ago we had buried Grandma Mary
Beavers in her place between Tucker Beavers, Sr. and Tucker
Beavers, Jr. I read the article again and a third time, picking up
things I had not noticed before. Uncle Zenas Meeker was living
on Culp Mountain and Mr. Oliver Lee had moved from his
Dog Canyon ranch to Alamogordo.

A weight seemed to settle on my shoulders and I shivered but
I wasn't cold. Even as I walked away, my eyes beheld that
headline: MURDER ON BEAVERS RANCH. People I didn't
know—Tucker Beavers, Bet Sommes—had died; people I knew
suffered—Grandpa Bob; Pecos Pete Kidd never rode again;
Aunt Mary could never pass the cemetery without stopping at
the graves and shedding tears; Grandma Presilla, Aunt Eda B.,
and Aunt Sue Ellen all were affected by what had happened
over thirty years ago. And I had to find the whole story on
wallpaper in a stranger's home. Even though I had seen
Grandpa's scars from the fight, I realized that men carry scars
on their hearts too. Grandpa would get very quiet sometimes as
he rested by the fire and Grandma would whisper to me,
"Shhhh, Dempsey, he's remembering, let him be and he will be
back in a minute." He always "came back," but it seemed even
behind those smiling eyes there was a sadness, a memory of
something lost.

Little did I know then that there was much more than the

murders on Beavers Ranch that caused that sadness in Grandpa. These walls told me. These walls *could* talk. I went back and wrote down in their proper order the articles I had already found. From here on, I wrote the articles down in the notebook, word for word.

Chapter 8
The Trouble About Texas

If man will only realize that it is unmanly to obey laws
that are unjust, no man's tyranny will enslave him
—Gandhi

I didn't go back to the walls for a couple of days, but eventually
my boredom overtook my dark thoughts and I found myself
perusing the walls as I passed through to or from the barn. The
horses must have been bored too, for they were restless and
enjoyed the challenges of wading deep snow or walking atop the
frozen crust until they were tired and readily returned to the
shelter of the barn. We didn't have a thermometer, but I know
there were days on end that the temperature didn't get above
the teens and the wind blew—hard—and the sun would near
blind a person.

Tired of reading *Ben-Hur,* I leafed through the notes I had
made about articles on the wall and ran across the two about all
the accounting books burning at Robinson and the armed state
auditors in Socorro about the same time.

"Coop, have you seen anything about trouble in the Rio
Grande Valley with tax collectors or bandits in 1881?"

Cooper closed his book with a sigh. He knew he would get
no peace if I wanted to talk and there was no use to fight it, "I'll
look." He leafed through his notebook and read some. "Yeah,
here it is, it's from *The Socorro Bullion,* June 10th, 1881. I found
it in the hallway on the . . . right side goin' to th' barn."

"What did it say?"

"Didn't *say* anything, read something about a special interest law."

"Guess I'll hafta go see for myself," I said. I bundled up and left the fire. It didn't take any time to find the article. The headline caught my eye:

THE SOCORRO BULLION
Friday, June 10, 1881
A LAW FOR SPECIAL INTERESTS

A new law was rushed through the legislature in the wee hours of the last day of the 1881 session that will greatly affect business in the lower Rio Grande Valley. Parties interested in promoting their own interests and fortunes have passed a law that places an import tax on any merchandise imported from Texas. We wonder how our southern neighbor likes this attention.

Many merchants hereabouts are asking how such a special interest law that punishes open and free commerce could be passed. We have been assured that this issue is far from over.

Someone must have been reading the papers as they pasted them up, for right next to that page was a paper from El Paso that had a related article. It wasn't the last time I would find things together like that.

THE EL PASO DAILY HERALD
Thursday, June 9, 1881
CHALK ONE UP FOR THE SANTA FE RING

Acting true to form, the Santa Fe Ring has sneaked through the New Mexico legislature a law that favors their minions in the world of commerce. Specifically, the law places an odious tax on all merchandise imported into that state from Texas. The intended result is to force commerce in the lower Rio Grande Valley to look north for their supplies by placing more readily available merchandise at a heavy handicap. We are afraid that this law will precipitate a second War Between the States.

Might have known. By now, we had learned that to look for related *subjects*, it was easier to find by looking for related *dates*, so I began looking for any paper published within the year 1881. I found the following articles and placed them in their chronological order:

THE SOCORRO BULLION
Thursday, September 1, 1881

Auditors and tax collectors from Santa Fe have descended upon local businesses to determine that they have complied with the new taxation on Texas merchandise. We wonder why they come so heavily armed.

THE ROBINSON BLACK RANGE
Monday, September 5, 1881

Tax collectors and auditors from Santa Fe were surprised and dismayed to discover that the books and records of our local merchants have succumbed to a tragic fire that destroyed the office of Martin & Samson, bookkeepers for virtually every business in town. The books had been gathered for audit to determine taxes due from each company. Mr. Samson said the visit by the state officials was entirely unexpected and the unfortunate fire has made their visit unfruitful and unnecessary.

THE LAS CRUCES RIO GRANDE REPUBLICAN
Monday, September 12, 1881

Resistance to the so-called Texas Tax has forced the State tax collectors to patrol the roads looking for contraband merchandise. *While we deplore this special interest law, we are dismayed to find normally upstanding and honest merchants defying law.*

Well la—di—da, Mr. Republican, when has it become more important to obey a law than to have good sense or ignore th' fact that th' law was bad? I'll bet you wouldn't jump off th' top of th' Organs if it was *"The Law,"* yet you would urge ever'one else to!

And lo and behold, not far away, I found this Santa Fe paper article:

SANTA FE WEEKLY GAZETTE
Tuesday, November 15, 1881

Our correspondent from the lower valley informed us this week that freight traffic from the south has slowed considerably since additional agents have been sent to patrol the roads in search of smuggled merchandise.

While we sympathize with those who view the import tax as odious, we are dismayed that normally honest citizens and merchants have chosen to flaunt the law instead of complying as reasonable upstanding citizens should.

Horsebiscuits! So . . . it is reasonable and upstanding to obey an odious and unfair law just because it is under the mantle of law. These are probably the same people who hold more allegiance to *law* than to *justice*. How ignorant and spineless can people get? If they had been around in colonial times, they would have paid the tea tax without a murmur . . . well, they *might* murmur. Thank God they weren't there!

EL PASO MORNING STAR
Tuesday, October 4, 1881

Freighters tell us that traffic up the Rio Grande Valley has been especially heavy recently as merchants and businesses begin to stock up for the winter months when much of the freight traffic will be impeded by the weather.

TULAROSA SANDS
Friday, December 2, 1881

Our curiosity was aroused by the passing in the night of an unscheduled train and inquiries of the stationmaster found that the Special was from El Paso to Santa Fe. Later, a telegram came to our desk from our Santa Fe correspondent and relieved our curiosity. It seems that the Special had one boxcar and was sealed, to be opened by the State Auditor only. Imagine his surprise and consternation when upon opening the car he discovered his agents inside dressed only in tar and feathers!

It was a tale told many times by the old-timers about how the "Santa Fe Auditors" had been sent home in a boxcar and how a little later some of the very same men had reappeared as bandits harassing and robbing freighters along the roads. This last story tells how the Texas Tax was abandoned:

THE SOCORRO BULLION
Thursday, January 12, 1882

The discovery of a fresh grave in the Jornada that has yielded the body of one of the road agents plaguing the roads has led us to the conclusion that Messers. Colt and Winchester have taken to riding the freights.

The aroma of fresh coffee and cornbread brought to my attention that my stomach had been talking to me for some time and I headed for the "kitchen," which doubled for the living room and dining room. I ate in a hurry and got back to those talking walls as fast as I could.

"What about washing th' dishes?" Coop called.

"I'll get them after supper."

"If there's any supper," Coop growled. He hated cooking almost as much as he hated washing dishes.

The Ferris Good Sense Corset Waist advertisement had another code written under it and I looked up the next ad. There was another Ferris Good Sense Corset Waist ad with a young girl, shoulders bared, low-bosomed corset—very fetching. In part it read:

A FLEXIBLE CLASP
Ferris Good Sense Corset, Waist No. 317, is especially designed for growing girls.

As suspected, there was another code. In fact, we discovered that every female scantily clad or undergarment advertisement on the walls had a code, top and bottom. Those darn Fereday boys!

CHAPTER 9
THE TROUBLE AT PINETOP

A wise man feareth, and departeth from evil: But the fool rageth and is confident.

Proverbs 14:16

The bunkroom was a treasure of articles about Tucker Beavers. It took me several days to collect all the information the papers held and put them into some sort of order. This is the story I found:

THE EDDY ARGUS
Tuesday, April 13, 1886
MURDER AT PINETOP

Word comes from The Pinetop Crow *that a young man of that community was murdered the night of April 4th & 5th. Riley Giddens, son of prominent merchant John R. Giddens, was seen in an altercation with an unknown person under the light of the Town Hall the night of April 4th. A shot was fired and the assailant was seen to take the gun away from young Giddens and beat him severely with it. He then made his escape, leaving Giddens bleeding and unconscious.*

Giddens was carried to the doctor's office where he expired at 2:17 AM April 5th without regaining consciousness.

Sheriff Pat Garrett is in charge of the investigation. Anyone having information about the incident should contact him.

TULAROSA SANDS
Wednesday, April 21, 1886
SUSPECT IN PINETOP MURDER SOUGHT

Sheriff Pat Garrett is seeking the whereabouts of Tucker Beavers, Jr., a suspect in the murder of Riley Giddens on the night of April 4 & 5th. Beavers was last seen the afternoon of April 4th. He is described as 21 years old, of slight build, about 6 feet tall with dark hair. He left to resume working in the range roundup in progress at that time in the basin and has not been seen since.

It is known that Beavers and Giddens had difficulties in the past and it is feared that the events of April 4th & 5th are the culmination of their quarrel. Anyone with knowledge of the whereabouts of Tucker Beavers, Jr. is urged to contact Sheriff Garrett or Deputy George Ryles at Pinetop.

THE PINETOP CROW
Thursday, April 29, 1886
AN EDITORIAL

The naming of Tucker Beavers, Jr. as suspect in the death of Riley Giddens has sharply divided our community. Some claim that Tucker would not have killed Giddens in such a manner and then run off. Others feel that Beavers's flight is sure evidence of his guilt. The fact that the two had difficulties in the past lends weight to their argument.

Witness descriptions of the assailant closely resemble the description of Tucker Beavers—and a hundred other men in this region. The shot fired that drew attention to the conflict was very likely fired by Riley Giddens. Witnesses say that his assailant was seen to take the gun away from him. It was later determined that Giddens owned and carried the gun at times. This would lend one to speculate that the killer may have been acting in self-defense.

Our community has known for some time that the Beavers and Nealys have intended to follow their stolen herd and seek justice for their fallen. It is an unfortunate coincidence that Tucker Beavers would choose this time to leave unannounced—if that is indeed what he has done.

We do not know which combatant started the fight. We are not sure if the shot fired took effect or missed its intended target. And most important of all, we do not know the identity of the second man in that fight.

THE PINETOP CROW
Thursday, November 4, 1886

Unverified reports are circulating here that Tucker Beavers, Jr. has died in a gun battle in the province of Sonora, Mexico. Beavers is being sought for questioning in the murder of Riley Giddens in April of this year.

The next item to appear chronologically in our story is the earthquake of May 3, 1887. It seems that Tucker was on his way home when the quakes struck and he returned to Bavispe to give aid to his friends there. That delay would have devastating results for our friend. Because it had some value to the story, I copied down some of the articles about the quakes:

EL PASO MORNING STAR
Monday, May 9, 1887

From our sister publication in Tombstone comes this report of the earthquake that shook us slightly on May 3:

EARTHQUAKE
Everyone Runs Out in the Street

The Movement Up and Down

At six minutes past three this afternoon a severe shock of earthquake was felt in this city. At first, as a reporter of THE PROSPECTOR was sitting at his desk, he thought it was a heavy ore team or freight wagon running away, and stepped to the door to see if he could catch an item, when someone hollered earthquake, which was good news for the reporter who immediately pulled out his watch and counted the seconds while it lasted, and by his timepiece it lasted about 35 seconds. After the first shock was over, he began rummaging around for particulars. The first man he met was Palmer Seamans, who said it was a dandy—it stopped all the clocks in his store.

The second shock occurred about eight minutes later, but was very slight, just causing the people to step out in the street, and lasted about two seconds. The third shock was hardly felt, it occurred about fifteen minutes of four o'clock.

THE SOCORRO BULLION
Thursday, May 12, 1887
TALES FROM THE EARTHQUAKE

Fantastic stories are emerging from the center of the late earthquake, some true and some no doubt enhanced and expanded by the teller. Without comment, we present here a few of the stories gleaned from local papers and some eyewitness accounts:

From Tombstone: Two men rode in from their ranch in the Sulphur Springs Valley, reporting the eruption of a huge geyser of water from a fissure 4 or 5 feet wide and 100 feet long. The water shot high into the air and formed a lake the two men waded their horses through.

All the buildings on Slaughter's San Bernardino Ranch have collapsed. There has been no report of any injuries.

Reports from Mexico indicate that the quake was much more severe there. Several towns and ranches are totally destroyed, including Bavispe. There have been several deaths.

Several forest fires have led people to speculate that a volcano has arisen somewhere in the mountains of Mexico.

Many springs have dried up and several more have appeared in other places. Some of the springs have warm water, some smell strongly of sulphur.

Dr. George Goodfellow of Tombstone is organizing an expedition to Mexico to lend medical aid and search for the volcano.

THE PINETOP CROW
Thursday, May 26, 1887

Word has reached here for the second time that Tucker Beavers has died in Mexico, this time due to the late earthquake that devastated that region.

It is a sad commentary that in this modern age of telegraph and telephone that communications over large distances in some areas of our world are so unreliable that news is passed by word of mouth or rumor. Until more reliable reports are given, the family holds out hope that Mr. Beavers is yet alive.

Somebody wanted people to think Tucker was dead. I wonder who and hope fervently it was not a Nealy or Beavers—or Brown for that matter.

THE PINETOP CROW
Thursday, December 29, 1887
A CHRISTMAS WEDDING

Miss Lucinda Nealy and Mr. Rance Brown exchanged vows in a candlelit Christmas evening ceremony in the Pinetop Union Church. The young couple hosted a reception at the home of

Mr. Brown's parents after the ceremony.

Family legend says that Tucker and Aunt Cindy were very close and the news (rumors, it turned out) of Tucker's death influenced her to consent to Uncle Rance's pleas to marry him.

The next paper skipped to March, 1888. It was an article confirming Tucker's return from the dead—or Mexico:

THE PINETOP CROW
Thursday, March 22, 1888
A PRODIGAL RETURNS

To the surprise and delight of his family, Tucker Beavers, Jr. has returned from Mexico and dispelled all rumors of his demise.

He reports that the organization that had robbed this region of cattle has been destroyed, largely by the earthquake of May, 1887. We suspect that his activity in the area may have accomplished as much as the earthquake in eliminating the rustlers and thieves.

Mr. Beavers told this reporter that he was greatly surprised at the murder of Riley Giddens and had not known of it until his return.

TULAROSA SANDS
Tuesday, March 27, 1888
GIDDENS MURDER TO BE DISCUSSED

The district attorney will present the case of the murder of Riley Giddens to the Grand Jury for consideration.

Not too long ago, señor hemp would have been judge, jury, and executioner—and quite possibly very wrong. Fortunately, our society has progressed far enough along the road to civilization that we are content to let the law, no matter how slow, take its course.

TULAROSA SANDS
Monday, April 2, 1888
GRAND JURY SESSION ENDS

The spring session of the Otero County Grand Jury ended March 30. The last item considered in this session was the murder of Riley Giddens at Pinetop two years ago. The jury indicted Tucker Beavers, Jr. for the murder.

THE PINETOP CROW
Thursday, April 5, 1888
MURDER SUSPECT ARRESTED

Tucker Beavers was arrested April 3 by Deputy George Ryles for the murder of Riley Giddens in April of 1886. Beavers has engaged J. G. Burnett as his council. Trial has been set for October 25, 1888.

It seemed that from this point, the story spun faster and faster to its conclusion.

TULAROSA SANDS
Thursday, October 25, 1888
GIDDENS MURDER TRIAL BEGINS

The wisdom of hiring J.G. Burnett as his defense lawyer became very apparent yesterday when Tucker Beavers went on trial for the murder of Riley Giddens. Mr. Burnett quickly discredited both witnesses for the prosecution, establishing that Bill Evans could not positively identify the assailant and that Duncan "Doc" Shull was too visually impaired to identify the man.

The prosecution rested after the testimony of the witnesses and the trial was continued until 9:00 Friday morning when the defense is expected to call Mr. Beavers to the stand.

TULAROSA SANDS
Monday, October 29, 1888
TRIAL ENDS IN TRAGIC FASHION

The much-anticipated murder trial of Tucker Beavers, Jr. ended suddenly last Friday morning when the defendant and Deputy George Ryles were gunned down on the steps of the courthouse.

The defendant Beavers, escorted by Deputy Ryles and preceded by defense attorney J.G. Burnett, was climbing the steps to the courthouse when a screaming man pushed through the crowd and shot deputy Ryles and young Beavers. The assailant is identified as John R. Giddens, father of the deceased Riley Giddens.

Assailant Quickly Subdued

Giddens was quickly subdued by the crowd and two deputies who had been momentarily separated from Ryles and his prisoner by the press of the crowd. Giddens was manacled and marched off to the jail. As he was hustled away, Giddens called for lawyer Burnett to represent him, to which the shaken lawyer roared, "No!"

Shooting Victim Dies

Deputy Ryles survived the attack with some broken ribs and the loss of a quantity of blood. He is expected to fully recover.

Tucker Beavers was shot in the chest at point-blank range and was attended on the steps by his mother and Mrs. Lucinda Nealy Brown, a close friend. After some whispered words for the two stricken women, Beavers died. Arraignment for the attacker had not been set at the time of this printing.

I read the story again and again. It was unreal, like a yellow-

99

paper dime novel, yet it had happened to someone so close to my family. Even the editorials that followed did not soothe my feelings.

THE EL PASO DAILY HERALD
Thursday, November 1, 1888
ASSASSINATION USURPS JUSTICE

The cowardly murder of Tucker Beavers on the steps of the Tularosa Courthouse stole the young man's right to a fair trial in addition to his life. The consensus of the legal profession is that the witnesses for the prosecution had been effectively discredited by the defense and that very likely Beavers would be a free man today. Instead, his grieving family and friends are preparing for his funeral.

Who can fathom the mind of the murderer, John R. Giddens? His seeming conviction that Beavers had murdered his son defies the real possibility that another had fought with and killed his son.

The recent events have run their course and Tucker Beavers will not have his opportunity to prove his innocence in the murder of Riley Giddens. Instead, his name will forever carry the stigma of guilt to the observer; and his loved ones will know the bitterness of a young man robbed of life and justice by an unwarranted act of vengeance.

For the present, Otero County officials have no plans to investigate the Giddens murder any further. In all likelihood, the matter will be quietly laid aside and hopefully forgotten. "Is there no justice for this poor widow's son?"

LAS CRUCES BORDERER
Tuesday, November 13, 1888

The Pinetop Crow *reported in their last edition that the funeral of Tucker Beavers, Jr. was attended by virtually everyone in that part of the country. Beavers was assassinated on the steps of the Tularosa Courthouse by the bereaved father of the man Beavers was accused of killing.*

The conviction that Beavers was innocent of the murder is pervasive on the east side of the basin and feelings have run hot against John R. Giddens, Beavers's assassin. He has been moved from the Tularosa jail to an undisclosed location.

I was sad and bothered for a long time.

CHAPTER 10
THE MYSTERY OF THE MURDER

Five Thousand Hardware Stores display this sign in their
stores:
The **WINCHESTER** Store
They sell Winchester Roller Skates, Pocket Knives, Rifles,
Fishing Tackle, etc.
WINCHESTER REPEATING ARMS COMPANY, NEW HAVEN,
CONN.

The snow line had been creeping up the mountain very slowly—
too slowly. There was too much snow for Nap to make it to
Pinetop and all creation above the snow line was frozen solid in
spite of a bright sun. To say that we were restless would be an
understatement. Even the horses were restive. We were running
out of supplies and firewood and had about decided to leave
when on the way to the barn one morning I heard a gunshot far
down the mountain.

As I reached the back door, it opened and Coop asked, "Did
you hear that?"

"Shore did, bet it's Nap at th' snow line an' I hope he has
food or our parole papers."

"Let's go find out." Coop drew his pistol and fired it into the
air—almost—he was under the eave and the shot brought down
splinters and wood and snow on us.

"Dang, Coop, if I want a shower, I for sure wouldn't take it
with you!"

Both horses were saddled and standing in the pathway by the time Coop came back with his coat. In keeping the path to the barn clear, we had built up quite a windrow of snow on both sides. They had a struggle getting over the south pile and when they did, they fell through the crust on the level snow, their bellies actually dragging below the surface. There was nothing to do but go single file, taking turns breaking trail. It was a mile before the level snow dropped below horse-belly-high and both were soaked with sweat and puffing. We would have rested them, but they didn't think standing in thirty inches of snow was restful and insisted on moving on. We didn't object.

"Where do you think he is, Demps?"

"I would guess right where the snow line crosses the fence." And that is where we found him.

"Howdy boys." He was sitting on the wagon tailgate swinging his legs an' grinnin'. It was the first time we had seen him in over six weeks.

"Whatcha know, Nap, is it clear for us t' quit hidin' out?" Cooper asked. The pile of gear in the wagon told me the answer to that.

"Nope, storm ain't quit a-ragin' down th' mountain. Doc Shetley says March will most likely be th'worst time."

"Well, you can tell Doc Shetley an' th' rest of 'em that come th' first of April, I'm gonna be grinnin' at Aunt Cindy's door."

"Most cert'nly will, Demps, an if'n I can find that infernal shotgun, I'll hide it."

"Ya don't hafta hide th' gun, Nap, just th' shells," Cooper said.

"How are things at the two ranches?" I asked.

"Doin' well, Demps, doin' well. No one else has taken ill. Miz Cindy stayed in the bunkhouse 'til she was sure she hadn't taken th' flu, then came on back to th' house. She's been awful quiet since she come back. I almos' wished you two were down there t' give her somethin' t' stew over. Me an' yore pa buried Mr. Bob in th' cemetery. We both thanks you for diggin' th' grave."

"Wish I—we—coulda done more."

"T'were 'nough fer me an' yer Pa, that's f'sure. If we woulda had t' dig that grave, we'd have been up here stranded with you boys. Barely got home afore that storm hit as it was."

"It was a doozy up here," Coop added.

"I saw the grave th' day that storm hit, that was th' same day you laid him to rest?"

"Yup."

"Wow, that really was close!"

"You bet, Josh had t' stay with us a couple of days b'fore he could git home."

"Nap, do you remember when Riley Giddens was killed?"

"Shore do, Demps, I was repin' for th' Rafter JD when it happened. Someone rode out to th' roundup and told us about it that morning . . . no, it wasn't just someone, it was Miz Cindy an' Miz Kizzie Stark, come t' git ol' man Stark. He was justice o' th' peace er somethin', had to be there for th' inquest. We was sure surprised it had gone that far."

"What had gone that far?" Cooper asked.

"Feudin' 'mongst th' young folk. They were split up atween th' Santa Fe Ring an' Texas Smugglers. Not many were on th' Ring's side; Giddens was mouthiest amongst them an' he kept things stirred up."

"I thought that was a town feud, what was Tucker Beavers in it for?" I asked.

"Don't recollect he was much, but he did whip th' tar outa Giddens fer notifyin' the Dolan gang about their cattle drive to th' reservation. One of those toughs they sent out t' stop us roughed up little Green Nealy an' made th' mistake o' braggin' t' Tuck about it. Tuck whacked him across his face with his .44

an' knocked him out of his saddle—almost started a gun battle right there, only we were a little faster an' got th' drop on that gang. It shore was a close call. I shook for a month after that whenever I thought of it."

"That was th' only time they fought, wasn't it?"

"S'far es I know, Demps, but there was a lot of jawin' b'tween th' two if they happened t' git together. Mostly, they avoided each other."

"Bet that was hard t' do in a small community," Cooper said by way of asking.

"Th' community was not as small back then as you would think. There was a lot goin' on an' a lot more people in th' country than they is now," Nap hopped down and started rolling back the tarp over the wagon bed. "Gotta be gittin' down th' mountain, boys, Miz Cindy'll be lookin' for me t' tell her how you two're gittin' along."

"Was Aunt Cindy on th' Santa Fe Ring side?"

"Fer Goodness sake, Demps, whur'd you ever git that idée?" Nap grunted as he heaved a hundred-pound sack of flour over th' fence to my shoulder.

"Well she didn't like Tucker Beavers any."

" 'Nother bad idea. She was expectin' t' marry Tucker when he disappeared."

"Marry! Why she 'most always gits mad when someone mentions him around her."

"Seems t' me some people get mad and some people cry in those situations," Coop observed. "Maybe she would rather get mad."

"You may be right, Coop, I don't think I ever saw Aunt Cindy cry."

"Tough as nails," Coop whispered as to himself.

Nap stood still a moment, "She's cried some since Mr. Bob passed, gets mad if she sees I know it."

"Grandma said they shared secrets about something," I said.

"They was awful close, I took my life in my hands when I tried t' talk her outa goin' up there when he got sick, think she'da shot her way through a posse t' get to him."

"Hey, Nap, is that Kizzie Stark same as Miz Kizzie Simmons?"

"Well Demps, I can tell you don't know yer history. Yessir, Miz Kizzie of th' second is th' same as Miz Kizzie of th' first, you oughta knowed that. Here, take this bale o' sugar afore I drop it."

"Got any horse feed on there?"

"Only oats an' sweet grain, hay's mostly gone. We got a lot o' snow this year, it'll be a good growin' season."

"We'da fed our horses cornmeal th' last couple a days—if we'd had any." Cooper grinned at Nap. "You shore run your supply train close on th' starvin' timeline."

"If it ain't deep snow, it's deep mud 'at keeps interfering with this train's schedule." He reached under th' seat an' handed me a bag of newspapers, "Don't read those all at once, an' Miz Cindy said t' be sure an' tell you she's expectin' those book reports t' be done when you come down, says if you're through with them now, she'll take them so she can look 'em over afore you come down."

"Hah! Won't take her long t' look at Dempsey's blank pages," Cooper laughed.

I ignored his jab. "Nap, do you think Tucker killed th' Giddens boy?"

"They was men, Demps, an' *no one* ever b'lieved he killed Riley Giddens. Conly Hicks'll tell you that Tucker did his share o' killin' in th' war in Mexico, but if he had even thought he had killed Riley, he wouldn't have run. *Not one second* did anyone who knew him, *friend or foe*, believe Tucker Beavers would have run away!"

Nap surprised me. His conviction carried a lot of comfort for me. "Well who coulda done it?"

"Someone who would have run."

"You don't have any guesses?"

"A man don't spec-u-late on that out loud 'round here s' long as his suspect er any o' his kin is livin'. Yer on your own on that."

"You shoulda knowed better than t' ask, Demps," Cooper admonished in a severe tone.

"Coop, you're nervier than a busted tooth."

"Yeah, an' you're touchier than a teased snake."

"*Saint Cooper,* you're . . ."

"Sometimes th' best answer is silence, Demps." Nap grinned, "I gotta git."

"We gotta figger how t' get all this stuff up to th' house afore th' ground thaws," Cooper replied. "You didn't throw in a couple o' packsaddles, did you, Nap?"

"Sorry, boys, I didn't. Use your saddle blankets for an aparejo an' your saddles for a sawbuck."

"Ain't got much choice in that," I said.

"See you in a couple o' weeks. Wake up, you mules an' git!" He slapped reins and turned the wagon down th' mountain.

We had to make two trips apiece t' get all that plunder to th' house. Even though th' trail was pretty broken, our horses knew they had done something when we finished. We fed them some sweet grain and retired to cook a real meal for a change.

"It's just like Miz Cindy t' get mad instead o' cryin' when someone mentions Tucker, Demps. You know she'd do just opposite o' what you expected."

"Yeah, an' I keep thinking 'bout her kneeling by Tuck when he died. Someone who hated him wouldn't o' done that, prob'ly wouldn't have gone to th' trial."

"Not likely she would get to hatin' him for somethin' he

done *after* he died."

"I doubt he done anything after he died—'cept smelled a little . . ."

"Demps, that's th' worst profanation I've heard in an age."

"True, ain't it?"

"Shore it's true, but you don't go to a funeral an' sniff th' corpse, do you?"

"Don't go to funerals if I can avoid it."

As is common in situations where you go without for a while, we cooked too much, ate too much, and didn't sleep too much that night. We had been sleeping in the heated rooms since late fall and about 1:00 AM, I woke up thinking about Tucker Beavers and the things he had done. It was no use sleeping any more so I stoked the fire some and sat with my back against the warm rocks of the fireplace and read my notes. I made a list of the things the walls had told me and a list of things I didn't know. My "List of New Knowledge" ran like this:

1. Women's legs go all the way up. (Placed first to watch Cooper faunch.)
2. Tuck was accused of murdering Riley Giddens; J G Burnett was his lawyer.
3. He was murdered by John R. Giddens while going to his trial.
4. The prevailing belief is that Tucker did not kill Riley and that he would not have run away if he had beaten him.
5. Tucker had buffaloed a tough that had abused Green on a cattle drive to the reservation.
6. Rance Brown had shot a man with rock salt that was burgling his store.
7. The Rock Salt sale.
8. The Texas Tax War.
9. Riley Giddens's murder, Tucker suspected.

10. Aunt Cindy was to marry Tucker.
11. Tucker never cleared of murder.

My "List of Things I Don't Know" contained:

1. Who killed Riley Giddens if Tucker didn't?
2. Why did Tucker stay a whole extra year in Mexico?
3. What happened when Tucker got shot in Mexico?
4. Who did Rance Brown shoot with rock salt?
5. Who started false reports that Tucker was dead?
6. Why did Aunt Cindy marry Rance?

Looking over my lists, I decided that these walls hadn't told me everything and possibly would not ever answer the questions I had. Even so, I decided that they would get a closer examination starting in the morning when the light was better and the house maybe a little warmer. It was 4 a.m. when I fell asleep again and late when I awoke to the aroma of frying bacon and eggs.

"Shore smells good, Coop," I said as I pulled on my boots.

"If you hurry, you can have the horses fed and watered before it's all ready."

"I'm on my way," I called from the hallway before the door slammed shut. When I came back, Coop was already eating and reading my lists I had left on the table.

"Yours is in the pan," he said without looking up.

I got my plate, poured coffee, and refilled his cup before I sat down. "What do you think about my lists?"

"Mine would likely be longer than your lists, but yours needs some more re-search, I would say."

"The re-search will begin startin' this day," I said over my cup.

"Guess I should help," Cooper replied. He copied my two lists into his book. "Miz Cindy's gonna be put out if we don't fill out the book reports."

"She may be put out more when she finds out what we been doin' with our time."

"She'd understand if she'd been locked up in a house with someone who don't got enough brains t' grease a gimlet."

"Well, I thanks ye for th' compliment, Coop. I know it was hard t' come up with that, bein's you ain't got enough brains t' fry an egg in. Here, have some more coffee, it'll help your headache."

There followed a long conversation on th' relative intelligences of the two conversationalists, which would not endear either participant to their Sunday school teacher. By and by when the conversation dragged, we both got up and started reading the walls. Passing down the hall, I came across an obituary page of the *Alamogordo Sands,* formerly the *Tularosa Sands* until it moved to Alamogordo in 1900. What had caught my eye was the word "Pinetop," but the rest of that article was covered over by a newer paper. When I tried to peel them apart, instead of separating, they both peeled off the wall. A little flour paste repaired the tear and I discovered that when I rubbed the newsprint with a damp cloth, the top paper became transparent enough so that I could read the page below. The article I saw read:

Pinetop Pioneer Passes

Mr. Rance Brown, 45, early pioneer resident of Old Pinetop, died February 10th, 1899 in his home. He is survived by his wife, Mrs Lucinda Nealy Brown of the home and . . .

The rest of the article was not readable. The only thing remarkable about it was that I had thought it was later—1902 or so—that he had died.

CHAPTER 11
THE SILENT WALLS

The prayer was short enough For a hungry stomach.

—Napoleon Witt

That was essentially the end of our education from the walls if you discount the underwear advertisements some lonesome buck cataloged. I don't think he missed a single ad.

"Looks to me like we got a murder mystery on our hands," Coop said a few days later when we had completed our search of the walls.

"Yeah, we do, if we prove that Tucker didn't kill Riley, we'll have to find who the killer was—or is," I said.

"How we gonna do that? Th' walls quit talkin' about it."

"I guess we'll have t' talk to real people and see if they will tell us," I said.

"That may be harder than readin' walls, seein' how they have kept all this secret from you. I suppose it would be better if I did some snoopin' 'round instead of you."

"Might be, but I got an idea if we *both* poked around different parts of that tale, we might get a whole story without anyone realizing we're doin' it."

Cooper looked over our lists, "I shore would like to know who your uncle Rance shot with the rock salt."

"Seems pretty certain that it was Giddens, don't it?"

"I 'magine so, nobody else we know of fits th' bill, but from what we know right now, no one ever accused him of it." Cooper

111

wrote some notes beside his list.

With nothing else to do, I was forced to read Aunt Cindy's books and to save my hide and ears, I wrote reports on th' ones I read.

Sunday, March 30, 1919, it started snowing, and in the night, snow turned to rain and ground snow was making a fast retreat up th' mountain. We could hear creeks on both sides of th' house roaring in their canyons.

"Glory be we been set free!" I crowed and headed for the barn.

"Ain't you gonna pack anything?" Cooper called.

"I'll get that stuff later—about 1999," I called over my shoulder.

We didn't even eat breakfast for scurrying around and getting ready to leave that place. The horses figgered out what we were doin' an' we could hardly contain them long enough t' saddle up. Cooper mounted on th' run and I had a real time holdin' my horse long enough t' shut th' barn door. With the left rein draggin' ground and me pulling that cayuse in a circle, I managed to mount up on the right side—and that was a show—and hang on until we caught up with our pardners.

Thawed ground had turned to muck and mud and the horses slogged through it spraying mud all over our legs while the pouring rain soaked us to th' saddles. The rain stopped and just as we entered the barnyard, the sun broke through in all its glory. "I've got to heaven!" Coop exclaimed.

It shore looked it to me. Those soaked saddles must have doubled their weight and the horses were sure glad to be shut of them. We rubbed them with burlap bags down to the mud line and turned them out in the pasture. They ran and kicked like colts.

"Wonder where Nap . . ."

"He's right here," Nap called from the door. "Ye got clean clothes in th' bunkhouse an' orders t' clean up afore you go to th' house."

"Those orders agin," Coop groaned, "I ain't sleepin' in th' house anymore!"

"They's vacancies in th' bunkhouse now an' you won't have t' sleep in th' tack room this time." Nap laughed.

"I know where my assigned bed is and it ain't in th' bunkhouse an' I don't have a choice," I said. Cooper smirked and I popped his rear with a rein.

"Ouch, Demps, *I* don't make any rules around here!"

"You know how t' laugh at another man's discomfort, though."

"We been in a shower bath all morning an' I don't aim t' take another now. If I ain't clean, I'll never be," Coop declared.

I had to bite my tongue and Nap just grinned. Cooper was right, there was no need for further cleansing after being soaked all morning. We toweled dry and sat around in dry clothes until enough time had passed for us to have taken a bath.

"Ain't no use putting those wet boots on just t' walk to th' door and take them off again," I said. We stuffed them full of rags in the hope that they wouldn't shrink too much and barefooted it to the back door.

"Lookee there, two April Fools coming through the door."

"April Fools, my a . . ." Cooper caught himself in time. Six months without verbal discipline had taken its toll.

"Not so, Aunt Cindy, it's two prisoners broke free an' outa prison," I shot back.

"They talk like fools too," Aunt Cindy said to the cat. "Go on out where you won't get polluted by that kind of language. I suppose you two are hungry. If you can wait a little, we'll have supper early."

"Or dinner late," I added. "A couple of cold biscuits would

tide us over, Aunt Cindy."

"No Billy Seldom, we ate them all at breakfast, but some Johnny Constant is in the warming oven."

"What's she talkin' about?" Cooper asked on the way to the kitchen.

"Around here, biscuits used to be called Billy Seldom and cornbread was Johnny Constant."

"O-o-h, we never named our breads, but th' principle's th' same at home."

I handed him a chunk of cornbread and took one for myself. "Let's go talk to Nap."

He was sitting on the bunkhouse stoop braiding a horsehair halter and we sat and watched for a time, makin' small talk. When the conversation lagged, I asked, "Nap, would you tell us again about Tucker pistol-whipping a man on that drive to the Indian reservation?"

Nap eyed me with narrowed eyes. "Where did you hear that, Demps?"

"Seems like I heard it somewheres, but I don't know where or who said it." I grinned.

He studied his work a minute, looked up, and said, "We were moving the cattle along on their last day when we looked up and found Mr. Beavers surrounded by a crowd of riders and by th' looks of them, we all knew it wasn't good. Th' herd stopped and we moseyed up and crowded in so that there was a Beavers man between each owlhooter. Little Green was behind Mr. Beavers dabbin' his bloody nose and there was th' print of a hand across his face.

"Tucker Junior subscribed to the Pecos Pete theory of battle an' I saw that he had his hand inside his coat where his gun was. This scoundrel next to him said something to him about young-uns showin' proper respect to their elders and he still had an ugly smirk on his face when Tucker backhanded him across th' face with his .44. *Whack!* From th' clickin' of hammers bein' cocked, you would of thought we were in th' middle of a herd o' crickets."

"Is that all he done?" Coop asked.

"All he needed t' do. That man's eyes were swoled shut afore he hit th' ground—or nearabout."

"I guess you could call that pistol-whipping," I said, "Even if he hit him just once."

"We preferred t' call it buffaloed, only he hit him in th' face 'stead o' th' side of his head." Nap chuckled.

"And then Nate and Green robbed him?"

"I swear, Demps, where'd you hear about this, over at Lincoln? We didn't *rob* anyone, we *relieved* all of those fools of their guns and knives, and little Green and Nate got th' priviledge o' *disarming* the man who roughed up Green. Kept his weapons, too."

"Dempsey Nealy," Aunt Cindy called, "if you and Cooper want to eat any time today, you can get yourselves in here and lend a hand." The screen door slammed shut.

"Spring's too tight," Nap muttered.

"Th' one on th' door, or th' one in th' woman?" Coop asked over his shoulder.

"Might be both, Coop, might be both."

Aunt Cindy must have been glad to see us in spite of her attitude, which was bristly most o' th' time. She had a white cloth on the table and her best set of china stacked on the counter ready to spread. "Dempsey, put those plates around and Cooper you can get the silver chest down and put the silverware around, fork on the left and knife and spoon on the right—*stop*, wash your hands first—the two of you!"

I had not quite put th' last plate down when she gave another order; "Now, Demps, set glasses on the left side of the plates—Cooper, this isn't a chuck wagon, set that silverware neat an' th' same every place. Napkins are on the counter by th' pantry. Place one under each fork, and keep them folded like I have them."

She had the big cast-iron skillet on the stove and dropped a piece of newsprint into it. When it turned brown, she knew the pan was hot enough and plopped a thick steak in it. After a few minutes, she turned it and put three more steaks in the skillet. She liked her meat well done, the old way, and knew we would want just a little pink in th' middle of ours, even Nap. The room was full of wonderful smells. I could tell there was bacon fat in the green beans and the smashed potatoes were the whitest. Peeking through the warming oven window, I saw two ten-inch pies with golden crusts. Another pie with meringue topping was in the cooling window. I hoped it was my favorite, lemon pie. While the steaks cooked, Aunt Cindy opened the oven and pulled out a big tray of three-domed rolls. I drooled like a dog with a fresh bone.

"Don't just stand there staring, Demps, call Nap in and sit down." She forked the steaks on the plates while Cooper set the bowls of vegetables on the table and I called in Nap and fished a dish of butter from the cooling window.

Aunt Cindy stood surveying the table and with a nod of satisfaction moved to her place at the head of the table. Cooper pulled her chair out and helped her be seated.

"Why, thank you, Cooper, you're a gentleman."

Nap sat at the other end and the two of us took the sides. I almost reached for the potatoes before remembering my manners.

"Dempsey, will you say grace for us?"

"Yes, ma'am. Lord, we are grateful for your bountiful blessings, for this home and this table. Bless this food for our nourishment and bless the loving hands that prepared it. Amen."

"Thank you, Dempsey." She took her napkin, unfolded it,

and laid it in her lap. We watched her closely and did the same. "Cooper, take some beans and pass them on to Nap."

I watched and passed the mashed potatoes to Aunt Cindy. "Thank you, Dempsey." I only hoped there would be some left when it came back around to me.

"Here you go, Demps," Nap grinned as he handed me the bowl of beans.

I took a small helping and started to pass the bowl to Aunt Cindy. "Oh Dempsey, you're a growing boy, take more than that."

I felt my face warming, but put another spoonful on my plate.

"Good," she said, and passed the warm rolls to Cooper. He took one and was reaching for another when she smiled and said in a stage whisper as she passed him the butter, "Only one at a time, Cooper."

The butter was running out of his roll almost as soon as he put it in and he was about to take a bite when I nudged him with my foot and shook my head very slightly. Looking around, he saw that no one was eating and he set the roll down. When our plates were loaded, Aunt Cindy looked at us and smiled, "Now, boys, this isn't a working meal and we will have polite conversation as we eat."

Three "Yes, ma'ams," and that is just what we did. We learned news from the Tularosa basin and told about our confinement without mentioning the walls. The meringue pie *was* lemon and the warm pies were apple and fresh strawberry rhubarb. My favorite aunt cut me an extra large piece of lemon; Cooper and Nap chose the strawberry rhubarb.

"I believe I will have a piece of lemon pie and we will save the apple pie for tomorrow," Aunt Cindy said. She sat down and we ate. It was a special time and we managed to live through the ceremonies without any wrecks.

"How did you know we would show up today, Miz Cindy?"

Coop asked.

"We've been watching the snow line and when it started raining last night, Nap allowed the line would be above the house this morning, so we got busy."

"Knowed there wouldn't be any moss growin' on either one o' you scalawags once th' road cleared," Nap added.

"Dempsey, I have standing orders that you are to present yourself to the ranch as soon as you come down. It's a little late today, but you can leave early in the morning."

"I'm anxious t' see them too, Aunt Cindy."

"Folks thought it best not to have a spring roundup due to the epidemic, so the association has hired detectives to patrol and see that there isn't any maverickin' during th' summer."

"Was I you, I wouldn't be buildin' any fires and for sure would not be carrying any irons or loose cinch rings in th' basin," Nap said.

I looked at Aunt Cindy. "Sounds like there'll be a lot of cattle going to market this fall; why don't we round up what we got in our pastures and sell now? We can let th' pastures grow and restock from the fall roundup and avoid the low prices then."

"We've been talking about that. Your pa thinks that's what he's going to do . . . I haven't decided yet. Bluewater Ranch is overstocked and we would benefit by selling off there. The drought last year pretty well emptied the Sacramento range but this winter should bring it back pretty good."

I thought a moment. "Why don't you sell off most of the Bluewater stock, split the Pinetop stock with Bluewater, and let the Sacramento rest? It could be your winter range and you might not have to feed much. The extra grass could be baled for harder times or sale."

"If prices are low in the fall, you could buy up some of the roundup cattle," Nap suggested.

"I'll think on it; you just head up to home tomorrow and

when you get back, maybe I'll have a plan. I sure have plans for Cooper and Nap while you're gone."

An hour after dark, we were in bed. I slept between sheets on a feather bed for the first time in a coon's age; don't even think I turned over once.

CHAPTER 12
A WELCOMING BACK PARTY

If a man or woman is inclined to murder or violence,
owning a gun is not important.

—Barnabas Sackett

I was awakened by a jangling ringing in my ears that only
stopped when I heard Aunt Cindy shouting, "Hello . . . hello
. . . hello . . . yes, I can hear you just fine, is that you, Jane?"

Listening pause.

I jumped out of bed and into my clothes as fast as I could.

"Yes, Yes, they came riding in here a little after noon yesterday."

Listening pause.

"It was too late yesterday for him to start; he's going to ride
up first thing this morning." She repeated louder, if possible,
"Yes, I say, first thing."

Listening pause.

"Bring *what?* . . . I'll see that he does, anything else? . . . Well,
okay, goodbye. Dempsey Barnes, are you up?"

"Up and dressed, Aunt Cindy." I stomped on my boot—on
the wrong foot—and had to sit down and take it off, fish my
sock out of it, and put the darned boot on the correct foot. My
sock was heel-side-up but I stomped on the other boot anyway
as I stumbled down the hall.

"I find it more profitable to wake up early and *before* I put on

120

my clothes," she said in her dry voice. "Your shirt is buttoned crooked."

"Yes, ma'am."

"Well, don't just stand there, *fix it.*"

"Yes, ma'am." I turned around and started unbuttoning my shirt.

"Oh, for heaven's sakes, Dempsey, I've grown up with a house full of men and boys and it doesn't bother me a bit to see you dressing."

I said, "Yes, ma'am," but didn't turn around. My ears felt warm.

"Go tell those scamps in the bunkhouse breakfast will be ready in ten minutes and bring back an armload of wood when you come back."

"Yes, ma'am." I stumbled out the back door, buttoning my shirt. Nap was rocking on th' stoop, smoking his pipe. "Chow in ten minutes," I called as I headed for the woodshed. The woodbox was empty so I made a second trip; then split up some pine kindling and put it in the box behind the stove.

Coop and Nap came stomping in the back door. "Are you two washed up?" Aunt Cindy called.

"Yes, *ma'am,*" Nap replied. Cooper looked at his hands and spun around, heading for the washbasin.

"And you can wash your face and comb your hair while you're at it."

"Yes, ma'am." Seems like that's about all we say when she's around.

We sat down and Coop remembered to wait until after grace was said to start eating. We had a big stack of flippers with butter and Karo syrup and a big pan of risin'-up Billy Seldom. The bowl of eggs scrambled in crumbled sausage disappeared in a flash and before we knew it, we were staring at empty plates and dishes.

"My stars and stripes, Nap, you would think these boys had worked all day in the hay, the way they ate."

"I guess they *are* still growin' some, ma'am." He chortled.

"Th' only growin' I'm doing is pushing my stomach off'n my back bone," Coop said, "Demps' cookin' ain't a bit better than mine, an' I'm pretty bad at it."

"You can say that agin," I said, licking the last of the syrup off my fingers.

"Don't lick your hands, Dempsey, you've grown past the high chair."

"Yes, ma'am."

"Your mother wants you to pick up a bag of flour with that order of groceries she called in to the store."

"I wonder how much she ordered."

"She said it wasn't much, could fit behind the saddle if you want."

"Think I'll take a packhorse just in case," I said.

"Nap, I want you and Cooper to round up all the horses in the pasture and put them in the big corral. Then you can get them used to saddle and bridle and the mules need to be re-acquainted with harness and wagon. I'm thinking we will have a little roundup of our own soon. I'll go into town later and check out cattle prices.

"Demps, try to be back by Sunday night. Little Zenas has already told me I could have a couple of his boys for summer work and, if all is good, we will gather a herd to sell. At any rate, we will be moving cattle between the ranches this summer and we'll be busy."

"Yes, ma'am, may I be excused? I want to get going."

"Yes, you may. Nap, Cooper and I will clean the kitchen while you saddle up a couple of horses and hitch Suky to the buggy."

"I'm on my way, ma'am."

I grinned at Coop and he kicked me in the shin while he grinned across the table at me.

"It seems to me, Nap, that we are going to have to rearrange our seating at the table and put these boys at the long ends. Those long legs are getting mixed up too much across the table."

"Wouldn't be s'prised, ma'am, wouldn't be s'prised." The screen door closed behind him.

"Is there anything you want to send to the ranch, Aunt Cindy?"

"Not that I can think of but check with me before you leave town if you can."

That Polo Pony was standing outside the corral hanging his head over the high fence as much as he could and nickering at me when I left the barn.

"I heard him fussin' last night after we went t' bed," Nap called, "musta caught your scent from those horses you turned loose yesterday."

I walked around to the pasture gate and Polo met me there and came into the corral when I opened the gate. "You seem eager to go, ol' boy, did you have a good winter?" He was fat and sleek as an unweaned pup. "We'll have to get you toughened up b'fore we start workin' cattle, boy." I could hardly saddle him, he was so glad to see me, and eager to go. I caught up a packhorse and Polo nipped at him out of jealousy.

The trip to town was more of a run than a lope. The packhorse was winded when I tied him up at the store. The order was boxed up for a wagon trip and I had to repack it for the horse. The first thing I knew about anyone being near, my feet were kicked out from under me and I lay in the mud looking up at the ugly mug of Tub Marony.

"Howdy, Demps, didn't know you was back in town," he leered. "Nice of you t' lay yer coat out like this so my feet don't get muddy." His two cronies, Webb Simpson and half-breed Cheek Cloud, sniggered as they stepped up on the boardwalk. Tub stepped up on my chest, pushing me down into the mud, and when his hind foot came over to step down, I grabbed it and twisted hard until I heard it pop. Tub yelped as he fell to his hands and knees and I was up and rammed my knee into his backsides before he could move. He fell on his face and I stepped onto his back, my next step pushing his head into the mud as I jumped to the walk and grabbed Cheek by his bib, slinging him over the hitching rail. The posts gave way and he fell into the mud. Webb was slow and it wasn't hard to catch him and send him to his friends.

Out of the corner of my eye, I saw Tub swinging a haymaker fist at my head and I just had time to duck under and into him, landing an uppercut to his protruding chin. His teeth clanked together loudly and I knew he would need some dental work. I got a couple more punches to his gut before Cheek hit me low from behind and I dropped down hard on his back. The air went out of him and it didn't help any when Webb crashed down on top of us. He was astraddle me, knocking my head from side to side and all I could do was swing at his gut, so I hit him in the crotch as hard as I could. He grunted and it took another blow to stop him. He rolled over in a ball groaning.

As I stood, Webb swung at me with a fence post. The only thing that saved me was the canopy post that he hit first. It must have stung his hands, for he dropped it and squeezed his hands between his thighs. My blow to his head spun him around and I booted him into the street mud, with his hands still between his legs.

I stood over the wheezing Cheek and groaning Webb wiping mud and blood from my face and flipping it over them. "Yep, Webb, I'm back in town. Nice of you boys t' notice and welcome me like this. Haven't had this much fun since th' last time we met." I blew my bloody nose into Webb's face.

"You hit me a low blow," Webb groaned.

"Couldn't reach anything else," I replied, "maybe someday we can have a good fight one on one where we both have an even chance . . . but I doubt you would know what to do in that case. I'm goin' in an' pick up th' rest of my purchases including a brand-new .44 and smokeless powder. I would appreciate it if you boys would watch my gear for me while I am gone."

"I'll watch for you, Dempsey, these boys look like they won't feel much like doing anything for a while."

I turned and there stood U.S. marshal and retired sheriff George Ryles, grinning and his hand extended. I tried to wipe my hand clean, but it was no use.

"No problem, Demps, I'm used to dirt." He smiled and I felt his firm grip taking my hand. It hurt, but I didn't let on.

"It's good to see you, Sheriff," I mumbled through swelling lips.

"I was concerned about the boys for a minute there," he said, indicating the three bullies now sitting on the walk. "Thought I might have t' step in and help them out, but they got smart and quit afore they got hurt."

I could just grin at him, wiping mud and blood from my face with my shirttail.

"Let me pump while you wash off a little, you'd scare them store folks goin' in there lookin' like that."

"Fanks," I muttered. The water was cold and felt good and stung in places. My mouth felt three times its size and awful tender. By the time I was decent enough t' enter the store, I could barely speak. George sat on the window ledge and made small talk to the three bullies.

"It sure was good to see those three get their comeuppance," Mr. P.T. Wakefield, the store owner, said as I entered, "They do nothing but loaf around and stir up trouble."

Mrs. Wakefield came clucking from behind the counter and wiped at my face with a cool damp cloth. I didn't mind.

"You ate their lunch good, young man," P.T. said.

"Aow, but I sink dey got a sam'ich er two," I slurred. I didn't try to talk more, but indicated by motion and notes what I wanted. I got a new set of clothes, and really did buy a pistol and ammunition, just to be safe.

A trip to the barber's for a haircut and bath, the new clothes on, and I was pretty well fixed up—if I could only talk.

Since those three came out of the blue at me, I think I should explain our relationship. Galen O'Riley Marony was an Irishman straight from the heart of the old country. He came over in the midst of the Irish famine and stepped off the boat into the anti-Irish prejudice of Boston. In order to avoid starvation, he joined the Army and fought on the Union side of our late difficulty. After that ended, he found himself at Fort Stanton chasing Mescalero Apaches across the southwest. When fellow Irishman L.G. Murphy left the Army to establish his store at Lincoln, Corporal Marony went with him. One of his several daughters married John R. Giddens and another married a man named Webb, whence descended, through a daughter, Webb Simpson. Cousin Tub's grandfather was also the venerable Galen O'Riley Marony. They were Irish as paddy's pigs.

Being lazy to the extreme and with nothing better to do than rustle a few head of cattle or horses occasionally, the two decided to defend the honor of their martyred ancestor, Riley Giddens, and carry on the feud even if there had not been a feud before they thought of it.

We had met before with similar results as today's. Tub was big, but slow of mind and foot and so far I had been able to best him somewhat. Webb was more my size and we were a good match. Cheek? He was just along for the ride, not much for fighting, but good at what Indians are good at.

Marshal Ryles was sitting in the barber chair talking to barber Tyler Pike as he stropped his razors. "You look a little shopworn, Demps, but you smell better," Pike said.

"Fanks," I slurred.

"Gotcha somethin', Demps." The marshal tossed me a small paper sack.

I opened the sack and saw an odd object shaped like a cup with no handle. "It's a catcher's cup; they wear it to protect their manhood when they're catching. Too many of them were getting hit in low places when they were squatted down behind the batter. That thing came out a couple of years ago and it's selling like bad whiskey on Saturday night. I thought you might wear it when you are in the neighborhood of those boys."

"Fank 'ou." After trying two or three times to be understood, I wrote a note and handed it to George.

"O-o-oh, you want to know what happened when Tucker Beavers was shot?"

I nodded, " 'Ess."

"Sure, Demps, you should know. I was thinking the other day, that was thirty years ago and I have nightmares about it yet. If only I could have known . . ." His voice trailed off and he was silent for a moment.

"Not a thing you coulda done, George, th' deck was stacked aginst you from th' start. I was back in th' crowd and saw it all," Tyler Pike said.

"Pike, you've said that a hundred times, I guess, but it still rankles."

"We-e-el-l, we probably wouldn't think as much of you if it didn't bother you some." The barber folded his last razor and put it away. "I was just a young feller when it happened, Demps, down there gettin' my barber apprenticeship from old Snips Russell. He always closed the shop when court was in session, said he got lots of news he could pass on while he barbered, worst gossip in town. Made me go with him, too, off the clock.

"Like I said, I was in the back of the crowd waiting for the doors to open and the trial t' start when George, here, came up th' street with young Beavers beside him and two more deputies following along b'hind. People crowded around Tucker shaking his hand and givin' him encouragement and the two deputies got lost in the crowd.

"That John R. was over on th' edge of th' crowd at the foot of the steps. Snips had pointed him out to me earlier when he was 'takin' th' roll' as he called it. He knew almost everyone there an' if he didn't know one, he would speculate and make up some name for them. Anyway, when Deputy George and Tucker started up the stairs, John R. shoved his way through the crowd and as he got to them, screamed out, 'You murderer!' George went for his gun and Giddens shot Tucker square in the chest. I heard the second shot from under the stampede and didn't see what else happened. When I could finally get up, the two deputies had wrestled John R. down and George and Tucker were layin' on the steps bleeding. I remember old J.G. Burnett standing on the top step just staring at the bodies. Snips, being somewhat of a doctor, ran to the steps to help. Beavers's Ma had Tucker's head in her lap and Miz Cindy was holding his hand and leaning close, whispering to him.

"I thought George was dead. The bullet had gone through his shield and some papers in his pocket and into his chest. We ripped his shirt open and there was a ragged hole just below his nipple spouting blood. Snips got a compress over the wound and we tied it tight."

"I woke up feeling for my gun and trying t' get up while they were tying the bandage," George said, "They let me sit up . . ."

"Snips said sitting up would slow the bleeding and we had to talk fast to keep him from standing. I didn't think he was ever going to give up his gun. When he saw Tucker, he just wilted and cried. I saw Tucker open his eyes and heard him say, 'I love you both.' Then he died just as quiet as going to sleep."

It got real quiet for a few moments, just the wall clock tick-tocking and the warming sun causing the front window to tick as it expanded.

George stirred in his seat. "I was sure Beavers was our killer when we investigated the murder. His leaving town was too much of a coincidence to be believable, and going out of reach in Mexico cinched it for me. Pat Garrett wasn't all that sure and that shows you the difference experience makes. I spent a lot of time with Tuck and before the trial I changed my mind about him being guilty.

"Your grandpa, rest his soul, once told me he could prove Tucker was innocent, but that's all he would say about it. I think he had a good idea about who the killer was, too. I have a strong feeling the real killer is dead now."

"How about your wound?" I asked.

He pulled his shirt up and showed me the scar. It was ugly and there was an old incision running from the scar around his rib cage. "The badge and papers in my pocket slowed the bullet enough that it only broke two of my ribs and slid around between them until it lodged tight. Doc Rice cut me open around to the bullet and cleaned me out good. He found paper and pieces of that badge all through there," George said, indicating the track of the scar. "Even though the ribs were broken, he had to prize the bones apart to get the bullet out."

"Feelings was so hard against John R. that they kept him hid. They wouldn't even tell George where he was." Pike glared.

"I admit he could have been in some kind of trouble if I had met him," Ryles grinned.

"George, did you ever figure out who Rance Brown shot in his store?" Tyler Pike asked.

"Why, yes, we did, don't *you* know?"

"Never heard for sure, but I have my suspicions."

"The night Riley Giddens died, they kept him laid out at Doc's until they could hold an inquest. I stayed with the body and old Doc Shull sat with me and slept off his drinks. The sheet over the body slid off onto the floor and I went over to pick it up. They had opened up Riley's shirt to see if there were any other wounds and when I stooped to pick up the sheet, I saw a small red spot peeking out from under his right side. It got my curiosity up and I rolled the body on its side. His lower right side looked like he had the measles; there were so many spots on him. It had to be the rock salt. From the looks of the pattern, I was certain the bulk of the shot had hit him in the butt. I didn't look, just rolled him back and covered him up again.

"After the inquest, Old Man Giddens and his wife took the body and would not let anyone help them prepare him for burial. The next time anyone saw him, he was laid out in his coffin. I talked to Doc Rice at Tularosa and he said the man he had treated had rock salt in his right side and buttocks. No one knew about it but the doctor, Pat Garrett, and me for a long time but I guess the story finally leaked out somehow."

We questioned Rance Brown real hard about the murder, but couldn't shake anything out of him. "Well, I'll be switched." Pike patted his knees softly.

I was really feeling bad, my head ached, every tooth felt loose in my head, and my hands were swollen. The sun had settled well toward twilight when I rode in to Aunt Cindy's barn. I put Polo Pony in the corral, unloaded the packhorse, and crawled into one of the bunks in the bunkhouse. Coop and Nap came stompin' in from supper and found me.

"Sh-h-h, Coop, that's Demps sleepin' in here. Bet he's been up t' som'pin in town too late t' make it to Mountain Beavers." I spent a very restless and painful night.

CHAPTER 13
MARSHAL RYLES VISITS

Never interfere with nothin' that don't bother you.

—Cowboy philosophy

The spring sun hadn't come up when I was jarred awake by hard-soled shoes stomping across the porch. It had to be Aunt Cindy or another female, for they were the only ones who knocked on the door.

"Napoleon, Cooper, are you in there? Is Dempsey in there? Will someone answer me or I'm coming in." The door opened without pause and she strode two steps into the room. All I could focus on was a vague figure backlit by the open door. I had swung my feet to the floor and got so dizzy I sat with my head in my hands to stop the spinning.

"Is that you, Cooper? I'm lookin' for that Dempsey. He didn't show up at the ranch all night an' his mother is worried to death about him. I'm gonna skin his hide if he laid around and didn't go home like he was supposed to." It all came out in a rush like it did when she was mad and I peeked to see if she had the shotgun.

"Ish mm, Ampt Shinny," was all I could get between my lips. The corners of my mouth were crusted with blood and stuck together.

"Demps? What's wrong with you—are you drunk?"

"No, mmm."

All was quiet for a moment then I heard her step softly over to me. "Look at me, son, what has happened to you?" Her hands were cool on my neck and forehead and I heard her suck in her breath between her teeth. "Oh, my, my, Demps, it looks like you stuck your head in a hammer mill. Who did this to you?"

"Shaw Tup and Wepp in tow-n," I slurred.

She didn't say a word for a minute an' if I could have seen, I bet her jaw was set and her eyes was shootin' lightning. "Come on out here in the light and let me look at you." I stumbled to the door with her leading me by the hand. "My stars and stripes, boy, how did you let them whip you like this?"

I tried to shake my head and got dizzier, "I wh-hiph boph oph 'imm!"

"Did their faces look *this* bad?"

"Tup's teef an' lower." My face wouldn't grin.

"Well I certainly hope you fixed it so he can't reproduce! Sit on the stoop while I get some cleaning gear." Her footsteps faded until I heard the screen door slam, then open again. "Nap, Cooper, if you can hear me, get down here right now." The door slammed again. She was gone and it was blessedly quiet for a few moments. Obviously, Nap and Coop hadn't heard her; it wasn't healthy not to hop when she said to. I was kind of dozing, elbows on knees and head cradled in my hands, when I heard the screen door squeak open, then, *boom* went the shotgun. I nearly fell off the porch.

"That ought to get them," she said. I could see her nod in satisfaction in my mind's eye. As she walked across the yard, shot peppered down on the barn roof. Must have shot straight up.

"Uhs at rock sal-t?" My face was too stiff to grin; it must have looked awful.

"No, son, I save that for targets on the ground." She squeezed my shoulder. I heard a pan set down on the porch and she was wringing out a rag. "This may sting in a place or two, but we have to get you cleaned—*where are* those two?"

The warm water felt good and I steeled myself not to flinch when it stung. I could taste blood, must have cut my cheeks inside. Aunt Cindy worked on my face a long time, not saying anything, but an occasional cluck. I really didn't think I was that bad. I must have bled some in the night to make such a mess. We heard horses trot up to the barn an' she said, "It's about damned time."

Footsteps trotted 'round th' bunkhouse an' Nap asked, "What's wrong, Miz Ci . . . hell's bells, ma'am, *what has happened* to that boy?"

"I could ask you the same thing, Napoleon Witt, why did you let him go to bed like this and why didn't you tell me *last night* that he hadn't gone home?"

"Honest, Miz Cindy, he was asleep when we got to the house an' we figgered he had taken care of all that," Coop said.

I nodded my head as much as I could. My neck sure was sore.

"Who done this, Missy?" Nap asked.

"Best th' boy can tell me, it was that Tub Marony and Webb Simpson. Probably Cheek Cloud had his hand in as well."

"From th' looks o' those hands, you got some licks in," Nap said.

"I wphuphed 'um."

"My stars, I hadn't noticed. Cooper get a bucket of fresh well water and bring it here."

She was about done with my face and when Coop came back, I soaked my hands in the cold water, working my fingers back and forth and rubbing them. It felt good.

"Cooper, hitch up my buggy, I'm going to town," Aunt Cindy said, wringing out the cloth.

"Uh-uh," I said, shakin' my head.

"Hush up, Demps, I got business."

"Now Miz C . . ."

She cut Nap off. "When I got business, I got business, and it's none of yours," she snapped.

"It's some o' mine if'n youse gonna do somet'ing t' git yourself put in jail about." I hadn't heard Nap sass her back like that b'fore.

She stomped her foot, "*Cooper, git,* and do as I say! Nap, if you're going with me, go get your gun on, you're not dressed without it."

"Yes'm."

"Yes'm."

They moved off on their errands. "Amp Shindy, don'ph," I pleaded. I could imagine what my life would be like if it got out that a woman took up my fight for me, though I had no doubt who would win.

"Hush, Dempsey, I'm gonna take some of Rance's rock salt shells and run those three clear to th' river, and I'll give them their choice, Rio Grande or Pecos, my mind's made . . ."

"Hallo-o-o th' house." George Ryle's voice came from beside the main house and I heard him ride up to the bunkhouse rail. "Well, hello, Miz Brown, how are you this morning?"

"Get down, George, and have a rest, I think Nap has a pot on the stove in there, help yourself," she said by way of welcome. Leather creaked and he stepped across the porch. "Thank you, ma'am, believe I will." The door closed. "Howdy, Nap, goin' somewhere?"

"Now what's he up to, do you guess?" she whispered. "You do something he needs t' see you about?" I shook my head in spite of the pain.

George came back and sat down beside me. "How you feelin' this mornin', Demps?" He slapped my knee.

"Ho-kay."

"Nothin' so good as a woman t' fix up your bruises, hands

135

swole up any more?"

I held them up, dripping.

"Yep, swole more than yestiddy." He grimaced.

"You saw that happening and didn't stop it!" Aunt Cindy said accusingly.

"Come up just as Demps was finishin' up. Thought for a minute I was gonna hafta step in an' help those three out t' even up th' fight some."

"Of all things, a sheriff watching three thugs beat up on one man!"

"No, ma'am, I saw th' last of it and Dempsey Nealy whupped all three. Besides, a little fight ain't nothing an *ex*-sheriff should git mixed up in less'n he's got a dog in it."

"Humph, doesn't look like it was a little fight to me."

"I just came by to tell you the boys decided to take an extended vacation at the river and it will be a while before they come back."

I heard the buggy drive up and Cooper 'whoa' th' horse.

"Which river are they goin' to, I'm going to encourage them on their way," Aunt Cindy demanded.

"They started last night and got too much of a head start on you." George laughed. "Rance shore started a custom in this family with that rock salt."

I couldn't help grinning. "Hush your face, Dempsey, I've got a mind t' go huntin' them, anyway."

I wished I could talk plain to her.

"Oh, my stars! Your ma is waiting on pins and needles for me to call her back and I completely forgot! It's all your fault, Dempsey, we'll deal with that later," she said as she hurried off to the house.

Nap stepped out of the bunkhouse with two cups of coffee and handed me one. It was hot and I wrapped both hands around the cup.

"S'pose I can undress now that we aren't goin' t' town." He was chuckling.

George laughed softly with him, "Knew I would have to come out and head her off, but couldn't get away last night. Fortunately, she was delayed until this morning. I woke up every time I heard a wagon come into town."

Nap grinned. "I's shore glad you came by, you stopped our march off to war."

"May only have delayed it, Nap."

"We got t' git her mind on other things or we'll be marchin' f'sure." Nap stepped down and got in th' buggy. "I'll put ol' Solomon up an' maybe she won't notice."

"You have those dreams often?" George asked.

"Nawsir, but there's always hope." He drove the buggy back to the barn and we heard him shoo Solomon into the pasture.

The screen door announced the return of Aunt Cindy, "Your mom thinks you are going to work for me a few days before you go up, maybe that will give you time to heal. You're too ugly to be seen right now. Did you bleed all over that bed?" All this said in passing as she went into the bunkhouse.

"That door didn't slam right, Nap, what's wrong with it?" George asked the returning cowhand.

"Stretched th' spring, got tired o' that bein' my doorbell."

"Have you tried stretchin' th' springs at th' house?"

"She kept tying knots in 'em til I gave up." He sat on the edge of the stoop with a sigh.

"Would you look at this pillow? It's a wonder that boy has any blood left in him!" The screen door slammed. "It's soaked plumb into the pillow, I'll bet I have to throw away half the feather ticking."

"Oh, that's not so much, I've seen fellers bleed a lot more than that."

"Yeah, an' where did you bury them, George Ryles?"

"You're just too wound up about this, Cindy, the boy had a little set-to and whipped three men at once and got a little roughed up in th' process. Let's go get a cup of *your* coffee and set a spell until you calm some. Nap's horseshoe has melted in this pot and I need somethin' to ease me down a little."

"I haven't got time . . ."

"*I'll* put the boy back to bed, Miz Cindy, you go and entertain your guest," Nap put in.

With all this talk *about* me and not *to* me, I wondered if I had turned invisible too. "I'll go phack to phed here, Aun' Chindy, I'm okay."

"You'll come into the . . ."

"We'll discuss that later, Miz Cindy, right now, th' bunkhouse is quieter an' me and Coop'll watch the boy an' see he rests," Nap interrupted.

"A good idea, Nap. Now come on, Cindy, and get me some of that coffee that don't stand up in th' cup."

They moved off toward the back porch, Aunt Cindy giving orders over her shoulder. "Don't get back in bed with those clothes on, Dempsey; Nap get him another pillow . . . and put clean sheets on another bunk. You can get the pillow on his bed in here . . . make sure he has plenty of blankets . . ." The slamming screen door cut off any more instructions.

We relished the quiet a moment and Nap sighed, "That woman would march into hell and have it reorganized afore th' devil hisself knew what was happenin'."

"I'sh goin' t' phed, Naph."

"Good, Demps." he hurried ahead and ushered me to a clean bunk that had a fresh pillow on it. I lay down and when he laid another blanket on me it startled me so that I jumped. "Sorry, Demps, go back t' sleep." I heard one floorboard squeak as he left, but didn't even hear the door close.

CHAPTER 14
THE TEXAS TAX WAR

To shoot an unarmed man, to run sheep in cow country,
to change a brand, to steal a horse, to cheat at cards, or
string a fence are crimes. (Being the only crimes
recognized by the old time cowhand.)

—Mesquite Jenkins, Tumbleweed

I slept all that day and night and woke up the next morning disgusted that I let a little thing like a fight get me down like that. Aunt Cindy didn't waste any more sympathy on me; that was good. She just fussed at me for sneakin' in and not telling her, for bleeding on her pillow, sleepin' my life away, tearing up good clothes, and looking so ugly and swollen. It was good to get back to normal.

Aunt Sue Ellen came over the next afternoon and sat with me while Aunt Cindy went to town. I was relieved she didn't take that infernal shotgun. We sat in the front porch swing and talked. When the conversation tapered off, I asked her, "Aunt Sue, do you know much about the Texas Tax War?"

"Cindy said you came down the mountain full of questions. Where did you get all of that?"

"Oh, I read something about it somewhere and wondered what it was all about."

"The Santa Fe Ring got a law passed that put a tax on goods bought in Texas. Since most of our commercial business in the lower valley came from El Paso, it put anyone who didn't buy from the suppliers in the upper valley at a disadvantage.

"Riley Giddens had gone to Santa Fe with Jimmy Dolan from Lincoln during the senate session and he came back all smug and smiling. We didn't know why until the news of the tax was published. It caused a big stink and most of the merchants down here ignored it until the auditors showed up on their doorstep. *That* put the fat in the fire!"

"What did Uncle Rance do about it?"

"He ignored it as long as he could, then had pretty harsh words with Riley and John R. The Giddens got their merchandise from Santa Fe through the Murphy-Dolan store at Lincoln and could sell their goods cheaper if the Browns had to pay the tax. Several merchants including Rance got together and began smuggling goods from El Paso.

"That lasted until the tax collecters and auditors showed up at the store and practically took over. Some of the so-called collectors were the same thugs that had tried to interrupt the Mountain Beavers cattle drive to the reservation. They disappeared one night only to show up in Santa Fe in a boxcar, tarred and feathered." She laughed. "Rance said Riley Giddens missed the ride by two minutes when he left town on the gallop. During that time, Rance's hands were pretty beat up and so were Riley's, they say."

"You think they fought?"

"Only every time they met. They were pretty evenly matched and the championship passed back and forth between them."

"Why didn't they suspect that Rance had killed Riley?"

"Oh, my goodness, they did, but they couldn't pin anything on him except the fighting, and Tucker's disappearance was too obvious. That was just a coincidence, Dempsey, Tucker *did not* kill Riley Giddens."

"How could anyone prove that?"

"I don't know."

I could tell she was pained and near tears, so didn't say anything more.

After a time, she said, "Your Aunt Cindy and Tucker grew up together, you know. Tuck always took care of her and they were friends a long time before they became lovers."

I looked startled and she must have understood what I was thinking, "Oh, no, no, Dempsey, they were not lovers in the *intimate* way, but they loved each other just the same." There was just a hint of pink on her cheeks.

"I didn't know that until just lately," I said.

"I guess we have neglected to tell you youngsters the story. Even after thirty years, it's too painful to talk about."

"I understand, Aunt Sue," and I hugged her. She laid her head on my shoulder a moment, then sat up. "Ma said you and Tucker were real close."

"We were. He was always my strength, especially after Papa died. I was the one who told him Cindy and Rance were married, that was about the hardest thing I ever did."

"How did he take it?"

She looked at her hands in her lap a moment, "I think it broke his heart and some of his spirit. He wouldn't have stayed around here long if he had lived long enough."

We had been hearing the rattle of the buggy and a few moments later Aunt Cindy drove into the yard and up to the front steps, "Make yourself useful, Dempsey, and haul these things to the kitchen," she said as she came up the steps and plopped into the swing where I had sat. "I swear, Sue Ellen, I'm gonna start making out lists and sending someone else into town to fill them."

"Do you think that's a sign we're getting old?" Aunt Sue laughed.

"I'll tell you when I get there," Aunt Cindy snapped, then laughed and patted Sue Ellen's hand.

It took me three trips to unload the buggy, but I didn't mind. Those groceries and things just told me my good eating was going to last a little longer. I was approaching the front door from the kitchen when Aunt Sue's voice came into focus. ". . . wonder where he got all his curiosity about family affairs?" I paused near the door.

"I don't know, Sue, but I guess it's healthy he's getting interested in those things; he's about the age that family becomes important to him again."

"You mean we're getting smarter again?" She laughed.

"Yes, I think we are about over our stupid stage." Aunt Cindy laughed too.

With that, I made some noise and stumbled out the door. "Are you going to put up the buggy now, Mr. Grace?" Aunt Cindy asked.

"Yeth'um." I was a little tongue-tied.

"Give Solomon some oats, he's worked a little today."

I nodded and left on my errands. On my way back to the house, Aunt Sue drove out of the yard and Aunt Cindy was putting away groceries in the kitchen when I got there.

Saint Cooper laid the iron in the fire and threw the calf he had roped, while Nap struggled to hold mama cow away from the activities. "Keep that horse close, Coop, if somethin' turns loose here, you want to be on th' go."

"You ain't just whistlin' Dixie, Nap." He quickly cut the yearling bull, throwing the testicles on the coals. Coop rubbed liniment on the new wound and the freshly notched ear while he waited for the iron to get hot enough. The new steer bawled when he applied the brand to his left hip and his mama bawled and bucked against Nap's loop. His horse was near, sitting on his rump, feet braced, trying to hold the angry cow.

"Hustle, Coop."

The released calf ran to mama and Nap gained enough slack to flip the loop off her horns. Cow and calf trotted off. Coop rolled the fries over on the coals and, after a moment, speared one and handed it to Nap. The second fry was speared and he blew ashes off of it. Finding it too hot to bite, he waved it, making patterns with the steam.

"You gonna play with your food all day?" Nap had finished his and was licking his fingers.

"My tongue ain't seared over like yours, I haven't drank that much scalding coffee yet."

"Wish we could cut steaks off like we done those fries."

"Well, it wasn't all that easy, took us three calves t' find one properly equipped," Cooper said as he finished his treat. They had ridden over to the Bluewater Ranch checking out conditions and cattle and had found three unbranded yearlings. The fries were just enough to sustain life until they rode in for supper.

"Let's check out th' south fence and see how it survived the winter. If these cows drifted any, that fence may be leanin' toward Jericho." Nap turned his horse south and Cooper caught up with him. "Nap, did Tucker have a lot of trouble with that Giddens boy?"

"What you boys so interested in bringing up ghosts for, did you see somethin' up there last winter?"

"It was just th' walls talkin' to us," Cooper smiled.

"Walls don't talk, Coop, but haints do."

"If that had been a haint up there, I would have walked *on top* of th' snow gettin' away."

"Bet you would." Nap shook his head and chuckled. After a long pause, he said, "I only know of that one time Tucker and Riley fought. After that, they wouldn't have anythin' t' do with th' other. Nope, they stayed away from each other, wouldn't even stay in th' same building."

"Must have put a strain on things in such a small community."

"Don't know an' don't care, that was near thirty years ago an' would best remain buried, Cooper."

"They say Rance Brown and Giddens fought a lot," Coop persisted.

"Only every time they seen each other, seems one couldn't stop goadin' the other. Rance was as bad as Riley in that."

"Did they carry?"

"Dang, Cooper, you're shore persistent . . . word was, Riley carried all th' time, but Rance's pa wouldn't let him, said he wasn't as likely to get shot if he wasn't armed." He looked Cooper in the eyes. "And that's good advice for present company, don't take your guns t' town, and don't ride out here without one."

"Good advice t' live by," Cooper agreed. "Why wasn't Rance suspected of killing Riley?"

"He was, but I don't think he was suspected enough."

"You think he done it?"

"I think they didn't go far enough t' find out for sure he *didn't* do it, may have been some politics involved." Nap bit off a chunk of Lorillard Twist and returned the tobacco to his vest pocket. "How in th' world can a cow leanin' on a fence break th' bottom strand an' not th' top one?" He pointed to several spans of leaning wire, and to the bottom strand of wire that was broken and pulled from a couple of posts. Without breaking stride, Cooper turned east and Nap patrolled the fence west to the corners. They met back at the broken fence, not having found any other damage.

"Must have happened in that storm that came after we had driven them up here from the Sacramento," Nap said.

"From the looks of th' ground, there must have been some pretty big hail in it, look at those holes."

"Near big as a hen egg, ain't they?"

"But why did they push th' fence over in just this one place?" Cooper asked.

"Look at th' tracks, Coop, there weren't more'n eight or nine cows here. Now look up; see th' trees hangin' over the fence?"

"Well, I'll be, they weren't driftin'; they were tryin' t' get under those trees away from that hail, weren't they?"

"Shore they was an' that's why th' bottom wire's broke and peeled back, they were stomping th' whey out'n it." Nap spat a stream of tobacco juice on a large grasshopper too stubborn t' move away from the horses, "Git yore pliers, Coop, let's get this fixed afore dark."

They worked for an hour plumbing posts and retamping them into their holes, not talking much, but each man trying to do more than the other, as men proud of their work and eager to carry more than their share of the load are prone to do. Wire spliced, stretched, and restapled to posts and they were done. They caught up their grazing horses and headed for home.

"I think he done it," Cooper said.

"What? What'd you say?"

"I think he done it."

"Think *who* done *what*?" Nap asked, irritated that his thoughts had been interrupted by some inane word.

"I think Rance Brown killed Riley Giddens."

"Oh, for gosh sakes, Cooper, can't you git yore mind of'n somethin' an' let it go? What difference does it make now?"

"Nothin' but that Tucker Beavers was innocent."

"Shiftin' th' blame just shifts th' pain from one family to another."

"Not any Browns left but Miz Cindy an' she's already grievin' over Tucker."

"So-o-o let me line this up; you want Miz Cindy t' stop grievin' about Tucker bein' a killer an' start grievin' 'cause her

145

husband was?"

"We never thought of it thataway, Nap."

"Some things you can't dig up out o' th' past without throwin' th' dirt on someone else, Coop. It's best t' let those things be. It's like tryin' t' take th' blame off'n Custer an' puttin' it on Reno and Benteen for th' Little Horn massacre, they's just as many tryin' t' take th' blame off'n those two an givin' it all to Custer. Either way, th' only ones t' get hurt are th' survivors. Wait a hundred years when all o' them are dead an' then fix blame proper an' no one'll git hurt."

They rode a long ways before Cooper said anything. "I never thought about us lookin' for truth would hurt people, but I think you are right. It's too early, ain't it?"

"I thinks so, but it'll be pretty hard t' git Demps t' see that. Once he gits aholt o' somethin', he don't let go 'til it thunders."

"Would it be just as harmful t' figger out who Rance shot with th' rock salt?"

"I have thought on that a long time, and I think that it's not such a big thing in folks' minds because they's already decided who it was an' it ain't an issue either way," Nap said. "Who do you think it was?"

"Most likely, Riley Giddens."

"Yup, an' that's what most everyone else thinks too. It's a settled thing in their minds."

"Why ain't Riley's murder settled?"

" 'Cause that story never was finished and it's more important t' people than some rock salt in someone's ass."

"You mean b'cause a good man got th' blame an' it never was brought to a conclusion?"

"That an' no one believes if he done it, he would of run." Nap flipped a horsefly off his horse's ear.

"But they say he killed others."

"Killin' someone tryin' t' kill you or yours ain't murder,

them two things is diff'rent."

"I'm gonna quit lookin' for Riley Giddens's murderer," Coop said as he plopped his boot on th' floor.

"Why for?" I asked from my bunk.

"Nap says diggin' up dirt from one grave throws dirt on another."

"What th' heck does that mean?"

"If Tucker didn't kill Giddens, who would your prime suspect be, then?"

"I been thinkin' it'd be Uncle Rance," I said.

"And who's his widow?"

"Aunt Cindy, of course . . . and you think it would cause her grief if we were to think that she had married a murderer."

"Well, at last you started using your kidneys," he said, tapping his temple.

I lay back and thought about what Coop had said. I had not thought of our search hurting other people, but Cooper and Nap were right; if we proved that Uncle Rance was the killer, it would hurt his people, including Aunt Cindy. I wouldn't want to do that . . . and just as important to me, I don't want my family to go on living under the stigma of having a murderer in the family. I've seen how it affects them and how it influences the attitudes of friends and neighbors—even after thirty years, for gosh sake. They can't tell me to let things lie and forget the past when they don't forgive and forget themselves. That's not justice.

"I'm gonna keep lookin'," I said.

"Huh? What you say, Demps? I was asleep."

"I say I'm gonna keep lookin'."

"Ok, but don't tell anyone." He turned over and went back to sleep.

Don't tell anyone, that's a good idea, I thought as I drifted off.

CHAPTER 15
A BUSTED TRAP

When you see 'Pache sign, be keerful, 'n' when you don'
see nary sign, be more keerful.

—Buffalo Soldier

You would think that by 1919 all Indian troubles would be
over, but that wasn't the case. Folks lost cattle and horses on a
fairly regular basis. The trouble is, if the thief could get his stock
to the reservation without being caught, he was home free
because the agent would not let anyone search on the reservation for his property; and even if it was found, he would not
make the Injun thief return the stock regardless of brands,
claims, or witnesses.

It made for hard feelings and secret invasions of the reservation by ranchers set on regaining their property. And if they
took a little more than they lost, it was considered payment for
all the trouble they had retrieving their property, but that only
perpetuated the back-and-forth. At one time, the theft of a cow
or two was overlooked, for it kept the Indians fed and not likely
to go on the prod. Honest agents and decent food put an end to
beefing by the Indians. The stealing nowadays was all for profit.

The summer of '19 was especially bad with the price of beef
being high after the war ended. Ranchers in the Tularosa Basin
and around suffered most because the Indians would steal cattle
here, take them to the reservation, and when they had a good
herd, drive them east to a remote spot on the rails without be-

ing seen by many people—and those who did see would look the other way because the enriched Indian would spend his money there.

It got so bad that the sheriffs of four counties, Lincoln, Otero, Doña Ana, and Socorro, appealed to the Army for help. The usual troop sweeping Mescaleros out of the Guadalupes sent over Lieutenant Andrew B. Clifton with six Buffalo Soldiers and two scouts to look into the situation.

They passed through Piñon one afternoon and camped just outside of town. Coop, Nap, and I rode out after supper and visited with them some. Nap spent his time visiting with the soldiers while Coop and I visited with Lieutenant Clifton. The lieutenant was not familiar with the west side of the mountains and asked if there was someone who could guide them to the basin. Of course, we knew of two who were very familiar with the area and assured him we would be there early the next morning to lead the squad west.

Soldiers turn in with the sunset and when we went to get Nap, we found him talking with the men in a strange language, a mixture of English and some language we had never heard. As we rode home in the gloaming, Coop asked, "What was that language you were talking in, Nap?"

"Some people call it Geechee an' others call it Sea Island Creole English."

"Where'd you learn it?" I asked.

"I growed up with it on the Carolina Sea Islands where I was born. Come time I left th' islands, I couldn't speak a word of American."

"You had t' learn English?" Coop was incredulous.

"What language did you grow up usin'?"

"English."

"An' now you can speak Mexican and some 'Pache, an' when you go 'round Dodge City you speak some German, an' mebbe some Pueblo in th' valley. We're a reg'lar blend of Babel, ain't we?"

"How did Geechee come about, Nap?" I asked.

"Donno, just know my people on th' islands speaks it."

"Did the Buffalo Soldiers all know it?"

"No, just a couple of them, I knowed their families on the islands. It shore was good to talk to them in the old tongue."

"Does it make you homesick?" I asked.

"Naw, I come too many miles for that, these mountains is home now—an' might near any place I lay my head."

"Why did those two soldiers wear those Indian headdresses with horns and all?" Coop asked.

"Those weren't soldiers, they were Seminole Negro Scouts."

"They were Negroes."

"No, Coop, they were *Seminole* Negro Scouts," Nap asserted.

"What's a Seminole Negro?"

"I know," I said. "They are Negroes who escaped from southern slaveholders and lived in the swamps of Florida with the Seminole Indians. Some were enslaved to the Seminoles and some lived free with them. There were even 'tribes' of former slaves that lived separate from the Indians in their own villages and had their own languages. They fought Seminole, Cherokee, and Anglo."

"That man has partaken of the Tree of Knowledge," Nap exclaimed.

"But *they* are Negroes in warbonnets," Cooper persisted.

"Seminole Negroes are *not* just plain Negroes, they's Injuns in th' *form* of a Negro," Nap said forceably. "They trail and hunt an' fight like an Indian, and they have the endurance of an Indian. Negro soldiers can't do near as good at those things as th' Seminole Indian."

"And besides that, they are Baptists," I added.

"Baptists?" Coop yelled, "now I know you're lying—the two of you!"

"It's th' truth, Coop."

"I don't believe you—one word of it," he exclaimed. "Baptist Seminole Indians, my ass!" He loped on ahead.

"Wait and see," I called, and me and Nap had a good laugh.

"If he stays around long enough, we'll have that boy ed-u-*cated,* shore," Nap said.

The house was dark when we got there, so I left a note on the back screen door tellin' Aunt Cindy where we would be for a couple of days.

Nap refused to carry the message for us. "I seen her kill th' messenger too many times."

When we got to the soldier camp at 4:30 next morning, they were ready to mount up and go. We didn't even dismount. Cooper rode beside Lieutenant Clifton and I fell in behind them next to First Sergeant West. "Where are your scouts?" I asked.

"Oh, they's likely two–three miles ahead of us," he said, "they git up an' leave *early.*"

"Cooper," I nodded toward his back, "doesn't believe they are Indians."

"He ain't alone in that." The sergeant chuckled. "An' all them doubtin' Thomases ain't got white skin, neither."

Parts of the trail up the canyon were narrow and we rode single file. I noticed the troops rode with their carbines across their saddles. Their eyes constantly searched the rocks and slopes above.

"Don't like this place, 'specially where it's narrer," the soldier behind me muttered.

"Mescaleros might kill a lone man in these places, but I never heard of them attackin' a bunch of people this close to the reservation," I said.

"Was they wearin' uniforms, they might."

"It doesn't seem they have any deep love for soldiers, especially Buffalo Soldiers," I said.

"Dat's sho' right," the man whispered and we watched the slopes.

It seemed even the horses were glad to be out of the canyon when it widened onto the slope to the ridge. The two scouts were waiting just below the ridge and the officer called a break while he conferred with them. Girths were loosened and bridles removed so the horses could graze on the sparse grass. I noticed the soldiers were scattered around, sitting with their rifles across their knees or standing, rifles in hand. All eyes were busy watching and Sergeant West walked below the crest of the ridge and looked over the ground on the other side. It was a level of awareness I had never seen before.

Lieutenant Clifton called the troop and we gathered around him. "The scouts have found a fresh trail of several men driving a herd of cattle and horses over the ridge. It is heading north toward the reservation; we are going to attempt to catch them before they are safe on the reservation. We'll be riding hard until we are closer but I want you scattered to keep the dust down."

"Lieutenant, this is the Rim Trail and it goes through the woods most of the way. I don't think dust will be a problem, but an ambush may be," I said.

He looked at me and nodded, "Very well, we'll ride in columns of two so long as we are under the trees. If I signal, form a skirmish line and follow me."

The scouts had disappeared over the ridge and we rode north on the east side of the ridge into the trees where we could cross to the trail without being seen. By alternating walk with lope, we made pretty good time in spite of the poor condition of the troops' horses. The south fence of the Pinetop pasture had been cut and the herd driven through. The thieves had spent the night at the old town. The fire was warm and we knew they were close.

Several spans of fence had been cut at the northwest corner of the pasture where the herd was driven through and Cooper got mad. "Guess who's gonna be building fence next week, Demps."

We rode another five miles or so before the lieutenant called a stop, and while we rested, I proposed a plan to the sergeant: "Just up ahead there is a gully that runs up the hill to another ridge that nearly parallels this trail. If some of us rode hard, we could get ahead of those Indians and some of us left behind could drive them into an ambush." I drew out the plan in the dirt and West studied it, asking questions. After a while he nodded, "Sounds like a good idea to me." He rubbed his chin in thought. "The problem is that we have a shavetail lieutenant just out of the academy an' he don't take suggestions well. We're gonna hafta get him t' feed th' plan back t' us as if it was his idée. I'm gonna think on this a minute afore we talk to him." He studied the map and walked around looking at the terrain before he came back, nodded at me, and rubbed the map out. "You stay here until he calls you up," he said low.

I lay down and pulled my hat over my face as if I were going to sleep a little, but I could hear the conversation between officer and sergeant.

"Seems lak th' hurrier we go, th' hurrier those Injuns go, Lieutenant."

"I've been thinking the same thing, Sergeant West, if we don't catch up with them soon, we're going to chase them right on the reservation."

"If we was a-*tween* them and the res, lak we was over in Eddy County, it'd be sweet."

It was quiet for a moment, then the sergeant said, "We's

ready when you are, sir," and stood up as if to go.

"Sergeant, bring one of those cowboys over here."

"Yessir."

I lay and heard West approach. He kicked my boot and I jumped as if he had awakened me. "The lieutenant wants t' talk to you," he said in his official military voice.

I scrambled up and followed West over to the officer. "Nealy, do you know the country up here?"

"I growed up runnin' these ridges, when I wasn't dodgin' 'Paches,"

"Is there any way we can get ahead of those Indians and between them and the reservation?"

I scratched my chin, seeming to be in deep thought. "There might be a way . . ."

"Tell me about it," he interrupted.

"A feller would have t' do some hard riding . . ."

"What are you thinking?" The lieutenant shure was impatient.

I wiped off a place in the dirt and started drawing with a stick. "This is the trail the Injuns and us are on. Right up about here, maybe a half mile, is a gully that runs up the mountain to a ridge that 'bout parallels this rim. If we was t' get up there, by riding hard, we might be able t' get ahead of 'em."

"Would they be seeing us?"

"Could ride below th' ridge and they wouldn't. It's pretty open under th' trees, but it's sidlin', be a lot o' slidin' if you weren't careful."

"How far does that ridge go up the trail?"

"Several miles, then it turns away and ends in a slope down to a gully off of Cox Canyon. If you had to, you could go down into that gully and follow it back up to th' trail." I thought a minute, "That gully's deep enough to hide a man on horseback 'til he's almost to th' trail."

"Where's a likely place t' stop th' herd?" Sergeant West asked.

I thought, then said, "If you come back thisaway on the trail a bit so they couldn't get to the gully, they would be trapped between the bluff on one side," I pointed to the cliff to the left of the Rim Trail, "and the steep hillside on the right. They'd be sorta boxed in where the animals would be hesitant t' go down that steep slope, but you'd have to be careful th' Injuns didn't jump their horses off down that hillside."

"Is it open with trees like here?"

"No-o-o, that's an old burn an' th' trees there are small an' it's pretty brushy."

"A good place for an ambush?"

"Yeah, I'd say so."

The officer sat back on his heels a moment and looked at our map. "You're saying that if we followed this ridge, it would end, and down the slope is a gully that would bring us back up to the trail?"

"Yessir."

"And if we guarded the gully, there'd be no way to escape but down a steep slope?"

"Well, that or to turn around and go back down the trail they came on."

Lieutenant Clifton studied the map a moment and thought. "Go up this gully to the ridge, run the ridge and down to another gully, up it to the trail?"

"That, or if you got far enough ahead of them, you could just turn and come to the trail 'most any place along here."

The lieutenant stood up. "Sergeant, call Corporal Adams."

Sergeant West turned and hollered, "Corporal Adams."

A short square-built man with a slouch hat and bowed legs hurried forward and saluted. "Corporal, I want you to ride ahead and stop those scouts. Send one of them back here to us and keep the other with you and these two guides. When the sun is four hands high, start up the trail after the herd, but don't push too hard. The rest of us are going to try to pass them and set up an ambush."

"Corporal, we are going to separate the herd from the Indians and we will drive the herd down this gully," Sergeant Adams said, indicating the one they would come up to the trail in. "You say this runs into Cox Canyon, Nealy?"

"Yeah, and Cox Canyon would get you plumb away from the reservation."

"Good. Adams, be sure you and the ones with you aren't in the line of fire if we engage the Indians."

"Yassuh." He saluted and hurried off to his horse. I motioned to Coop and we followed as Sergeant West was calling "saddles" to the other troops.

"We gonna capture th' whole tribe by ourselves?" Cooper asked as we caught up with the corporal.

"No, the lieutenant is gonna try t' head 'em and we'll drive them into an ambush."

"All we's gots t' do is not drive ourselfs into no ambush," the little corporal said.

"It'd be just like those Apaches t' do that, wouldn't it?" I agreed.

"Yassuh, 'n' it sho do pay t' keep your eyes peeled." The soldier slowed to a walk and we moved cautiously up the trail, spread out so as to give smaller targets.

The slightest movement to my left caught my eye and I was bringing my rifle up when I saw the horned headdress of one of our scouts. He grinned and stepped out onto the trail. "Herd stopped. Injuns waiting."

"Now, what could they be waiting on?" Corporal Adams mused.

"More help coming." The scout squatted in the shade.

I dismounted and drew our map again in the sand. "The troop has gone up to that ridge over there and is trying to head the herd. They don't know about more Mes-co-leros coming down the trail. The lieutenant wants you to catch up with him."

The scout nodded, "I go," and stood looking up the hill a moment before he mounted and plunged into the woods, straight up the mountainside.

"That'll git him ahead of th' troop." Adams chuckled. "Like t' see their faces when he pops outa th' bresh."

"If he don't get shot to rags," Cooper observed.

"Not likely t' happen with that feller." Adams shook his head, then turned back to the trail. "We'll mosey 'til th' other Seminole finds us."

"Them ain't Seminole Black Indians, are they?" asked Cooper.

"You heered him a-talkin', didn' you? Sound like nigger talk to you?" Adams asked.

"No . . ."

"Well, they ain't jist black men, they's *Black Seminoles.*" The corporal had obviously heard this before and took exception to anyone asserting the scouts were just black men.

Coop didn't say anything and I was sure he was not convinced. It takes more than a wink or a nod for a blind man . . . and speaking of blind men, we heard a noise behind us and whirled to see the second scout sitting his horse across the trail grinning at us. "Herd resting," he said.

I could tell the corporal was as put out with himself as I was with myself for not seeing the Indian *and his horse* as we passed. Cooper was agog. "Where'd *he* come from?"

"Well, it weren't th' sky," Adams grunted.

We told the scout the plan and he nodded, got down, and squatted in th' shade of his horse. "Rest," he commanded.

We rode under the trees and picketed our horses. Adams measured the sun. "We got most of an hour," he said, and lay down close under a fallen log with his hat over his face. In less than a minute he was snoring gently.

In a world without timepieces, one common way to tell time is by hands. With the arm extended, the sun moves about four fingers or one hand to the hour. Therefore, with the bottom of the extended hand resting on the horizon, the number of hand widths above to the sun approximates the number of hours until, in this case, sunset. I've used this method of telling time many a day with a good watch in my pocket.

The scout led his horse over and sat down with his back to a tree trunk, his rifle across his knees and the horse's lead wrapped around his wrist.

I sat down against the log and Cooper said, "Might be snakes under there."

"Not likely this high on the mountain," I replied and lay my sombrero on top of the log. I was just dozing off when the unmistakable sound of an arrow swished by my ear and I heard the double thump as it went through both sides of my hat and carried it off the log.

Coop's eyes were big as saucers as he motioned to the vacant log.

"Don't worry, Coop, and keep your head down," I whispered, "he could have done th' same thing to my punkin head if he'd a-wanted to."

"I believe that!" he said.

The scout had disappeared, his horse's lead dragging the ground and his rifle lying beside the tree. We watched and listened and wondered for what seemed an age. The scout came back as quietly as he had left and resumed his seat. "Gone," he grinned. I wondered what he meant, but I didn't see any bloody scalp or other sign, so I scooted further down on the log and waited.

Corporal Adams slept on, undisturbed. Presently, he stirred, stood up, and measured the sun. "Time to go," he announced.

I reached over the log and picked up my hat. The tail feathers had not gone through the hat and the momentum of the arrow had carried the hat with it over the log. Adams looked at the arrow running through the hat and unconcernedly asked, "Didn't have it on, did you?"

When I put it on, the arrow shaft rested on my head, the hat brim a good two inches above my ears.

"Nope, didn't have it on," Coop chuckled.

As carefully as I could, I removed the arrow and stuck it in my bedroll.

We moved up the trail at a slow pace and found where the thieves had rested. Not far beyond that, we heard the soft lowing of cattle and knew they were near. "Spread out, slow down, and don't shoot unless you have to," Adams whispered.

If I were those cattle thieves and this close to home, I would have been pushing that bunch as hard as possible. Instead, they were moving slowly up the trail, even letting the animals graze a little.

"Just like they're goin' up th' trail t' Dodge," Coop said in passing. "What in the world are they doing?"

"I'm just as puzzled as you are, Coop. Seems like they're lollygaggin' on purpose."

Corporal Adams joined us. "You don't see what they's doin'? It's plain as day if you looks at th'whole pie. They's goin' slow up th' trail so's the troop'll head 'em an' come atter them an' their buddies from the Res can come in ahind 'em an' trap our boys atween th' two."

"Why, I'll bet you're right," Cooper said. "We need t' warn the troop."

"Those boys got all th' information we's got. They'll have it figgered out soon enough an' you wait an' see whut's in store for these Injuns."

"Th' only thing that ain't figgered out is what they plan t' do with us, knowin' there's only four of us followin' them," I said.

"Ef youse had my hair, you wouldn' hafta worry 'bout losin' it." The corporal chortled.

Cooper felt a chill on the back of his neck and rubbed it away. "Well, we ain't got time for a shave, so what's we gonna do?"

John Q. Adams tipped his hat back and scratched his nappy head, "We gotta wing it. We'll line up wide across th' trail an' you follow my lead. I got a feelin' that herd's gonna speed up some time soon an' we just might be their starters."

We spread out and walked along. It wasn't just accidental that Cooper and I were put in the middle, the corporal and scout taking the exposed outsides. I can imagine how someone who believes in ghosts feels walkin' through a cemetery at night. My skin got that crawly feeling and my back between my shoulder blades expected t' be shot any minute.

"How much farther to the gully?" I hadn't noticed Adams ride near and it startled me. Some Injun fighter you are, I thought of myself.

"I think maybe a half mile or a little more."

"Are you *sure?*" The little man looked at me intently.

"Yeah, we're about a half mile from the gully."

"Good, keep your eye on me and do what I do." He rode back out to his position on th' left flank. A little ways along, he motioned, hung his rifle on his horn, and drew his pistol. We followed suit, except I noticed the scout kept his rifle out. I don't think he had a pistol. Corporal Adams spurred his horse into a trot and we stayed abreast. The closer to the herd we got the faster we ran, and a hundred yards before we got there, Adams fired into the air and yelled. At first the startled herd stopped, then the lead steers broke into a run and the rest of the herd followed. I didn't waste my shots into the air, but directed them toward the nearest Indians.

Even though they knew we were there, I don't think they expected four men to run in among them like that and stampede the herd, but it didn't take them long to get over their surprise and bullets were whizzing everywhere. I rode low on my horse and whispered sweet things in his ear. We actually rode into the back of the herd and I yelled and quirted the animals around us.

Suddenly, an Indian loomed out of the swirling dust and animals and hurled his lance at me. I sat up and the lance whizzed in front of my chest. I heard a horse scream as the lance hit him and the Indian was lost in the dust again.

Up ahead, I saw the troop mounted in a skirmish line beyond the mouth of the gully. They were waving the herd into the head of the gully and firing at Indians, front and rear. Lieutenant Clifton yelled as we passed, "Stay with them, Adams." The scout left us there and joined the troop.

I holstered my empty gun and drew my rifle. Several of the Indians were staying with the herd and we had a running fight for a few moments until it got too hot for them and they melted into the woods. The gully got steeper and rougher, forcing the animals to slow and soon they were at a walk, blown and sweaty. I could feel the heat from their bodies. The ravine was too narrow to let them spread out, but we could let them string out in a long line and get cooled.

The lance that missed me had struck a horse between his ribs and he stood head down behind us a ways. He had run with the herd as far as his waning strength would let him and I hated to shoot him, but it was necessary to end his suffering. The vision of him laying on his side, the lance sticking straight into the air stayed with me a long time.

Cooper and the corporal were reloading their weapons when I caught up with them. We could hear firing continuing up the mountain. Gradually, it faded to an occasional shot.

"Th' battle's over, but th'war goes on," John Q. Adams said. His face had turned gray with dust, only showing the ebony of his skin where the sweat had run.

Cox Canyon was broader than the side gully and we were able to let the herd spread out in a little meadow and rest.

"Shore wish that lieutenant would hurry and git here, them Injuns'll have this herd back in no time an' th' three of us can't do a thing about it but maybe git kilt," the soldier said. Wiping his face with his bandana only served to mix dust and sweat into mud.

We laughed. "Looks like what we need is a good washin'," Coop said.

We found a little pool in the creek and while two of us kept watch, the other washed until we had resumed our pre-stampede identities.

It was easy to drive the herd and keep it together within the confines of the steep-sided canyon and we drove them along at a reasonable pace. The horses gradually migrated together at the rear of the cattle, preferring our company to that of the bovines.

Lieutenant Clifton caught up with us at the Rio Penasco, a couple of troopers riding double behind their buddies. We decided to take the herd to the Bluewater Ranch. Where the river takes a sharp turn toward Mayhill, we climbed out to Mc-Donald Flat and over the divide into Bluewater where we pastured the cattle, except for one slick-sided steer, behind a five-strand fence and separated out the horses. Old Bill Evans, who lived in the old ranch house, swung the gate open and hazed the horses into the corral.

The troops were in a jolly mood, joshin' an' jokin'. When Corporal Adams joined them, they razzed him for preferring to herd cattle over fightin' Indians. "Iff'n I hadn't been herdin' at th' time, you niggers would be th' meat in a 'Pache san'wich," he rejoined to the raucous laughter of the men. "B'sides, I done got my quota o' 'Paches for this year."

"Yuh, gots *boff* of 'em *a'ready*?" a tall man with a big drooping mustache asked.

"Two times zero don' come out t' two," another called.

Bill rode with us to the barn. "Lots o' brands on them horses, Demps; you boys been to a roundup on th' reservation?"

"We rounded them up and that bunch of cattle in th' horse pasture *before* they got to the reservation," I replied.

"Hope you rounded up a few Apache cowboys too."

"We made it plenty hot for them," Lieutenant Clifton answered. "Found blood in a couple of places, but don't think any of them were hard hit. They'll be on the reservation a few days licking their wounds."

"Good fer them," Bill nodded.

CHAPTER 16
A TALK WITH BILL EVANS

The cow-men are good friends, virulent haters, and if justified in their own minds, would shoot a man instantly, and regret the necessity, but not the shooting, afterwards.
—Frederic Remington

Bill eyed the steer we had driven down. "Them Rafter JD blacks shore do make good meat, don't they?"

"They do, Bill, and I'm sure they would be grateful enough t' donate one steer t' feed th' troops that returned their stock to them," I said.

First order for the troops was care for the horses. They were "undressed and rubbed," watered and fed, before they turned to their own carcass feeding.

They took the calf and soon had him skinned and hung from a singletree. There were coals in the fire pit and we stoked it with hickory and oak wood until a good fire was going. Bill produced a kettle and the makings for a son-of-a-gun stew breakfast were simmering in the pit. A huge iron skillet came from the chuck wagon in the barn and did good service cooking thick slabs of steak.

"If I'da known you were coming, I could have had a big pot of frijoles ready," Bill said, to the groans of the troops.

"Don't want no 'forty miles a day on beans and hay' when we gots beef," Sergeant West grinned.

"How about t' go with th' stew fer breakfast? Good steer

tallow with it should sweeten th' pot some."

"Steer tallow would sure beat that alkie-watered stuff we usually cooks in," Corporal Adams said.

"It's as good as done." Bill busied himself fixing the pot of beans while the steaks cooked. The sun had set when the last steak was cooked and eaten, and the troops were rolling up in their blankets after Sergeant West had set the watches. All was soon quiet and we moved into the house to bunk. We sat around the fireplace talking about the adventure we had.

Conversation lagged and sleep was near for all of us when I asked, "Bill, what do you remember about the night Riley Giddens was killed?"

He nodded and chuckled, "Well, obviously I *remember* a lot more than I *saw*, according to lawyer Burnett." He thought a moment. "I was working for Jim Hunter on Rancho Perdido in th' basin and had come in t' pick up our mail and some groceries and naturally that took up all the daylight of that first day.

"I was some put out at th' delay, but decided t' cool my ire with a few beers an' maybe a shot or two of tarantula juice. I wouldn't say I was drunk when I made t' go about midnight, but it was long after my bedtime an' I was plenty cooled off." He paused. "Doc Shull was takin' in fresh air on th' spit-n-whittle bench and we jawed a little. I was just getting in the saddle when I heard the gunshot.

" 'What the devil?' Doc said and trotted off up th' street.

"My cayuse shied an' it took me a moment t' get settled, then I trotted towards th' sound, for a shot at that time of night never is good news. Doc was peekin' 'round th' corner when I rode by. We both saw two men struggling over a gun and one got it away from th' other and hit him with it several times.

"Town Hall light was bright enough we could see that much, but not their faces. When he heard my horse, he dropped the gun and ran around the corner of the building into the dark. I didn't know who it was layin' there 'til Doc come huffing up and said, 'That's Riley Giddens—an' I would swear that man who ran was th' Beavers boy!'

"I didn't know Giddens, but I did know Tucker Beavers and thought at th' time it was mighty strange that *he* would run. I just natural took Doc's word for gospel an' never thought about it again. A crowd gathered an' here come Rance Brown from their store across th' street with a door. We put Giddens on it and carried him to th' doctor's office where he died.

"Of course when it was found out that Tucker had disappeared the same day, suspicion turned into fact for a lot of people. I had a lot of time to think about it and some things about that night came to mind, like why was Rance Brown sweatin' so much his clean clothes was soaked, and why did it take him so long to get there when he was sleeping in the store? George Ryles told me later that the store door was open when he came up and that was before Rance showed his face. He never said a thing about seeing th' fight, but if that shot woke him up, he sure would have seen what me an' Doc saw, maybe more.

"I had a lot of time t' think things over th' next two years and I don't to this day think Tucker Beavers killed Giddens— and I don't think Rance Brown is all that innocent of it."

"You think Rance did it?"

"What I am *convinced* of is that a man like Beavers would not have run after a fight, and what I strongly suspect is that Riley Giddens and Rance Brown met and Giddens tried to shoot Rance who took th' gun away from him and whipped him with it."

A thought suddenly struck me, "Did Riley have shoes on?"

"Yeah . . . yeah he did," Bill nodded. "They were moccasins."

"Soft soled!" I exclaimed.

" 'Course they were."

"The door to the store was open . . . Riley had on soft shoes and his gun . . ."

"I heard Riley's pa say th' gun was Riley's."

"You're thinkin' Riley went to break in th' store knowin' Rance was in there and he intended to kill him, aren't you?" Coop said.

"What does it look like to you?"

He thought a moment, "I think you could be right, easy."

"Well, I'm pretty *sure* you're right," Bill agreed. "A fellow would be justified pistol-whipping someone who's come to kill him. Th' bad thing is that he ran and that put a whole 'nother light on th' thing."

"If he hadn't run; if Tucker hadn't left th' same day; if Riley's shot had hit his killer—even just a little bit . . ."

"And if that prosecuting attorney hadn't told me not to say anything more than answer the questions asked me . . ."

It was quiet for a very long time, only the ticking of the stove as it cooled down.

"You gonna stir that up again, Dempsey?" Bill Evans asked softly.

"I don' know, Bill."

"Three dead men . . . what difference does it make now?"

"I don't think justice was served . . ."

"Won't mean a thing to those three, Demps," Cooper said, "but it would bring up hurts to a lot of others."

Of course they were right. It was the concern of every person I had talked to. Maybe it would be best to let it be. To prove that Tucker Beavers was innocent and maybe that Rance Brown wasn't would open a lot of old wounds that, if not healed, were at least not foremost in anyone's mind. Who would benefit from exposing the truth after thirty years? Maybe Tuck's brother or sisters, surely not Aunt Cindy. I didn't know how she felt about it, maybe she no longer cared; I just didn't know.

Coop drifted off to bed and Bill set his chair on four legs and slapped my knee. "Put another stick in afore you go to bed."

I sat there until cold crept up my toes and fingers. With two sticks in the fire, I found an empty bunk and slept.

I wouldn't believe six troops and two scouts could eat half a steer if I hadn't seen it myself, but when they packed up to leave in the morning, there was only that half to wrap up and send with them. We sopped up S.O.B. stew with Bill's biscuits and ate beans swimming in beef juice for breakfast. I took only one helping as did Coop and Bill, but it was amusing to watch those hungry troopers clean up the rest. All I saw that they had to eat was hardtack and a little venison jerky they had made themselves.

They took the horses with them and I hoped no one came to claim them. The horses they rode were about all used up. Lieutenant Clifton told me the only horses they got were rejects and condemned horses from the other cavalry units. The officers were able to purchase their own horses and were better mounted. Feelings were mixed about the Buffalo Soldiers, but I never heard a mumbling word from those who were rescued or protected by them.

Bluewater was a little remote and after we conferred, we decided to drive the cattle back to town where their proper owners could reclaim them. It was interesting to look at the differences in cattle from different ranches. Just in driving them those few miles, we got to where we could identify th' ranch they came from by their appearance, not seeing their brands.

"Some folks take more pride in their herds than others, don't they Demps."

"Yeah and those that do, go about it in different ways. Those Durhams belong to the Rocking R, an' you see a lot of Hereford in those black, white-face Rafter cows. Rancho Perdido still has a lot of Longhorn blood in theirs."

"Probably need them in that desert range," Coop observed.

"They ain't a better cow if there's five or ten miles b'tween water and grass," Bill said as he spurred away after a straying steer.

We got home late and drove the cows into the horse pasture at the house. Nap saw us ride in and had a pot of coffee on and supper in the skillet when we got to the house.

"Miz Cindy's gone to th' Beavers Ranch for the night, should be back some time tomorry."

"I need some groceries for Bluewater, them Buffalo Soldiers ate half a Rafter JD steer an' all my beans 'n' biscuits." Bill laughed.

"Them boys is might near bottomless, ain't they?" said Nap.

"We need to spread the word about the cows we brought back, guess we'll ride in with Bill in th' morning," I said around a bite of steak.

"You know she'll be full of ideas an' orders when she gits back, be sure you git back afore she does so's I don't hafta take on th' whole load," Nap ordered.

I looked at Coop; that order might just depend on our mood after we go to town.

CHAPTER 17
THE WALLS TALK AGAIN

> How perverse does a man have to be to take a round
> world and slice it into squares with bobwire?
>
> —Old Vaquero.

The slamming screen door announced her return. "Dempsey
Nealy, are you out here? Cooper, where are you?"

"We're out here in the barn, Aunt Cindy."

"Well come here a minute." She started talking the instant
we rounded the corner and she could see us, "Have you finished
repairing that Pinetop fence? I've got some things to do; first, I
want you to . . ."

"We ain't started that fence yet, Aunt Cindy, just now loading th' wagon."

"Don't interrupt me when I'm talking, young man, I'll send
you back to the Beavers Ranch."

"And pa would switch my legs with a hickory switch an' send
me right back."

"You're a *man*, Dempsey Nealy, and if you allow *anyone* to
switch you, I'll switch you again when you *do* come back!"

"In the first place, I ain't goin', Aunt Cindy, and you can't
fire me, 'cause you never hired me."

The corners of her mouth twitched as she surpressed a smile
but her eyes twinkled, "I swear, you are the beatinest one for
getting someone off the subject, now I've plumb forgot what I
wanted you to do. Go fix that fence and git right back here. If

I'm not here, there will be a list of things you and Cooper are to do on the dining table. I've got other things for Nap to be doin', so you leave him alone."

She turned and I called, "Yes, ma'am" to her back. The screen door slammed.

"Dempsey, if you get me fired along with you, I'll whip your ass," Cooper promised.

"I'll fight my own battles, Coop, an' you can fight yours. Light a shuck, let's git."

We went out through th' pasture gap, not giving Aunt Cindy opportunity to salute us with that shotgun. The climb to Pinetop was plumb peaceful except for Coop occasionally worrying about gettin' fired b'cause of my mouth. The lower fence was easy to repair, but they must have had some leisure cutting the upper fence, for they cut it every span and a couple of posts were broken off. We had to hunt up more posts and string new wire, and a new problem arose we had never considered before—how to dispose of a wad of ten-foot-long barbed wire pieces. I wanted t' find those Apache wire cutters and make them necklaces out of it.

The light failed us before we finished the fence repair, and it looked like we had a half day's work to go. After some discussion, we decided to go down to the Fereday house for the night and make sure everything was in order there. By the time we put the mules up and drew water for them, it was pitch-black dark. We had left a load of wood on the hearth and it had not been disturbed, indicating no one had visited since we had escaped the winter there. We ate a can of tomatoes and a can of peaches apiece by the light of the fire and retired to our bunks.

"I found somethin' for you, Demps," was my wake-up call. I couldn't believe that streak of sunlight across the floor. "Why didn't you wake me up, Coop?"

"I was busy an' I didn't want you interfering, look at this."

I lay back and collected myself before I got up, "What did you find?"

"It's about Riley Giddens's death." He pointed to a place on the wall where the top layer of paper had peeled and revealed the paper beneath. The paper was *The Pinetop Crow* for April 8, 1886. It gave an account of the events of April 4th and 5th, but there was nothing new in it that the other papers we had already read didn't have until I got to an article about the coroner's inquest down at the bottom of the page. It listed the coroner and jurors and their deliberations and the conclusion that they had come to: ". . . that the deceased, Riley Giddens, had died April 5, 1886, as a result of a severe beating by person or persons unknown."

There was nothing new there, but a little article below caught my attention:

A LONG SAD JOURNEY

Two brave young women, Kizzie Stark and Lucinda Nealy, made the long ride down the river last Tuesday to the spring roundup to take the sad news of young Riley Giddens's death and tell Kizzie's father, Paul, that he was needed for the coroner's inquest. Paul Stark hurried back to Pinetop and the girls followed on their tired mounts at a more leisurely pace.

Miss Nealy had ridden in from Mountain Beavers Ranch Monday morning to spend a few days in town with her friend Miss Stark when she was greeted by the sad news of Giddens's passing. "It has been a very sad time for all of us, especially the young people who were so close," Miss Nealy said after their ride. Miss Stark was too upset to give a statement.

I cut out the record of the inquest and the article about the girls' trip and repasted the sagging paper back over the older paper. Our appetites were whetted for more news from the walls and after breakfast we toured the house again. I found where John R. Giddens was sentenced:

TULAROSA SANDS
Tuesday, November 6, 1888
GIDDENS ARRAIGNED

A greatly subdued and disheveled John R. Giddens appeared before Judge Webb today. When asked how he pled the charge of murder in the first degree, he replied, "Not guilty" in a barely audible voice.

Judge Webb then took the occasion to invoke the rarely used right to recuse himself from hearing the case because of his close association with the trial of Giddens's murder victim, Tucker Beavers, Jr. "I am reluctant to even set bail in this case because of my involvement," he explained. He ordered that Mr. Giddens remain in protective custody and returned to his undisclosed place of incarceration until the State decides to change venue or appoint a special judge to hear the case.

Mr. Giddens was kept under close guard in the Tularosa jail and removed to a safer location some time in the night.

Some slick lawyer from Santa Fe brokered a first-degree murder charge down to manslaughter and John R. was sent to jail "for life," which meant "for a few years."

Cooper found an announcement that the Browns had bought the Giddens's store and stock; then way down low to the floor he found the announcement of John R.'s death:

ALAMOGORDO SANDS
Tuesday, May 1, 1917

RENOWNED PRISONER DIES

Word comes from Santa Fe that a locally known man has died in prison. John R. Giddens, who shot then deputy George Ryles and his prisoner on the Tularosa Courthouse steps, has succumbed to old age and heart problems at the age of 68. He had been considered for earlier release because of his health, but none of his kin survived him and there was no one to assume responsibility for his care. He died April 23, 1917, and was interred in the prison cemetery April 27th.

It was such a sad way to end life—and things would be so different today if he had let the law take its course. His blind act of rage had condemned a young man most likely innocent of the charges against him, left his family to bear the sorrow and stigma of the accusation, and left a murderer free. Even as removed as I was from the times and events, I was angry with John R. Giddens. I was repulsed. "Let's get out of here, Coop, I'm sick and tired of this place."

"I think I am too, what a shameful, sorry thing that was."

We had wasted half a morning at the house and hurried to finish our job and leave for home by noon. We drove quietly into the back of the barn about an hour before sundown. That trail through the pasture gap was gettin' well used.

"Awful quiet, ain't it?" Cooper asked.

"Yup, a good sign. I'll sneak into the house and see if there's anything on the table for us."

"I'm checkin' on the beans in th' bunkhouse, you about starved me today."

"Don't hurt a bit to miss a meal once in a while, Coop."

"Speak for yourself," he said over his shoulder. "I've missed too many in my short life an' it's gonna take a while t' catch up."

The house was quiet and the back screen door squeaked like

a pump organ hittin' high C. I propped it open with my boot and tiptoed to the dining table. Sure enough, there was a long list propped up against the spoon cup. I grabbed it and made a quiet escape, the only noise the squeak of that darned door as it closed. I was sittin' on the step putting my boots on when a familiar voice behind me said, "Afraid you might wake someone, Demps?"

I turned, "Hi, Aunt Polly, how are you?"

"I'm just fine, Demps." She laughed and came out and sat on the step beside me. "What have you been up to, sneaking into th' house like that?"

"Just trying to keep things calm and quiet," I grinned.

"You're safe for a few minutes; your aunt has taken a bowl of soup over to the Simmons', Miz Kizzie has a cold."

"Not the influenza, I hope."

"It doesn't seem so," she said, slipping her shoes off and resting her feet in the sparce green grass around the stoop.

"I just found out from a wall that Miz Kizzie and Aunt Cindy had ridden all the way down the river to find Miz Kizzie's pa at the roundup when Riley Giddens got killed."

"Walls can't talk, Demps." She smiled and felt my forehead for fever. "I remember those days like it was yesterday and others still feel pain from them. Go lightly, Demps, go lightly."

"Yes, ma'am, I understand."

We were quiet for a moment, only the crickets singing a soft song in the grass. "Cindy left for Kizzie's right after Sunday dinner and she was in town when the fight took place. Later in the afternoon, Tucker left for the roundup and we didn't see him for over two years. His mother must have aged twenty years worrying about him. Of course, all us kids were mad at him for leaving us behind on his big adventure. Rance was especially mad, but he would have had to sneak off like Tuck did to get away from Dad—and I really think Dad would have gone after him." She laughed.

"I didn't know Uncle Rance very well, I was too young," I said.

"He was a good big brother to me, even to Parmelia and she was three years older than him. He and Tuck and Cindy grew up together on the ranches. They were all very close. Cindy always bragged that she could do anything they could—except pee names in the snow." She laughed and blushed very prettily.

I could only grin and feel my face warm, "John R. got off pretty easy, didn't he?"

"He wouldn't have if he had been tried in Tularosa, but when the judge excused himself from the trial, John was tried where that Santa Fe Ring held sway and got off easy. If he had ever come back to this country, a lot of people would have put him to work stretching hemp—and I might have been one of them! Tucker Beavers was a fine young man and I loved him. If I had been a little older, I would have given your Aunt Cindy a good run for his attentions."

"I sure have been learning a lot of family history lately." I laughed and hugged her.

"Losing Tucker was a hard time, but we had some good times too. Did anyone ever tell you about the time we ate bear sign and all went swimming together?"

"I haven't heard that," I said.

She told me how Uncle Rance and Tucker had thrown sweetening-covered Green and Nate in the creek; Rance had pushed Tuck in and Parmelia had been pulled in by Rance after she had pushed him. Aunt Polly told me how the rest of the girls had skipped down the hill hand-in-hand and right off the bank into the water and how much fun they had until Nate and Green threw up seven doughnuts apiece.

"Oh, the scolding we girls got for getting all our clothes wet and how Parmelia was told that she was too old and mature for such goings-on. The ladies hadn't turned their ire on the boys and when they went to find them, the boys had escaped to the Far Pasture. We didn't see them for a week, except for Cindy, who helped them round up those wild cows."

Saint Cooper had come out and listened to the swimming party story. "Nap has a big pot of beans in pork tallow on the stove. They're good and hot and there's a tin of sody crackers too," he grinned.

Aunt Polly acted shocked. "And you didn't invite us to eat with you? For shame, Cooper, I can tell you ain't no saint."

"I'll get us some, Aunt Polly," I said, and fixed us both up with a bowl of beans with the crackers and steaming cups of coffee. We sat on the stoop and ate our supper. Presently, we heard the buggy roll into the yard and the front door screen slam.

Aunt Polly smiled, "Guess who's home?"

"We know," Coop groaned as he headed for the unknown.

We heard her quick steps coming down the hall. She must have waited until she was halfway to the back door to start talking. "Polly Ann, what are you doing sitting out there, we've got perfectly good chairs on the front porch, have you seen anything of those two boys, I need one of them to put up the buggy and feed Solomon—oh, there you are, Dempsey go get the buggy, did you finish the fencing, where's that scamp, Cooper?" And that was all in one breath.

Aunt Polly stood, slipping on her shoes and laughing. "Have you been drinking too much coffee and tea again, Cindy? You sound like that wall clock when it's been wound too tight."

"I just might well be, someone has to be wound up around here or nothing would get done. Come in here and let's visit awhile. I'll brew us some tea and we can have a piece of pie at the dining table."

Polly laughed again. "I was just telling Dempsey about the

time we had bear sign and went swimming in the creek, remember?"

"Oh, yes, I remember and I remember the scolding we got when we went to the house in all those wet dresses."

"Rance and Tucker ran off to the Far Pasture before their moms got ahold of them."

"The cowards. Don't you think I didn't let them know about it that week while we were branding those wild cows."

"That's when Pecos Pete was still riding, wasn't it?"

"Yes," Aunt Cindy nodded. "He just showed up one day and Tucker kept him. We never would have gotten those cows if it hadn't been for him and his brush-popping dogs." They sipped their tea, each lost in her own thoughts. "You didn't tell him about the *next* time I went swimming with Tucker, did you?"

"No, we hadn't gotten to that—yet," Polly laughed.

"And you damn well better not *ever* get to that, Polly Ann." Cindy's smile belied the fact that she meant what she said.

"You really loved him, didn't you, Cindy."

"Oh, but I loved them both . . . but I have to admit I favored Tucker more. Had he lived . . ." Her voice trailed off before she admitted that thing she held in her heart that no one else ever knew.

"Had he lived and you being married to Rance, *I* would have had a chance with Tucker."

"That you would, Polly, that you would," Cindy Brown said, relieved that dark corner of her secret thoughts had been passed over.

CHAPTER 18
EL PASO

The history of El Paso is naturally divided into two parts:
(a) from the end of Noah's flood to the arrival of the
railroad. (b) from then on.

—Owen P. White

It took four things to happen that spring for me to have my first
visit to our Mexican ranch. First, the spring roundup was
cancelled; second, we got the cattle sold and dispersed as we
had planned before May; third, Nate Beavers's wife was expect-
ing their third child any day and she insisted that he stay home.
That pretty well assured that I could go to the Playas Valley
with Uncle Green.

The fourth event literally fell in place when Uncle Green's
horse fell on him while they were trying to climb out of a gully.
By th' time we found him, his broken leg had swelled up so big
he had to split his pants leg to make room for it. Doc Shetley
hoisted his leg up in traction and fed him morphine until the
swelling went down and he could set the break. A cast from his
foot to his butt put an end to his ambulating for a while.

It looked for a time like Uncle Nate was back on the trip
until we all sat down for a big three-family Sunday afternoon
dinner. He should never have brought the subject up.

"Looks like all the supplies for the Mexican Beavers Ranch
will be loaded on a car at El Paso by Friday. Dempsey and I
will leave for the train Wednesday."

All was quiet for a moment and I almost ducked under the table. Aunt Cindy dropped her knife on her plate so hard she chipped it—and that *really* made her mad. "Nate Beavers, you have been away when two of your three children were born. You have no business leaving now and Green's broken leg is not enough to excuse you to go. Who do you think will take care of this ranch with Green in a cast and you galavanting off?"

"The boys . . ."

"If you think three or even four boys hardly out of their diapers can run this ranch, it would seem to me that you and Green have been wasting your time running it instead of doing something constructive with your lives. It's gonna take you *and* those boys to keep this place up and be ready for a fall roundup. Dempsey and that Cooper boy are well able to take the supplies to Conly and the Mexican Ranch."

Nobody can rightly claim that Aunt Cindy ain't cocked and ready for any occasion. Her speech gave the other women time to get primed and she had hardly quit before another took her place. I'll have to say that there was very little repeating in their talks and by the time th' last speech was made, poor Nate was overloaded with reasons why he was not going to the Mexican Beavers Ranch. All he could do was glare at his plate and such of us men that still had our noses above the table.

It was very quiet the rest of the meal and we escaped as soon as we could without being called cowards.

"He really grabbed the hot end of the iron, didn't he?" Coop whispered.

"I think he got busted good," I replied.

"You ever been to the Mexican Beavers?"

"Nope, and it's about time I did."

"What do we have to do?"

"We'll ride to El Paso and pick up the supplies and see that they get safely to Conly at Pothook." I slapped him on the back.

"Nate and Uncle Green always talk about how much fun it is down there. I can't wait to find out for myself."

"What do we need to take?"

" 'Bout ever'thing, I guess, and that would include saddle and bridle. Conly will have horses for us to ride to the ranch."

When a man decides t' go somewhere, he just ups and goes, which is far from what a woman does. We spent the next three days "getting ready" as Aunt Cindy interpreted it. In the end, we rolled up our belongings in our bedrolls, picked up our saddles, and rode to Paxton Siding for the train—which is exactly what we would have done without female help.

In the late 1880s, Phelps Dodge began building a railroad along the Mexican border from El Paso to Tucson to serve their copper mines in Arizona. Later, they extended their line down into Sonora, Mexico, to their mining operations there. The El Paso and Southwestern line sure made it easy to travel that country. Before it came, we would have gone by horseback and wagon and it would have taken us near a month to get there across some of the most desolate desert in the country.

Now, I need to explain something about the Mexican Beavers Ranch: It was established by Tucker Beavers and Conly Hicks after they had taken over the ranch that had been run by the cattle thieves in the lower Playas Valley in Mexico. The new ranch was very successful, running cattle and sheep with the original Mexican sheepherders who had been dispossessed of their homes and range by the thieves. Conly married a local girl and stayed on as foreman of the ranch. They were very success-ful and the sheepherders shared in the bounty of the operation, unlike the peons of other operations in Mexico.

About 1910 the peons of Mexico had enough mistreatment and began to rebel against the government of Porfirio Díaz and the system that kept them in bondage to the elite ruling class.

Scattered rebellions grew into general revolution and the aging Díaz was deposed. Enter Pancho Villa and his army in northern Mexico and exit the Mexican Beavers Ranch, cattle, sheep, and people. The whole ranch, save for a few young revolutionaries who joined Villa, moved north in the Playas Valley and established their ranch under the Hatchet Mountains. Their range extended from the Darling creeks south to the border.

It was a perilous time when every man went armed and the ranch fought against revolutionaries who would drive off sheep and cattle by the herd to feed Pancho's army. Villa fed his army a steady diet of hatred for the Gringos, and in March of 1916 he and his army invaded the United States, attacking Columbus, New Mexico, and the Army camp there. After doing much damage to the town, he was repulsed and left the States minus over a hundred troops. That was the beginning of Pershing's futile great pursuit of the rebel.

Even though the ranch was now in the United States, we still called it the Mexican Beavers Ranch. We didn't have to haul supplies to them as we had in the past, but it was our custom to do so, even after the trains ran. We used to order supplies from merchants in El Paso and pack them up in a regular wagon train for the long trip to the Mexican ranch. Now, two or three times a year, Conly would telegraph an order or travel to El Paso to purchase supplies for the ranch and a small store they ran in Playas.

This year, we were picking up some white-face bulls that we had ordered to be delivered to the EP&SW yards at El Paso, and we were going to see to their safe delivery to the Mexican Beavers. The chance to see new ground and the hint of high adventure was enough to set our feet eagerly along the southwestern trail.

Coop couldn't get over the fact that the trip to El Paso would only take two or three hours, depending on the number of stops we made, and he had his watch out when we boarded the train. It seemed we would no sooner get up to speed than we would have to stop and pick up someone flagging us down. Like a trainer timing his horse on the track, Coop had his watch out as we pulled into the station, "Ha, three hours and twelve minutes, I knew they couldn't do in 'two or three' hours."

"Yeah," I said. "They only beat us by, say, thirty-six hours horseback, what they braggin' for?" Even in broad daylight and watchin' the country fly behind at twenty-five, thirty miles an hour, it seemed unreal that we would be seein' El Paso "three hours and twelve minutes" after leaving Paxton Siding. We had our gear transferred to the EP&SW line and walked downtown to see the sights and check in with our supplier. Their large adobe warehouse was dark and cool and for a moment I didn't notice that the man standing at the counter was Conly Hicks.

I sidled up and greeted him, "Hey, Conly, how you doin'?"

He spit and said, "Howdy, Dempsey. Why I'm just fit and fine, fit an' fine." He shook my hand and extended his to Cooper, "And you must be the Saint Cooper that Cindy was telling me about."

"Yes, sir." Coop shook his hand. "Glad to meet you."

"All our plunder is gathered and ready to load as soon as an empty car is available and the bulls are in the pens. They're looking good," Conly explained. "Let's mosey downtown and see th' sights."

At the first clothing store, I bought bibless overalls and shirts for Coop and myself. We walked down to El Paso Street in the old part of town.

"She shore ain't what she useta be back in the '80's," Conly said, a little sadly, I thought. "This time o' day, th' early crowd would be gatherin' at their favorite watering holes for an early start on th' evenin's festivities." He gestured at the empty streets, only an automobile or two sitting along the sides. "How about a cold one, boys?" he asked as he steered us toward a slightly rundown building with a faded sign that announced the Acme Saloon. It was pleasantly cool in the dark room and, at Conly's nod, the barkeep set up three cigars and three mugs of beer on the bar—surprisingly cold beer.

The barkeeper made small talk as he worked. Presently, he said to Coop who was standing at the end of the bar, "You're standing in a famous spot, there, young man."

"How's that?" Coop asked.

"That's John Wesley Hardin's favorite place to stand when he drank here."

"Hm-m-m, that's neat." Conly stood up straight and looked at the favored spot. "What made this so important?"

"Lean up against the bar and look in the mirror."

Conly complied and said, "Oh-h-h, he could see who was coming in the door behind him, couldn't he?"

"Yes, only he wasn't looking when Old John Selman came in and put a .45 slug in th' back of his head." He pointed to a dark stain in the wood. "That's John Wesley's blood there."

Coop had a funny look on his face and moved his mug off the dark stains. He looked uncomfortable and Conly and I moved down the bar to give him room to move away from that famous spot. "Might be an unlucky place t' be caught standin'," he muttered.

"It shore was for him." The barkeep grinned. "Local customers always leave that spot vacant in case John comes in." He smirked.

"Bet he never does," I said.

"I don't know, I have fellers tell me they seen him standin' there from time t' time. 'Course it's gener'ly after an evening of beers chased with tonsil varnish."

"After that, a man's either seein' lots of things or only the insides of his eyelids," laughed Conly.

"Yeah an' then there's those that can drink all night an' stay sober, *they* are th' ones I keep an eye on an' my scattergun close."

"A feller has t' be awful mean t' do that, don't he?" Conly chuckled.

"Gen'erly they are plumb oily," the barkeep agreed.

Our glasses empty, we said our goodbyes and left for the sunshine of the street. Coop inhaled a deep breath and flipped his cigar away. "Think I've seen enough of the ol' place."

Conly laughed, "Folks say if that bloodstain could talk, it would stand up and crow. Let's go down and look at the bulls." He haled a taxi buggy and we rode across town to the EP&SW cattle pens. One of the pens was full of white-faced red bulls two and three years old. Except for being road hungry, they looked pretty good. They had been taken good care of; there wasn't a broken horn among them. Conly pointed to one whose horns were turned in. "We'll be dehornin' him afore those grow into his head. Maybe his next pair will grow normal."

"Looks like you got about twenty or twenty-five of them." They moved so much I couldn't get a good count.

"Twenty-one, just in case something happened to one of them on th' trip. They got this far good, but th' next ride's gonna be a *leetle* rougher."

"Hows come?" Cooper asked.

"Road's rougher. Too many places tore up by 'Paches an' Villistas—and that's not countin' a few washouts." He added, "We have rooms at Hotel Paso Del Norte and it's getting on toward sunset. I promised The Muchacha we would meet them there for supper."

"You brought Eledina with you!" I exclaimed.

Conly nodded, "Eledina, her rifle, Little Conly, and th' two older girls."

After Aunt Cindy, Eledina—The Muchacha—was my favorite

woman of that generation. Just like Aunt Cindy, she could ride and shoot as well as any man—and on top of that she was the prettiest woman in the Playas Valley, *either* side of the border. I vaguely remembered the two girls; they were just giggly girls the time they came to Pinetop ranch and I ignored them as much as I could. Tucker Hicks must be three or four now. Everyone called him Little Conly because he resembled his father so much. I had never seen him.

We hurried back to the hotel and Coop and I got haircuts, cleaned up, shined our boots, and put on our new clothes. We got to the lobby a half hour before we were to meet Conly and the women and sat in the ample plush leather chairs, Cooper watching people as they passed. I picked up an edition of the *El Paso Daily Herald* and read.

"Demps, Demps," Cooper whispered, kicking me sharply. "Looky there!" He was tipping his head and cutting his eyes sidewise toward the stair.

"Aw, Coop, it's just a girl . . ." I began, then caught my breath as I realized that I was looking at Eledina, only twenty-something years younger, "Wow!" I whispered. A giggle from the landing above called my attention to another girl skipping down the stairs behind her sister, "Wait, Ana, I'm coming with you," she called.

"Mee too, Cepa, mee too!"

I beheld a cherub carefully descending the stairs, both hands on the railing above his head and his toes searching for the next step below. "Wait, Cepa, here me come," he called.

Both girls stood at the bottom of the stairs and waited on the tyke, who could only be Little Conly in the flesh. Four steps from the bottom, he turned loose of the railing, and turning to his sisters, held his chubby arms up and jumped. "Catch me-e-e," he cried in midair.

The girls were caught off guard and off balance as both tried to catch the child with the result that all three fell at the foot of the stairs; the child plopped on the second step laughing at the girls tangled on the floor.

"See, I told you they went all th' way up," I whispered to Coop as we stepped to the rescue.

Eledina's Image was rearranging her skirts over her legs as I reached her. "Here, let me help you up," and I offered her my hand. She looked up and I have never seen such blue eyes on an olive-skinned beauty in my life. I almost forgot to breathe.

"Oh, thank you," she smiled, seeming not to be the least embarrassed by her predicament. It was good she rose on her own strength, for I was suddenly weak as a kitten. She held my hand a moment, then turned to Little Conly who was clapping his hands and laughing. Coop was lending his hand to Cepa.

"Tucker Hicks, you know better than to do that," blue-eyed Ana scolded, but she couldn't hide her smile.

I scooped the child up and he pushed away, not in alarm, but curious, "Who you?"

"*I* am Dempsey Nealy and *you* are Tucker Hicks of the Mexican Beavers Ranch."

"You, Dimsy?" he asked, his eyes growing wide.

"Why, yes, he is," Ana said, a little surprised. "I almost didn't recognize you, Dempsey."

"I think we all have changed since we last met," I laughed.

Tucker kicked and pushed away. "Mee hungry." His chubby legs pumped toward the dining room and we followed.

A waiter stepped out in front of the boy and he stopped so suddenly he teetered on his toes. "Does the gentleman wish a table?"

Tucker stared in awe. "Yes," I said, "he wishes a table for seven."

"Very good," the man said to the tyke. "This way, please."

Tucker raised his eyes to us and Cepa said, "Follow him, Tucker."

The waiter led the way to a table in the corner, the boy pattering behind confidently—after he had made sure we were coming too. Ana took my arm as we walked. Her hand was warm. I awkwardly followed Aunt Cindy's instructions on the proper way to seat a lady, and Cooper on the other side of the table helped Cepa into a chair. Little Conly was trying to clamber into the chair with a booster seat beside Coop.

"Well, I see you have all met," the real Eledina said behind me, and I turned to see her smiling up at me. "My, how tall you have grown, Dempsey." She gave me a hug and I led her to the seat at the end of the table beside Little Conly.

"Thank you, Dempsey." She looked at me and she was as beautiful as ever.

"I guess I'll take a chair at the foot, here." Conly grinned as he sat at the other end.

"Papa, he Dimsy," the cherub said, pointing his spoon at me.

"I know, Little Bit, he's big, isn't he?"

"Lo-o-o-ng," the child corrected.

"Conly, would you please make the proper introductions." Eledina smiled.

"Of course, Saint Cooper, this is my wife, Eledina, the scamp next to you is our son Tucker Hicks, the lady on your left is Cepa Hicks, our daughter, and the lady next to me is our daughter Ana. Ladies, this is Saint Cooper of the Pinetop, Bluewater, and Sacramento ranches, New Mexico."

"We are glad to make your acquaintance, Mr. Cooper." Eledina smiled.

"And that, ladies and gentlemen, is the last formality to be had at this table tonight," Conly announced. He took the menu from the waiter and looked it over. "We will have the oyster soup and please serve the salads with our meal. For the main dish, the men will have steaks, and the ladies will have the veal cutlets, all well done. We'll have the cauliflower with cheese sauce and . . . the white rice. French bread and will the ladies take tea with their meal?"

"I think a nice wine would be appropriate for the main course," Eledina said.

Conly's eyebrows lifted and he glanced significantly at the two girls.

"It will be all right, the girls should become acquainted with proper meals." Eledina encouraged her husband.

"Might I suggest a light champagne?" The waiter smiled.

"That would be fine, and a ginger ale for the boy," Conly added.

"Also a glass of milk," Eledina instructed.

The waiter nodded and wrote in his book. "I shall bring the drinks now and shall I bring the milk with the meal?"

Eledina nodded and turned her attention to the boy, who was holding Coop's arm and chattering a thousand words a minute. I had to laugh at Coop's discomfort—it was obvious he had never been around little ones very much.

"Tucker, where did you get your name?" I asked.

"Mamma gived it to mee. She take it from the man who get us our ranch."

"Did he lose his name?" I asked

His face clouded in thought, "When he died, he gived it to Mamma."

"We gave it to you to honor Tucker Beavers and in the hope that you grow up to be like him," Eledina said. I could see her eyes were misty and Conly was watching the boy closely. "He was a very brave man, Tucker, and we would be proud if you grew up to be like him."

"*I* will grow up to be just like you, Papa—and Tucker Beavers too." He nodded as if that issue were decided.

"Cooper, tell Tuck about the rattler you killed last week," I suggested.

"You did?" The boy's eyes widened.

I turned to Ana, "How was your train ride?"

"Hot, long, and dusty," she laughed. "If not for the Villistas, I would have preferred horseback or even buggy and four days' travel."

"Are the bandits much trouble?"

"They don't bother the eastbound trains since there isn't much on them except ore, cattle, and sheep, but they will be a real menace when the loaded trains head west."

"So they prefer flour and beans to mutton, silver, and gold," I said.

"Silver and gold in the desert don't feed starving men," she said. The tone of her voice spoke of sympathy for the dirty, ragged, and starving army of peons struggling for their independence and dignity.

I, too, hoped for the success of the people against an oppressive system of servitude. This thing called freedom was a precious commodity and those of us who possessed it were indeed fortunate. I even understood Pancho's hatred of the Americans who allowed his enemy's armies to march across United States soil to reinforce those forces he had surrounded against the international border. He suffered the disastrous results of that betrayal, but possibly did not know that the orders came from Woodrow Wilson, even while he and his administration professed neutrality. Would that Pancho could loose his army on Washington instead of the innocent citizens of Columbus, New Mexico, and other U.S. citizens caught up in this conflict.

"I would fight with Pancho if I were a man," Cepa said, and the table was suddenly quiet. I sensed that this discussion had come up before and there was tension between daughter and parents on the subject.

"Many of us would, Cepa, but freedom is more precious to those who have fought and gained it for themselves," I said. "It has been left to us to stand aside and encourage them when we can."

"And we must not sacrifice our own freedoms to give them freedom," Cooper added.

"That sounds a little selfish to me," Ana said.

"Ah-h, but it is," Coop said. "If we reach down and give them a hand up, we are helping them from a position of strength. If we sink to their level, we might end up serving them. *We* must stay strong."

The approach of our waiter with a bottle of champagne in a bucket of ice saved us from any further political conversation. A second waiter distributed stemmed wine glasses and, with a flourish, filled Tucker's little glass with bubbling ginger ale. The delighted child took a big drink and it promptly spewed out of his nose. Cooper grabbed the glass while Tuck's mother applied a napkin to the sputtering face. The girls giggled and I wondered what their reaction to the champagne would be.

"Take little sips, Tuck, and it will just tickle your nose," Cooper instructed as he held the glass up to the boy's lips. Tucker took a small sip and immediately rubbed his nose, "It's spitting at me!" he exclaimed.

"Let me see." Cooper held his glass for the servant to pour some of the ginger ale in his glass. "Well, I'll be, Tuck, it's spitting at me too! Do you think that's what tickles your nose?"

"Me bet it is," the boy replied.

Cooper took another sip and the boy watched intently. "Is 'at tickle you?"

"Yeah, it does, isn't that funny?"

"You like it?"

"Pretty good, isn't it?"

"I don' know, Coo-per, I don' t'ink so." He shook his head in

191

doubt. Our attentions were drawn to the waiter who expertly opened the champagne with a pop and not much fizz. He first poured the glasses for the ladies, then for the men. The girls watched the glasses closely, observing the bubbles gently rising through the golden liquid.

Conly nodded to me. "Dempsey, I suppose it would be proper for a toast."

He caught me completely off guard and I stifled the toast I was composing in my mind to two smiling blue eyes. "Uh-h-h, yes, sir," I stammered as I rose. I looked at Cooper for help and he mouthed, "Over the lips and through the gums . . ." and I glared at him an instant.

"Here's to Tucker Hicks, may he leave his boot prints on the land beside his father's, and here's to the three loveliest ladies in all New Mexico."

"Hear, hear." Coop and Conly raised their glasses while the ladies glowed and Tuck sipped ginger ale. We sipped the wine and it was amusing to watch both girls wrinkle their noses at the tickle it caused.

"Bu-r-r-r-up." Tucker burped. His eyes widened in surprise. "The bubbles did it, Mamma!" he whispered in awe.

"Try to burp quietly," Eledina admonished, as she gave Ana a warning glance. I dared not look at her, and when my eyes met Cepa's, she choked off a giggle behind her napkin.

"This champagne tickles my nose just like the ginger ale, Tucker," said Ana.

"Will it make you burp too?" he asked, still awed by the newfound novelty.

"Ladies *do not* burp, Tucker," Eledina said, and I wondered who she was addressing, for she was looking at Ana. I could see that Eledina was becoming upset and I understood how she felt. Here was a rare opportunity to show the girls how to act in polite society and the occasion was slipping away, awash in ginger ale and an uninhibited four-year-old boy. Cooper looked at me and nodded his understanding of the situation. "Tucker, we are going to have a special dinner, now, and I want you to help me out."

"What we gonna do, Coo-per?"

"Well, first of all we have to mind our manners, that means not to burp out loud and not to interrupt when anyone else is talking. Second, we have to see that the ladies are comfortable and taken care of. You are sitting by your mother, so you have to see that she has everything she needs before she asks for it and engage her in polite conversation."

"I don' know those big words, 'ingage her in polite conv, con-ver . . .' what's 'at, Coo-per?"

"The most important part of that is to be polite and talk to her."

"Like, I would ask your mother, 'How was your trip, Mrs. Hicks?' " I said, "and Mrs. Hicks would reply . . ."

"It was long and dusty, Dempsey, but I enjoyed the scenery and it is so nice to be here and shop in the town," Eledina said.

"Then, Tucker, I would turn to Cepa and say something like, 'I hope you are pleased with your room here at the hotel, Miss Hicks.' "

"Oh, the rooms are very nice," Cepa replied. "I especially like the view of the street; and the maids are so helpful."

"Father, how was your day, did the cattle arrive safely and did you see them?" Ana took up the conversation and while Tucker listened and sipped his ginger ale, the meal proceeded in a much calmer fashion.

The Muchacha smiled.

CHAPTER 19
THE THIRD BATTLE OF JUÁREZ

Poor Mexico, so far from God and so near the
United States.

—Porfirio Díaz

1919

It turned out to be a most enjoyable evening with the Hicks family. Someone was playing the grand piano and we sat and listened until Tucker got restless. We decided to take a walk before bedtime—after the desk clerk convinced Conly that it would be perfectly safe to stroll down the street a few blocks. I led the parade with Eledina on my arm; Cooper escorted Cepa. Conly with Ana kept watch over the nearly deserted street from behind. He still could not believe that El Paso had become safe for gentle folks to venture out at night.

Tucker with his short legs set the pace and he spent much time staring into store windows and chattering to one or the other of us about a hundred things. On the way back to the hotel, he grew tired and I took him up on my back. We hadn't gone a half block until he was asleep, his head on my shoulder and his arms around my neck.

We parted in the hotel lobby, the ladies retiring to their rooms with the sleeping tot and the men returning to the bar. "How soon do you think we will be ready to leave?" I asked Conly.

"The girls haven't finished their shopping," he sighed, "and they are having some gowns made which I'm sure we won't leave town without—I would guess we will not leave before the third day from today."

Cooper grinned, "That'll give us time to look around a little ourselves."

"That'll just about give us time to finish loading the car with our supplies and the bulls ready to load before we pull out," Conly corrected.

I grinned, knowing Conly's sigh was not for the time wasted by the ladies shopping, but for his shrinking purse. We would not have much time on the town with all the things we had to prepare for the road, and the little details to be rounded up here at the last would take the most time. Conly pulled out his tally book and leafed through several pages of supply lists. On a page of hotel stationery, he had listed supplies he had been unable to purchase at the mercantile. "We're gonna have to shop around town for several things," he said as he tore the list in half and handed one piece to me and the other half to Coop. "You two need to find these items while I see to the bulls. A veterinarian is coming in the morning to examine and inoculate them. There'll be two buggies out front for you at seven o'clock. See how many of those things you can round up by sundown and the one that accomplishes the most can have his pick of the guns in th' showcase at the warehouse."

Cooper eyed me with that "I'm gonna have that gun" look and I knew the race was on. "With that, gentlemen, I shall retire to my room." I rose and paid the tab. Followed closely by Coop and Conly, I climbed the stairs to our room and drifted off to sleep thinking about the list and places I could go to find the supplies.

I don't know if I heard the first shot, but the next half dozen shots were just bringing me out of a deep sleep when the boom of a cannon not far off rattled the windowpanes, and I found myself standing in the middle of the room. Cooper was shucking on his pants and I hurried to dress. People were running in the hall and there was much excited talking. I heard snatches of conversation, "Pancho Villa's attacking Juárez . . ." ". . . he's crossing the river!" "They're shooting people on 8th and 9th Streets!"

Still barefooted, I opened the door just as someone was about to knock on it and almost got hit with a small fist. A vision with large blue eyes and wearing a pink gown said, "Papa wants you, hurry!" She turned and padded barefooted down the hall and I followed. Cooper overtook us as we entered the Hicks's suite. Ana disappeared into one of the rooms and Conly began giving us instructions. "Villa has attacked the Carrancistas in Juárez. He is driving them back to the fortress. If he wins, he is just as likely to cross right on over the river and attack El Paso. We must leave town as fast as we can. I am going to the railyard and convince them to hook us up and move us out of harm's way.

"Dempsey, those bulls are in the pens down by the river. I need you and Cooper to drive them west along the tracks out of the war. We'll load them at a safe loading chute down the road somewhere."

Eledina emerged from a bedroom with a sleepy Tucker in tow. "Eledina, there will be a buggy at the door for you and the girls. Wait here and when Demps and Coop drive the cattle by, follow them. Hopefully, I will be along soon with the train." The Muchacha nodded. Her grim look and the set of her jaw told me she was well in command of the situation and ready for action. Conly buckled on his pistol and picked up one of *four* rifles leaning on the wall by the door. Without a look back, he strode down the hall. Coop and I hurried after him and hauled our gear out of our room. Both girls had appeared dressed and were instructing porters to load the luggage on the waiting buggy. I gave the suite a quick look and noticed that there were only two rifles left and Tucker was asleep on the divan.

"Mother has gone after Father," Cepa said at my elbow. I noticed for the first time that she wore a gunbelt. I picked up the sleeping Tucker, and after looking around, Cepa picked up both rifles and closed the door behind us. Ana, wearing a gunbelt, was herding the laden porters down the stairs and I glimpsed Cooper's hat bobbing in the lead.

Small arms fire was a continual roar and artillery boomed a periodic cadence. The buggy was just pulling up to the door and a panicky man demanded that it take him and his wife away. He was in the act of taking over the buggy when Cooper forced him away, his gun ready if needed. "You got two good feet there, mister, and they can take you away as fast as this buggy can in this traffic. The lady is welcome to ride with us if needed."

"Never mind, we can take care of ourselves," the lady said. "Come on, Herbert, we're walking." She turned with a toss of her head and joined the crowd leaving the battlegrounds, the chubby man puffing after her.

I handed my drowsy bundle to Cepa and said, "Coop, you stay with the girls. I'll drive the bulls down the tracks and meet you out there somewhere." I turned and trotted off toward the cattle pens down by the river. It seemed that they were in the middle of the battle and I hoped they weren't all shot up. Glancing back, I saw the girls and Cooper in a heated discussion of some kind. Ana now had Tucker and he was protesting at the top of his lungs. As I turned the corner, I saw Cepa take up her rifle and turn my way. *Dear Lord, don't let that girl follow me,* and I ran.

CHAPTER 20
THE LITTLE VILLISTA

You can't hold a girl with a lock and bolt, any more than
with a vault.

—Old Russian Saying

I was running down El Paso Street toward the river and the
street here was almost deserted. There was an occasional figure
peeking through a window or around a door and I glimpsed
people on the flat rooftops. As I approached 8th Street, I heard
keening and a few houses down that street, a crowd was
gathered around the steps of a house where a woman lay, obviously dead. On the corner of 9th, several people were gathered
around a shrouded body laid out on a door. Bullets whined
about and I called a warning as I passed. When I looked back
the shrouded figure lay alone and Cepa was halfway to me from
the corner I had turned. "Go back, go back," I yelled. Should
have saved my breath. Just past 9th was the railroad and the
pens were on the sidetrack to my left. I turned toward them and
ran for the gate. The gate was tall and the latch a little low for
some reason. As I stooped to release it, a bullet splintered the
rail where my head had been and drove a dozen splinters into
the side of my face. I heard a shout of laughter from the river,
and looking across, saw two figures standing on the roof of a
house derisively waving their rifles at me.

When the gate swung open, I had to sidestep the rushing
herd. One bull lay still in the middle of the pen. I heard the

chuf-chuf of a train somewhere east of me. As the last cow left the pen, I snapped a shot at the snipers and turned and almost ran over a breathless Cepa.

"You're shot!" she exclaimed. "Who did this?"

As if in answer, a bullet smashed into the board next to our heads and another shout came from the snipers. "Those . . ." and out of respect for the lady, I will refrain from pronouncing the name she gave them. Cepa knelt and, resting her rifle on a plank of the pen, took careful aim and fired. It took the smallest moment for the bullet to strike home and its victim slowly toppled forward off the roof. As his companion stared down, a second bullet spun him around and he fell from sight on the roof.

"You *do not* shoot my friends, you dirty Carrancistas," Cepa screamed. She shook her rifle at the empty roof. Tears were streaming down her cheeks and she was shaking. I grabbed her and held her to me. "I am okay, Cepa, it's just splinters from the board, I'm okay."

"Oh," she said in a small voice, and holding her hand I turned to follow the cattle. They ran up Ochoa Street and slowed to a trot about halfway to First Street where they would have to turn left to pass the hotel and return to the railroad tracks beyond. Leaving Cepa behind, I ran to turn them west down First. With the help of a passerby, I managed to turn them. It was quieter here and the softened boom of the artillery served to keep the herd moving instead of scattering and seeking somewhere to graze. The street had cleared of traffic and beyond the hotel I could see our buggy moving along very slowly.

The press of the buildings kept the herd together, and with me running ahead on one side and Cepa on the other, we kept them out of the side streets. I had no idea how without a horse or two we were going to keep them together outside of town where the land was open. As we approached the end of the street and open country, I heard a noise and looking back saw a rider approaching. It was a boy riding bareback and only a halter to guide his horse. I was about to speak to him when he bare-heeled his horse and headed off a wandering bull. After that, he worked hard on one side of the cattle while I worked the opposite side afoot and Cepa kept the herd moving from behind.

We reached the buggy, new cattle pens and chute, and exhaustion all at about the same time. Coop and Ana hazed the cattle in and closed the gate while Cepa and I sought the water pump. The boy rode up and sat there grinning at us as his horse drank from the trough.

"Thanks for all your help," I said. "Can I pay you something?"

"Nah, unless you have something t' eat." He hopped off the horse, threw the halter rope over his shoulders, and shooed him back toward town.

"Your horse?"

"No, I just borrowed him. He'll go back home now."

"And you'll have t' walk."

"Ain't goin' thataway, I'm on my way to Tucson."

"Best you kept your horse for that, it's a long way and dry," I said.

"Kept th' horse an' I'da been a horse thief." He stuck his head under the pump and I pumped for him.

"You did ask permission to ride him, didn't you?" Cepa asked.

"Asked th' horse first, he said 'yes.' Didn't see anyone else t' ask."

Ana giggled, "An uncaught horse thief."

The boy only grinned at us. "Where are you headed?"

"We're going west to our ranch as soon as that train comes," Ana said.

"Train's already gone through, missed it myself," the boy said. He stepped into the watering trough and washed dust off his feet and legs.

"If th' train's gone through, where could it be?" I wondered.

Ana sighed, "With Mother and Papa involved, you never can tell what's going to happen."

"All we can do is wait here and see. We're safe for now, so we might as well make ourselves comfortable." I started to wash my face and winced when I touched my left cheek. There were still splinters in my face and I cautiously felt for them.

The girls descended on me, one with a wet cloth and the other with tweezers, and I was soon de-splintered and washed, though some of the places continued to bleed some.

"You got spots on your face, Demps," Tucker observed.

"Yes and I think Cepa has one or two, also."

The boy looked and gave a little gasp, "You do, Cepa, you do."

Cepa smiled and then the memory of how she got those splinters came back and she teared up.

I led her away from the crowd. "Cepa, you needn't worry about what you did, it was right."

"But I *killed* those men."

"It was kill or be killed. In a sense, they forced you to shoot them by shooting at us. I imagine Villa still has a bounty for any Anglo killed by his men."

Her tear-rimmed eyes were big. "Those were Carrancistas."

"No, Cepa," I whispered, "they were Villistas shooting at Americans from Mexico—and they would have killed you if they could." I refrained from telling her about the heads of U.S. citizens stuck on poles across Chihuahua.

"No, it couldn't be."

"Yes, Villa has poisoned his people with lies about the Americans and made them hate us as much as they hate the Carrancistas."

"Here comes a train!" Cooper called, pointing west.

"There's our ride, I hope. I won't say a word about this. It's just between you and me unless you speak." She nodded and wiped her eyes and we hurried back to the pens.

CHAPTER 21
CONLY HICKS, ENGINEER
(AS TOLD BY THE ENGINEER HIMSELF)

Come all you rounders, if you want to hear
The story told of a brave Engineer
Conly Hicks was the rounder's name . . .
With apologies to Casey Jones

I saw Eledina hurryin' after me half a block behind, but I didn't slack my pace. The sooner I got to that train, th' sooner she would be out of danger. I had awakened the engineer and lined out what I wanted before she caught up with me, red-faced and puffing.

"Conly Hicks, you saw me and didn't even slow down to wait on me," she puffed.

"I was waitin' on you here," I grinned, "sooner we got here, th' safer you are."

The engineer was adamant. "I ain't gonna move this train 'til th' track's clear an' I get an order."

"All right, I'll get those things for you while you start building up steam and get ready t' roll," I turned to the office, The Muchacha beside me. The stationmaster was busy on the telegraph and couldn't talk for a minute or two. When he turned to me, he said, "All eastbound traffic has stopped, westbound trains are still moving. I have an order for your train to leave as soon as possible. We're not going to let those Villistas steal any trains."

"Good!" I said, "We are ready, just have to stop and pick up th' rest of th' family and my beeves somewhere along the line."

"I hope they are well away from the shooting, and by the way, we *won't* be stopping at the pens to pick up those beeves, they're right in the middle of the battle."

"Won't have to, my men are driving them out of town. Is there another pen and chute west of town?"

"There's one about two miles from the edge of town. They shouldn't miss it if they follow the tracks."

"I'm sure they will," Eledina said rather dryly.

We followed the stationmaster out to the train where he had a conversation with the engineer. It seemed the engineer was balking at moving the train right through the war zone and the stationmaster got pretty hot about it, "You will take that train west as soon as you can or you can give up ever running a train again *anywhere, for any line,* I'll see to that!"

That engineer and his fireman turned as if to leave and I grabbed his arm so tightly he flinched. Leading him toward the engine, I said to the stationmaster, "We are on our way!" To the engineer, I whispered, "Get on, I have a plan."

"I'm not . . ."

"Shut up and listen to me," I gritted. "Get this thing rolling and I will tell you how you will be safe like you were in your own bed." He glanced behind him at The Muchacha with her rifle ready, and the determined look on her face made him think less of mutiny. We all climbed into the cab and I explained my plan. The stationmaster watched until the train started moving, then returned to his telegraph.

Quickly, the engineer showed me the controls, "This is the throttle, set it about here for the proper speed. It should get you about 30 to 35 miles per hour. Pull it all the way out and the engine will idle. Push this lever forward as it is now and the train will go forward. Straight up is neutral and back is reverse. You cannot be moving forward when you shift it for backward.

Here is the brake, move the lever to neutral before you apply the brakes. Watch your boiler pressure and keep the needle out of the red. You should have plenty of water so long as the tanks don't get shot up." With that, he turned and jumped off the train, his fireman having already bailed.

Eledina stared at me wide-eyed, "You are the driver?"

"Only until we are out of town, the crew will meet us there if we get through." I pushed the throttle and the train gained speed. Already, the sounds of battle were louder and I could see flashes of guns and artillery ahead. "Get down behind this steel wall and stay there."

A ping or two of lead hitting steel told me we were becoming a target and I ducked down beside Eledina. Glancing back, I noticed the empty cattle pen and was relieved. The pings became heavier and I prayed for the water tanks to hold. The pinging stopped just as if we had run out of a hailstorm and the hail had suddenly stopped. We were out of danger from flying lead. I peeked out and saw that we were past the battleground and moving through the last of town. People were standing by the tracks waving frantically for us to stop, but I couldn't have stopped in time to pick them up. If I had, we would have been overrun and I would never have gotten that engine moving again. It was best to keep going, and that is just what we did.

I must have been looking out the left side of the train when we passed the loading pens on the right. Anyway, we missed them. It was fun driving a train—until things started going t' hell on me. First of all the train started slowing down, and when I finally found the pressure gauge, it was 'way low, so we threw some more wood in the furnace. That helped for a little while, then I got worried about the water. If we ran out, the boiler would blow and I didn't want us to be near when that happened.

While I was pondering that, Eledina hollered, "We've just

passed mile post ten."

"Ten miles? That's too far!" I wrestled the lever to neutral and the engine blew off a cloud of steam. *Then* I remembered to pull the throttle back. When I applied the brakes, we stopped so suddenly we both slammed into the front wall.

"Just where did you learn to drive a train?" Eledina growled as she wiped dust and dirt from her dress. There was a black smudge on her cheek and her hair was awry from watching out the window like she had seen engineers do. "Any more driving like that and I'll take my chances walking."

I pulled the big lever to reverse and cracked the throttle a little and we began to creep backward. "You'll have t' leave on th' run, for this train ain't stopping for nothing." I grinned at her and she stomped my toe with the butt of her rifle.

Time sure gets discombobbled on a train. It didn't take us any time to get ten miles out and cre-e-eping in reverse we were still outpacing a horse at a good lope. Steam pressure was creeping up and I wasn't stoking th' fire an' I didn't know what to do t' get the pressure down when Eledina called, "There's the cattle pen and there's the girls."

It was a blessed sight to see, but the most blessed was the sight of those two railroad men hot-footin' it to us. I stopped the train, hopped down and helped Eledina down, and gladly gave over the engine for proper care. The engineer hurried up the steps with hardly a glance at us and went to work trying to salvage the engine from my mishandling.

We hurried to the pens and a waif trotted to his mother prattling like a Jaybird. "Mamma, did you drived the train? You beated us here and left us, where did you go? I'm hungry. Papa, that Injun-ear said you might break his train, did you broke it? I'm hungry, Mamma."

His bare feet and legs were muddy to his knees and I grabbed him before he could get to his mother. "I know someone who's been wading in the watering trough," I held his legs out away from me.

"Me did, Papa, and we all washed off in the pump."

"Someone needs another washing, I think."

The boy looked at his mother and exclaimed, "An' I know who—Mamma, your face has dirt on it."

I smiled as Eledina blushed. "Your papa did this to me, Tucker, what should we do to him?"

"He needs washing too, Mamma." Down he squirmed and ran to the pump. "I can pump for you, see?" He vigorously pumped short strokes and water trickled from the spout. "See, Mamma, see?"

The girls held a mirror for Eledina while she cleaned her face and fussed with her hair, and I suffered through a trickling wash at the pump. "Thank you, Tuck, that was good."

Noises from the engine reassured me that the engine had not been permanently damaged and soon the train backed up to us. Cooper shoved the cattle car door open and the engineer expertly lined it up with the chute. While we loaded the animals, the ladies and a lad strange to me loaded our luggage into the passenger car. The train consisted of a passenger car behind the wood hopper, a boxcar loaded with our supplies, and the cattle car last. There was no caboose or conductor because of our hurried departure.

That engineer still had a burr under his saddle and we had to run to catch the passenger car before he built up speed and left us trying to catch the cattle car. Dempsey just missed the handrail and had to settle for the boxcar steps. He climbed over the rail pronouncing special blessings on that pansy engineer. I had to agree with him, and at the same time I was relieved to be on the way out of the battle.

Clancy

We couldn't get into the passenger car until we stored the luggage that was thrown and piled helter-skelter and blocking the aisle. In front of the properly stored baggage sat the youngster I had noted before.

"Hello, young man, where you headed?" I asked.

"I be Clancy, on me way to Tucson, Mister Hicks." He cocked an eye at me from under a battered, sweat-stained bowler hat and his accent told me he was Irish, not long off the boat or the streets of Boston, New York, or some other large eastern city.

"Why are you going there?" I asked, seating myself across the aisle and hopefully out of any drafts wafting from Clancy's person. To say he was filthy was to understate the facts, though I know of no other more accurate description.

"That be where they ha'e taken me brother, Patrick."

I sensed a story, "Who?"

"That damned priest, Father Murphy, stole him right off the street and took him to the parish house where he was tortured by the Sisters," Clancy spat.

"Tortured? How was he tortured?" Dempsey asked. He had judiciously taken a seat in front of the boy and opened the window.

"They shaved his hair, took away all his clothes and *burned* them, then they *washed* him!" He shuddered, "Head to foot."

"Didn't leave him naked, did they?"

"May well ha'e bean, they put a *gown* on him and made him wear cloth slippers, like a lassie."

"Then they fed him!" Cooper exclaimed.

"An' he slept in a bed!" Dempsey added.

Clancy lowered his head and scraped his horny feet on the

floor, "Aye, they do it," he muttered barely above the noise of the train.

"How did brother take all this mistreatment?" I asked.

"O-h-h he not like haircut and bath, he screamed at the gown, but me thinks he liked the food and the bed." Clancy's chin was on his chest and a tear washed a streak down his cheek. "But they take me baby brother away, said he couldn't sleep in our box no more, couldn't go barefooted in the street. They take me only kin in the world and they put him on a train with other childs and taken him to live with people in Arizona." After a moment, he muttered, "I go to get him back."

"What is he talking about, priests stealing children and shipping them off?" Cooper asked.

"They call them 'orphan' or 'baby' trains, Coop," Dempsey explained. "They gather orphaned street urchins and care for them and find people in the country who are willing to adopt them and raise them away from the cities. They say there are thousands of orphans wandering the streets of places like New York and Philadelphia," Dempsey explained. "Catholics want them raised in Catholic homes and there was a riot over in Clifton a few years ago when the priests were going to give blond-headed white children to Mexican immigrants who hardly knew English. The white folks took the children away and ran the Catholics out of town, priest, nuns, and all. They barely missed a good tar and feathering."

"I remember that," I said, "but we didn't get the whole story down there in Bavispe." Forty years I have lived with the Mexicans on both sides of the border and I have grown to love them and their simple ways, though they can be exceedingly exasperating at times, I don't remember having the racial prejudice many or most Anglos have.

"Why didn't they take you too, Clancy?" Cooper asked.

"Too old, nobody would want me."

"But they shouldn't take your brother away from you."

Dempsey shook his head, "Brothers and sisters get separated all the time and few ever know what happened to their kin, Coop."

"Well, that ain't right!"

"That may be so, but is it any better to grow up on the street living in a box and begging for food, no way to be educated or dressed or warm?" I asked.

The train whistle blew and we began to slow down. Eledina was standing over me with a pile of clothes and bundles in her arms. "We're coming to a water stop and the engineer has agreed to stay over a few minutes." She gave Clancy one of those looks any man who has been around women understands, but obviously, Clancy has not been privy to that knowledge. There he sat totally ignorant of what was to come while its significance bore fruit in three minds.

"O-h-h-h, me," Demps groaned as he unbuttoned his shirt. Coop was shucking his boots and digging through one of the packs; he came out with two pair of moccasins, one of which he handed to Dempsey.

"Clancy, let's go out and watch the watering." I leisurely walked to the rear door, followed by Clancy and two mounds of sundry clothing. The watering was already going and the big six-inch pipe was pouring into the water tank. When it was full, the fireman flipped me the pull chain and capped the tank. With a little toot, the engine backed up and the boys laid their bundles on the cowcatcher.

I pointed to a cloud of dust rising across the desert south of the tracks. "See that dust, Clancy? That's a bunch of Apaches hoping to catch the train. They're all about here and a fellow wouldn't last five minutes away from this train. I tell you that for your own health, for you are going to get a shower right here and I wouldn't want you running off to lose your scalp to some wild Indian."

As I talked, Dempsey and Cooper had positioned themselves either side of the boy, prepared to force the issue and probably to take a shower with him. To our surprise, Clancy shouted, "Oh, boy," and began stripping off his filthy rags. In no time he had a cloth and soap and I was pouring water from that big pipe over his head. He scrubbed and scrubbed himself and sang an Irish ditty as he worked.

Coop and Demps were grinning with relief and the engineer and fireman were standing on the walkway either side of the boiler watching and laughing. The boy lathered himself twice, washed his head twice, and after the last rinse, I raised the pipe and turned the water off. "Tank's almost empty, Clancy, get some clothes on."

New underwear where there had been none before, new shirt and overalls, and we had a new boy. He picked up the sombrero, set it on his head, and nodding to us barefooted it back to the passenger car. Heads out the windows quickly disappeared as the boy mounted the front steps and we heard applause as he entered the car.

"You don't smell, Clancy," a little voice piped.

Two long toots of the whistle and we were on our way. Next stop, Playas Valley and home!

CHAPTER 22
PLAYAS
(DEMPSEY'S STORY)

Only a fool argues with a skunk, a mule, or a cook.

—Ramón Adams

It was good to be on our way and out of the paths of flying lead. Conly joined Eledina and Tucker at the front of the car and the rest of us scattered about. Cepa told the others about our adventures dodging bullets and herding bulls and we laughed and joked about our foibles and fun. I suppose we didn't get loaded and on our way until about noon, and as the afternoon wore on, the heat and rocking of the train lulled us until most of us slept. Only Clancy stayed awake with me, watching out his side of the train at the vastness of the desert. I watched out my side and remembered a young man that rode alone across this very plain before the trains came. Riding at night to avoid Indians, he went looking for retribution for the murders of his father and friends, and I wondered if I would have been brave enough to do the same.

It seemed we had to stop for water more often than we did north of El Paso, and the fireman agreed, explaining that their EP&SW engines were smaller and the AT&SF engines had bigger water tanks. The chaos in Mexico had just about depopulated the border region and the communities along the line were mostly deserted. Very few of our stops had even a stationmaster, which was a grand name for telegraph operator and water tank filler. Several of the water tank sidings were occupied by eastbound ore trains waiting for the all clear signal from El Paso. Our crew took a lot of joshing from the engineers of the ore trains because they had to back up so our donkey engine could drink. They were anxious to hear news about the battle and worried about how long they had to stay idle without food and other accommodations. They didn't mention the very real possibility that they could be subjects of a visit from renegade Indians and bandits and I noticed that almost all of them were armed.

I know what you're thinking; this is 1919 and the Indians have all been tamed and become civilized, but no one had told the Indians that and they were still on the prowl for any mischief they could get into. Contrary to popular belief back east, there were still Indians living off the reservations, especially in the wilds of the Mexican Sierra Madre. The unsettled conditions in Mexico had also attracted scoundrels of the white variety and many an outrage laid to the Indians or Villistas were the work of white men. Often the gangs were mixed, Indian, white and Mexican working together. The Three T's—trains, telegraph, and telephones—had changed a lot of things, but there was still a lot of taming to do.

Our last stop was Hermanas and we all got off the train to stretch our legs and walk on ground that didn't shake and roll. Little Tucker was sleepy and fussy and Eledina dug out snacks for all of us. We stood around eating and talking while the engineer and fireman sat on the rails and ate their suppers.

Conly was especially quiet and Eledina motioned for me to talk to him. As I walked up, he said, "This is where we met Tucker Beavers back in the spring of '86. That's Tito Jimenec's store," indicating the only building in sight. "It hasn't changed a bit."

When Conly said, "*We* met Tucker," he meant his three buddies, Slim, Gabby, and Shorty, partners with him in some sort of ranching operation south of Hermanas, quite likely stocked with cattle of dubious ownership and unknown origin.

A faded sign over the door listed: Groceries, Hardware, Tack, Beer, Whiskey, and Billiards. "See what Slim wrote on the sign?"

I moved closer until I could read the scribbling between the words. After Tack, it read, *when in stock,* and after Whiskey, it said, *always in stock.* I grinned at Conly.

"When Tito heard our plans to go after the bunch that had stolen our cows with the Beavers's stock, he and his double-barreled 'shootgun' insisted that we pay our tab. I don't think there was six bits between us and all our money on the hoof had been stolen so Tucker paid the tab. I thought then that he was awful foolish going off into the desert with four strangers and all that jingle in his belt, but later on, I realized that it wasn't foolishness, he was that good at discerning character—and he was brave too."

He turned and looked south across the tracks. "Down there a couple of miles or so is an arroyo with a spring and a big cotton-wood, 'bout th' only one of its kind around. That cottonwood was our ranch house and that spring our only reason for stayin' there—that an' th' dearth o' close neighbors." He smiled at the memory of those wild days.

A toot of the whistle and the hiss of steam called us back to the train and we chuffed off on the last lap of our journey. It was still daylight when we got to Playas and pulled off the main line, nose to nose with a big ore train engine parked on the sid-ing. "Six hours from El Paso and it would have taken us three, four days horseback." Coop wondered at our speed. "Why, we would hardly be out of earshot of that artillery!"

Our first duty was to unload the bulls and water them. Without access to the chute, we hooked up the ramp provided and once the first bull ventured off the train, we had our hands full avoiding a stampede for the water trough in the pens. A little grain and a little hay and they settled down for the evening.

We found Conly with four or five sweating men unloading the boxcar and pitched in to help. Two wagons stayed busy running between train and store until the car was empty and the storage room bulged with new merchandise. Ladies and tot had disappeared and when we had finished, Conly led the whole crew across the alley to a large adobe house. We had to throw out three washpans before we were all cleaned up and that was just in time for our call to supper. The whole back end of the house was a large dining hall and the long table was laden with steaming dishes on one end. I suppose that table could hold twenty people on those long benches. There were ten of us and we only took up one end of it. A large Mexican-American lady stood in the doorway to the attached kitchen and surveyed the layout. A word from her and two young ladies appeared with tall ewers of coffee or cool tea and passed down the table filling glasses and cups.

Clancy's eyes sparkled, "Glory be, Patrick, would you look a' that?" he whispered.

"Clancy, come sit here by me," Conly called, and the boy moved cautiously as if in a dream that might suddenly disappear. He carefully stepped over the bench and sank slowly to the seat as if it might not really be there, never once taking his eyes off the dishes.

"Now, this is probably not anything like the food you have been used to, so I'm gonna educate you about it all," Conly began . . .

"But first, you will say grace." Eledina stood in a doorway to the front of the house. She had changed from her road-grimed dress to a pretty dress called an evening gown and looked greatly refreshed after her trip. The girls did not reappear, having eaten and retired for the night.

"Of course, I will say grace before we eat." Conly smiled and waited until the kitchen help assembled near the doorway. Clancy quickly removed his forgotten sombrero and all bowed, "Bless, oh Lord, this bounty you have provided and bless the hands that prepared it." All said the "Amen," and the devout Catholics crossed themselves. I remember Nap's saying, "The prayer was short enough for a hungry stomach."

We had a lot of fun teaching Clancy how to eat this strange food. His experience eating food was limited to what he could pilfer or work for here and there, but no one had taken the time to educate him on the intricacies and manners of eating Mexican food. I doubt the food he got lasted long enough for anyone to teach him the whys and wherefores. He was almost desperately hungry and it was several days before he slowed down long enough to savor the food.

He didn't know how old he was. "Somewhere about twelve or thirteen, I imagine," he guessed, but I doubted that. By his size, I would expect him to be more like nine or ten with the experience of a twelve or thirteen year old. It was no small feat he did, coming from the city of New York to Playas, New Mexico, with nothing but his will to carry him through. He didn't remember his last name, so assumed the old Irish name of Wilson. It was politically inspired, but didn't get him into the White House to see cousin Woodrow.

Eledina tried her best to convince the boy to wear shoes but he refused; even the threat posed by cactus needles didn't deter his resolve. "Those feet are so tough, you would do better taking him down to the smithy and getting him shod," Conly laughed.

"We tried that one day," Coop said, "but th' nails kept bending."

If you wanted to find Clancy any time of the day, you went to the kitchen and there he'd be, munching on something stolen or given to him to get him out of the way. Finally, Tina, the cook, took him by the ear and showed him the woodyard. "Eef you eat, you work about here. So long as I have thee fire wee weel have food for you to eat, No wood, no food, *comprender*?"

Clancy *comprendered* and Tina never had to look for fuel so long as Clancy was around. He took it as his duty to see that the kitchen stayed well stocked with whatever was needed and most of all to make sure Tia Tina was happy.

We all loved our cook, Tina Esquival. On the range, the vaqueros called her Pequeñita Tina, equal to Tiny Tina, but never within her hearing. She was the spring that made everything tick in the household. "Household" included the Hicks family, and all the hands working on the range or in the store, plus any of the many shepherds that might be passing through or bringing sheep or wool to be shipped. It was a large task and kept Tia Tina and her staff of two to four girls busy.

I doubt that the lady was more than eight inches over four feet tall and I'm pretty sure she was as broad, but her energy seemed boundless and she could be found in the kitchen or dining room almost any time of the day—except Sundays. Sundays were her day of rest and that is just what she did. If the priest was in town, there was always Mass; then after that, you could find her rocking and knitting on the front veranda if weather permitted. Sometimes she would commandeer some vaquero to take her in the buggy for a ride over to Playas Lake to watch the birds that congregated there. If there was no Mass, she might ride over to Old Hachita to visit and decorate the graves of her family. It was an all-day trip, but very early Monday morning found her refreshed and busy.

Monday morning breakfast began at six o'clock and *huevos rancheros* were served all day long. Tuesday through Saturday breakfasts began at four o'clock. There were always hot frijoles, tortillas, and the meat of the day—beef, mutton, or pork— available only if served by one of the ladies. Entry to the kitchen was restricted and rigidly enforced, sometimes with a broom, sometimes with a pan, possibly with a knife. There is a legend of a vaquero who dared violate the law who had a long scar across his forearm. No one doubted the legend.

CHAPTER 23
THE MEXICAN BEAVERS RANCH

> To build a house is one thing, but to make it a home
> is another.
>
> —Bendigo Shafter

It is said that the Playas Valley was once a huge lake before the Lord took the water somewhere else. If it was a lake, it sure was a long one and I would like to have seen it. Now, the intermittent streams from the mountains on either side run into the valley and sink into the sands. The northern boundary of the Mexican Beavers range is marked by the two Darling creeks flowing into the valley, about ten miles south of Playas. There isn't a legend about how two creeks flowing into the valley from opposite mountain ranges got the same name—there are a dozen.

The tale I like best is about two friends, Pablo and Jose, early day vaqueros from Hachita, who loved the same girl, Querida. She promised to marry the one who built her a hacienda on a range where they could tend the sheep she had received from her many admirers.

Pablo chose to build near the most reliable stream that flowed out of the Animas Mountains on the west side of the valley. "So my Querida can see the sun rise over the mountains."

Jose's choice for Querida's new home was on a hill east of Pablo's site overlooking the valley and near a stream from the Little Hatchit Mountains, just as reliable as Pablo's.

On two prominent points in the foothills, where they could look across the valley and watch their rival, the two began constructing adobe houses; a jacal was not good enough for the lovely Querida. Both named their stream "Querida" in honor of the maiden. All through the long hot summer they labored, watching in dismay as they perceived that the other was matching their work brick for brick. Each could see that the other had finished the front of his home even to the point of installing windows and door. Soon, it seemed, the other would have his hacienda finished and ride off to claim the lovely Querida.

As the streams dried up, the two had to move farther and farther out into the valley to find moisture for making their bricks until one day they looked at each other across the marsh at the sink of the stream from the east. At first, they didn't speak, but the heat and the work took its toll on their patience and they began to argue, curse, and swear until only lead could settle the argument. They fired at the same instant and Pablo fell. It was a moment before Jose realized what he had done; then with a cry of agony, he ran to his friend's side. "Pablo, Pablo, what have I done?" Tears streaked his cheeks. A long ugly cut along Pablo's head just above his ear marked the path of Jose's bullet and a small puddle of blood stained the mud. With trembling hands, Jose bound his head with strips of cloth torn from his own shirt. He dragged his friend to the shade of a willow and made him comfortable and prayed to the saints to spare his friend.

Presently, Pablo stirred and Jose gave him water, and as he lay there, the two friends talked about how foolish they had been. Long into the night, they talked about how selfish it was that a woman should choose a husband on the basis of how nice his house was. It was decided that the two would confront Querida and tell her she must choose the one she loved most for her husband. When Pablo had grown strong enough, they rode to Hachita—and found the lovely Querida married to the lazy Felipe, round with child, and living in a jacal.

They never returned to their Playas Valley haciendas and it was with great satisfaction that they watched their Querida grow fat and ugly among her many children. The Anglos who heard the story and found the ruins of the two adobes called the two creeks "Darling," that being the English equivalent of querida. Excuse me for making a short story long, but I thought you would like to hear it.

At the sink of the Animas Mountains' Darling Creek, Conly dug a long tank with a dam across the middle of the long sides. Water from the spring runoff would always fill the first half of the tank and it was a day of celebration when the overflow ran into the second half. Most years, both halves of the tank filled. Conly dug a well and built his house nearby and it was not long before the sheepherders joined him and the little community was called Placita Hicks. Their hopes that they would be out of the way of the Villistas were not fulfilled, but the visits came less often.

It was a strange arrangement to us, but the use of the range was dependent on the proximity of Pancho's ragtag army. If they were near, the herds stayed on the northern range. When Pancho waged war elsewhere, the southern range from the border north was grazed. Even when the Villistas were gone from the country, there were plenty of thieves and outlaws around, and Conly and his shepherds and vaqueros made a pretty formidable force to deal with. For the most part, the misbehavers stayed away, but there was still an occasional loss of beef or mutton to the poor starving natives who stayed in spite of Villista depredations. So far, these losses could be tolerated—especially if the native was related to a vaquero or shepherd fortunate enough to be under the protective umbrella of the Mexican Beavers Ranch.

Conly set the third day after our arrival to drive the bulls south to the range, and that was just the schedule the bulls set, for they were very restless in their pen the night before and when we rode up and opened the gate, there was a rush for freedom. We didn't have to keep them moving, just pointed in the desired direction, and they set the pace.

We hadn't gone five miles before we began to see Beavers cattle. We gathered those that were close and by the time we reached the home range, we had a pretty good herd. By late afternoon the herd was several miles south of the Placita, and Conly called a halt to the drive. There must have been three hundred head of cattle when we quit the drive and the new bulls had mixed in well with them. Conly had culled all his old bulls the fall before and the new bulls' services were in need. We left the herd to disperse over the range and rode back north to the ranch house.

"There are still a lot of cattle on the sides of the hills north of the Darlings, so tomorrow I want to start another sweep and move our cattle back where they belong," Conly said after supper. We were eating on the plaza because so many of the hands and shepherds had come in to welcome Conly back and see the new cattle. He spent a lot of time talking with them and just as the sun settled behind the mountains, we saddled fresh horses and followed the dust of the half dozen vaqueros north to Playas. Midnight found Coop and me groping for empty bunks in the bunkhouse and it seemed I had just dropped off to sleep when everyone started dressing for the 4:00 a.m. breakfast.

Cooper groaned, "It's just as bad as a trail drive, all work and no sleep."

"I'm not sure that bunk is any softer than the ground," I said.

"Too much traffic around here to sleep outside," Coop answered, "feller's liable t' get run over."

"I think I would be awful careful where I throwed my bedroll," I agreed.

The dining room was full and we filled our plates and sat outside on the stoop and ate. One of the girls came out and refilled our cups. We were just sopping up the last of breakfast when we heard a mass scraping of benches and boots from inside.

"Herd's on th' move, Coop, better get out of the way." Our move was just in time to avoid being hit by the screen door as the vaqueros hurried through and headed for the corrals. We put our plates down on the step and followed.

"Your horses are over here, Demp-sey." And I followed the sound of the voice to find a young vaquero with two horses bridled and tied to the corral fence beside the place where our saddles hung on the top rail.

"Thanks," I said and the boy disappeared into the gloom. We saddled up and joined the crowd riding south. Conly gathered us at the south end of Playas Lake just as the sun peeked over the horizon.

"I have a feeling there are more Beavers stock north of the Darlings than we suspect, so we are going to clean out one side at a time, starting on the west side of the marsh." The marsh ran south from the end of Playas Lake to just south of where East Darling ran into it. "I want you to ride up every gully," he continued, "and round up every Beavers cow you find. Run them down here to the valley and some of us will turn back what's not ours and keep the Beavers cattle moving south. The chuck wagon and cavyyard will be over by the marsh about halfway to the Placita. What we catch today we will drive back into Beavers range and we'll clean out the east side tomorrow." He divided the men into pairs and assigned areas for them to cover. Cooper and I were left on the plain with a foreman named Sergio and another man because we were not familiar with the ground like the others. As soon as the men left on their assignments, Conly rode on south to see to the cavyyard and chuck wagon.

"Lets no man ride the range alone and then there he goes—alone," Sergio complained. It was obvious he cared a lot about Conly and his safety. We rode north on the west side of the lake so we would be sure to be north of the first cows to be rousted out.

"So, you two are vaqueros for the northern ranch?" he asked as we rode along.

"I am working for the Pinetop Ranch out of Piñon," Cooper said.

"And I am also working for the Pinetop," I added. "My father is Josh Nealy of the Beavers Ranch."

"Ah-h-h, Meester Joshua," he nodded, "why he not come?"

"They're shorthanded while Uncle Green is laid up with a broken leg and Uncle Nate has a newborn child. That's the reason we got to come."

"It's good and you are welcome," Sergio added.

"We came hoping to see the old placita in Mexico and to find out more about Tucker Beavers," Cooper put in.

"Ees vera' dangerous there, now." Sergio's smile faded. "I too long to see thee placita of my youth. To lose it thee second time is almos' unbearable. I theenk it is thee reason my mother she die so young."

"It must be especially hard being run off by your own countrymen."

"Sí, they no like Mexicanos to bee successful if they are not. Why must fighting for your leeberty take away someone else's?"

"I sure don't know that answer." Cooper shook his head.

A bunch of cattle burst out of a gully a quarter mile south of us and trotted out onto the old lake bottom. "Looks like we came too far north," I said, spurring after the cows.

"Go hold them," Sergio called. "There will be some come out up here and wee weell wait for them."

Another bunch of cattle burst out of a gully farther south and I looked back to see Elias, the second vaquero, riding after me. I passed by the first bunch and rounded the second one while Elias took the bunch nearer him. We bunched them together as other cattle poured out of the hills. Sergio and Coop were gathering several head as they trotted out and pointed them our way. We had to work fast to catch up with all the cows on the flats and several men rode out of the hills to help or we would have lost a good number of them back into the arroyos. There was no chance to weed out the other brands, though we let some that broke out of the herd go.

The morning passed in a welter of dust, sweat, and bawling cows, and I was surprised when the cattle started milling until I saw the chuck wagon over by the willows and realized it was noon. Cookie threw his hat in the air and half of the vaqueros rode hell-bent for the wagon while the rest of us herded cattle. It helped for the cattle to mill some, for it made it easier to cut out the foreign stock and send them on their way.

One by one the first shift came back on fresh horses and one by one the second shift rode in for frijoles and fresh horses. By the time I rode back to the herd, it was strung out in a long line marching south to the Darlings and water. It was easy to cull out the strange beef by the time we got to the creeks. The tanks were fenced off to keep the cattle from fouling them, but there were plenty of watering troughs available for the cattle.

As the cattle came off the water, we pushed them south with emphatic instructions not to stray back north of the range again. Didn't do much good, but made us feel better at the time. The dust was heavy and darkened the sky until I realized that the sun had settled for the evening. We rode back to the ranch house where the chuck wagon was dealing out steaks and beans and tortillas. After supper we mounted fresh horses and rode north to be ready for the sweep of the eastern foothills.

"We ain't ridin' all th' way back t' Playas are we?" Cooper asked as we rode north with the crew.

"I don't know, Coop, but I don't intend to. Some place near where tomorrow's roundup begins is a spot with my name on it and I intend to lay me down and sleep right there," I replied.

"I believe my bed right nearby has already been turned down and awaits my arrival."

We followed the crowd when they turned right and took a trail through the marshy ground to the east side of the marshes. Not far ahead of us, we saw a fire and when we rode to it, there sat another chuck wagon with pots of coffee boiling and there was even a big pot of frijoles for anyone so disposed. A cup of coffee served as our nightcap and soon the camp was quiet. I found a soft spot, lay down, pulled my feet up to fit my blanket, and slept.

The second day proceeded much the same as the first, only there seemed to be less cattle on this side of the marsh. As a result, we finished somewhat earlier and were looking to a long restful evening when one of the men who had choused a bunch of cows south rode up with a bloodied man riding behind his saddle.

"Señor Conly, they have taken my sheep!" he called in anguish as he tried to dismount. Someone caught him as he fell and helped him stand. "They took *all* of them." His tears were from a mixture of pain, sorrow, and anger and it took a few moments for him to calm down enough to tell his story. "They are not Villistas, Señor Conly, just common thieves and they killed my dog, poor Rosa, and shot me. I pretended to be dead until they left and have been walking to find help. I heard them say they were taking the sheep to the Smuggler Hills where a man who doesn't ask questions will buy them."

"I suppose his name would be Aquilero Rivera," Conly said.

"Sí, it must be that man, he is *El Diablo* himself." The shepherd could no longer stand; his head sank to his chest and the two vaqueros who had held him up gently eased him to the ground.

"Get Cookie over here to take care of him," Conly ordered. He began looking over the crowd and calling names. Cooper and I stayed close. If there was going to be any action, we would be in on it regardless of what Conly or anyone else said about it.

"This may not be the only flock they hit. I want the rest of you to ride two-by-two and check every sheep camp. Don't try to be *bravos,* unless you have the advantage. Their safety is first; we can always buy more sheep and cattle, but a good man is much harder to replace and much more valuable." Pointing to five men standing in a group, he said, "Take Cookie and the shepherd to the Placita and guard it. Don't let any strangers enter there. The women and children are to stay within the houses."

To the others he called as they left on their missions, "Sheep may not be the only thing they gather. Be alert for any sign they have gathered cattle anywhere."

"Well, it looks like we have some exploring to do in the Smugglers," Conly said. "What say we mosey over there and look for strays, be they sheep, cows, or men?" Without any further talk, the six of us mounted and, each leading a spare horse, started across the valley to the southwest.

The three men Conly had chosen were Sergio, Nava, and Lupe, and the names recalled a story of other times. It clicked! These were The Muchachos less one whose name I could not recall! I looked at them with renewed interest. Plain men they were not, but their manner bespoke men of confidence and experience, men not afraid to face danger, men who stood where others retreated. Sergio was watching me, his eyes reflecting amusement. "You know us before, no?" he asked.

"Sí, *Payaso*, I do."

"Is it safe for these two muchachos to ride with us?" Nava teased.

"Try and stop us, Nava, I know your adventures when you were much younger than we are and played with sweaty dynamite." I grinned.

"Ah-h-h the muchacho has been educated, I see," Lupe grinned back at me.

"What is this all about?" Cooper seemed to always be in the dark and showed his frustration.

"Do you remember me telling you about the muchachos who helped Tucker and Conly fight the cattle thieves?"

"Yeah, I do, are these the ones?"

"All except one," I said.

"Benito is *alcalde* at Playas, but he has gone to Deming on some business," Sergio explained.

"Probably, he has escaped to a quieter land," Lupe crowed. The bachelor was referring to Benito's house full of little feet and loud mouths, something Lupe actively avoided.

"Someday you may know the joy that comes with the birth of one from your loins," Nava admonished.

"I fear he loves the sounds of silence too much." Conly laughed.

We were all tired from two days of hard work and little sleep and the conversation lagged. The moon rose and we rode on at a pace that preserved our mounts. The Smuggler Hills are set aside a little east of the Sierra Madre and got their name because they provided sanctuary for those who smuggled sundry items to and from the countries whose common boundary was but a short ride south. Bleached bones and mounds with crude crosses spoke of violence witnessed by the hills and men who no longer talked of such things. An old stone shack with a stone-walled corral attached to it snuggled in the hills just above Smuggler Creek on the west side of the hills. This was the logical place for thieves to establish their headquarters and this was our destination.

We found a little water in Deer Creek and watered the horses. Due west of our watering, the Smuggler Hills loomed up in the moonlight. Hilo peak on the south end of the hills was the highest, though not by much. There were lower passes between the hills and Conly led us through the one just north of Hilo. We crossed Smuggler Creek and rode up the divide between Smuggler and Rough Creek. Presently, we stopped and the men gathered and searched the hills for signs of the shack and its corral.

"It's halfway up the hills from Hilo and set back in one of those arroyos," Lupe said.

Sergio beat dust off his sombrero on his pants leg. "I think it is a little more than halfway unless the *proscrito* have moved it."

"I know of no *proscrito* with the ambition to move rocks from under his bedroll, how much less would he move rock walls?" asked Lupe.

"There should be a light, shouldn't there?" Cooper asked.

"It seems to me that these men would not choose the most obvious place to hold their stock. They should know that would be the first place someone would look for them." I had kept quiet out of respect for their experience, but that seemed too obvious to me.

"You're right, Demps, I would think that they have more than one place to gather and hold the flocks and herds," Conly said, "but the corrals are too convenient to pass by."

Lupe lifted his sombrero and rubbed his forehead, "Water will be their greatest need and Deer Creek has the most reliable water. Already, these other creeks are drying up."

Even as we talked, the Smuggler Hills began to stand out plainer against the graying eastern sky. It wouldn't be long until someone with a glass could see us up here on the divide. It seemed the west side of the hills got darker and darker against the light of the dawn. A light winked at us from between two of the hills and Nava exclaimed, "There! There is the rancho, I told you it was there." He slapped Sergio's shoulder.

"It does not seem that they would be so brazen as to keep stolen stock there, although it would be a good place for their headquarters. They could say they are hunting or looking for strayed stock and keep the stolen flocks and herds somewhere else where there was plenty of water and grazing," Cooper said.

"We should find a place to rest awhile and make plans and I know just the place." Lupe turned west and Sergio groaned, "Not on Rough Creek."

"Sí, sí, 'tis Rough Creek for me-e." Conly sang as he followed Lupe down a narrow gully.

CHAPTER 24
ROUGH CREEK

I'm goin' back to Arkansas
Where you don't have to climb to get to water
And dig to get to firewood.

—Discouraged Pilgrim

If ever a stream deserved its name, it's Rough Creek. The bottom of the ravine it flows through is such that it has no defined streambed; the path of the water—when it ran—depended on the obstacles deposited by the last flood. In places the solid rock bottom was washed clean. Other places, rocks and gravel had piled up and directed the flow elsewhere or made an effective dam that would be eventually washed away to choke off flow in another place. Scattered across a wide bottom were huge boulders ranging from wagon-sized to house-sized and larger. They didn't move with the floods, but served as bastions against which the smaller materials washed and piled. Thankfully, it was a remote stream with limited flow, for it could be a deadly monster when aroused.

Lupe led us downstream through this maze of boulders, sometimes stopping to check his position against some landmark until he was oriented to his satisfaction. Both banks of the stream became vertical solid rock walls. It made me nervous, for should a cloudburst occur somewhere upstream, there would be no escape. We came upon a rock wall that almost blocked the entire bottom of the ravine; only narrow channels either side of the wall provided outlet for the water.

231

"This is *El Roca Represar*," Nava explained, indicating the rock. "Some wonder how it got here, but the wise know only the Creator God could have placed it."

Looking up the sides of the ravine, I could see where the water had risen when the narrow channels had been blocked or the flood was so great the water piled up behind this rock dam. I kept looking upstream for that telltale wall of brown water that would seal our doom in this trap.

"That top water line marks the top of El Roca down there. After it reaches there, the water flows over the top of the rock," Conly explained.

At the dam, Lupe chose the right passageway though it seemed no wider than the left side. "This side is wider, but you need to walk through. It helps the horse if you carry your saddle for him," he grinned.

I was glad I followed his advice, for if the saddle had been left on the horse, it would have been badly scuffed. I doubt a larger horse could have squeezed through there. As it was, the horses were very nervous and we almost had to blindfold a couple before we could persuade them to follow us.

"We call this *al yegua apretar;* pull the mare through and behold the mare and foal on the other side," Sergio grinned.

"I believe that!" Cooper was pale and sweaty. He didn't like tight places.

Passing through the chute was like passing from one world to another, for on the downstream side of that big block was a meadow in the middle of the creek with much grass, some mesquite, and willow trees for shade. There were deer and antelope tracks aplenty. In the middle of the island was a camping place surrounded by the willow bushes—a cozy spot not visible from the hills above.

El Roca was wedge shaped, tapering down to the surface of the island on the downstream side. Standing on the top, one could see far up the creek. I pulled out the coffee pot. "Where can we get water?"

"Up there." Lupe pointed up the rock.

"Why is it that out here you have to *climb* for water?" Cooper asked.

"You can contemplate that while you *dig* for firewood," Conly grinned. In this arid country, the best firewood was mesquite roots that had to be dug up.

I carried the coffee pot up the rock and on the flat top found several *metates* where the Indians had pounded their grains into flour. The holes were full of water and I dipped out a potful, straining out the wigglers with my kerchief.

"Don't worry about the wigglers, Demps, they just add flavor to the coffee." Sergio had followed me up the rock. "A nice place for the *metates*, no? The ladies could pound their corn while watching for the enemy."

"Was there always an enemy?" I asked.

"It seems that is the way, doesn't it? Always, the enemy."

"And maybe the enemy is looking at us right now and thinking, 'Always, the enemy.' "

Sergio grinned and turned back to the island, "We must be the *hidden* enemy, sí?"

Two days of hard work and little or no sleep took its toll on us and we hardly finished our breakfast before we were rolled in our blankets asleep. I awoke just after the sun passed its zenith and looked around the camp. The horses were all there and contented with their forage. A long drink of water and I crawled under the deeper shade of a willow and slept. When I awoke, the sun was behind the Sierras and it was dark and cool. Another trip up the rock and I soon had coffee boiling and the salt back frying in a lake of lard. Nava came in with an armload of wood. "The smell has called me to your fire, Demp-sey, I think I could eat *en su totalidad* and drink the grease—and still be hungry."

"Me too." Cooper stretched and wiggled his bare feet into the cooler sand below the surface.

"Watch you don't step on something that stings or sticks," Conly warned.

"I doubt your feet are as tough as Clancy's," Sergio observed.

"Do you suppose he was barefooted all the way across the country?" Cooper asked.

"I wouldn't be surprised," I said. "He for sure was barefooted most of the way to get them that hard on the bottoms."

Supper over, we got our heads together to plan out our strategy for ridding the range of thieves. "We don't know how many owlhoots we're up aginst and where they are, so we're going to need to spy out the land before we do anything," Conly said. "We need to look over the Hills and find the water, for that will be where they keep the animals."

"I don't think they will keep them here long," I said.

"And the question is, where are they taking them?" Sergio was drawing a map in the sand. "They are not likely to take them into Mexico unless they are going to Chihuahua and that's a long drive."

"What about Bavispe?" asked Lupe.

"The sheep and cattle have been practically eliminated around Bavispe by the Villistas," Conly said. "I don't think there will be much of a market there until Pancho and his army are gone for good."

"If not Mexico, how about Arizona?" I asked.

Conly thought a moment. "Arizona may be the place. Not many of those ranchers look closely at the brands and they are in need of livestock."

"But not likely sheep," Nava grinned, "The rancheros are only for cattle."

"If not Mexico or Arizona for the sheep, why not the railroad?" Lupe asked.

"Good point, Lupe." Sergio drew on his map. "They would have to drive them to the railroad somehow and their best way is up the Animas Valley." He drew a long line west of the Playas Valley to represent the Animas. "They would drive them south from here a little way to the San Luis Pass—here—and then up the valley to the tracks, probably at Animas."

Conly rubbed his chin, "From there, they could ship east or west. If they went west, they could take them all the way to California where there is always a market for mutton or wool."

"You really think they would ship east right through Playas?" Cooper asked.

"Why not? The train would not stop at Playas, and we would never know unless we watched and stopped every train—and the railroad is not likely to let that happen." Conly was drawing the railroad on the map with El Paso on the east and Tucson on the west. "First, we need to know what they are stealing. If it's sheep, we know they are most likely to drive them either north or south in the Animas Valley. If they steal cattle too, they will most likely take them west into Arizona where New Mexican brands become invisible at the state line."

"Either way, they would be passing through San Luis Pass?" I asked.

"No-o-o, not necessarily," Sergio said. "They *could* drive up Indian Creek and down Double Adobe Creek where there would likely be more water."

Lupe shook his head. "That's not a pass and it is pretty rough climbing over the top."

"Sheep could not make it over there, but cattle could," Nava interjected.

"Wait a minute, wait a minute," I said, "we're chasing herds and flocks we don't even know have been taken. If we heard

about the first flock they have taken, then they haven't had time
to drive them away and most likely they are still in our valley
gathering herds and flocks. What we need to do is prevent them
from leaving with our stock."

"You are right, Demps, let's stop the stealing before we chase
down any that have left the valley," Conly said. "The thing we
need to do is find the thieves and what they have taken here in
the valley. Sergio, I want you and Nava to ride up Deer Creek
and find water and any stock that may be there. Turn up Indian
Creek to the divide, then down Double Adobe Creek. Cooper
and Lupe will ride up the Playas Valley looking for signs of herd
gathering and try to determine where they are headed. Lupe, I
want you to gather all the men you find, be sure they are well
armed and send part of them over Whitmire Pass and down the
Animas to meet Sergio if he makes it that far. Sergio, if you
haven't found anything by the time you are opposite Gillespie
Creek, scout back down that creek to the valley. Anywhere you
suspect something's happening, check it out, but don't try to be
a *bravo*, ride for help. If I have to bury any of you, I'll feed you
to the hogs first."

Sergio grinned with the rest of us and asked, "Where are you
and Demp-sey headed?"

"We're checking out the Smuggler Hills."

"He saves the best for himself, Sergio," Lupe grinned.

Nava snickered. "And if they act the *bravo* and die, we will
gently carry Demp-sey to the Placita hallowed ground and we
will take Conly's bones after the hogs and bury him outside the
fence and his epitaph will be: Here lies a *Bravo Tonto*."

Conly grinned. "You may put that epitaph on my stone, but
The Muchacha will see me under hallowed ground, of that I am
sure."

Chapter 25
A Visit to Smuggler Ranch

Hell hath no fury like a woman . . .

It was time to travel light and we sent the spare horses with Lupe and Cooper to drive back to Placita Hicks. Sergio and Nava disappeared into the chute and we heard them saddling up on the other side. The rest of us rode down Rough Creek to Deer Creek, and it was full dark when we got to where Smuggler Creek entered Deer. With the spare horses staked in a little ravine where they would be out of sight, the four of us rode up Smuggler Creek.

After a time, Lupe whispered, "There is the ravine where the stone house is built."

"It's the next one, isn't it?" I was pretty sure he was mistaken.

"No, this . . . listen!" We all froze and listened. The sound was far away and sounded high pitched like an animal screaming. The echo bouncing from hill to hill only added to our confusion.

"Where is he?" Cooper asked.

I started riding slowly up the trail listening. As we passed the mouth of the second arroyo, the noise became louder and more distinct.

"It seems to be coming from that gully." Lupe turned his horse and rode into the mouth of the gully. Within the walls of the gully, the sounds came more discernible. "That's a little dog!" Cooper exclaimed.

"One of those bag dogs," Conly spat.

"What in the world is a bag dog?" I asked.

Lupe snorted in disgust, "The señoritas of Mexico have a little dog they call the Chihuahua that they carry around with them in fancy bags hanging from their shoulders. They are nasty tempered little rats."

"Just as soon bite you as look at you," Conly added. "I am more wary of little dogs, they'll sneak around and bite you from behind. A big dog will face you down and you know what he will do." The shrill yapping of the bag dog stopped.

I lowered my voice, "Then I would guess the hacienda is up this arroyo."

"I would say so, and not too far," Conly opined. "Let's ride up and see."

"You mean just ride in like we didn't know what they were up to?" Cooper asked.

"I mean ride in like we *did* know what they were up to . . ."

"And offer to sell them a few head of Beavers stock at a discount."

Conly smiled, "You read my mind, Demps; it's dark so they won't recognize us if we stay out of the light and we just might get away with it. Spread out and don't let them bunch us up. We'll ride in there just like we belong."

He turned up the narrow trail and I pulled my rifle and laid it across my lap as I followed. Halfway to the house, a man rode out and blocked the trail, "Who is there?" he asked.

"Vaqueros looking to sell some cattle," Conly answered.

"We are not interested in buying cattle, go away."

"Ah-h-h but these are sleek and fat and cheap cattle." Conly spoke a little louder and the dog resumed his yapping. The door to the house opened and the yapping dog raced to us. Evidently, he considered all of us as enemies, for he attacked the guard's horse, nipping at his heels and causing the man to divert his attention to remaining seated and getting rid of that demon at his horse's heels. Taking advantage of the guard's predicament, Conly rode up to the porch. With his hat pulled low and looking at the ground, he addressed the man standing in the doorway. "We have a small herd of Beavers cattle we would like to sell."

"Why do you think we are buying stock?" the man asked. His voice was gruff and gravelly. Just then the little dog gave a cry of pain and the man called, "I'll have your hide if that dog is hurt, Jose."

"It is not me, but the horse that kicks at the dog, call him off before he is killed."

The man on the porch ignored the man and resumed his conversation with Conly, "We are only here to hunt the jaguar, not to buy cattle."

"We can provide them at a very low cost to you, señor."

"Why do you hide your face?"

"If you do not know my face and I do not know your face, we will not lie if the authorities ask us if we saw who took the cattle."

There was a long pause and the guard turned and trotted off down the trail, more to be rid of the yapper than anything involving duty. The dog, satisfied, climbed the steps and sat at his master's feet, panting. A soft voice called and he turned back into the house.

"We are only hunting," the man began again, "but I could be interested in a few head if the price is right."

"These are good cows, many with calf by side. They would be worth three dollars a head, four dollars with calf."

"Does this look like th' stockyards to you? I will give you four bits a head and five with calf."

Conly shook his head, "It is worth much more if we work to gather them—and the work is dangerous."

"Th' danger is you might get lead poisoning," the man sneered.

"Sí, that is a good possibility." Conly sat a moment as if in deep thought, "We would sell the cattle at one dollar a head and four bits for the calf."

Something, a glint of light, or a sound from the rock-walled corral, caught my attention and I was suddenly very aware of our surroundings.

Lupe was a few feet to my left and murmured, "I saw it too, Demp-sey."

"There is another to the right at the corner of the house," Cooper whispered from somewhere to my right.

No tellin' how many more there are layin' out here in the dark and there's the one behind us somewhere, I thought. *How are we gonna get out of this?* "Do you see any more?" I whispered.

"There is one to my left slightly behind us." Lupe whispered so softly it seemed to be something in my head instead of my ears.

A pebble rattled off to our right beyond Cooper. Our surround was complete—and we still didn't know how many more there were.

The man on the porch turned toward the door, "Four bits a head and five with calf is my price, take it or leave it."

Conly's shoulders seemed to sag in resignation. "You drive a hard bargain, señor." He turned his horse slowly.

The man in the door turned back. "I hear there are people in the Animas at the foot of San Luis Pass who are buyin' cattle, you might try them. *Don't bring any stock here.*"

"Sí."

You never saw four people more careful not to make any sudden or unexpected moves in your life when we turned and followed Conly down the trail. My shirt was wringing wet and sweat stung my eyes. I needed a long drink of water.

"Goodnight, señores," came from somewhere above us as we passed the trail guard, and my reply sounded like a frog croaking.

Without another word, Conly led us back down the creek and we gathered and watered the horses at Deer Creek before turning up Whitewater Creek, which at that time of year would have been more aptly named Nowater Creek. After a couple of miles, Lupe turned away from the trail and pushed through the cedars to a small clearing. I wondered how in the world he found it in the dark.

We unsaddled and rubbed the horses before hobbling them all. Leaving the clearing to them, we crawled under the cedars to sleep.

Conly asked, "How many did you count up there?"

"There were six counting the trail guard," Lupe said.

"I saw two silhouetted against the sky up on the roof," Cooper said.

"That makes eight and we don't know how many more there were, especially in the house," I added.

"Two to one ain't half bad." Conly chuckled.

"Sí, we have overcome worse," Lupe agreed.

"What were your odds when you attacked the cattle rustlers with Tucker?" I asked.

There was a long silence and I thought the two were not going to answer. I lay back and closed my eyes.

"There must have been fifty or more of them," Lupe said.

"Our advantage was that they were scattered over the range and not all in one place," Conly added.

The tones of their voices had changed and I felt a pang of guilt in even asking. "I'm sorry if talking about it bothers you, it's just that I have never heard the whole story of how the Mexican Beavers Ranch came to be."

"You *should* know and at another time we will tell you; but for now, the thing we need is to sleep and figure out what we are going to do with these range thieves. Let's pile up some sleep first," Conly said.

I was inclined to agree with him, but the question of that battle long ago and the possibility of a near battle had me keyed up. It was a long time before I slept—and it was troubled with vague disturbing dreams. I finally gave up and built a fire. It took the water from three canteens to have enough to brew coffee. When it was boiling good, the aroma awakened the others and we gathered around the fire and finished off the coffee.

"Any ideas about this situation?" Conly asked,

"There *have* to be more than eight men," Cooper asserted.

"I don't think the men at the hacienda are the ones gathering stock," I said. "It would be too obvious for them to bring the cattle to the stone corral. I think they are just the headquarters bunch and there are others on the range."

"I would not like stealing a bunch of cattle and driving them over the pass to a place and people I do not know. The price might be much lower than the quote and hard to collect."

"You are right, Lupe. We will have to deal with them sooner or later, but first, I think we need to cut off the head of the snake," said Conly.

"We need to know what is going on out on the range before we do anything else, I think."

"I agree, Coop, we should do as Conly first said, you and Lupe scout the Playas while Conly and I watch the stone house."

"I don't know, Demps." Lupe shook his head. "It might not be safe for you to stay with *Bravo Tonto* after last night."

I rubbed my chin. "I suppose you are right. Should he ride with you and I stay here or should he stay and I leave?"

"I would say that a lone *Bravo Tonto* would be safer for the rest of us. You should come with us," Cooper said.

"Good enough," I said and made to rise.

"Now wait a minute, fellers," Conly grinned. "How many of you got shot last night?"

"None," Cooper said, "but you just knocked ten years off the end of my life with that trick you pulled."

"You'll be so stove up by then you'll be glad to go early," Conly laughed.

"*That* should be entirely my choice, Conly Hicks." Coop tried to look severe, but couldn't. We all grinned.

After a moment, Conly said, "Let's stay with our original plan, Coop and Lupe take the extra horses and sweep the Playas, and Demps and I will watch the rock house. Maybe we can get a better picture of how many are there and you can send more help back here. Send the first armed men you find to meet us at the junction of Deer and Smuggler creeks by sunset tonight. If they leave their dogs with the flocks, they should be safe for a day or so."

With that, we saddled up and left our hideaway. Conly turned up Smuggler and I followed. We took the first ravine, and while I held the horses, Conly erased our tracks back to the trail. We rode as far as we could and then climbed up and over the divide between the first and second gullie. This put us well above the hacienda, and a couple hundred yards above it we found comfortable spots under brush cedars and settled ourselves down to watch. There were four bedrolls laid out on the roof, two occupied, and we counted thirteen horses in the corral. There was no smoke from the chimney and we took it that they were either very early risers and breakfast was over or that they were very late risers and breakfast would come nearer noon. No one stirred.

A warming sun and singing crickets soon had me nodding and it was a fight to stay awake . . . Conly's kick brought me up and I followed his gaze to the brush among the boulders beyond the house. There wasn't anything apparent for a long time; then when he moved, I saw a man sitting there watching the trail beyond. Conly held up one finger, then pointed to the right of the trail. This guard was more restless than our first one and I caught sight of him almost immediately. Conly held up two fingers.

A door closed and two men stepped off the porch and went to the corral. They caught two horses and rode down the trail. That made six men counting the two sleepers on the roof. The back door opened a crack and a rifle barrel emerged, the man behind it obviously taking his time to show as he looked over the hills. He stepped out, followed closely by a woman who was obviously in a hurry, and that little yapper, a fawn-colored little dog who busied himself sniffing and marking his territory. I imagined how the investigating coyotes laughed as they smelled the little scamp's markings.

As the woman disappeared into the cedars an eighth man casually strolled out the door and looked around. He picked up a stick of wood from the woodpile and tossed it over his head onto the roof. The thump of the stick hitting the roof brought both sleepers up, guns in hand. Some words were exchanged and the sleepers rose and dressed. They disappeared into a corner of the roof and in a moment emerged from the back door. I grinned at Conly and he nodded.

As we watched, the woman returned from her trip and passed the guard by a wide margin. By her demeanor, we could tell she was very angry and we caught snatches of her Spanish vitupera-tion as she approached the men gathered on the back stoop. She slammed the door as the yapper skidded to a stop to avoid decapitation. He yelped twice and the door opened a crack to let him in. A few moments later, we heard the front door slam and in a moment a ninth man sauntered around the house to the amusement of the little group on the stoop.

"I believe the house is now empty of men," I whispered, and

Conly nodded agreement.

"Seven to two ain't bad odds, Demps, but we can wait 'til the other two come back if you want to make it more even for them."

"It might be safer to wait and see which side that woman would be on. Right now, I'd be reluctant for us to take her on two-to-one."

"Good idea." he grinned, then said seriously, "We still don't know for sure what these men are up to, though I have a good idea it isn't for good or jaguar hunting. We need to know their reasons for being here before we start a war."

I nodded agreement and we watched the men a little longer. One of the men tried the door and found it locked from within. With a shrug of his shoulders, he joined the others sitting on the stoop and rolling cigarettes. Soon a cloud of smoke drifted above their heads and they lounged about waiting for things in the house to cool off.

It looked like a long wait.

CHAPTER 26
HORSE THIEVES AND DREAMS

There ain't much paw and beller to a cowboy.

—Ramon F. Adams

For nearly an hour we watched five men smoke and try the
door latch until, finally, Conly signaled and we retreated to the
place where we had come over the divide, between the gullie.
"No use wasting our time watching them loll around, let's see if
we can find out anything around front."

He led the way to the horses and we rode down to the creek.
"The two who rode out came this way by the looks of these
tracks," I said.

"Let's follow and find out what they are up to."

We proceeded cautiously, me reading sign and Conly keeping
watch. When they turned down Deer Creek, their tracks joined
the tracks made by Cooper and Lupe and their little herd and it
was hard to follow them. In the Playas, the tracks all stayed
together and I was sure now that Cooper and Lupe were the
prey of our quarry.

"Horses coming." Conly's warning brought my eyes up from
the trail and I saw the dust approaching at a goodly pace. Conly
cut for the rocks at the foot of the Smugglers and I was right
behind him. With the horses hidden, we settled behind our
picks of the boulders and watched.

"Eight head and two riders, one hurt," Conly called softly.

"Two of those horses have saddles," I replied. There was no

question whose horses they were. One of the riders lay low over his saddle and the other spent his time keeping the horses moving.

"Dempsey, when they get in close range, stand up on that rock and holler at them."

"You want me to commit suicide?"

"I got you covered."

We watched the herd near with sweaty palms and bated breath. When they got within a hundred yards, Conly called, "Now!"

I scrambled up on my rock, my rifle to my cheek, and hollered, "Hey," as loud as I could. Even as the lone herder turned, his gun was coming up and I fired. He toppled from his horse and the rest of the herd ran a few yards and milled in confusion. The wounded man sat up and tried to bring his pistol to bear and Conly shot him out of his saddle.

I was mad, so mad I could have shot Conly. "You made me the target and didn't even shoot?" I hollered at him.

"I shot him, Demps, you didn't hear the sound."

"No you didn't!" I yelled, "I shot him or I would be dead right now!" I was so mad I was shaking and my rifle pointed at Conly's feet. All I had to do was raise it and fire.

The man leaned his rifle against a rock and said, "Come here and see." He walked to the fallen man and rolled him over. Ripping his shirt open, he showed me two bullet holes over the left breast within two inches of each other. My knees got weak and I sat down, shaking at the realization at what I had almost done. The sounds of our two shots had exactly coincided and had seemed as one. Naturally, I thought it was mine.

"I'm sorry, Conly, I should have known."

"If I hadn't seen you fire, I would have thought I was the only one who fired. It's Ok, Dempsey."

He grabbed the reins of the fallen man's horse and rounded

up the horses while I recovered from my anger and fright. My knees were wobbly when I walked over and caught up the reins of the horse Cooper had ridden off on. There was blood on the saddle and the horse's shoulder. "Cooper's been hit," I called.

I looked at the two bodies and Conly called as he rode up leading our horses, "Leave them be, we got more important business." I jumped in the saddle and with Cooper's horse in tow on one side of the backtrail and Conly leading Lupe's horse on the other side, we loped up the valley.

It was past noon, we were still following the trail, and my tongue felt like it was swelling. I had stopped sweating. "Take a long drink, Demps, or you'll soon be no good for anything," Conly yelled at me. I drank and felt better. My horse was tiring and needed rest, but we had to keep moving.

All at once, the trail of the horses ended in a mill and Conly called, "I've got footprints." There came a shout from the rocks at the foot of the hills and there stood Lupe waving his hat. Cooper was lying in the shade of a stunted bush, his shirt wrapped around his ribs and a big bloody spot on one side.

"He took a bullet across his ribs, then tried to bleed to death," Lupe rasped. "It's gonna take a lot of stitches to close that up."

Conly handed Lupe his canteen and I took mine and gave Cooper the last of it.

"He's been calling for water and we didn't have any." Lupe sounded better after he had some lubrication.

"You left it on your horses and they took them," I said.

Conly went to their horses and returned with two nearly full canteens, "We got them back for you." He grinned and unstoppered the canteen for Lupe. I gave Cooper another long drink and washed dirt and grime from his face.

"Fell off my horse when I got hit," he grinned at me.

"You had a big breakfast, there wasn't any reason for you to eat dirt," I said.

"I got one of them before I got shot."

"You sure did, Conly finished him off for you."

"You got the horses back?"

"Of course we did, Lupe, you didn't expect us to nod and tip our hats to those two when they had your horses, did you?" Conly was looking over the horses as he spoke.

"What we gonna do, Conly?"

"Looks to me we got a full-fledged war on our hands. Cooper can't ride in his shape, so I'm going to take the best horse and ride hell-for-leather to the placita and send a wagon back for him. Then I'm going to gather an army and we're going to clear the valley of vermin. One of you stay here with Coop and the other one go back and gather up those horses and bring them up here. You can take them back to the ranch house."

We switched Conly's saddle to Lupe's horse and without another word, Conly left on the run. "Hope he doesn't kill my horse, he's a good one," said Lupe. "I'll go get the horses if you will stay here with Cooper."

"Sure, Lupe, you deserve a break from nursing duty."

"Some nurse he is, jumping off his horse and dragging me up here. Laid me on an anthill and went off taking potshots at desert rats while they tried to eat me alive."

"The rats tried to eat you?" I asked.

"No, the ants, dummy." Cooper closed his eyes; that was about all the talk he had strength for.

Lupe and I switched his saddle to Cooper's horse and he rode south to gather the horses. I sat beside Cooper and gave him water and washed his face. After a while I broke off cedar limbs up on the hill and made a better shelter over him. I gathered firewood and out on the plain away from the rocks set up a fireplace ready to light. It would probably be after dark before either wagon or Lupe got back and they would need a light to navigate to.

It was hot and very still on that arid hillside. As I sat and listened, I could hear the small life of the desert, a cricket singing his early evening song so soft and low that he can only be heard when nothing else speaks. A tumblebug struggled with his ball of fresh dung, pushing it with his hind legs as he crawled backward to his hole. I wondered if he had eyes in his backsides somewhere to see where he was going. In this environment, he couldn't afford a lot of unproductive activity.

As I thought of it, I wondered what he was doing out here in the first place. By some accident or act of nature beyond his control, he was put in this place and he has made it his home. He should be up by the corrals or out where the cattle graze and there is plenty of his kind of food. Yet, here he was struggling up the slope to his home when home could be much more convenient in another place.

People are like that, I thought, just like the people of this valley. When it's not very, very hot here, it's very, very cold, and it's almost all the time very, very dry, yet they stay. They could go where the climate is much milder and friendlier, but they stay. Why? I asked a vaquero this once and he shrugged his shoulders and said, "Because this is home."

Home, what defines "home"? Home is where family is, where the familiar is, where comfort and refuge are, and for most of us, it takes something extreme or violent to uproot us from this thing called home. Yet we can give up comfort and refuge and the familiar, even family and the human—no, the whole balance of nature—to strive to stay or return to that place, that range, that spot on the earth where we feel "at home." Is it because it is familiar? I think so, but it goes beyond what we can see and feel and hear. It is something familiar deeply hidden from our conscious senses, something we search for and long to find, and all you can say is that it's—home.

Cooper groaned and brought me back from my thoughts, "Water, Demps." I gave him a long drink and worried if there would be enough to last until the wagon got here. Lupe and I didn't drink any, saving it for Coop. If we had to do any more than what we were doing now, we would be in real trouble. I longed to hear the rattle of a wagon that I knew was hours away.

The shadows of the Smuggler Hills crept across the Playas and the cricket was joined in chorus by his cousins. The tumble-bug hurried by on his way for another ball of dung. Daylight or dark, there was only so much time before the moisture was gone and his opportunity for food was quite litterally dried up. As the shadows deepened, I walked out, and after several tries got a fire lit. I would keep a flame going until all were here. We would be safe in the rocks if the light drew unwelcome company.

All kinds of bugs were drawn to the light. The proverbial moths were busy flitting about dancing with the flames. A shadow flickered across the light and a moth disappeared in mid-flight. A bat had the first bite of his supper. There would be many more bites as the night marched on—and many more bats feeding.

Coop drifted into a restless sleep and I drew my knees up, lay my head on my arms, and dreamed. A figure, dark and small, approached the fire and squatted by it. He was completely naked except for the woven sandals he wore. His hair stood in all directions from his head and down to his hairy shoulders. Beside him lay a long stick and I could see a flint blade affixed to the end. The throwing stick of his atlatl was tied to the spear. I could see he had a belt of some kind and a small bag was tied to it. He raked a flat rock away from the fire with a stick, and taking a few items from the bag laid them on the hot rock, occasionally stirring them with a twig. When they were done to his satisfaction, he raked a few into his hand and bounced them from hand to hand until they were cool enough to eat. His meal finished, he stood, picked up his weapon, and disappeared from the fire.

The snort of a javelina brought me fully awake and I listened to him rooting through the underbrush. A squeal or two told me I was hearing a sow and her brood and they were too close. I felt around until I found a good-sized rock and threw it at the sound, "Git out of here, you hogs, go on, leave," I hollered. I ran my rifle through the brush making as much noise as I could, and to my relief the pigs moved off.

"Javelinas look like a ball of fur with a butcher knife run through it," Coop muttered as to himself. I gave him another drink and with the last drops from the canteen washed his face and folded the cloth over his forehead. I don't think he had any fever, it was too soon for that, but the cooling had to help.

More wood on the fire brought the flames higher and as I turned back to Coop's shelter, I saw away north a tiny light. I stood and watched and it didn't seem to be moving. An hour crept by and I added more fuel to the fire. That light was still out there. It was brighter, though I couldn't tell that it had moved at all.

It must have been more than an hour later that I heard a bell and horses and a voice not much more than a whisper rasped, "Hello, the camp." Try as I might, no sound would come out of my mouth more than a sort of growl. Then in a voice strong and clear, Cooper called, "Come in friend and show yourself."

"Thanks, Coop," I said and patted his arm. He started and I realized he had spoken in his sleep. Lupe walked into the light of the fire on the opposite side of his horse from us, and I rose and walked slowly into the light until he recognized me and relaxed. Neither one of us could speak much above a whisper, and if we didn't get water soon, we would be in real trouble.

Lupe had made a bell mare out of one of the horses and the

others had stayed with him—the bell mare was a gelding. That light out in the Playas seemed even brighter and I realized that it wasn't apparently moving because it was coming straight to us. The sound of a horse loping toward us sent us into the dark, alert for trouble.

The horse stopped and a voice called, "Dempsey . . . Lupe . . . Cooper?" It was Cepa. All we could do was walk into the light of the fire. She rode up and flung herself off her horse, "What's wrong, are you all right?" Halfway to us, she stopped with an exclamation and returning to her horse lifted a large canteen from the horn. "Here, drink this." And we did, gratefully.

While Lupe took his second sip, I was able to say, "We have Cooper up here in the rocks where it's cooler." It was a strange thing to say, for with the setting sun, it had gotten progressively cooler until we had covered Coop to keep him warm.

I took a burning stick from the fire and led Cepa up the slope to Cooper's shelter. The flickering light made the man look pale and gaunt and Cepa fell to her knees beside him, touching his head to see if he was fevered, looking at our rough bandages and clucking over the amount of blood on them.

Coop stirred and looked up, "I see an angel, Demps, do you see her?"

"Sure do, Coop. This angel's named Cepa."

"Cepa? How did you get here?"

"I rode as fast as I could, Cooper. How do you feel?"

"Bad, Cepa, bad." He turned his head and drifted off to sleep.

"Papa didn't tell us much, just that Cooper had been shot and to get down here and help him."

"—and you had to ride in the night alone knowing bad men were about, to come to see for yourself," I teased.

"Not by myself, I came with the wagon."

"Looks to me that wagon is still some miles off," Lupe observed.

"Well, I came ahead of them, they were too slow."

"Didn't want to kill their horses, I imagine."

"Dempsey Nealy, you know I wouldn't kill my horse riding down here. I came ahead to bring you water and see if I could help in some way." She stomped her boot for emphasis.

"Well, it's for sure your water saved me and Lupe from considerable discomfort, and we have plenty for Coop's needs now."

"There wasn't another drop in the camp and Cooper would be suffering soon without it," Lupe added. "So we thank you for your help."

"Are you going to tell me how this happened or is it some secret of yours?"

"I don't know myself," I said, "Lupe and I have been too busy to talk. We found people at the stone house and they were not too friendly so your pa sent Cooper and Lupe for home with the spare horses and he and I stayed and watched the house. Two men rode out and when we were through watching the house, we trailed them—until we knew they were trailing the horse herd. We met the herd headed back south driven by these two men and they had Lupe's and Cooper's horses with them. We didn't talk with them too much, just brought the horses back up here."

"Only *we* have two saddled horses in the bunch now," Lupe added.

"We left those two horse thieves lying around down there a few miles."

"Without horses or water?"

"They won't need either—ever again, Cepa."

"Good! *Damn* horse thieves and killers!"

I was startled by her vehemence, "Cepa!"

Even in the firelight, we could see her blush and we laughed. She grinned a little and said, "It isn't right that people should kill and steal another man's livelihood."

"They will always be until we make it unprofitable or too dangerous for them," I said. "Lupe, tell us what happened when those two caught up with you."

"We saw them back there behind us and thought it might be you and Conly, so we moseyed along until they caught up with us. They accused us of stealing the horses and Cooper drew his gun. He got a shot into one of them before they got him. I fought back, but when Cooper fell off his horse, I jumped down and dragged him out of danger. The men tried a little to take us, but the wounded man and I convinced them to leave. They took the horses with them."

I took up the story. "We were following them out of the hills when we deduced they were following the herd, then we hurried on. When we saw them coming with two saddled horses in the bunch, we hid in the rocks and when they got even with us I stood up and hollered. They went for their guns, but didn't get off any shots."

"That was foolish of you to stand up like that," Cepa scolded.

"I'm not good at dry-gulching." I didn't mention that her papa had told me to stand. We had been hearing the rattle and jangle of the wagon for some time and in a few minutes, it pulled up to the fire. A figure jumped down from the seat and said, "Cepa, don't you *ever* run off in the dark like that again!" Ana strode into the light, her demeanor showed both anger and relief. "What could we have done if you were not here when we drove up? You could be laying out there hurt and dying and we couldn't do a thing about it."

Two vaqueros tied their horses to wagon wheels and disappeared into the darkness. Another man who had driven the wagon handed down a kit to Lupe and began dipping water from a barrel for the horses. No one had to tell the horses what to do; they all gathered around the tailgate and drank in their turn.

Lupe handed the kit to Ana and picked the lantern off the wagon. They hurried to the shelter and I decided to stay out of the way. Not knowing where the two guards were, I climbed up on the wagon seat with my rifle, turned my back to the lights, and let my eyes become accustomed to the dark. A faint glow on the eastern horizon told me it was near midnight and the moon was on the rise. Even a quarter moon would give some light for us. I sat there long enough for the guards in the dark to see where I was, then slipped down into the bed and leaned against the sideboards, my back to the fire.

The desert chill began soaking into my bones and I found a blanket and wrapped up in it. Gradually, I warmed, then got too warm. I awoke with a start when the wagon shook and someone climbed over a wheel into the bed. A shadow against the stars whispered, "Dempsey, are you in here?"

"I'm here," I said in a voice more raspy than I expected.

"I brought you more water, you should drink a lot of it." Cepa kneeled beside me and handed me a canteen. Her voice was quivery and when I took the canteen, her hand was icy cold. "You're cold, get under this blanket."

She didn't need another invitation and wrapped the blanket around her and snuggled close to my side, shivering. "We re-bandaged Cooper's side and stopped the bleeding. The bullet took quite a bit of flesh with it and we will have to wait until we get to the ranch to sew it up. Mamma and Pequeñita will know better how to do that."

I grinned that she knew Tia Tina's range name, "Who is Pequeñita?"

"You know." She elbowed my ribs and laid her head against my shoulder. "It's cold out here, how did you get so warm?"

"Blankets do that."

"We brought food enough for a meal for all of us, then we will take Cooper to the house."

"Sounds like a good plan." We didn't talk for a while and she gradually warmed until she relaxed and slept.

Someone stirred the fire and I got up and stretched my cramped legs. I gently lay the sleeping girl over, gave her another blanket for a pillow, and quietly climbed down. We had left the four mules in harness all night, not knowing when we would need them, and I felt guilty. The driver came from the back with four filled nosebags. Without saying anything, he handed me two and motioned up the near side. The mules understood and there was no trouble putting the bags in place. Getting them back was another story.

Now that I had time to think about it, I wondered why Conly and Eledina had allowed these two girls to ride down here at all, much less without an older woman who if nothing else would act as a chaperone to the girls.

Ana was working with the driver laying out food on the tailgate of the wagon. "How did you two steal away without a chaperone?" I asked.

"Oh, we have a chaperone, Demps, my Tio Raul." She indicated her helper, the driver. "He is the best chaperon Mamma could find."

I grinned and thought to myself, *He'll be the best unemployed chaperone if the women find out that he let Cepa sleep beside me in the wagon.*

"I watch you closely when my child Cepa sit with you in the wagon, Demp-sey, you were much the gentleman." Tio Raul grinned and I wondered how close I had come to having a knife at my throat.

People were stirring and Cepa hopped down from the wagon

and trotted up to the shelter. I found a coffee pot already loaded with coffee and added water from the barrel. It was soon nestled in hot coals in the fire.

As I rose to leave, I stumped my toe on a rock that had been pulled away from the circle of rocks. In a little depression on top lay a roasted fennel seed.

Chapter 27
El Tigre

A man-eating tiger is a tiger that has been compelled,
through stress of circumstances beyond its control, to
adopt a diet alien to it.

—Jim Corbett

We ate a quick breakfast of cold bread, meat, and hot coffee.
Tio Raul told us that Conly had gathered several men and
headed for Whitmire Pass. It was his intention to clean the
countryside of thieves all the way to the stone house and then
clean it out. Cleaning the house out would be a job since it was
built like a fort and we would have to cross open ground to attack it. Lupe and I decided that it would be good to ride across
the valley to the marsh at the foot of Hachita Valley and make
sure the thieves had not been into any mischief over there.

The nurses had seen to it that a sturdy door with a thick
mattress was brought along and it took all of us to move Cooper
over to the bed and carry him down to the wagon. Getting to
the placita was going to be hard on him and it would be a very
slow drive.

With Cepa's horse tied to the tailgate and both girls watching
Cooper, the wagon started and we rode with them a few miles
north until we were across from the Hachita Valley. Had it not
been for Cooper, both girls would have insisted on riding with
us. I was thankful for a woman's nursing instincts when there
was no fuss as we left.

Already, the breeze was hot as a blast furnace and we drank deep and often. I was worried our water would not last, but Lupe knew of a spring up Hachita Valley a ways that did not fail. Nothing stirred in the Playas, but when we got to the Hachita there were signs that a flock of sheep had preceded us to the spring. Considerable cattle tracks showed that the spring was a popular watering hole. I hoped they had not trampled the spring into a mudhole.

Instead, it was a pleasant surprise to find the spring contained in a stone well-house under ancient cottonwoods and oaks, ringed by willows. A pipe ran out of the building and spilled into a large concrete trough. Overflow from that only ran a few feet to a small pool in the creek bed. Adobe ruins melting back into the ground gave evidence that the place had been occupied at one time. Horses and men gladly drank deeply of the cold water and we refilled our canteens.

The sheep had watered and moved on up the creek seeking shade and graze. We found dog tracks but no shepherd tracks and cautiously rode after the flock.

Just the slightest hint of dust in the air told us we were approaching the sheep, and we tied our horses in the shade of the cedars and proceeded on foot, Lupe on one side of the valley and me on the other. If times had been different, it would have been amusing to see two men stalking a flock of sheep. Sad to say, caution and guns were necessary.

The sheep were unattended except for the dog and when Lupe whistled he became so excited he jumped up and ran across the backs of the flock to the man. I stood against a cedar and watched man and dog across the flock. After an enthusiastic greeting, Lupe fed the dog, then sent him to turn the flock back down the valley. I joined him at the horses.

"He has been injured by some animal, but he will be Ok. He held the sheep a little too close, but that is because he was nervous about being alone with the flock. I am worried about the shepherd. It seems that the flock is too far east for him to be chosen to go with Conly. We should search for him."

The flock drank at the spring again as we passed. I sure wished we could have tarried there awhile. That trough looked good enough for a bath—and we both would have benefitted from one.

As we moved down the valley, we spread out and looked for any sign of our missing shepherd. I found his camp just inside the mouth of the Hatchita Valley where the north and south branches join. There had been a great struggle and the signs showed that the shepherd had been attacked while asleep. His blanket was torn and bloody and there were furrows where a body had been dragged away. Not far from the camp, the drag marks ended and that is where we found the first plain tiger prints. I should explain that the animal called "tigre" in the far southwest is really the jaguar. I bow here to the native custom of naming him *tigre*.

He had picked up his quarry and carried him off into the brush. I started trailing the big cat and Lupe called, "No, Demps, we two cannot follow the cat. It will take several hunters to track that one down and we are too late to help the poor man. We will call for help at the placita and hunt that killer down."

It took a pretty strong argument from Lupe to convince me to leave off trailing the killer, but in the end, I yielded to his experience. I certainly thought the two of us with our guns could handle one cat but I had never encountered one that could lift and carry away a human body. Maybe Lupe was right. Still, I left very reluctantly.

Two things now begged for—demanded—our attention: thieves on the range and a man-killing tiger in the Hatchitas— and here we were stuck with a flock of sheep without a shepherd. I have a recurring dream that I am stuck knee-deep in mud and a wall of water is rolling toward me and I can't move. Fortunately, the water never gets to me before I awake, but here I was awake, stuck with a flock of sheep and two dangers rolling toward me. It was the same feeling as in the dream.

"Look, Demps, I see another flock out in the valley and they have two men with them. I will call them to come this way and we can shed these sheep." He rode ahead and I was left with the flock and dog. Fortunately, the dog knew what to do and we moved on toward the other flock. Soon, Lupe returned with a boy riding behind him. As they neared, the boy jumped down and whistled to the dog. They had a happy reunion and the boy took charge of our flock.

We turned to leave on our mission when the second shepherd began calling and running toward us. He arrived out of breath and after a moment asked, "Where is Pablo, señores, this is his flock?"

"He was taken by a tigre," Lupe answered.

"El Tigre? A tigre has taken Pablo?" the man asked, unbelieving.

"Sí, my friend, we found his camp and there was much blood in his bed. The tigre dragged him into the brush, then carried him away."

We watched as the reality sank into the old man's mind and the agony on his face was hard to behold. "He is my nephew, like a son to me, and now he is gone," he cried. Tears were rolling down his cheeks. "Where have you laid him?"

"The tigre has taken him," I said, feeling numb and helpless.

"No, no, we must not let El Tigre have him, we must take him to his people, to rise from the Holy Ground with them at the Calling. We cannot leave him to be eaten and his bones scattered in the wilderness."

"It will take many men to beat the tigre from the hills and kill him. We are too few," Lupe said gently, for the old man's grief was profound.

"I will go and find him."

"The tigre will not let you take him and you will die, also," I said.

"It matters not, I must find Pablo and bring him back." He turned and went to the young shepherd, giving him instructions about the combined flocks.

"Is he going after that tigre alone, Lupe?"

"Si," Lupe sat disconsolate, in the throes of indecision.

"We can't let him go alone."

"I know, Demp-sey, I know."

"What do you want to do?"

"I want to tie that old man up and march him off to the placita, but that would only mean that he would have farther to come back here and find Pablo and he would bring half the family with him and for sure someone would get hurt."

"We four are surely enough to find one tigre," I said. Lupe's method of hunting tigers, pumas, and javelinas was by using beaters to flush out the quarry for easy killing. I had been on many a puma hunt with just two of us and maybe a dog or two for tracking and we had been successful and safe. Surely, we could hunt this tiger the same way. After all, carrying his prey would force him to leave a plain track.

"We would have to leave the young one with the sheep and that would only leave three to hunt El Tigre."

"That will be enough, Lupe, we won't even need a dog to follow that tigre's trail."

"I think it will be enough to get us killed," Lupe said as he watched the old man divide his lunch with the boy, take up his ancient rifle, and start for the mountains. "He marches off to his death," he murmured as he turned his horse to follow.

Instead of taking the old man up on his horse, Lupe walked with him, leading his horse. I rode beside them for a while, but that didn't work so good at their pace, so I took Lupe's horse and rode ahead. Horses watered and staked, I began looking at the sign around the camp. The poor man had no chance. The jaguar had a death hold on him before he was half awake and it was a clean kill. The puzzle was why the animal had attacked a human when there were sheep there for the taking. The presence of the dog would not have deterred the animal from taking his meal. The fact that the man had no warning meant that the dog had been somewhere else, probably with the flock.

Even after the animal picked up his quarry, he was easy to track in the sand. He left no sign on the rock ledge he climbed up to, but the occasional drop of blood marked his trail well enough. Lupe and Fernando, the old shepherd, caught up with me on the rock ledge and I led them along the trail.

The cat followed a kind of bench around the mountain. Above, the slope rose very steeply and rough, below was thick brush that would have been impossible for the cat to carry his prey through. If his habits were similar to the mountain lion, he would not have gone much farther before he stopped, maybe fed again, and buried the carcass under brush and leaves. He would have then found a comfortable spot to doze and watch over his meal. Often, this would be back along his path somewhere so he could watch for anything that may be following his trail. Lupe and the old man were holding back and they were watching both sides of the trail.

The bench ended abruptly and the brush grew across the trail and up into the jumbled boulders of the upper slope. I stopped and took a long drink from my canteen. The heat was stifling. Lupe was squatting in the shade of a dwarf cedar watching the upper side of the bench and the old man was not in sight. The canteen stoppered, I turned to resume my tracking when I heard a low growl from the cat. I froze. He had told me I had come close enough.

"Do you see him?" I asked in a low voice. It was a dumb question, for the cat was sure to be out of sight.

"No," came Lupe's answer.

I slowly backed up away from the trail. If I had chosen my retreat in the right direction, the threat to the cat and his meals was relieved and he would not feel he had to defend his property or territory.

Near Lupe, I scooched down under the sparse shade of another cedar and watched the mountainside. "Where is Fernando?"

"He went into the brush when you stopped and I have lost him."

"Not good."

"No, and he is liable to do something foolish that will get us all in trouble," Lupe said.

"Did you hear El Tigre growl?"

"Yes, but where did it come from?"

"Wish I knew." The faintest rustle of a branch where the tiger's trail entered the brush caught our attention, but we could see nothing. It could have been El Tigre or the old man, we had no way of knowing.

The cat growled again, this time a little louder, indicating that he perceived the threat to him had grown. "Up there?" Lupe pointed up the hill with his gun.

"More to the right, I think." Sweat stung my eyes and I was very thirsty again. We dared not move.

"That must have been Fernando over there?" Nothing was sure.

There was movement on the boulder Lupe had been watching as the cat rose and turned to jump down behind the rock. I jumped up, "He's on the move, Lupe, after the old man." I ran into the brush where the cat's trail had disappeared.

"Mi Dios," Lupe muttered as he entered the brush. It was a prayer.

My prayer was that the cached body was to the right of the trail so that we would have a shorter distance to run than the cat and could cut him off, staying between him and Fernando.

"I have found him," the old man called and my prayer was partially answered. He was to the right, but further along into the brush than I had hoped. The jaguar was not stalking prey, he would be running flat out to remove the threat to his food.

We almost made it, but I could hear him crashing through the brush to our left and he was going to pass in front of us before we could reach his path. "Look out, Fernando," I yelled as I ran to intercept the cat. Behind me, Lupe cut to the right, hoping to meet the cat just before he found the old man. I was within twenty yards of him when he ran by and my one shot took him just behind the shoulder. He rolled over, biting at his side where the bullet hit. In a second he was up, running again, but slower. I lunged through the tangling brush, trying to catch up to him as fast as I could. Again, he fell and bit at the source of his pain. Again, he rose, shaking his head and trying to run to his cache. I couldn't shoot now, for Fernando stood directly in line watching the big cat approach as if he were resigned to his fate.

Lupe fired and I jumped at the sound as the cat crumpled into a heap. He shuddered and was still. Fernando stood fixed, not ten feet away from the animal. Had he not been wounded by my shot, that last ten feet would have been made through the air as he attacked Fernando.

My head ached and my knees felt like they would buckle any moment. I found a fallen log no bigger than a fence post and sat down. "Drink, Demp-sey, drink deep and long," Lupe called from somewhere in the brush. I heard the old man weeping.

It was several minutes before I felt strong enough to stand. Lupe still nursed his canteen and both of us wished for something stronger than water. Fernando sat by his nephew's torn body and keened softly, rocking back and forth. His sorrow was touching and I was moved.

"Come, Fernando, you must tell your family and prepare for the burial. Lupe and I will bring Pablo to you."

"No, señor Demp-sey, I am family to Pablo and I must bear his pall."

"Are you not the *patrón* of the family?" I hoped. "Your duties are more important than this. Your son out there with the flocks can escort Pablo to the burial, but if you are not there to prepare the way, there will be nobody else to do it."

The old man struggled with the decision and while he did, Lupe returned to the camp for a blanket to wrap the body with and I examined the jaguar. El Tigre was old and when I opened his mouth, he had few teeth. There were only two fangs left, the upper right one and the lower left one. This would have made it very hard for him to catch his prey and harder yet to tear flesh and eat. I had noticed the missing toe in his tracks. There was one gone off his front right foot. It was an old wound. His coat was dull and rough, but it was my intention to have it.

"Fernando has seen the wisdom of returning to the placita to make arrangements, Demps, and I will take him there after we move the body to the camp. The boy, Benito, will stay with the sheep until someone is sent to take his place. I will bring back a wagon and coffin for the body." Lupe was still somewhat shaky from our adventure as was I.

"That is good, Lupe, I will stay with the body until you return."

CHAPTER 28
BREAKFAST WITH THIEVES

Wine is a mocker, strong drink is raging: And whoever is
deceived thereby is not wise.

—Proverbs 20:1

Fernando led as Lupe and I struggled through the brush and
heat with Pablo's body. It took some time to reach the camp
and we carefully laid him under his canvas shelter. Once his
mind was made, Fernando was in a hurry to leave for the placita
and I loaned him my horse. It was only a few miles to the vil-
lage and I expected Lupe to return by early morning.

We returned to the tigre after Fernando rode away and hauled
the animal back to near the spring. He was heavier than Pablo.
We hung the carcass in a tree and I skinned him after Lupe
rode away. The animal was gaunt and tough and I doubted the
meat would be good so after taking his hide and claws I dragged
the carcass back into the brush as far away from camp and
spring as my strength would allow.

Just before sunset, Benito brought the flock to water and I
walked with him behind the sheep. He was dusty and hot and
his cheeks were tear-stained. When the flocks were safely bedded, we returned to camp. I would not let the boy see Pablo's
torn body, but his face was untouched and we washed it and
left him uncovered. The boy sat beside the body and we talked
long into the night, about Pablo and their adventures together,
about their family and life on the range. The boys had aspired

to become vaqueros and both had the skills, but the pressing need was for them to shepherd the family's sheep. They viewed this as a temporary occupation and waited for the opportunity to ride after the cattle as the vaqueros did. Now there was only one to ride and his sorrow was touching. Toward dawn, we both dozed some.

I had coffee going and salt back in the pan when the boy arose and sent the dog after the sheep. Soon they passed camp and when they were spread over the valley grazing, Benito and dog returned for breakfast. To my surprise, the dog ate frijoles as readily as he ate the meat. Benito laughed. "Mama not allow him in the house after he eats the frijoles."

"I can understand that," I said.

A dust arising from the valley announced the return of Lupe with a wagon and several passengers. Fresh horses were tied to the tailgate. Pablo's mother and her sister, who was Benito's mother, were in the wagon with two older gentlemen who must have been of some kin. The women were upset and the more so when we refused to let them see more of Pablo than his face. Already there was an odor and his lips were drawing away from his teeth in his death smile. We placed him in the coffin and nailed it shut.

Lupe was very quiet and close-mouthed and I sensed something was afoot other than the works of El Tigre. He motioned to me and began saddling one of the horses. I threw my saddle on the other horse. Benito drove the wagon back toward the placita with the women passengers while the two men saw to the sheep and camp.

"Coop is doing well," Lupe said, as he mounted, "and the others there with lead poisoning are doing as well. However, there will be more than one burial at the chapel today," he said, the grim look on his face and determined set of his jaw told me we were not going to be in attendance at the funerals.

"What's happening?" I asked.

"Conly and the men have met several men attempting to steal sheep and cattle. Anyone who opposed them was shot. They have had several gunfights and now they are chasing them through the mountains toward the stone house. We are to ride across to Bennett Creek and down the valley looking for any trouble that may be there and eliminate it."

We turned and loped down into the valley and across the plain. "Who are these people and why do they think they can get away with this?" I asked as we rode.

"We have been told that Aquilero Rivera has let it be known that he will buy any cattle or sheep that are brought to him, no questions asked. He has made the rock house his headquarters and all he intends to do is buy the stolen stock—at his price, of course."

My anger was growing by leaps. "He reaps the rewards while the trash and robbers do the stealing and killing. He looks to wipe our range clean." I pulled my rifle and checked the load. My pistol was loaded and I inserted a round in the empty chamber. It was hard to keep from overworking the horses as we rode.

It must have been the last water on Bennett Creek where we crossed and the horses drank. The chopped-up ground told us that a flock of sheep had watered there as recently as last night. It had come from the direction of Ash Creek and returned the same way. Ash Creek ran underground most of its way to the flats, and as a result, grass tended to grow quite well there late into the dry season. There was almost always a flock or two along the creek and it seemed that this flock had not been bothered by thieves. Just the same, we determined to check it out and warn the shepherd of the danger.

There is not much of a divide between the two creeks and from the top of the slope we could see the flock grazing high up the creek against the hills. Their shepherd was not in sight, probably sitting in the shade somewhere watching. Lupe and I rode a hundred yards apart on either side of the track looking for signs that hadn't been obliterated by the passing flock. We found the trail of a bunch of cattle that crossed the tracks of the sheep at the same time and both of us turned off to examine them. The herd was being driven south away from me and toward Lupe. I backtracked a ways and the best I could determine there were three or four men driving the herd. They were in a hurry.

Lupe waved and we met where cow and sheep trails crossed. "We have to warn that shepherd and we need to catch the cattle before they leave the valley. You ride up and warn him and I will stay on the cattle trail until you catch up."

Like a fish needs spurs, I thought. "No, Lupe it is too dangerous to meet up with those men alone and the shepherd will not know me. You ride up and tell him and I will mosey *slowly* down this cow trail until you catch up. You can cut across country and I will wait on you at that boulder down there if I get there first." I indicated a large rock sitting alone on the valley floor about a mile beyond Bennett Creek.

"But I will know if the . . ."

"I will not be shot by a scared shepherd who probably would not believe anything I told him, even with my dying breath."

Lupe grinned and shrugged and turned his horse toward the flock. I rode slowly down the track of the cattle, studying the horse tracks I could find. There were four riders for sure, one on an unshod horse and one with only forefeet shod. *Don't think much of your horse, do you?* I thought. Lupe caught up with me before I got to the boulder and I picked up my pace.

Our quarry made dry camp past Bluff Creek and moved on south. We were not more than four hours behind them.

"They will be without water until they get to Deer Creek and the cattle will be slowing down. If we are lucky, we might catch up with them before dark," Lupe said

"At the very latest, we would have a surprise for them when they wake up tomorrow morning," I answered. We slowed our pace to save the horses, now that we were confident we would catch up with them within the next ten to twelve hours.

"What then?" I asked.

"What do you mean?"

"What do we do when we catch up with them?"

"We will be ready for anything, but let them determine what we do," Lupe replied.

"My inclination would be to shoot first and ask questions if anyone is able to talk after that."

"Well, it's sure I won't be waiting more than an instant for them to decide what to do." Lupe laughed out loud.

"Understood."

There had been water at Walnut Creek, but the cattle had fouled it so much our horses could only get a sip or two from water-filled tracks. The water was thick and muddy, just before the chewing stage. There certainly wasn't enough water for the whole herd—we guessed around a hundred fifty head—and the vaqueros must have had a time turning them away from the wet spot.

As the sun sank behind the Sierra Madre, it became more and more apparent that the herd would be pushed on to Deer Creek in hopes of finding adequate water. It was there, but the herd would have to scatter up and down the creek to find enough for all of them. Once they scattered the thieves would have to wait until morning to gather them. There was no more need for us to rush. We had them any time we wanted.

"Where do you think they will camp?" I asked.

"Probably up Deer Creek at least to the end of the Smugglers to have adequate water for the cattle," Lupe opined. "I would say somewhere in there, probably on that island at the southeast corner of the hills."

I had seen that island and the campsite there; it would be a good place to stay all right, though it would be pressing to call it an island without any water around it. "We should wait and hit them in the morning early."

"I was thinking the same thing, Demps, catch them asleep."

"All four of them should be in camp with the cattle scattered, they won't have to ride herd all night."

"Probably sleep late." Lupe was checking his handgun for the tenth time. The bullets were all there still.

"You got them new silenced bullets?"

"What's that, silenced bullets? Never heard of them."

"They don't make any noise when you fire them. The way you been reloading that gun, I thought you might have been firing some," I said.

"I can't remember if I filled the chamber under the hammer, that's why I keep checking."

"It must have a dozen bullets in it by now."

"Yeah, and how about yours?"

"It's only got two bullets in it, I guess."

We rode up among the rocks above Deer Creek's little island and made dry camp without so much as a cup of coffee. The warmth of the rocks kept the cold away until the small hours, when the cold caught up with us and chased sleep away. I got up and the big dipper said it was near four o'clock.

Lupe stretched and stomped his feet awake. "Might as well go see what's for breakfast on the island, hadn't we?"

"I'm ready," I said, and we saddled up and rode down the hill. The thieves must have been cold too, for their fire was a beacon to guide us.

"Are those big lumps scattered around the flats cattle bedded down or just boulders?" I asked.

"We'll avoid them like they were spooky cows; don't need some kind of stampede to announce our arrival."

We tied the horses a couple hundred yards from the camp and crept up to the fire. There were four saddled horses picketed nearby the camp and there were four bodies wrapped up in blankets, feet to the fire.

"There's only four of them." Lupe signaled across the fire, and all were accounted for.

I was puzzled why someone hadn't stirred some until I spied two near-empty whiskey bottles among the sleepers. Lupe walked up to the fire opposite the sleeping men and I joined him. "Sleeping off a good drunk, I'll bet," I whispered.

Lupe grinned. "Sure enough. You watch over them while I fix breakfast." I walked around behind the sleepers' heads while he dug through their packs scattered around and found the food they had. It wasn't much, but the coffee was soon bubbling away and, boy, did it smell good. A small pan with a dab of lard and fatback bacon was frying, its aroma making my mouth water.

One of the men groaned and sat up, or rather he sat up and then groaned. I could imagine his pain. He sat with his head in his hands for several minutes; then with another groan he looked around, found a bottle with a little left in it, and fumbling with the lid, he turned the bottle up and drained it. All he could see of Lupe was a shadowy figure cooking over the fire and it was several minutes before he was alert enough to count heads and figure there was one extra man in camp. He watched the cook intently and like a wolf stalking a mouse slowly drew his gun from under the blanket. That's when I buffaloed him just above his ear. He never saw me and fell like a rock. I left him where he fell, for the others were stirring and I knew I was soon to be busy.

"Good morning, muchachos," Lupe called cheerfully,

"breakfast will be ready very soon and the coffee is ready now."

The men froze for a second and then scrambled for their guns. I fired a shot into the sand beneath a reaching hand and it recoiled, stung and bleeding. The other two men, somewhat slower, sat still, their hands in plain sight.

"What is wrong with Jose?" one asked, indicating the unconscious man.

"He sleeps," I said, "but he will rise again. It will be good if you do not move until I say you can."

"Sí, señor." One nodded, then groaned and held his head with both hands.

"What in the world did you drink last night?" I asked.

"It was the tequila, señor," one said.

"I think I eat the worm," another groaned. Slowly and cautiously two of the men lay back down. The one with the bloody hand sat still and groaned. He had smeared blood from his hand all over the side of his face and looked a mess. I suppose he was still too drunk to feel much pain in his hand. I pulled up on his collar and said, "Stand up."

As he arose, I secured two handguns and a large knife from his person. His buffaloed friend groaned and I removed his pistol and bowie knife before he was fully conscious.

"Chow's on," called Lupe cheerfully; no one seemed hungry but me. Our prisoners were very docile and no trouble while Lupe and I ate our breakfast.

"Where were you going with our cattle?" I asked as we finished eating. All we got in reply were sullen stares. "They are not your cows and we have every right to hang you for the thieves you are unless you can give us a reason not to." Of course, it wasn't our "right" by law, but they understood the "law" of local custom and that it was liberally applied in the border regions without reflection or regret.

"There are men over San Luis Pass who will buy the cattle

without question, señor; with that monies we would feed our children."

"Your 'children' live in a bottle in the cantinas," Lupe spit. "Your seed wasted in the belly of a whore."

I was surprised at his vehemence. Upon later reflection, I realized that the life of an honest man was just as cheap as that of a bandit in this country and Lupe's anger was justified. More than one of his friends and kin spilt their blood in the sands over nothing more than another man's greed and lawlessness. It was a time when "an eye for an eye" was a gentler law than they were forced to live by. The man who had spoken shrugged. He knew the "law" they lived under.

"This, then, is what we will do," Lupe said. "We will take these cattle over the pass and see what these men pay you for them. You will help us and show us where to go. Perhaps by doing that you may purchase back your lives and return to your 'children.' "

"I would choose death first," said the man with the bloody head, and I marveled at his misspent loyalty, for it was a sure thing that the buyer over San Luis Pass felt no such loyalty to him.

"You have made your choice." Lupe raised his gun.

"No, Lupe," I said, "he may be of some use to us otherwise." My mind raced to find that "otherwise use," and there was none. But that pause gave Lupe time to reflect and he lowered his gun. "We have no use for these men if they do not help us drive the cattle to the buyer-thief."

"We will *all* help you if you will release us when the deed is done," the man who seemed the eldest of the four said.

"Even the bloody ones?" I motioned to the two injured men.

"Los ensangretado, sí."

"How can this be?" Lupe asked.

"It is our pledge, before God," the man said.

"The word of a thief?"

"The word before God of a man who would steal to feed his children," the man replied somewhat bitterly.

"Where do you come from?"

"Bacerac."

"You are hungry there?" Lupe asked, disbelieving, for it was a fruitful land.

"Villistas," was all the man had to say for us to understand their plight.

Lupe sat back on his heels and thought a moment. "Our range is full of thieves stealing our stock and killing us and you ask us to believe you steal for the life of your children. It is a hard thing to believe."

"We have harmed no one, only taken the cattle. Aquilero says he will pay us well."

"You cannot eat silver."

The man shrugged, "It is easier to carry and the Villistas also have little interest in what they cannot eat. We would not keep the cattle two days, but it is still possible to purchase grain and meat in certain places."

Lupe shook his head. "This is still hard to believe, amigo."

"I have a suggestion, Lupe."

"Then you must tell me, Demp-sey, for I am at the end of my rope here."

"If these men are telling the truth, let them gather the cattle and move them slowly south while we attend our urgent business in the Smuggler Hills. We can catch up with them and help drive the herd over the mountain and clean up the thieves there. In exchange, we will help them drive some of our cattle to Bacerac to feed their families and restock their land. If they are honest, they will be here and if they are not, they can only escape without the herd."

"Would you agree?" he asked the men and four aching heads

nodded agreement. "Then it is settled. You will gather the cattle and slowly graze them to the trail over the pass and we will catch up with you there."

"We will leave your weapons at the base of that hill over there." I pointed to a small hill at the tip of the Smugglers. When we return, we will hold up a white flag so you will know us."

Four heads nodded cautiously and I noted that none fell off. Without further adieu, we left for our horses.

"I doubt there will be much accomplished by that bunch today." Lupe chuckled.

"It will be interesting to see what they will choose to do," I said. Without further talk, we rode to the hill where we deposited the weapons and headed up Smuggler Creek for a meeting with the unknown.

CHAPTER 29
SMUGGLER CREEK SWEEP

A big country can breed big men.

—Bendigo Shafter

As far as we knew, Lupe and I were the only Beavers men on this end of the Smuggler Hills and signs along the trail seemed to confirm that. "So-o-o we are on our own here and Conly is driving desperate men our way," I said.

"Looks that way." Lupe hardly took his eyes off the ground, but there was no encouraging indications that anyone had preceded us.

"Well, hold up, Lupe, let's think on this some."

"What is there to think on, Demp-sey, we know what we have to do."

"I'm not worried about *what*, I want to know *how*. We don't know how many are running from Conly and his bunch. We don't know how many have made it to the stone house. If they make it there, we could spend the rest of the summer smoking them out of that forted-up place."

"That would not be good. If we could prevent them from reaching the house, we could clean them up quicker and with a lot less trouble."

"Now you're thinking, Lupe. It would be best if we could stop their running *before* they reach the house. We don't know where anyone is, so if we hurry, we could get past the trail up the draw to the stone house if Conly hasn't gotten there already, which means we should get a move on and not worry about sign anymore," I said.

With that, we picked up our pace considerably until we approached the second arroyo where the stone house was. Here, we detoured down into the creek bed and stayed as much out of sight and sound as possible. When we came back to the trail, there was no sign that more than one or two riders had passed. We began looking for a place to set up our little trail block and about a mile past the stone house, we found the place we needed.

Boulders that had rolled down from the Smuggler Hills, when they were much higher and it was much wetter, had forced the trail into the creek bed between high banks. It would be no trouble for us to hold off a lot of men here. With the horses hidden, Lupe chose a large boulder on the right of the trail for his perch, and I built up a rock fort on the left side where I could defend any approach toward Lupe and see the full width of the creek bottom. Anyone coming down the trail would be in our crossfire the moment he stepped into the creek.

Waiting is the hardest part of any war. After all the hustle and bustle comes the waiting. I hate it. We thought the wait was over when the first shots echoed down the valley. They seemed far away at first, but as time passed they got nearer and louder. I took a long drink from my canteen. There was a half-gallon left. This war better not last long.

There was a rustle and movement where the trail came down into the creek bed and a man stepped into the open. His clothes were ragged and his only weapon was a bloody machete. Lupe signaled to hold my fire and we watched as three more men appeared and walked our way. Lupe signaled that the fifth man was his and I shifted my aim to the man with the machete. From the corner of my eye, I saw the fifth man appear and I fired with Lupe. My shot hit the knife near the handle and it rattled on the gravel as thief number five screamed and fell, the leg of his duck pants turning crimson. One of the men in the creek was unarmed and threw up his hands. Another dove for the pistol dropped by the wounded man Lupe had shot. As he came up with the gun, I fired and he fell. Almost simultaneous with my second shot, a bullet splattered the rock an inch from my head and showered my face with stinging shards. "Behind us, Lupe," I yelled and when I looked, he had disappeared. A reflection from a gun barrel told me where my attacker was and I ducked as another bullet whistled off the rocks where my head had been.

Where is Lupe? Is he hurt? How many are behind us? I chanced a glimpse at the creek bed and the men there were running, two toward me and the others back up the trail they had come down. Two quick shots convinced my attackers they were running the wrong way and they turned back. Where is Lupe?

Another glint from that infernal rifle barrel warned me to duck. He was sure making it hot for me and I fired back to no effect except to make *him* duck for a change. I sprinted for the boulder Lupe had been on. He wasn't on the ground and I called again.

"I'm here, Demps." His voice came from behind me, hidden in the rocks. "Go back and guard the trail and I will get that sniper behind us."

I turned back, but that fort was too exposed so I stayed by the trail. The creek bed was empty except for one body. The wounded man had been carried to safety. We seemed to have arrived at some stalemate; the firing upstream tapered off to an occasional shot, and all I had to do was fire at anyone stepping into the creek bed.

It was growing hot and I snuggled back under the shoulder of the rock where it was shady. Someone kept stepping into the creek and I kept sending him lead messages. I had just sent my last messenger and leaned back under the rock when I noticed the tiniest bit of sand rolling off the boulder. Someone was on top of the rock and I was pretty sure it was not someone in sympathy with our cause.

Being careful to stay under the shelter of the rock, I backed around behind the boulder. From my new position, by looking around the corner, I could still cover the trail, but the spang of a bullet on the rock told me that my sniper friend had seen me move. If I lay flat on my belly there would be a rock between me and his last position. If he moved higher, I would be in trouble. Another trickle of sand told me the stalker was thinking I was still in my old position.

Someone attempted to enter the creek and the instant I fired a man dropped off the boulder, facing my old position in a squat and firing. All he hit was rock and before he could turn, I put three bullets into him. He sank to the sand with a sigh and was still. A shout and shot from the creek bed warned me of a rush and three quick shots from behind me crashed into the rock just above my head. A man appeared running up the bank and I shot him as he was vaulting the body of the man from above. He landed and took another running step before collapsing close enough to me I could touch him. A head appeared over the creek bank and I snapped a shot that convinced the man to stay where he was.

My empty pistol and the rifle being no good in close quarters convinced me it was time to move to new ground so I crawfished back into the rocks until I could safely stand and run. As I reloaded, men were running down the trail and I couldn't do a thing about it. I chanced a peek at the sniper's position and was greatly relieved to see Lupe there. He was shooting at men along the trail between us and when I was sure he saw me, I dropped down and crept toward the trail. Horses were coming at a trot and I stepped out ready to fire when Conly called,

"Hold, Demps, friends."

"Hold yourself, Conly, you're riding into a trap. Lupe is up there and the bandits are somewhere in the rocks between us."

He dropped down off his horse as the others behind stopped. "From the looks of things, you two have been busy down here." He grinned through streaks of sweat, dust, and powder smoke. A long scratch along his cheek oozed a little and his overalls were torn to shreds.

"We got a new thing back east you could benefit from," I said, "they're called chaps."

"Didn't have time for 'em. Say, you got some water there?"

"It's not much, but you can have it."

Conly took the canteen and shook it. "It'll do," and he handed it to a man beside him. "Take that back to Juan and make him drink all of it. Tell him we are near the end of the mountains and there will be a wagon there to take him home."

There must have been a dozen men standing around us and Conly said, "Now, men, let's clean this up." We scattered into the rocks and sweeping toward Lupe's position pushed the bandits together. With only an occasional shot here and there, the culprits were soon bunched in the trail, hands in the air. It was surprisingly easy.

There were fifteen men, mostly Mexican with a few Americans, guarded by men whose demeanor demanded strict attention to the business at hand. Another group of prisoners, no more than seven, was gathered in a separate spot and were guarded even closer than the large group. I had to smile, for the guards looked as bedraggled as their prisoners. There was little for a stranger to discern the difference except for the red sashes our men wore around their waists. Nava walked up with a big grin on his face and a new sash around his waist. "We are to shoot any man not wearing a red sash," he said to Conly, "may I shoot this Gringo?"

"He's armed and dangerous, Nava, I think I would give him a red sash instead."

"Very well, amigo, I will give him my old sash; it was getting too trail-worn for a man such as me and I had to make a new one." He handed me a dirty torn sash and by turning it wrong-side out I could tell it was red—just barely.

I looked up at Lupe, ready to show him my red sash, and saw him standing with Sergio, who was sporting a new sash. Lupe's sash looked well worn.

"I suppose you have cleaned out the rock house also," Conly said.

"No, we came up here to prevent the men you were chasing from getting to the rock house."

"I see, so there is one more thing to do before we finish here." Conly lifted his hat and wiped his forehead with a bloodstained handkerchief. "Do you have any more idea how many men are in the house?"

"No, just the ones we counted; I guess, seven men, one woman, and a yapper."

"They shouldn't be too hard to handle, only I would not like to shoot the woman."

"She hasn't chosen her friends very wisely; if she shoots at me, I shall shoot back," Nava said. He had not suffered for the lack of female company as we Anglos had north of the border. That dearth of Anglo women in the west and on the range has influenced the American vaquero to look with favor on the ladies of Spanish-Indian descent and their unions have improved the stock of both races.

"We can give her the opportunity to leave before the fray begins," I said.

Nava looked puzzled, "What is a fray?"

"A battle."

He looked relieved, "One should say it plainly."

"One would never learn new words that way," I replied.

"Ah-h-h I do not need all those new words when the ones I have are adequate."

Conly chuckled. "Same here, but we are not getting closer to ending this thing standing here jawing. Let's make a plan and do it. We need every man we have to clean out that place and we're going to have to guard these people at the same time." '

I looked around and counted heads. "We only have fourteen men and that's not enough to do both jobs at once. We're going to have to dispose of these men before we can take care of the men at the house."

"I know what we should do with these." Nava motioned to the prisoners.

Conly looked at the men and shook his head. "No, Nava, we don't have enough rope or tree limbs and we need to save our ammunition for the ones in the rock house. Only those in the other group had guns, these men were here to herd the stock, not fight. They have done this for many reasons, I suppose, but from their looks I would say that they are hungry and more than a few of them have hungry mouths at home they worry about.

"Let's march them over to Deer Creek where we all can get some water and we'll deal with them there. Leave those seven here and double their guard. We can walk the rest with no trouble."

"I have an idea about how to keep the gunmen," I said. "Be sure they are all unarmed, march them up to the rock house, *and* guard the house so *none* of them get out. We can be assured that way that no one from the rock house will sneak down here and free these birds and they will have to feed and take care of them for us."

"You are taking the chance that there won't be arms there for them."

"Even if they do, they can only have a fixed amount of ammunition and food. Most likely we can starve them out pretty quickly."

"It has to be quick, we have a ranch to run," Conly said.

Nava was grinning. "You have a perverse mind, Demp-sey, and I think your idea might work. The house is built around a seepy spring that has not much water. All those people and horses will quickly use up the water and there will be thirst."

"What is this 'perverse' word?" I mocked. Nava only grinned.

"It would work to our advantage to keep both groups bottled up and we don't have the men to do both and march these herders away." Conly thought a moment, "Ok, let's do it." He gave orders to the men holding the larger bunch, then motioned for the guards to bring the gunmen to us. "We are going to take you men to your boss at the rock house. I'm sure he will welcome you with open arms, food, and water. You will stay there until we decide what to do with you."

The smirks and grins among the outlaws showed that they were amenable to the plan. I hoped fervently that the plan went our way. It was a gamble, the only one I could see that had a chance of working and that quickly.

The men readily marched in front of us and Conly sent a couple of their guards back to help with the large group. Sergio joined us and Lupe stayed behind to oversee the movement to Deer Creek, where we fervently hoped there would be adequate water. All of us were beginning to suffer for the lack of it.

At the arroyo, I saw a glint from a lookout partway up the trail and knew there was company coming. He would have to be puzzled about us, some walking and some riding, so we hoped he would not be alarmed right off. Sergio's rifle was across his saddle and I held mine pointing down just in front of my leg and out of sight.

The guard rode out across the trail and before he could make any moves, three rifles barked. His sombrero flew from his head and his horse collapsed under him as he jumped clear. He snapped two shots at us as the prisoners yelled, then turned and ran up the trail. A second guard ran out and followed. It took us a moment to calm the men, then I ordered, "All of you, take off your shoes."

There was a moment of disbelieving silence and Sergio called, "You heard, put your shoes in a row along the trail."

They grudgingly complied and resumed their walk up the trail. We counted shoes and found them all there. Tender feet and sharp gravels slowed our progress, but we soon came within sight of the house. Nava and Sergio had climbed either side of the arroyo and flanked the trail to avoid any escapes.

Just out of rifle range, we dismounted and hid in the rocks while encouraging the men to proceed to the house.

I could tell by his voice that the man who came out on the stoop was the same one Conly had talked to that night we rode in here. It must be Aquilero Rivera. "You men go back. We don't want you here. Go away . . ." Two shots rang out and little puffs of smoke showed where Nava and Sergio were. Rivera staggered back in the doorway. Even from a distance we could see the dark stain spreading on his pants leg.

The group of prisoners had faltered for a moment, but when Rivera disappeared, they hurried toward the house. Instead of going for the barred door, they ran to the corral wall and climbed over. Soon the place was quiet and all our prisoners secured—for the time being.

CHAPTER 30
LUCINDA BROWN ARRIVES

It took real men to capture the Old West, But it took
women to tame it.

—Old Pioneer

Conly left Sergio and three men to guard the house and ap-
pointed one man to ride with us to acquire supplies for them.
We hurried back down the trail. "There should be a chuck
wagon and a couple of other wagons at the junction of Smuggler and Deer creeks. Hopefully, we will have food and water
there."

It was past midafternoon and I asked Conly, "How we were
going to keep the herder prisoners together after dark?"

"I hope we don't have to worry about that," he replied
without any further comment.

We rode weary horses down to the two creeks and it was a
great relief to see a chuck wagon set up and a fire burning. The
prisoners were there, all seated on the ground eating frijoles and
rice with tortillas and drinking steaming coffee.

As I watched, a vaguely familiar figure came around the chuck
wagon and helped the cook at the tailgate. It was a woman, but
not any of the Hicks that I could tell, yet her quick and sure
movements were very familiar to me.

Conly was staring too, "Who is that, Demps, do you know
her?"

"She's familiar, but not one of your girls . . . Oh my gosh,

Conly, that's Aunt Cindy!"

"Can't be."

"Trust me, I know that woman and it *is* Aunt Cindy."

"What in the world . . ." Conly grinned and shook his head in disbelief. ". . . I think you're right, Demps."

Aunt Cindy noticed our approach and with a word or two to the guards standing nearby, took up a gun leaning on the wagon wheel. She walked out toward us, the shotgun in the crook of her arm. "Better stop out of range of that scattergun, Conly, she's liable to use it even if she knows who we are."

"Son, don't think you are giving me any new ed-u-cation, I've been around the world a turn or two." Conly laughed and took off his sombrero. "Hello, Cindy, it's Dempsey and Conly."

"Just the ones I've been looking for." She raised the barrel slightly and I stopped. "Oh, don't be skittish, Dempsey, I'm not going to shoot you—yet. Come on in and make yourselves comfortable." She motioned and two young boys ran out and led all our horses away. "I'll give you time to wash up before you two do some explaining." She was distracted by things happening around the wagon that needed her supervision. Cookie gave Conly a pained look that pleaded the need for relief. Conly shrugged his shoulders, palms out, and surpressed a grin by immersing his face in wash water.

The roller towel was too wet to dry anything, so we dried on our shirttails and headed for the grub line. As we ate, Aunt Cindy brought a campstool over and we conferred quietly. "What do you make of these men, Cindy?" Conly asked.

"They're just common folk, shepherds and vaqueros, not naturally outlaws."

"That's what I had about figured. We have the bad ones holed up in the Smuggler House. These men were told that Aquilero Rivera would pay them for any stock they could steal, no questions asked. His gunmen would make the play and these men would drive the stock somewhere to be sold."

"We caught one crew with a bunch of cattle who were told to drive them over San Luis Pass and there would be someone there to buy the cattle," I said.

"That would be the bunch we saw coming up here. They were holding a herd and when we would have approached, they waved their hats and we left them."

"I need to see them. Conly, what do you say we drive some cows over the pass and see what is going on?"

"I want to go with you. Let me see to these men and we both will go."

"Are you two just not used to thinking right? Those men are out there without food and you want to take them on to God knows where without eating? Dempsey, you bring those men here and we will feed them, *then* you can go on about your rat killing."

"Cindy, you want us to bring those men in here? Are you sure you want to sleep here tonight surrounded by a bunch of throat cutters?"

"Who's gonna be sleeping? Certainly not me and these are not cutthroats, they're common men trying to feed their families. Now git, Dempsey, before dark. You can finish eating when you get back. That herd isn't two miles back."

"Yes, ma'am."

The ride on a fresh horse didn't take long and I waved my white rag on the end of my rifle. It looked like they had found all their strays, and when they rode up, I sent three of them to the wagon with instructions to give their weapons to the woman there and eat. I figured Aunt Cindy would be less likely to be shot than a man. Besides, she had that shotgun. The other man and I slowly herded the cattle toward the camp until one of the vaqueros rode out and relieved the fourth man so he could eat.

When another man rode out to spell me, I gave them instructions to bed the herd and I roped a yearling heifer and dragged her to camp. Cookie didn't have to ask what to do and the cow was soon dispatched and various portions spitted over a larger fire. The aroma of that meat would trouble our sleep tonight—if we slept at all.

Conly had been moving among the prisoners talking to one or the other and as the sun set, he called everyone's attention. "I have been among you and think that you are not killers but men desperate to feed your families and driven to this end. Beavers Ranch is not one to stand by and watch their neighbors starve, therefore, we will help you. In the morning, I will give each of you two pesos. They will be marked in a special way and you have the choice of spending them as you please or after one month from today you may bring one of the pesos to me at Placita Hicks or Playas and I will redeem it for food or two lambs, male and female, so you may build a flock with them. I will redeem the pesos for one year only."

There were nods of agreement among the men and one stood to reply. "Thank you, Señor Hicks; this is a very generous thing you do and we will be ever grateful." He looked at the men seated around him a moment, then said, "I must tell you that there is still trouble among us. That man is one of the Rivera men." He pointed to a man sitting amidst the crowd and the men around him nodded agreement with the speaker. The man rose as if to run and a sharp word from the nearest guard stopped him in his tracks. Several of the men held the outlaw and brought him to Conly. "You are a Rivera man?"

The man affected a defiant attitude and looking Conly in the face said, "Sí, and I will dance on your grave when Aquilero comes."

"Aquilero is tied up right now and won't be able to rescue you for a while. Maybe tomorrow you will see him."

"And maybe tonight," the man spat.

"We will fix for you a place where you can watch for him," Lupe said, and with a nod from Conly led the man to one of the chuck wagon wheels.

"Don't you dare tie that man there where he'll be underfoot; tie him to one of those other wagons out of the way," Aunt Cindy ordered.

The chastened Lupe turned and disappeared into the gloom with his charge.

As the light failed, so did the men who were prisoners no more and they slept where they lay. Guards faded into the gloom or came to the fire to fill their plates and eat. Drops of fat from the turning meat sizzled in the fires and the smoke that rose tickled our noses and taunted our appetites. Aunt Cindy moved her chair back into the shadows and, with a blanket around her shoulders, watched.

I went over and sat on the ground beside her. She laid her hand on my shoulder and patted softly. "Aunt Cindy, how did you get here?"

"Just like you did, Dempsey, I rode the train."

"I *mean*, why did you come?"

"I came because I had a feeling, Demps, did you ever have one of those?"

"No, ma'am—only when I knowed somethin' was wrong."

"Knew. Like the time Riley Giddens was killed, I knew Tucker would be blamed."

"How did you know that?"

"Well, I just saw how the stars were lined up, Dempsey, an' that's all I'm gonna say about it." She did that, dropped a hint or two about that time, then shut up and it was no use talking any more about it.

"What did your feeling tell you about us?"

She pulled her blanket closer and settled deeper into her

chair. "Just that something was wrong. I get here and up comes Cooper with a bullet in him and you are out here on the plain in a war and my 'feeling' was right. Those girls were too busy playing Florence Nightingale and I was underfoot. I had to come see what kind of mischief you were into. Next time you start a war, you be sure to tell me first."

"We didn't start this one, Pancho Villa did and Aquilero Rivera took advantage of it. We have to finish it or leave the Mexican Beavers to them."

"Well I'm damned if I leave those scoundrels a crumb or a cow pile. I only regret there aren't more cottonwoods around here to decorate."

"The rock house has some pretty strong vigas." I grinned at her vehemence. She was a force to be dealt with when her dander was up—which was most of the time.

"I brought rope, what are we waiting for?"

"We got to be sure no one is at our back. As soon as these men are out of the way, we'll clean up the rock house. They will leave at dawn and we can attend to business."

"The sooner the better for me."

"Aunt Cindy, you are not going to war with us, if I have to sit on you."

"We'll see about that, young man, and you better watch your tongue."

I laughed at the thought of me sitting on her. "I won't start a second war in the middle of this one unless I have to. You are too important to risk in a little ol' thing like a range war. Pa sent me to watch after you an' you know what would happen to *me* if I let you make war with us."

"Watch after me? You just wait 'til I get aholt o' that Joshua Nealy."

"You wait 'til I can be there t' watch." I laughed and she laughed with me. "I'll roll my bedroll out under the chuck wagon, Aunt Cindy. You can sleep there and I'll bunk with one of these others."

"No need to do that, I brought my own bedroll. It's in the wagon if you will get it for me, but I doubt I'll have much use for it tonight."

I wondered what would prompt her to bring her bedroll out here—and I suspected the telegraph at Playas had a lot to do with her "feeling."

CHAPTER 31
A HOUSE CLEANING

Adventure is just a romantic name for trouble.

—Louis L'Amour

I don't know where Conly had those pesos hidden, but he produced a pile of them and spent a good portion of the night marking twenty-eight of them for the peons to have. Pots and pans started clanking about four o'clock and by dawn's light, men were lined up ready to load their plates with tender beef, frijoles, and biscuits. Our captive bandit was largely forgotten until he called out. He had to wait until all were fed before he got to eat.

At the end of the chow line, Aunt Cindy handed each man two marked pesos. While they ate, Conly repeated the promise about the coins. The men seemed well pleased with the proceedings and conditions and Conly urged them to leave for their homes as soon as they had eaten, something they were glad to do. Soon, the camp was empty save Beavers Ranch men and our prisoner.

Conly called us together and gave us instructions. Lupe and I were to climb up the first ravine and guard the back of the rock house. The rest were stationed around the house and corral so that no one could escape. Aunt Cindy was helping Cookie, but I know she had her ear on us. When we rode out, she was busy at the chuck wagon. It was a waste of breath to warn Conly that Aunt Cindy was liable to show up at the stone house; he must have had experience with her before. Lupe and I broke off and rode up the first arroyo and climbed over the divide. This time we got within a hundred yards of the house and were still high enough on the hill to have the advantage over anyone trying to escape by the back door.

We settled down for a long wait, something I don't have the patience to do much of. Toward noon with the sun beating down on us, I began studying the house. There were no windows on the back side of the house and hardly a place to look out from. Of course, the roof was empty, though bedrolls were scattered around on it. If someone could get against the walls, he could do some damage without much danger. Come late afternoon, Lupe and I would have the sun directly in our faces and be at a hazardous disadvantage; come night, that roof would be lined with men and we would *all* be at a hazardous disadvantage.

I called softly across to my pardner, "Lupe, this isn't gonna be good for us from now until daylight with the sun in our eyes all afternoon and men on that roof after dark."

"I was thinking the same—it may be that we should be a lot farther away or much closer." He grinned at me.

"You well know I ain't backing off."

"Sí, we must worm our way down until we are closer, much closer." He began crawling his way down the hill toward the house and I paralleled his route on my side of the ravine. It was really slow going, for the slightest slip sent gravel skittering to the bottom, and if a watcher could not hear, he certainly could see the dust stirred up. Just below the barren boulders of the gully was a band of cedars so thick they formed a solid barrier we had to crawl under. They had been cleared away from the house a good fifty or sixty feet, and crossing that space from the back would be a problem.

A disturbance over Lupe's way startled me and I began crawling his way. It was with little relief that I saw that he wasn't fighting a man, for in his gloved hands was a squirming animal. A faint whiff told me it was a polecat. "What in the world are you doing, Lupe?"

"If you hold his tail down, he cannot spray," he answered. He had a death grip on the animal's hind legs with the tail tucked tightly between.

"This is a new version of having El Tigre by the tail." I grinned at him and backed away a little. "What are you gonna do now?"

"I don't know, I don't know."

"Hold on, I think I can help." I took off my shirt and long johns top. Tying the arms in a knot close to the shoulders, I turned the top wrong-side out and crawled over to Lupe. "Stick your friend through the tail and neck and I will fold the tail over him; just don't turn loose of that tail." We worked the animal through the shirt and I folded the tail over him with Lupe still holding on to his legs through the neck hole. Quickly, I tied off the shirttail with a leather thong and we had a bag, of sorts.

"Now what?" Lupe asked.

"We need a box or something to drop him in and run."

"We don't have any boxes, Demp-sey."

I glimpsed the house. "But we might have a chimney."

"I have no wings to fly there."

"Hang on," I said needlessly, and I crawled over for a better look at the house. The chimney was on the south end of the house, opposite the corral on the north. It was made of the same stone as the house, rising outside of the rock wall. The nature of the construction made it easy to climb anywhere along the wall, the corner of the chimney being the easiest.

I think the seed of an idea was sprouting in both of our brains and Lupe was beside me studying the situation. "We can make it to the wall without being seen and it would be easy to climb the *chimenea*, but not with one hand."

"Let's gain the wall, then we will solve the other problems," I answered. The skunk must have liked the darkness of the bag, for he had almost ceased struggling. I hung our two rifles in a tree and we crawled to the edge of the clearing.

"I think we can make it," Lupe whispered.

"You go and I'll cover you."

He rose from his knees and trotted across the clearing to the house. It was easy, maybe too easy, and my hackles were up as I sprinted across the open ground. Nothing happened. There was a hasp for a padlock on the back door and I closed it and locked it with the nail hanging there for the purpose. I led to the chimney corner, gun in hand, and studied the wall. It would be child's play with two hands. "You have any ideas?" I whispered as I stepped back.

"Is that you, Demp-sey?" came a voice and we both jumped.

"That's Sergio," Lupe said. "Where are you, amigo?"

"In the chimney corner."

"Peek around and don't shoot," I said. Sombrero rim, crown, and nose appeared until he could see us, then Sergio stepped around the opposite corner of the chimney. "What in the world are you doing in the chimney corner?" I asked.

"I might ask you the same thing, amigo, but I wonder more about what Lupe is doing with a skunk by the tail." He grinned at his friend's predicament.

"He's looking for a box to put him in and we think we have found one," I said, patting the chimney.

"Ah-h-h, I see, but it is too far for you to reach from here, my friend."

"It may be I could reach it if I stood on your head," Lupe growled.

"No, no, you must go on the roof; you would not want to

miss the view from there." Sergio's grin was infectious and even Lupe could not avoid grinning. "Come with me to my side of the chimney and there may be a way." From Sergio's side of the chimney dangled the man end of a lasso that was looped over the chimney. "I have been on the roof and secured the trap door so that the bandidos cannot climb up to the roof any more. If one of us pulled from the top and one held him at the bottom, I think a one-armed man could climb."

It only took me a minute to climb the wall with the rope, and by the time I was set, Lupe had the rope tied around his waist and was stepping on the first toehold in the wall. It took longer with Sergio pushing on his backside and directing his toes to the next step, but we got Lupe to the top with only a minor slip or two. He was soaked with sweat and pale.

"See, there is your box, amigo. We should remove the bedroll before you drop your friend in." Sergio indicated the chimney and bedroll stuffed into the flue.

I pulled the bedding out and the noontime sun shone directly into the flue. Someone below stuck his head into the fireplace to see why the light suddenly appeared just in time to cushion the falling bundle. The tail came up and there was a scream, then much yelling and scrambling around in the room below. Shots were fired, more screaming, dog yapping suddenly turned to crying and yelping.

All three of us must have seen the gun barrel enter the flue and ducked. Buckshot, soot, and rock shards blew out of the hole like a chimney fire, and I slammed the bedroll into the flue in time to catch the second barrel's blast. "Must have made someone down there mad," I said.

"Poor *mofeta*, poor, poor *mofeta*," Lupe mourned.

"I didn't know you were so close to her, compadre." Sergio patted his companion's shoulder in sympathy.

Noise of the pandemonium below suddenly came from a different direction, and we rushed to the front of the building in time to see a crowd of men boiling off the stoop, guns firing. A man with a shotgun turned toward us and we all three fired as the shotgun bore down. Its blast tore the air above us and the man crumpled. Others were firing at us and we ducked below the wall. Firing was coming from the rocks as our allies took up the battle.

Caught in the open as they were, the bandits had no chance and it was only a few moments before the firing ceased. Men appeared from the rocks cautiously surrounding the men in the yard. A shot from the door of the house felled a man in the yard and was answered by a dozen shots. We heard a gun clatter to the floor and the soft thump of a body falling. Somewhere in the house a woman screamed and the dog whined.

"We've done about all we can do here," I said as I headed for the chimney.

"Hold, Demp-sey, we now have a ladder to descend," Sergio said as he retrieved his rope. Lupe signaled to the men that we were going inside.

At the trap door, we held a quick consultation and on signal, Sergio lifted the door and I dropped through to the floor. My first sight in the gloom was a man at the door bringing up his rifle as he turned. My shots caught him full in the chest and he fell on his face. I jumped aside as Sergio dropped through the hole. "Lupe's hand is still asleep and he will come slower," he whispered hoarsely. The horrible stench in the room seemed to soak into our clothes and skin. Our eyes burned and I gagged.

There was no more movement in the room and it took a few moments for our eyes to adjust from the noonday glare to the gloom of the house. I thought how fortunate it was that the man I had shot was silhouetted in the door. If he had been in the dark, I would have never seen him—or anything else, for that matter.

Something moved under a table against the far wall and the lap dog whined in a corner of the room. "Come out from under that table," I called and the woman removed the blanket from her head and slowly crawled out. Rising, she paid us no attention as she headed for the door. "Hold your fire," I yelled and the woman safely stepped over the bodies in the door and on to the stoop. The whining dog limped after, tail between legs.

Someone outside called, "All is safe, amigos, you may come out now," and we gratefully left the house, but we didn't leave the stench of that skunk. I smelled my hand and arm. They stank. My clothes were saturated with the odor and if it hadn't been for the two women standing there, I would have stripped them off . . . *two* women? I looked again and there stood Aunt Cindy talking to the woman from the house. They didn't stand too close to each other, and that blamed shotgun rested in the crook of my aunt's arm.

Bodies were scattered around the steps, some of which would never move of their own accord again. One man leaned against the stoop groaning and I noticed his chest and legs were peppered with shot—number two buckshot.

Conly walked up, a big grin on his face and blood staining his cut shirtsleeve. "Dear Lord, Conly, where was Aunt Cindy in the battle?"

"Standing by me, Demps—and close enough for that scatter-gun to take effect." He ripped off his shirtsleeve and I tied it around his wound. It was just a grazing shot.

"What now?"

"We will clean up this mess, pick up the pieces, and go back to ranching again," he said.

Several men were attending to our wounded man when Aunt Cindy waded in and shooed them away, barking out orders no one dared ignore, and the place gradually assumed some sort of order. Only four of the bandits were uninjured and they sat tightly bound in the shade of the cedars.

Nine bodies were laid in a row across the front of the house, and Aunt Cindy and the woman tended three wounded bandits. The skunk odor permeated everything and when I went to speak to Aunt Cindy, she berated me for ruining the house so we couldn't use it, ignoring the fact that we had rooted the bandits out with the skunk.

The sun sank behind the mountains and we were grateful for the coolness that crept up the valley. Someone built a fire and we were sitting around just resting from the day's exertions when Sergio nudged me. "Lupe look at the house," he whispered. I watched as a black and white figure sniffed at the door, then furtively ran along the wall and off the porch.

"*Mofeta* is well," Lupe murmured.

CHAPTER 32
SAN BERNARDINO

"Viola, I want to ask a favor of you. When I die, I do not
want to be buried in Tombstone. . . . I want to be buried
where there are people."

—John Horton Slaughter

"What are we gonna do with these prisoners?" I asked Conly as
we rode down Smuggler Creek to the camp. We had spent the
evening before helping our captured bandits dig a mass grave
for their compatriots and a restless night guarding the survivors.
Aunt Cindy had taken our wounded men, all four of them, and
the woman down to camp the evening before. She would take
the men back to Placita Hicks in the remaining wagon. I offered
odds that she would be in camp when we got there, but no one
would take me up, too many knew her.

"The lady wants to return to Tombstone now that her
'husband' Rivera has passed on and I think Sheriff Slaughter
has an interest in some if not all of the rest. I am going to send
them to his ranch, San Bernardino, in Arizona."

Water was a problem. The seep at the rock house was totally
inadequate and with the horses from the corral plus our posse,
we were beginning to hurt. Progress down the creek was slow
until the horses smelled water and all of us perked up. Aunt
Cindy (I *told* you so) and Cookie had cooked up a huge meal of
bar-b-qued beef and frijoles and we enjoyed it to the last bean.

Aunt Cindy and Conly were having an intense conversation

as I walked up and I heard her say, "I haven't seen Viola and John in years and while I'm this close, I'm going to see them. It will probably be the last chance I get."

Conly scraped his boot in the dirt, making circles with the toe. "I was planning on sending the men cross-country from here, but since you are going, I guess we will send them all on the train."

"Good enough, Conly, I'll pay fare for all of them since I am the one causing all the trouble." And with that she marched off to attend to something at the chuck wagon.

Conly looked at me and grinned, "You would think she ran it all, wouldn't you?"

"Pretty much does," I muttered so she wouldn't hear, and got a sharp glance from her. She *couldn't* have heard that.

"You'll have to go with her, Demps, and keep her from shooting those bandits and that woman."

"Doesn't like the woman?"

"Lady of the Night would be a nice name she didn't call her."

I sighed, was it to be my life's calling—escorting a willful woman around the country trying to keep her out of trouble? I loved Aunt Cindy, but she surely was a trial—almost *all* the time. Conly just looked at me and grinned.

It was a day's travel to Placita Hicks, turned hospital, where Saint*less* Cooper recuperated under the watchful care of two lovely girls and another long trip to Playas, where a flag fluttered for a westbound train to stop and pick up passengers. As we were closing and sealing the cattle car the prisoners were in, a horse clattered up and Ana hopped down with a valise. "Wait for me, I'm going with you."

My day was made.

"It will be so nice to have you along, dear, we can become more acquainted." Aunt Cindy had Ana by the arm and escorted her to the passenger car. I trudged along behind with the luggage.

The smell of that skunk was everywhere. I had washed, changed my clothes, washed again, and still smelled like skunk perfume. Eledina had taken pity on the woman and given her a change of clothes, but that only diminished the smell a little. She said only one or two of the men got sprayed directly, but all of them soaked up the stench. I kept my distance from the women and downwind as much as possible. The poor little yapper must have gotten a load, for he stank worse than any of us. He stayed deep in his bag and only came out for the necessities.

The woman and I sat in the back of the car while the untainted passengers found seats for themselves in the front. Once we were moving, we discovered that the air in the car circulated from back to front. It only took a moment for all to reverse their sitting arrangements. Aunt Cindy held her handkerchief to her nose as she passed and Ana wrinkled her nose and grinned at me. That skunk had done us a great service, but I guess every blessing has its curse.

The El Paso and Southwestern Railroad dipped down from Playas to the Mexican border south of Bisbee, then ran northwest to Tucson, bypassing Tombstone by a few miles. Aunt Cindy had telegrammed Bernardino Station that we were coming with prisoners and several men met us there. Sheriff Slaughter had instructed them to take the prisoners on to Tombstone to the current sheriff of Cochise County. A buggy was waiting to transport us to San Bernardino Ranch. I rode in the back, dangling my legs over the tail and watching the country roll by while Ana and Aunt Cindy chattered.

It was 1887, I believe, when an earthquake down in Mexico had flattened San Bernardino. Of course, Mr. Slaughter had built back a little distance from the old house and mission ruins, this time with a nice ranchhouse for Miz Viola. The Slaughters were sitting on the front porch when we drove up and both rose and greeted Aunt Cindy warmly. Miz Viola hustled the women into the house "to freshen up" and I stepped forward to shake John Slaughter's hand.

His grip was firm, his dark eyes keen and piercing, John Slaughter was only five foot six inches tall in his prime and now was somewhat less. On his swollen feet were soft slippers, his boots being too painful to wear. Though he was friendly enough, there was a reserve about him that limited any relationship with him to casual friendship.

I took the chair he offered and we spoke of weather and cattle a few minutes. He gave an exaggerated sniff or two and grinned, "I smell a story, son, tell me what have you been up to?"

So, beginning at the time we saw our first bloodied shepherd, I told him about our little war. Occasionally he would interrupt with a question or two and when I mentioned Aquilero Rivera, he described him perfectly. He could put a name to other men I described and occasionally gave a little background into the man's life, then he would apologize for the interruption and signal for me to continue.

When I told him about dropping the skunk down the chimney, he chuckled and murmured, "Poor skunk." I laughed and told him Lupe's "Poor *mofeta*" remark.

When I finished, he rocked a moment, nodding, and said, "You've done the country a service, son, and I must drop Conly Hicks a note of congratulation." Laughing again, he added, "Was a time Conly couldn't be found in Arizona, but he has done well for himself and the people and his trespasses have been largely forgiven over here.

"Beavers Ranch in the Sacramentos, is that the same as the old hero of Bavispe, Tucker Beavers?"

"Yes, sir."

"People down there still revere his name. He did much good there after the quake of '87. It was a tragedy that he was killed."

"Yes, sir, we don't believe he was guilty of killing Riley Giddens."

"Neither do the folks down here that knew him. Folks say that he wouldn't murder and he wouldn't have run." He sat a minute, looking out over the river, "Life makes some funny turns sometimes, doesn't it?"

Miz Viola had been to the door a couple of times during our conversation and left without saying anything. Now, she opened the screen a crack and said, "John, dinner is ready."

I must have reflected my consternation at entering the house with my odor, but Mr. Slaughter looked at me and nodded, "We'll be right there, Mrs. Slaughter." He motioned to the corner of the house and said, "Washbasin's between the dining room and kitchen doors. You can come into the dining room there." He waited to rise until I had turned the corner.

The water in the olla was fresh and cold and the roller towel bright and unused. I wished my wash had taken away the smell of that skunk, but it hadn't.

Mr. Slaughter and the ladies were already seated when I went in. He indicated the empty chair opposite Ana and Aunt Cindy. As I sat, he said, "Mrs. Slaughter, our young friend has had a close encounter with trouble and he is very hesitant to come into our house. If, perchance, you get a whiff of a familiar odor, just know it is the smell of innovation and success."

"I know all about it, John, and the young man is welcome." She smiled at me as Ana hid her mouth behind her napkin and Aunt Cindy beamed. "Sometimes the smell of success is not so sweet, but it is success all the same, young man."

I thought of the smell of horses and cattle, a cow lot or horse stall, and had to agree with her, but that is the first and only time I ever heard skunk perfume put in the same category. We had a pleasant meal and afterward, Mr. Slaughter had one of his vaqueros show me around the ranch grounds. All was exceptionally neat and clean and the horses in the lot were of first-rate quality. At supper, I returned to the house and we spent a pleasant evening on the porch talking and visiting.

Mr. Slaughter provided Ana with a beautiful Morgan mare to ride and we rode around the ranch the next day. I certainly enjoyed that, though I paid little attention to the country. We rode north along the river since I didn't want to chance straying into Mexico. There was as much of the San Bernardino Ranch in Mexico as there was in Arizona and the line was not plainly marked. Ana was fun to be with and we talked and laughed the day away. She teased me about my "pomade," but she still held my hand.

Aunt Cindy met an old friend on the train back east and they talked all the way to Playas. That left me to entertain Ana and after a while she lay her head on my shoulder and slept. I didn't mind at all.

The fourth Muchacho, Benito, was at Playas when we got there, but he had little time to visit with us because of the press of Playas business. We hurried to Hicks to see how Cooper was faring, but needn't have worried with Cepa in attendance. The stitches had closed a wide gap in his skin and must have been pretty painful. His whole side was a deep purple bruise and they were afraid of infection. It was plain he would not be going anywhere for a while—and it was just as plain that he was in no hurry to go, either.

Eledina and Conly were gracious hosts and Eledina said she had not seen Conly so enthused about company in a long time. He arranged his time so most of it could be spent with us, especially Aunt Cindy.

One evening as we all were sitting on the plaza watching falling stars, Aunt Cindy said, "Conly, tell us about Tucker and the things he did down here."

It became very still and no one spoke until Eledina said, "Sometimes we cry about those times and sometimes we laugh, I think it would be good for us to laugh tonight." In the gloom, I saw a slender hand on Conly's arm.

"It is good to laugh and it is good that Lupe and I are here to see that Conly doesn't stray from the truth too far," Nava said.

Eledina's hand patted the arm softly.

"The first time we saw Tucker was at Hermanas when he came in on our all-night pool tournament and beer party to get his breakfast. There were four of us, me, Slim, Gabby, and Shorty. It was a sort of celebration because there was no work to do on the range because the Injuns that came through with the Beavers herd cleaned out our range too.

"We were impressed that Tucker had traveled that far alone and not encountered trouble on that Injun infested plain. He told us he was going to find his cattle and avenge the murders of his father and ranch hands—single-handed, mind you.

"Had we known more of him, we wouldn't have been so skeptical." I could hear him chuckle and Nava said, "Sí-sí."

"We figgered we better ride along and see if we could keep this kid out of trouble, maybe get *our* cattle back in the process, so we elected ourselves his guides and took out across that desert. It was another time we thought Tucker foolish to strike out with four strangers into the desert with a lot of jingle in his pocket, but we didn't know him that well then—had to teach him how to drink water in the desert and almost got shot for the teaching."

Conly told us about the water drinking lesson and how they scouted out the range, met the people displaced by the invading ranchers, and planned to retrieve their cattle. When the young men in Antelope Wells were kidnapped by the ranchers, all their plans were cancelled and they plotted to free them. It was a desperate plan, fraught with unknowns. This is where The Muchachos and The Muchacha, Eledina, came into the picture. "And now we will tell you the truth of the matter, since Conly does not know what we did with Gabby," Nava interrupted. "We had at Antelope Wells a box of old dynamite that we decided to use on the outpost guard camps and line shacks . . ."

". . . It was old and sweaty and we didn't know that sweat was not water," Lupe interjected.

"Gabby showed us when he flipped a drop on the wall and it popped. You can bet we were much more careful then. Sergio took Tucker, Conly, Slim, and Shorty south to a shortcut trail over the mountains to the back of the Placita . . ."

". . . A story *I* will give you when the time comes," Sergio, who had joined us, said.

They told us about the brush arbor guard camp and how The Muchacha had lured the guards away, much to the embarrassment of Eledina and delight of the rest, especially two young girls who heard the story with us for the first time.

The story of the fight was not so much fun to hear, especially the loss of Gabby, Slim, and Shorty and the shooting up of Conly and Tucker. Tucker's escape was a miracle in itself, how he survived under that huge gate, escaped with the little horse and spent the winter in the Sierra Madre, hurt and alone.

"No one could have recognized him when he rode into Bavispe that night," Conly continued. "He was the most dirty, shaggy bum you have ever seen. I pretended to know him, but it wasn't until he was washed and shaved and clipped that I was really sure. What a reunion we had. The town was full of Antelope Wells refugees and we celebrated the return from the dead as it were of Tucker Beavers the fighter."

"We determined to burn Tucker's old clothes," Nava added, "and they wouldn't burn! It took a roaring brush pile."

"I was drawn to this Tucker and admired him greatly and Conly was jealous." Eledina laughed and squeezed Conly's arm, her head on his shoulder.

Sergio told us about Tucker becoming a Baptist "priest" and conducting the marriages and we laughed, especially when we heard the row the Catholic priest made on his next visit. "It was touch and go there for a while whether the old priest would crucify Tucker or not. In the end, he relented and even enjoyed a laugh or two about it."

"Tucker was quite popular with the ladies, but he kept his affections for his sweetheart back in Pinetop, whoever she was." Conly put his arm around The Muchacha's shoulders and we watched a star streak silently across the sky and disappear behind the Sierra Madre.

"He left for home the third day of May of '87 and got as far as the abandoned Antelope Wells before the earthquake hit. As soon as he could, he returned to Bavispe, disregarding any danger that might come from his enemies at the placita."

"He found Bavispe in ruins and rescued a baby who was in an iron pot with its dead mother covering it," Eledina said, "And he found us in the camp outside of town, Conly busted up and me battered and bruised. The people were dazed and lost and Conly urged Tucker to make some sense of it all."

"And he did," Conly continued. "He began organizing the people, set up a hospital and morgue, organized rescue teams and cleanup crews, read scripture at the funerals.

"Doctor Goodfellow from Tombstone came down with medical supplies and treated the injured. He was very interested in the quake and I helped him look for a volcano that we suspected erupted and caused all the fires in the hills.

"All the time he had been back, Tucker had been limping from the wound in his backsides. Doc found the bullet in his hip and the second time he came down, he removed it. Tucker insisted it was in his hip, but we all knew it was in his ass, Doc told him so. It was a year before he felt it was right for him to return home."

"The letter he had written to us still lies somewhere under the ruins of the first San Bernardino ranch house and we never received it," Aunt Cindy said. "We had two messages—rumors, really—that Tucker was dead, once after the big fight and once after the quake. We were engaged"—I gave an involuntary start; I had never heard that—"and when the second rumor came that he was dead, Rance convinced me to marry him, much to my regret, I might add."

We were all very quiet for a few moments and I felt the tears in my eyes. Ana squeezed my hand in the dark but that didn't comfort much.

CHAPTER 33
JOURNEYS BEGUN, JOURNEYS ENDED

Forever is composed of nows.

—Emily Dickinson

One morning a couple of grimy boys dropped off a boxcar outside Playas. When the dirt was washed away, we found Clancy and his brother, Patrick, back from Tucson. The boy could have been Clancy five years younger and he idolized his big brother. Clancy resumed his job as kitchen aide and wherever he was, Pattie was too. It near drove Tia Tina mad. Aunt Cindy had to step in and put the quietus on the two boys. She was the only one who could make the two toe the line, and *that* was to no one's surprise. To calm Tina's nerves, she promised to take the two boys back to Piñon with us.

Saint Cooper slowly healed—too slowly for Aunt Cindy—and four of us returned to the ranches without him. On the train back, I rode with Aunt Cindy while Clancy and Pattie sat behind us and chattered in their Irish language. We listened to them as much as we talked.

"Such a beautiful language, Dempsey, almost like a song."

"Yes, ma'am, it is."

After a moment, she said, "Dempsey, I have made out my will and a copy of it is under my jewelry case at the house. Should something happen to it, Burnett and Son Lawyers in Tularosa have a copy. I've made you executor of the estate"— she held up her hand to quiet my attempted protest—"I'm not

313

planning on dying soon and if you are plenty mature enough now to handle the job, you will be better equipped when I go."

"I don't like talking about this, Aunt Cindy."

"Well, we're going to this once and not again. I have given instructions for the dispersal of my estate and my burial and I want you to follow those instructions to the last dot and tittle. You're the only one I know who will. The others have too strong ideas about what's right and proper."

I quaked inwardly. Hopefully her instructions would not get me into too much trouble, but I wasn't too sure of that.

"Now, tell me, Dempsey, when did you get so interested in family history and where did you get so much information about us?"

"When we were at the Fereday place all winter, we got so bored we started reading the walls . . ."

"You read newspapers instead of my books!" She slapped my knee hard enough to sting.

". . . There were articles about the rustling and killing at Mountain Beavers and the cattle drive to the Indian reservation and . . . about Tucker's trial and murder. I didn't know about that, Aunt Cindy, why didn't someone tell me? And I didn't know you were engaged to Tucker."

"I had never spoken of that until the other night, Dempsey, and none of the rest of the family knows about it, so you and the Hicks were the first to know. It would be best to keep that between us. Too many people I love would be hurt by the knowledge."

"Yes, ma'am, I understand."

"I was deceived, Dempsey, and it has been the bitterest pill." Her chin quivered—I never saw her cry—and she turned and looked out of the window.

My head was full and spinning. The engagement, executor, detailed instructions for what? I could only guess and my imagination was very fertile that day. True to her vow, we never spoke of the will again. Instead, our days were filled with work on the three ranches, cattle and horses, and family.

Clancy made a good cowhand, and spent all his money seeing that Patrick was educated. He went away to school and came back a doctor; he now practices in Las Cruces.

While we were away on a roundup and drive to the tracks, the Fereday house burned to the ground. "Lightning," Aunt Cindy pronounced. She didn't care that we had full view of the mountains from the basin and that lightning would have had to come out of clear air. Nap and I figgered that "lightning" rode sidesaddle and carried a can of kerosene. The walls spoke no more.

Cooper stayed with the Mexican Beavers Ranch and eventually married Cepa. We had a great time at their wedding and when we returned home, Ana came with us to attend college at Alamogordo.

Nap didn't come in one night and I found him next morning leaning against an adobe wall at Pinetop, his horse grazing nearby. We buried Napoleon Witt in the cemetery there among his friends, the Nealys, Meekers, Browns, and Beavers.

Ana visited often and when she finished school, came to Pinón to teach. She finally convinced me to marry her and it was the best catch I ever made. The school board had a rule that no married woman could teach, so we live at the ranch and have a son and daughter.

Aunt Cindy used to tease me, "I have never understood how a ten-pound girl could wrap a hundred-fifty-pound man around her little finger so tightly." She passed quietly in her sleep June 10th, 1936, full of vim and vigor to the last. We had a hard time finding her will. Ana finally found it inside those old notebooks she had given Cooper and I to make our book reports in during the flu epidemic in '18.

While I opened and read her will with much trepidation, Ana read my notebook, which was pretty much a history of the families around Pinetop. A yellowed newspaper clipping fell out of the book. Ana picked it up and read aloud:

A LONG SAD JOURNEY

Two brave young women, Kizzie Stark and Lucinda Nealy, made the long ride down the river last Tuesday to the spring roundup to take the sad news of young Riley Giddens's death and tell Kizzie's father, Paul, that he was needed for the coroner's inquest. Paul Stark hurried back to Pinetop and the girls followed on their tired mounts at a more leisurely pace.

Miss Nealy had ridden in from Mountain Beavers Ranch Monday morning to spend a few days in town with her friend Miss Stark when she was greeted by the sad news of Giddens's passing. "It has been a very sad time for all of us, especially the young people who were so close," Miss Nealy said after their ride. Miss Stark was too upset to give a statement.

I was only half listening and trying to wade through all the "therefore's" and "wherefore's" of the will. Something was wrong with the article and it kept interfering with my reading. I picked it up and read again. The second paragraph didn't ring true in my mind, *"Miss Nealy had ridden in from Mountain Beavers Ranch Monday morning . . ."* what was it?

Aunt Polly had said something that day sitting on the back porch when we were talking about the time Tucker left, . . . *later in the afternoon, Tucker left for the roundup . . .* no there was more . . . She said, *Cindy left for Kizzie's right after Sunday dinner . . .* Sunday dinner, Sunday dinner. I read the sentence in the article again; "Miss Nealy had ridden in from Mountain Beavers Ranch *Monday* morning . . ."

Ana intruded into my thoughts, "Dempsey, you're as pale as

a sheet, what's wrong?"

"I know Tucker Beavers didn't kill Riley Giddens, I have the proof."

"That's wonderful, darling, how did you find out, is it in the will?"

"No, it's in this clipping and my head."

"How is that?"

I pointed to the telling sentence in the article. "It says that Aunt Cindy got to Miz Kizzie's Monday morning."

"Yes, and what does that tell you?"

"Aunt Polly told me that Aunt Cindy left for Kizzie's *Sunday* after dinner and Tucker left later."

"Then where was she all ni . . ." Ana's hand flew to her mouth, ". . . Oh, oh-h-h, oh, Dempsey, that can't be right, Aunt Cindy would never do . . ."

"We're talking about *Aunt Cindy*, Ana."

"You believe . . . ?"

"That time I first visited the Mexican Beavers Ranch, she told us she was engaged to Tucker."

Ana was speechless, reading the newspaper clipping again. "Oh, Dempsey, what does this all mean?"

"It means for sure Tucker was with Aunt Cindy when Riley Giddens was killed. *And* it means that Uncle Rance most likely killed Riley, got away with it, and married Aunt Cindy, that damned triple play he was always bragging about."

"This is terrible, Dempsey, what shall we do?"

"We won't tell a soul. All three are gone now and it would do no good to dig up old ghosts. Aunt Cindy left hint enough in her will for all the others to see."

"What is it?"

"You'll see."

Epilogue

History is not elegant. Failure is not glorious.
Success is not permanent. Knowledge is not
  absolute.
And survival is not a birthright.

—David E. Stuart

So many things are lost or overlooked by historians, a ghost town, ranches taken into national forests and military reservations, cemeteries grown up in weeds, ruins of a ranch house burned long ago. Little things? Maybe, in the overall schemes of the world, but not little to those who lived in those times past. Things like who lived in the old town, what happened to the people at the ranch house, who were the people buried in the old cemetery and what were their lives like? And the occasional visitor to Pinetop Cemetery today, working on genealogies or just looking for lost relatives, wonders why the wife of Rance Brown is buried next to a man named Tucker Beavers, Jr.

ABOUT THE AUTHOR

"I want to write about things no one else has written; I want to represent people of the times as accurately as possible," **James Crownover** said in a recent interview. "After all, there are just so many steely eyed killers in the world and a whole lot of everyday people doing everyday jobs that do extraordinary things a few times in their lives. Nobody talks about them much." We leave it up to you, the reader, to decide if the two-time Western Writers of America Spur Award winner has hit his goal with *If These Walls Could Talk.*

The employees of Five Star Publishing hope you have enjoyed this book.

Our Five Star novels explore little-known chapters from America's history, stories told from unique perspectives that will entertain a broad range of readers.

Other Five Star books are available at your local library, bookstore, all major book distributors, and directly from Five Star/Gale.

Connect with Five Star Publishing

Visit us on Facebook:
    https://www.facebook.com/FiveStarCengage

Email:
    FiveStar@cengage.com

For information about titles and placing orders:
    (800) 223-1244
    gale.orders@cengage.com

To share your comments, write to us:
    Five Star Publishing
    Attn: Publisher
    10 Water St., Suite 310
    Waterville, ME 04901